To Marger
Wishing you every

THE WHITE CUCKOO

by

Annie Ireson

Best Wishes
Annie Ireson
x

First published 2012 by Fast-Print Publishing of
Peterborough, England.

www.fast-print.net/store.php

THE WHITE CUCKOO
Copyright © Anne Ireson 2012

ISBN: 978-178035-478-1

All characters are fictional.
Any similarity to any actual person is purely coincidental.

A catalogue record for this book is available from the British Library

An environmentally friendly book printed and bound in England
by www.printondemand-worldwide.com

This book is made entirely of chain-of-custody materials

For our son Michael
Always a part of our family

Acknowledgements

Firstly, I should like to thank my husband, Bob for putting up with my night-time writing sessions, and my children, Emily, Garry and Nicky for listening to and reading excerpts of the novel. Also thank you, Lee (favourite son-in-law) for giving me a man's point of view on an important aspect of the story, and Kelly and Christie (daughters-in-law to be) for your love and support. My grandchildren, Tyler, Sophie and Charlie, are my inspiration.

I would especially like to thank Andy Sipple for his continued and unfaltering belief in me as a writer and for pointing out that a man wouldn't know a woman's dress size. Also thank you, Heather Jackson, for your friendship and support on my journey to publication, and especially for coming on the Writers' Holiday with me twice, despite really being a photographer.

Without the encouragement and friendship of Jane Wenham-Jones and a lovely group of writers who were brought together by her book 'Wannabe a Writer?' I would not have had the courage to publish this novel. So thank you, Jane and all the 'Wannabes', from the bottom of my heart. You are all lovely people and deserve success.

Thanks also go to Sue Lyons and my friends and colleagues at the day job for being so supportive, and the readers of the first drafts of *The White Cuckoo*, especially the two RNA New Writers' Scheme readers and Nicola Minney, who put so much work into giving me valuable feedback.

Any book about the strange and elusive cuckoo needs an ornithological adviser. Many thanks, Dave Bishop, for your most interesting lesson on the behaviour and habits of cuckoos and for finding out that an albino cuckoo has never before been spotted in Great Britain.

Lastly, thanks go to the talented Craig Hayward and Jamie Rae of Fat Zombie for designing such a fabulous book cover, and the unknown lady behind me in the restaurant queue at the National

History Museum for the eavesdropped conversation that gave me the idea for the novel.

CHAPTER ONE

Harry opened his eyes to a lattice of blackthorn just inches from his face and the rasping, hot sound of Jessie breathing in his ear. A nearby crow's raucous call jolted reality into his fitful sleep and he flinched with the discomfort of Jessie's knees digging into his side.

"Is it any better?" he asked.

Jessie shut her eyes, bit her lower lip and shook her head in reply.

"Did you get some sleep?"

Jessie shook her head again, and grimaced as she clutched her treasured gold locket in her fist, grinding it under her chin as the pain of the contraction worsened. Under the rough, grey blanket that covered them both, Harry shifted slightly to ease his aching back. As his own stomach cramped painfully and gurgled with hunger, his fingers subconsciously curled around the stock of the shotgun at his side. There was no God — there couldn't be. What sort of God would make Jessie's baby come now, before they had found somewhere to live? Desperation prickled behind his eyelids. Running away with Jessie had seemed the proper, grown-up, thing to do, but he hadn't realised how hard it would be to survive in an indifferent world with only a shotgun, a handful of old cartridges and a few basic belongings between them.

"I'll have to shoot another rabbit today," he said in the broken voice of adolescence. "Perhaps the pains will go away if you eat something."

Harry knew Jessie was trying hard to be brave for his sake. She never wanted to cause any trouble, did Jessie. He saw the terror in her eyes and with it came an innate sense of loathing for her parents, who hadn't believed her when, hysterical with fear and shame, she had told them she was having a baby after being raped in the stables by Frederick de Montpelier, the Earl of Fawsden's eldest son. What had been more important, their jobs at Fawsden Hall or their daughter? They'd chosen their jobs and left him to care for Jessie, abandoned and

1

cast out of her home because of the dreadful shame she had brought them.

"Don't leave me, Harry. Please don't leave me here on my own. I might die. I might bleed to death." Jessie held her breath, clenched her teeth and groaned as another contraction built. "I think it must be coming."

"I'll just go and fetch you some more water from the stream." Harry didn't know what else to say. He felt awkward and embarrassed and didn't want to think about what women's things he would have to deal with when the baby came out from between her legs.

"No," Jessie cried as she drew up her knees further. She clutched at Harry's arm. "Don't leave me here on my own. Please don't go ..."

"Perhaps we should just go back to the Hall," Harry said, his voice almost a whisper.

Jessie shuddered. "I can't ever go back there, Harry. No matter what happens to me."

Harry let go of the shotgun and shifted onto his side, propping himself up onto his elbow. He pushed a lock of fluffy red hair away from Jessie's eyes, and then bent forwards to hold her in an awkward embrace as the painful contraction subsided. The baby was most definitely coming and it was much too soon. It would be stillborn. He'd have to bury its little body somewhere in the woods. With a surprising pang of sadness and regret he realised just how hard it would be to bury Jessie's tiny baby, despite the anguish and trouble it had caused. Conceived in an act of brutality and violence, the poor little soul had caused as many flying feathers as a fox rampaging through a pheasant pen, but even so it didn't deserve to have its life snatched away before it had even begun. The baby was innocent and pure and he had grown curiously attached to it as it had grown from a tiny spark of unwanted life into a kicking mass of arms and legs in her belly.

He had been ready to be a father to Jessie's baby. Everyone had blamed him, in any case, so what difference would it make? Every child needed a father and although he might be only fourteen, Harry was determined to be a good one. The three of them, together, would make their own way in the world. That had been his plan, anyway,

2

until everything had gone wrong and Jessie's baby had started to come before its time.

"I'll be really quick," he said as he slid out from beneath the bush. The bed of bracken crackled underneath him and the avian symphony of a mid-summer's dawn would have infused him with limitless energy and enthusiasm for the new day, had the circumstances been different. He stood up and rubbed his eyes. The burden of responsibility and sleeping on a pile of bracken had made his shoulders ache and they crunched and cracked when he flexed them. He breathed in deeply, inhaling the earthy, fertile smell of the countryside as he looked for a suitable place to relieve himself. It had been his idea to run away and now it was all going badly wrong. But he'd go back and kill Frederick de Montpelier one day. There would be a chink, somewhere, in the armour of nobility and he would have his revenge for the atrocity Jessie had suffered. His day would come. He just had to bide his time.

Harry felt uneasy as a nagging finger of fear replaced the tight fist of anger in his heart and began to prod somewhere behind his breastbone. It was dangerous for a woman to give birth prematurely, that much he did know. A sudden panic quickened his breathing, as if he had just sprinted through rain sodden, unharvested fields of corn. He couldn't bear to live without Jessie. They were the best of friends and it had always been so, right from the first day they had played together as toddlers in the grounds of Fawsden Hall, where his father was a gardener and her mother was the head cook.

He desperately needed to find them work and lodgings: somewhere permanent to live. What would they do in winter? Where would they end up? He knew that to try and achieve justice for Jessie was futile — no one would listen to the testimony of a fourteen-year-old gamekeeper's apprentice against that of the well-respected Earl of Fawsden and his cunning, devious sons. Nobility was above the law. Nobility had the money to corrupt and poison the legal system; everyone knew that.

Harry buttoned up his trousers and rubbed his eyes, blinking rapidly to focus through the early morning blanket of mist. His gaze fell onto the dull silhouette of a church in the distance. He pictured a scene in his mind. The parson's wife would soon be busy in the

3

kitchen of the vicarage, preparing breakfast. She wouldn't turn them away, would she? She would know what to do. Jessie needed urgent help and he had no other choice. He closed his eyes and lifted his gaze to the sky. He took off his cap, wrung it round and round in his hands, and then spoke out loud, feeling embarrassed, even though no one could hear him.

"Dear God. I know I ain't devout. I know I ain't never bin to church or Sunday School. But please God, if you're there and can 'ear me now, from the bottom of me 'art please save Jessie and her little baby. Amen."

Remaining still and silent, Harry kept his eyes closed tightly shut. He filled his lungs with damp, peaty air and focused on what he knew he had to do to save Jessie. It didn't matter about himself. As long as Jessie was safe, he would be content.

It was the high-low call of a cuckoo that made him open his eyes. His gaze, bathed in the wisdom of a childhood spent in the midst of the sights and smells of the countryside, panned the bushes and trees in the direction of the call. Eventually it rested upon a lone bird perched in an immature tree alongside the blackthorn bush where he and Jessie had spent the night. At first, he thought the bird was a dove, but the unmistakable call confirmed exactly what this bird was and the evil place it had come from.

Harry shook his head in disbelief. The bird's crested head twisted round and round, and its strange, predatory eyes fell on him. The rare albino cuckoo, shy and secretive by nature, flapped its wings and flew off into the undergrowth. Harry set his jaw in an angry, resolute glare at the place the cuckoo had rested as he made his way back to the blackthorn bush, the appearance of the strange bird strengthening the certain knowledge that, one day, Frederick de Montpelier would pay for the terrible things he had done to Jessie.

He bent down.

"Jessie," he whispered. Kneeling on the blankets that covered the bracken bed, he touched her shoulder with a gentle, concerned hand. "Can you get up? There's a church over there, and where there's a church there's a vicarage. We can get some help."

**

4

Polly-Anne Staverley sat down on the back doorstep and wriggled her bottom into a slight indentation in the stone. At ten years-old, she was the eldest of the vicar's children, and it was her job to get up early and lay the kitchen table for breakfast. She would do that soon but, before she did, she would spend just a few minutes sitting in her favourite place in the whole world, listening to the crystal sharp birdsong of the first day of summer whilst running her fingertips through the soft, silky ears of the family's spaniel. She breathed in and savoured the sensuous smell of dewy grass and freshly turned earth as she waited for the magical moment when the sun would melt away the mist of early morning and bathe the earth in the life-giving warmth of summer.

She felt a little tingle of excitement and drew her knees up underneath her chin. Pulling her dress over her knees, she revelled in the importance of being the eldest child in the Staverley family.

The dog nuzzled her hand with its cold, wet nose and she stroked its head. Inside the house, the threadlike wail of a newborn baby kissed the air with a thousand golden promises, and Polly jumped up, suddenly breathless with excitement. It felt just like Christmas — no, much, much better than Christmas. She giggled out loud and shivered with pleasure at the glorious happy feeling. She'd felt fit to burst with pride when her father had emerged from his bedroom late last night, a huge, proud grin splitting his face and tears in his eyes at the news he had another daughter and, at long last, Polly had a baby sister.

"Good morning, Polly."

Polly twisted around and grinned at her father standing in the kitchen doorway. His shoulders pinned back in a no-nonsense, business as usual kind of way, he reminded Polly of the day she had watched the changing of the guard at Buckingham Palace. His jolly red face beamed at her, as he stood tall and straight. He tucked a folded newspaper under his arm before adjusting his white clerical collar.

"Is the kettle boiled?" He waved the newspaper in the direction of the stove as he strode towards the kitchen table. "I didn't get time to catch up with the news last night with all the excitement of the birth, so I thought I'd have a quiet few minutes before breakfast."

"I was just going to light the gas," Polly answered. "How's Mummy?"

"She's very well. It was an easy birth, being her fifth. Your baby sister's very hungry though, so I thought I'd leave them to it and come down and make breakfast for us all. It'll give Auntie Gwen time to deliver her usual lecture about staying in bed and lying-in for the next two weeks." He shook his head subconsciously and tutted as he unfolded his newspaper and studied the headlines on the first page.

"She never wants to stay in bed when she's just given birth, Polly. Your mother is an intelligent woman, so why does she do it? She knows lying-in is essential for a woman's recovery from childbirth." He lowered his head and looked at Polly under his bushy eyebrows, waggling an authoritative finger in her direction.

"You, my dear Polly, must help me make sure that Mummy rests for a couple of weeks. We'll work out a plan between us so that she can get herself acquainted with your new baby sister without having to worry about household chores or chasing around after those boisterous boys of ours."

"Once I've laid the table, Daddy, can I go up and have a little peek at the new baby?" Polly asked.

"Of course you can," her father replied. "But make sure you don't wake the boys just yet."

***

With their spare clothes and other belongings bundled together in two rough grey blankets, tied with twine and hidden safely under a hedge just outside the village of Lyverton, Harry and Jessie made their way up the lane past the church. Harry's eyes panned back and forth searching constantly for the vicarage. The mist had begun to dissolve into a watery blue sky, but there was no sign of a church house. The lane contained only three rows of thatched-roofed, tiny, whitewashed cottages and a handful of grey slated stone houses all linked together with a haphazard array of outbuildings and barns. There were no wrought iron gates or sweeping gravel driveways.

Jessie stopped and steadied herself with a pale hand on the stone wall that bordered the churchyard. She groaned as she doubled over, clutching her abdomen, her breath coming in short light gasps. "It hurts so much, Harry. Find someone to help me … please …"

6

Harry took off his cap and wrung it in his hands. His broken voice rose and fell in a melodic lilt. "I don't know what to do, Jess. There's no vicarage 'ere." He stood on tiptoe, and made an exaggerated gesture of shielding his eyes from the emerging sunlight. "I'll 'ave to knock on someone's door. They'll know where the parson lives." He stepped forwards and with respectful gentleness drew Jessie's shawl around her shoulders, being careful to avoid touching her breasts.

"You wait 'ere, m'ducky," he said, guiding her gently back onto the church wall for support. "I'll be back soon."

"Don't leave me!" Jessie wailed, her huge dark eyes filling with frightened tears as the contraction reached a climax.

"Harry ... no!" She reached out to him as he backed away. "I'll be all right in a minute ... when the pain passes. Harry, please ... don't leave me here!"

Harry held her in his arms as the contraction gradually eased. "Listen," he said. "I reckon I just heard a baby cry." He stared intently at an upstairs window in the house opposite the church as the distinctive sound of a newborn filled the deserted lane. His heart filled with optimism. Bright, floral curtains flapped gently at the slightly open window, almost beckoning him towards the house as the sun broke through and bathed its grey stone walls in a warm, buttery glow.

"We'll knock on the door of that house over there and ask where the vicarage is. You'll be safe soon, Jess. The parson's wife will know what to do. Where there's a church, there's a parson, even if there's no proper vicarage."

***

The clunk of the heavy, cast iron knocker rattling on the oak front door made Polly jump as she spread an embroidered tablecloth over the kitchen table in preparation for the family's breakfast.

"Who on earth is that at this time of the morning," her father said, folding his newspaper and reaching into his waistcoat pocket for his watch. "I bet it's old Mrs Parker, bringing some flowers for the church as an excuse to have a first peep at our new baby. At this time of the morning too! Has the woman no sense of propriety?"

He sighed and took off his eyeglass, placing it on the table alongside the newspaper. "No peace for the wicked, eh, Polly?"

Polly followed her father through the hallway to the front door and watched as he bent down to draw back first the bottom bolt and then straightened up to tackle the stiffer top one.

The girl's boots were the first thing Polly noticed as the door creaked open. They were good quality, black leather, and not at all worn down. They were slightly grubby, as if she had just walked a long way through open fields, but they were not the boots of someone whose family was poor. As Polly stared at the girl's feet she was shocked to see a trickle of what she thought was urine running over the dark leather. The moment was ethereal, as if time had stopped and encapsulated itself in a bubble. Polly stood, mesmerised, as the urine began to drip from the instep of the boot onto a flagstone. The youth who accompanied her spoke, but Polly didn't look at him.

"Sir, can you help us please? My sister is ill. We've nowhere else to go, mister parson, sir."

Polly's gaze drifted upwards to the girl's face, which was hidden beneath tumbling curls of fine, coppery red hair as she leaned forwards, groaning in pain, with one hand steadying herself on the wall of the cottage. In her other hand she clutched a handful of her navy blue smocked dress over her abdomen. Polly's eyes widened at the growing pool of urine on the front doorstep. It was really sinful, it was, to be peeing on the front doorstep of her father's house. Could she not wait to use the closet in the yard?

"Harry," the girl wailed, with almost hysterical panic in her voice. "I'm ... I ... I can't stop myself ... something's leaking ... it's coming out. Oh God, please help me!"

Polly looked up at her father, and then stared at the youth the girl had called Harry. The girl had said *'oh God'* which was not allowed because it was taking the Lord's name in vain. Her father would be really cross. But to her surprise his face was kind and benevolent as he stepped forwards to catch the girl under her armpits just as her legs crumpled beneath her. As her father scooped her up into his strong arms, the girl let out a low, guttural growl. Polly had heard the sound before, only last night. It was the same animal noise her mother had made behind the closed bedroom door as she bore down in the last stages of labour, pushing her new baby sister from her womb. She looked at her father's face, which had turned a horrified ashen colour.

"Is this young girl about to give birth?" he hissed in a loud whisper, glaring at the youth with a deprecating, accusing scowl. "She is a mere child ... how old is she? Thirteen? Fourteen?"

Harry wrung his cap in his hands. His anguish was obvious, and a solitary tear escaped, which he brushed away with the back of his hand. He looked at Polly's father straight in the eye as he blinked back angry tears. "She's a month off fourteen; she ain't my sister but afore you go accusin' me — mister parson, sir — it ain't mine!"

Polly stumbled back into the house to make way for her father, who had scooped Jessie up into his arms, her crocheted shawl falling from her shoulders onto the doorstep. She held the door open wide for him.

"You'd best come in," her father said to the boy, a hint of compassion creeping around the hard accusation in his voice. "Don't worry, she's safe now."

Jessie screamed in Reverend Staverley's arms. The scream was high pitched and unremitting and ended in a low, rumbling growl as her womb bore down spontaneously to expel its contents.

"Oh Lord! Gwen! Gwen! Come down here quick," he shouted up the stairs. "Polly, fetch your Auntie Gwen down, she'll know what to do."

CHAPTER TWO
NINETY-NINE YEARS LATER

Day One
Monday, 25th May: 10:30 am

Tamasyn Hargreaves glanced at her mother's eyes in the rear view mirror. They were staring straight into hers, cutting deep into her soul. The eerie moment unnerved her, and she eased her right foot off the accelerator.

Almost two years had passed since Tammy had gazed into her mother's eyes, and yet it seemed like it was only yesterday. When Pippa was alive, she outwardly hid nothing from her daughter; yet behind the chestnut warmth prowled a dark reticence that kept its secrets well-guarded and veiled in mystery.

Tammy adjusted the mirror and her father smiled at her. Instantaneously, she smiled back. The strange moment passed with the spine-tingling realisation that she had inherited her mother's eyes and her father's smile.

As she approached the village, her inveterate obsession to, one day, come back to Lyverton distorted into a fearful uncertainty. It had startled her to see her own reflection in the rear view mirror. It was as if she had suddenly split into two people; the living, breathing woman in the car and the ghost of herself in the mirror. All her life, whenever Tammy had thought about Lyverton, she had always imagined herself going back one day, but the truth was she wasn't returning to the village. She had never before travelled along the twisting country roads of Northamptonshire, and if she was honest, she had always been frightened of what she might find there. An unexpected flush of warmth bathed her palms in sweat; she could actually hear distant voices whispering inside her head, drawing her in, mesmerised by unanswered questions of the past.

Tammy changed her focus and glanced in the mirror again. A middle-aged lady in a shiny black car was glaring over her steering wheel, only a few feet from her rear bumper. The woman scowled and shook her head from side to side. Tammy felt she should apologise for driving so slowly, so she raised a hesitant hand in silent acknowledgement as she began to accelerate.

The village sign stood proud, bathed in sunlight in a shimmering emerald sea of whispering long grass. Tammy felt a sudden fluttering of excitement tinged with apprehension. It was as if she was passing through a mythical gateway into a world beyond reality.

Lyverton.

Was this the beginning of the future or was it the end of the past? Was this where she would discover her roots, or was she about to lose her identity forever? She took a deep breath, bit her top lip in determination and jabbed her right foot down hard, speeding up as she approached the outskirts of the village. There was no turning back now. She had finally done it. She had, at long last, conquered the demons that for two years had danced around in her head, preventing her from fulfilling her deathbed promise to her mother and discovering the truth about Lyverton.

Inexplicably, the old Doris Day song, *Que Sera, Sera,* drifted into her consciousness and Pippa's voice began to sing to her. Tammy's childhood stirred inside her and everything in her remembered world suddenly appeared huge, sunny and glorious. She pictured her mother gazing into her father's eyes, singing softly as they sat either side of her bed trying to soothe her to sleep. She turned her head from one to the other: they were in a world of their own, and the ribbons of colour reflected in their eyes were identical. A halo of tight, soft, sun-faded auburn curls, shot through with a few strands of silvery grey, glistened around her mother's laughter-lined face.

Tammy gasped at the vivid memory as she slowed down to negotiate a sharp bend in the road. She remembered her mother's soft skin, devoid of make-up; newly scrubbed, radiant and shiny. She inhaled through her nose. She could actually smell the distinctive soap her mother used to use, and could feel the softness of Pippa's fine, curly hair entwined around her fingertips as she gripped the steering wheel. Her mother smiled at her father, and the tip of her tongue fleetingly touched her lips to moisten them as her gaze slid downwards and her eyes shone. The love her parents had poured into her at that

11

exact moment in her young life had gelled and formed itself into something so solid and substantial that, over twenty years later, the memory was so vibrant and alive, she could feel it beneath her fingers, smell the fragrance of it and actually hear her mother's voice.

Tammy remembered wriggling down into her warm bed, flinging up her arm and resting her hand, palm upwards, on her head as she brushed away her mother's goodnight kiss. She glanced in the rear view mirror again, took one hand off the steering wheel and subconsciously brushed the back of her hand across a damp spot on her forehead. She wondered why she hadn't noticed it before: her eyes *were* Pippa's eyes. Her mother's life was indelible, forever genetically entwined within her own.

Pungent, rambunctious hedgerows began to tame their wayward inclinations, gradually giving way to wide, newly mown grass verges and a row of red bricked and white cement-rendered terraced cottages with bloom-laden planters and hanging baskets adorning neat front doors.

Lyverton was even prettier than she had imagined.

The woman behind was tailgating again. The black car was so close Tammy could see her glaring eyes, frowning face and wobbling jowls as she muttered under her breath. Tammy's heart quickened. She felt like a lone, lost sheep, being rounded up by a beady-eyed Border Collie. Subconsciously she accelerated slightly.

The village sighed, opened its arms wide and drew its lost child back into its breasts.

***

Sitting outside the village tea shop in the warm, spring sunshine and wallowing in the sounds of the countryside, Tammy basked in the euphoria of a freedom so sweet she could taste it in the air. The wicker patio chair creaked beneath her as she bent forwards to lift up her mug of frothy, milky coffee. She took a sip and then put it down again as she remembered one last thing she must do before relaxing after her long journey. She opened her huge handbag, searched around in its bowel-like depths, and finally plucked out her mobile phone. The glorious sense of release she had felt just a few seconds before imploded into a mere dot as she ran her fingers through her unruly hair. Once the inevitable phone call was out of the way she could begin her quest.

The air around her squeezed the breath out of her lungs, and she took a deep breath as her father answered. A contrived, false mask of brightness brushed across her cheeks and tinted her pale, freckly face with a slight flush of colour.

"Hi Dad. I got here okay."

"Thank God ... good journey?"

"Yes. Thanks again for the sat-nav — it was brilliant; didn't get lost once."

"Good. Have you found anywhere to stay yet?"

Tammy sighed. There was one small problem she had momentarily forgotten about. She had hastily made up her mind to come to Lyverton only forty-eight hours ago and hadn't pre-booked anywhere to stay. It had been a sore point with her father, Alan, whose disproportionate fear at her wild, impetuous decision had almost made them have an argument. Two days ago she had finally begun to break away from the shackles that chained her to Alan: had she not escaped from him when she did, she would have gone completely insane.

"No. Not yet. There's a Travelodge just outside Fawsden ..."

"Well go and do it now, Tammy," Alan interrupted, his voice pregnant with paternal worry. "You don't want to find yourself with nowhere to stay!"

"I'll probably book in there for a few days," Tammy continued, ignoring the urgency in her father's voice. "Although I noticed the car park was filled with dozens of builders' vans. It looks to be pretty full."

"Builders?"

"Yes," Tammy said. "There's a new development site nearby and it's huge. It looks as if hundreds of houses are going to be built there, and the sign says there will be a school, a health centre and some shops, too. I think it's going to be practically a complete new village."

"Really?" Alan said, unable to disguise the surprise in his voice. "How far is this new development from Lyverton then?"

Tammy could feel disapproval burning into her ear. Whenever Alan had talked about Lyverton in the past, he'd enthused about the fantastic Northamptonshire countryside and how it was the Rose of the Shires: an unspoilt emerald jewel of Englishness, cemented right in the very centre of the country.

"It's on the outskirts of Fawsden, a few miles away from Lyverton."

She gazed into the distance towards the development site, where ancient trees, bushes and lush fields abruptly gave way to crude, Mondrian-like slabs of brown and grey, splattered with green and yellow dots of construction machinery and a couple of cranes.

"I can see it right in the distance. It looks like they've just started clearing the site and putting in the roads and drains," she said as she visualised her dad shaking his head in condemnation of government policy. Alan Hargreaves didn't want to acknowledge the need for new developments to house the country's rising population and how daughters needed to live in their own home instead of with their fathers. He didn't like change.

Lyverton had always euphemistically been referred to as *home* in the Hargreaves household, and Tammy had always known that part of Alan's soul had been left behind when he'd fled, terrified, from the grasping fingers of the seemingly idyllic, pretty village thirty years previously. Throughout Tammy's life he'd often talked to her about Lyverton, and she felt she knew this place. He'd never returned though, and neither had Pippa. The unspoken pact between her parents had been so solid she could have almost reached out and touched its cold, impenetrable surface. She knew Alan could never return — the pointing, accusing fingers and whispered comments about past scandals would persist for years in a village like Lyverton.

Tammy's mind wandered as her father launched into a lecture about old iron-ore quarries, listed buildings, biodiversity statements and the rare newts in the fields surrounding the village. Her father was a conservation officer at the local council in Yorkshire and, although Tammy usually found his work-related chatter quite pleasant, she was on holiday and to say she wasn't interested was an understatement.

"Can you remember if there are any bed and breakfast places in Lyverton," she interrupted, trying to change the focus of the conversation. She rolled her eyes and bit her lip. More than anything,

14

today, she wanted to distance herself from her father. In Lyverton, she was anonymous. She would be completely free to meander through touchy subjects and painful memories before finally fulfilling her mother's dying wish.

"The Red Lion used to have a couple of rooms. You could try there. You'll probably be more comfortable than at the Travelodge if it's crawling with builders. I can't tell you how relieved I am that you've arrived safely. I've been really worried about you all morning," Alan replied.

"I wish you wouldn't worry about me so much, Dad," Tammy said with a groan. "For goodness sake, I'm twenty-seven years-old. I'm perfectly capable of driving from one end of the country to the other. I'll ring you later and let you know where I'm staying."

"Sorry, love. You know I can't help worrying. You're all I've got in the world, Tammy. I don't know what I'd do if anything happened to you. For goodness sake be careful. People have long memories, you know. It won't take long before someone puts two and two together and realises just who you are."

"Dad," interrupted Tammy. "I'll be fine. Don't worry about me." She shut her eyes as familiar guilt descended like grey, sea mist dampening the bright, spring morning. She knew she was his entire world. She didn't need to keep being reminded — it just made things a hundred times worse. As soon as she could, she said goodbye to her father and thankfully dropped her mobile phone back into the depths of her bag, zipping it up with a flourish as if drawing a line under her old life, ready to start a new chapter.

Clutching her head in her hands, Tammy smoothed back her wayward, frizzy hair. Breaking the links in her biological chain had been so difficult it almost caused a physical pain in her chest, so she chased the suffocating feeling away by anchoring her thoughts to the present. She listened intently to a thrush nearby, singing its little heart out. Taking a sip of smooth latte, she turned her head to look for her tuneful friend, squinting against the midday sun in a sky devoid of a single cloud.

Tammy was the only customer at Marjorie's tea shop. Across the main road two teenagers sat on a wall, sharing a bag of sweets. They were swinging their legs, carefree and blissfully unhindered by responsibilities and commitments. As Tammy watched them — a boy and a girl dressed in scruffy, grungy clothing — she tried to imagine her father as a child in the village forty years ago. Had he once sat on that very same wall in the spring sunshine, having bought sweets from the village shop to share with his friends, grubby kneed, bare legs swinging over rough-hewn stone?

Tammy put down her mug, reached into her handbag and then turned her attention to a sheet of paper in her hand. She unfolded it and placed it on the wooden table in front of her, smoothing it out with her fingertips. She knew the names and addresses almost by heart, but she had a sudden compulsion to run her fingers over the indentations made by the pen — it somehow brought them to life. She spread her hand over the cool, silky paper and it was her mother's hand she saw. Faint freckles were just visible under the pale skin of winter, and the strengthening sun would soon coax them into a joined up mass of deep brown splatters. She twisted her mother's wedding ring around on the middle finger of her right hand. There was already a slight indentation: it was already carving its physical mark on its only offspring.

Tammy's eyes played across the names on the page, like a duet of pianists beginning a concerto, the orchestra still and silent in the background watching patiently for the conductor's cue. With a pang of sudden compassion, she understood how hard it had been for Alan to let her go, knowing that his only daughter had every right to find her roots, even though he, himself, had vowed never to return to Lyverton or speak again to any of the people who lived there.

Every name and address on Alan's list was spelt out in heavy, precise capital letters. Tammy smiled to herself. Her dad always wrote in capitals. She knew it was because capital letters were difficult to scan or read quickly. They forced people to decode them with clinical precision, leaving no place for the melody of a writer's soul to escape and sing to the reader. Alan was reserved and private and always hid behind a shield of capital letters.

Pippa's death had dragged all the smiles and laughter and every last remnant of heat and passion from her father until there was almost nothing left but a pale, thin shell. He was lost and disorientated, like a cold, lone cellist, suspended precariously on a bridge between bleak desolation and a wailing grief, the low dark notes scribing a testimony to his absent, detached presence in the world and his long forgotten smile.

Two days ago, Tammy and her father had both sensed the final, almost imperceptible twang of the last broken string of emotional control over her life as, with a reluctant sigh, he had handed her the list. At that moment, every one of her childhood fantasies about Lyverton had become real.

Tammy's gaze lingered over one name in particular and she shuddered. The naked capital letters slid from the page and thudded heavily somewhere behind her breastbone.

MARIAN TROUTMAN

Marian was the half-sister she hadn't even known existed until three years ago when a cancer-riddled Pippa had tearfully confessed to Tammy that she actually had an older sister, but even worse than that, Marian was the poor slaughtered lamb, sacrificed and cast out from her mother's life when she'd fled from the village with her father, never to be seen again.

There really was no going back.

***

Having finished her latte, Tammy sat back, clutching her list in the unfamiliar, but peaceful corner of rural middle England where thrushes warbled, bees buzzed and the pungent smell of hawthorn scribbled its untidy signature on the spring breeze. Not one of the people on her list knew of her existence. She had been conceived, born and raised in secret defiance of the ultimatum; it was as if an ethical rectitude of the highest order had conspired and whispered behind its hand to present her with a perfect but solitary childhood as she had grown up in blissful unawareness of the scandal, chaos and subsequent denial of the love of her lost family.

As Tammy mused over her ancestry, a smartly dressed mature lady

17

passed by, walking a white poodle. She nodded inquisitively in Tammy's direction.

"Good morning."

Tammy smiled at her and mumbled a returned greeting. The woman could be a relative. How would she know? A lone blackbird launched into its happy repertoire as if in competition with the thrush. Was the blackbird calling out to the village that its lost daughter had returned, full of optimism for a new chapter in her life? She stared at the nearby hawthorn bush, laden with tiny white flowers that breathed the distinctive smell of approaching summer into the air. She was suddenly envious of the microcosmic community where birds sang, brand new green shoots sprouted and blossom burst forth, insects buzzed and spring exploded life, colour and a tapestry of smells and sounds into its miniature world.

'The risen cream of all the milkiness of May time.'

A half remembered snippet from a long forgotten novel rose to the surface of Tammy's consciousness and she recalled that the hawthorn bush was said to harbour the Faery Queen and a cuckoo, according to Irish mythology.

Was she a cuckoo? A solitary bird perched outside the encapsulated world of the village, belonging nowhere and yet wanting desperately to become a part of the thriving, buzzing community.

Who was she?

Was she Tamasyn Hargreaves, only daughter of Alan Hargreaves and his late wife, Pippa, or was she just the perpetual wandering, lost offspring of their secret life?

The sadness that had always prowled around the edges of her parents' marriage dissolved into a knot of tightly wound anger in her throat. She tried to gulp it down as she tore her gaze away from the hawthorn bush and stared at the list in front of her. Her mother had slipped away from this beautiful world without breathing the life back into what must have been some of her most precious memories. Her half-sister had known Pippa had cancer, and yet this woman had chosen to ignore her mother's dying wish. Tammy couldn't really blame her though. After all, she had been deserted and abandoned in Lyverton. Why should she have cared that her birth mother was dying?

18

As she gazed at her father's list, she noticed regret behind every slight wobble in downward strokes and felt the tug of swallowed pride and heartbreak behind every single word her father had written. Why hadn't Marian Troutman noticed it in Alan's capital letters, too? His letter to her had gone unanswered. There had been nothing; not a single written word of acknowledgement. No phone call. No e-mail. Nothing. Tammy had been distraught. Her mother's soul had been wrenched from her father's heart with a helpless, wretched kind of sorrow that had corroded her frightened dark eyes as they gulped in the hazy images of her final moments of life on Earth with an unfulfilled longing for just one final moment to see her two daughters together — united at long last.

'Go and find her, Tammy.' Her mother's last words played themselves over again in her head. Tammy swallowed a lump in her throat and rubbed her eyes. A sudden rattle of porcelain on wood and a slight movement at her side had stemmed the unexpected, angry tears that had started to prickle behind her eyelids.

"Thank you," she mumbled, forcing a sideways smile at the amiable youth in a blue and white striped apron as he placed the bill by her side. His eyes gleamed like pure white pebbles against his smooth, black skin as he surreptitiously scanned through Tammy's list of names, his head cocked on one side. Tammy knew he was reading the list, but she didn't hide it away.

"She used to be my teacher," he said in a deep voice that didn't match his youthful appearance. His thin, bony index finger pointed to Marian Troutman's name.

"Really?" Tammy said, her heartbeat quickening. The youth hesitated, self-consciousness repressing any further spoken communication between them, but a huge smile split across his face.

Suddenly, she was swirling around the edge of a slowly rotating, deafening whirlpool; to escape would have needed a massive burst of energy. The spiralling waters of her parents' past fell away beneath her and it seemed a long way down. Tammy realised just how much was at stake for her father. Her lovely, gentle, wooden Dad, captured in his dark icy orbit of grief and loneliness. She flinched with the weight of knowing that she was his sun.

19

Not for the first time that morning, Tammy sensed there was no going back, but her father's grief and her mother's lost soul had followed her to Lyverton like faithful puppies.

Tammy blinked, and realised that the youth was speaking again, his words ringing in her ears. She hadn't heard a word he was saying.

"Pardon?" she interrupted.

He gave her a strange look and pointed across the road to the post office opposite the tea shop. The teenagers sitting on the wall lifted their hands and waved as Tammy followed the direction of his gaze.

"I said: she's just gone into the post office if you want to speak to her."

CHAPTER THREE

9:00 pm

The cream coloured walls and flowery duvet cover on the comfortable-looking bed were bathed in the golden light of the setting sun. The matching curtains blew gently at the open balcony doors as Tammy stood beside them for a few seconds, still stunned by the knowledge she had actually stood behind her sister in the post office, so close she could have reached out and touched her. She had heard her sister's voice, breathed in the light fragrance of her and watched as she had turned from the counter and brushed past her, out of the door and past the teenagers, who had been peering into the post office through the window.

The only other room to rent at the Red Lion was just across the landing from Tammy's room; it was occupied, but she hadn't yet seen her co-guest.

"He's a construction worker, employed on the new development site," Cynthia, the cheerful landlady, had said, beaming at her as she had handed over the electronic swipe card to her room that afternoon. "He's very quiet — a really nice chap. You won't be disturbed."

Tammy sat down on her bed and glanced at her watch. It was almost nine o'clock. Without warning, the smell and sounds outside her open window evoked another childhood memory and she recalled a conversation with a classmate when her parents had collected her from school one day when she was five years-old.

'Why does your mum look like a granny?'

'She's not a granny.'

'Is that man your brother?'

'No, that's my dad.'

That had been the very first time in her short life that she had been aware of the age-gap between her parents.

Tammy glanced at her watch again and wondered if she might just get away with losing her mobile phone for a few days. Instinctively she knew she needed to cut herself off from her life back in Yorkshire if she was ever to discover the truth about Lyverton.

***

Tammy made her way down the narrow stairs, the chinking of glasses, laughter and the smell of pub food drifting up to meet her. She decided to have just one drink and something to eat, and then go back to her room, read for a while and relax. She was exhausted from her journey, but the prospect of an interesting people-watching session beckoned, despite her tiredness.

She looked around and spotted an empty alcove beside a traditional inglenook fireplace. She made her way over to the table, sipping an ice-cold vodka and Coke. No one acknowledged her as she sat down. She might have been invisible.

Tammy didn't mind being on her own. In fact, she was quite enjoying it. Her mother's dying words to her repeated themselves inside her head: *'You need to live your own life now. You've wasted too much time already looking after me. Find yourself a decent man before it's too late and all the best ones are snapped up.'*

Then had come the promise: the one that had taken her almost two years to keep. *'Go and find her, Tammy. Please? Promise me you'll go back to Lyverton for me and find her. Tell her I always loved her ...'*

Tammy had promised. How could she not have done?

She sipped her drink and cast her eyes around the busy pub lounge. It felt oddly intimate and a brief sense of déjà vu unnerved her slightly. She sensed she was not alone. There was something surrounding her she couldn't quite describe. It was as if her frozen bones were warming from the inside and friendly voices were whispering gently inside her head, infusing her with life.

The sound of a young girl's voice outside the slightly open window attracted Tammy's attention and she turned her head to cast her eyes over the pub garden.

"Look, she's over there, sitting just inside the window," the girl said.

The grungy teenagers Tammy had noticed earlier stood outside the open window, just a few feet away. The boy's arm was draped protectively around the girl's shoulders and they were both staring at

22

her, wide eyed with a haunting innocence.

Tammy smiled at them; they were awkward and gangly, teetering on the edge of adolescence. They were dressed in very peculiar clothes, but Tammy supposed it was just a new type of teenage fashion. The girl raised a hand in acknowledgement. Tammy waved back.

"She's seen us," grinned the youth, and he raised a peaked cap in a cheeky salute.

Tammy gave a puzzled frown. For a fleeting moment, she thought the girl looked vaguely familiar.

A shriek, followed by a shrill, piercing laugh sliced through the air and Tammy jerked her head around, away from the window. A woman at the next table was squealing with laughter at a white-haired man sitting next to her. The woman slid her hand surreptitiously down her cleavage, retrieved a red glace cherry and held it up like a trophy. The white-haired man shrugged his shoulders, his palms upturned and feigned an innocent look, which made everyone else at the table laugh out loud.

Tammy felt suddenly very much alone. The people were obviously a family — something she didn't have.

She glanced back out of the window, searching for the teenagers again, but all she could see were families enjoying the warm evening sunshine and a couple of toddlers running around in the beer garden. The older children had obviously gone.

Her eyes dropped downwards and her gaze fell on her mother's silver charm bracelet. Pippa's voice began to speak again inside her head, as she fingered the charms one by one. *'The canary in the birdcage was for my fortieth birthday. The baby in the cradle came nestled in an envelope with the flowers Daddy bought me on the day you were born. The key with twenty-one on it — he gave me that on our twenty-first wedding anniversary, and the moon and the stars — he gave me those on our fifth wedding anniversary.'*

Tammy's gaze lingered on one charm in particular; a miniature silver bible. Whenever she had asked her mother about the event it represented she'd always shook her head and said she didn't remember. Then a dark veil would cloud her eyes and she'd shut out the world, just for a split second, before changing the subject. Tammy always suspected the special charm represented an event from her mother's past life in Lyverton, which was not to be talked about. Not ever.

Another old song drifted into Tammy's mind. It was on one of Pippa's old 1960s CDs. She imagined her mother's voice: *'Come on Tammy – snap your fingers and shuffle your feet – like this!'*

Pippa would grab Tammy's hand, start to sing, and they would shuffle around the living room. *'Doo wah diddy, diddy ...'*

Tammy felt like she was drowning in the turbulent sea of discontentment and unfairness that had lurked behind her eyelids all day, but she fought back the tide until she could return to her room. She still missed Pippa so badly, and remembering the sound of her mother's voice inside her head turned into a physical tightness in her throat. Why did she have to die? She hadn't been old. She was strong, funny and kind and had looked much younger than her sixty-eight years.

She stared at the woman nearby: the lady was throwing her head back, shrieking with laughter, enjoying her night out with people who were probably her husband, children and teenaged grandchildren. The woman looked to be about the same age as Pippa. Why couldn't the laughing woman have died instead of her? Why couldn't *her* children feel this dreadful pain instead? After all, they had each other to pull them through their misery and Tammy had no one, except her father, and the heavy burden of his loneliness and the shocking, unpalatable knowledge that she had a half-sister in Lyverton was stopping her moving on and building her own life.

Tammy felt guilty at the thoughts washing through her mind. The woman had done nothing to deserve to die, any more than her own mother had. She was perfectly entitled to spend a happy evening with her family at a village pub, being teased by her obviously doting husband when he'd cheekily dropped a red cocktail cherry down her cleavage.

Sounds of normality flooded back into her head. Someone had put an old 1970s song on the jukebox.

'Don't go breaking my heart ...'

Tammy gulped as her throat tightened and her nose tingled. The music provoked an almost-forgotten memory of the passion her parents felt as they sang to each other, and the song churned up two years' worth of grief in her heart. Her hands flew up to her face as she tried to stem the inevitable tide of tears that were welling up under her eyelids. The memory evoked by the lyrics was so strong she couldn't fight it back. Her parents were smiling at each other as the music started, then laughing out loud as they sang. Twirling ... whirling ... kissing ... Tammy had laughed and laughed until her tummy ached as her parents sang to each other, off key and out of sync. They had been in a world of their own. Then her father had picked her up and they'd flown and spun around the room in a happy haze, just the three of them, and when he had put her down again she had felt as if the floor was spinning beneath her, and her six-year-old knees had crumpled and she'd fallen over on the carpet, squealing with laughter. Happy. Oh, so very happy. What did it matter that her mother was old enough to be her grandmother? Who cared that her classmates had thought her father was so young, he was her older brother?

The tinkling laughter of the woman sitting at the next table merged with the music on the jukebox and sliced through Tammy's heart in a thousand sharp splinters. It had taken two years for the grief to rise to the surface, like the risen cream of May time, and for the first time since her mother's death she cried, the stinging, hot tears running through her fingertips and out of her nose and mouth.

CHAPTER FOUR

10:30 pm

"That girl over there is crying."

Paul Pepper was standing at the bar, alone, and his gaze automatically panned towards the subject of an eavesdropped conversation a few feet away from him. He raised his glass to his mouth and took a gulp of welcome, cold lager.

Cynthia, the pub landlady, was on the other side of the bar serving a customer. A few seconds later she leaned across to him and tapped him on the arm to attract his attention. She nodded in the direction of the alcove.

"That's the wee lassie who checked in this afternoon — she looks a bit upset to me. Can you go and see if she is all right, hen?"

Paul watched as the girl twisted her torso around on her chair, so that her back was towards them. Her chin dropped onto her chest as she rootled around endlessly in her handbag, obviously in distress.

He put down his half full glass of lager on the bar as the girl dabbed an inadequate scrap of already-used tissue over her eyes. Reluctantly, he negotiated his way over to the tiny alcove, pulled out a chair on the other side of the table and perched on the very edge of the seat.

"Here. Take these," he said extending his hand, in which he was holding a handful of fresh tissues extracted from a box behind the bar.

Tammy didn't hear him. She didn't even know he was there because her eyes were screwed shut, bathed in two years' worth of repressed tears that were flooding under the sodden scrap of tissue in mascara-tinted rivulets down her cheeks. She sniffed loudly and gave up with the tissue, trying to stem the flow with her fingertips.

Paul cleared his throat and reached out further, hesitating slightly before gently pulling her hand away from her face. He shoved the tissues into the palm of her hand.

"Can I do anything to help?"

Trembling slightly with embarrassment, Tammy pressed the soggy

26

scrap of tissue into her eyes again, letting Paul's tissues drop into her lap.

"It's okay. I found some in my bag," she finally said in a thick, nasal voice as tears escaped from her nose. She sniffed and then tried to wipe her nose with the rapidly disintegrating balled up piece of tissue.

Paul carefully plucked the clean tissues from her lap and handed them to her.

"Thank you," Tammy mumbled. "I'll be all right in a minute ... it's hay fever. It's all those grass cuttings and that smelly hawthorn blossom outside." She tried to force a laugh, but failed as more tears spilled over her bottom eyelashes.

"Aahh," Paul said, nodding in agreement, but unconvinced.

She dabbed at her eyes and cringed at the greyish streaks left behind on the tissue.

"I've messed up my mascara. I must look a dreadful sight."

Paul coughed, embarrassed. "I live here, by the way. I've got the room across the landing. I saw you check in earlier."

"Oh. Hi."

Paul extended his hand in a welcoming gesture. "I'm Paul."

"Tammy."

Tammy reached over the table and shook Paul's hand, trying to force a polite smile through her puffy eyelids and quivering mouth.

"Come on — let's get you out of here. You need to bathe those eyes in some cold water. Get rid of the pollen." Paul stood up, conscious that his gravelly voice was snagging the air as his chair scraped across the wooden floor. He cupped his hand under Tammy's elbow as she stood up too, clutching her open handbag with its wildly escaping contents in one hand and holding a piece of tissue to her nose with the other.

Paul was conscious that people were staring at them as he led her through the sea of curious faces and they made their way out of the door. His big hand rested lightly under her elbow as he guided her away from a woman's laughter and the unfeeling jukebox in the corner, belting out old 1970s songs. He opened the door to the staircase and felt her relax with relief when he shut it behind them. They climbed the stairs in silence.

27

Once they had arrived at the point on the landing where Tammy's room branched off to the left and Paul's to the right, she rubbed her hand across her eyes as, simultaneously, he swiped his key card in the lock. His bedroom door opened. Neither of them spoke.

Again, Tammy let him take her arm. As they crossed the threshold, she hesitated and pulled back.

"I ... I ... really don't think ..."

Paul bit his lip. He didn't know what to say, especially when she hid her face behind her hand and took an embarrassed step backwards. He let go of her arm.

"I'll leave the door open ... I, er ... I just thought I'd make you some tea or something."

Paul picked up a magazine rack and wedged it against the open door.

Muffled music from the bar and muted laughter swirled around the landing, filling the silence.

"Thanks," Tammy said, her voice muted and nasal. She let her hand drop, and for the first time Paul saw her face properly. Her eyes were red and puffy, smudged with mascara. Her cheeks were flushed and her tightly-curled, auburn hair untidy. His eyes instinctively fell to her breasts, which made barely an impression under her fitted white cotton shirt. Her jeans clung tightly to her slender, boyish hips, vulnerability seeming to shrink her somewhat. It was as if she was a newly-emerged butterfly, about to be captured in his huge, rough hands. He fought back a sudden urge to reach out and keep her safe, protecting her fragile wings from the harsh, indifferent world outside her cocoon.

***

His room was larger than hers — more like a tiny flat: L-shaped with a small sofa, coffee table and dresser as well as a neatly made bed. A tray holding mugs and a kettle nestled in one corner of the dresser. The room was cosy and lived in; not like a bed and breakfast room like hers. Tammy sat down on the sofa, wondering if it was wise to willingly enter a strange man's bedroom, but domesticity wrapped itself around her like a comforting blanket as the kettle burst into life,

28

crackling and hissing as it came to the boil.

Neither of them spoke. Paul bent down, his back to her as he opened one of the dresser doors to reveal a tiny fridge. Silently, he made the tea.

He turned to look at her over his shoulder and raised his eyebrows. "Sugar?"

Tammy nodded her head. "Yes, please."

Paul turned his back on her again as he vigorously stirred two mugs of tea on the tray; the sound of the teaspoon rattling in china mugs sounded crisp and sharp, like wind chimes in an open doorway. The sound swept away Tammy's embarrassment like a 1950s housewife brushing away unwanted cobwebs.

She studied the precise creases down the short sleeves of his blue and green checked shirt. The colours suited him and Tammy felt sure he must have a wife or girlfriend back home to iron his clothes and co-ordinate his wardrobe. There was no way he could possibly be single. Paul turned around, a smile crinkling at the corners of his eyes as he handed her one of the mugs. The sight of his slightly-tanned forearms fuzzed with blonde hairs made her heart nudge the inside of her chest with a tiny flip.

Paul sat down on the sofa next to her, but Tammy knew he was being polite and careful not to let their bodies touch. He perched on the very edge of the cushion, leaning forwards with his elbows on his knees as he sipped from his steaming mug. The pure, undiluted manliness he exuded seemed completely incongruous with the cosy, feminine room, but the way his sandy coloured, slightly wavy hair curled in the nape of his neck, and the way he was avoiding looking at her, made Tammy realise that he felt acutely self-conscious and vulnerable too.

Tammy heard herself begin to speak, but her voice was quiet, weakened by the unexpected avalanche of grief just minutes earlier.

"I'm sorry about back in the bar, just now. Thank you for rescuing me. I'm so embarrassed ..."

Paul turned his head slightly so that he was looking at her over his shoulder. He sat back further into the sofa, but his gaze quickly dropped from Tammy's. His reply was curt, clipped and measured.

29

"Not a problem. Glad to help."

"It was the jukebox ... the music ... not pollen at all."

"Aahh," he said, nodding as if he understood perfectly. "It's funny how music can sometimes do that ..."

His voice faded away and he took another breath as if he was going to add something else. He exhaled, changing his mind. Tammy was grateful he didn't ask any questions. She felt her body relax slightly into the soft cushions on the sofa. Paul stretched out his denim-clad legs and she noticed by the way his shoulders dropped that he was gradually relaxing too. They were not quite touching, but Tammy was conscious of the warmth of his body on the top of her arm.

***

Some time later, Tammy was acutely disappointed. Mesmerised by Paul's lovely smile and kind, twinkly eyes, she was desperate to talk about something other than environmental impact assessments, design and access statements and drainage systems. When she'd checked into the Red Lion earlier, and Cynthia had told her about the other guest who was staying at the pub, she had imagined he was a builder on the construction site. Now she knew she had been wrong. Paul *did* work on the site, but was based in the office as the site's civil engineer.

The boring conversation had been entirely her fault. An embarrassing, awkward silence as they had sipped their tea had forced her into making a throwaway comment.

"The housing estate on the edge of Lyverton is interesting," she had said. "I went for a walk around there this afternoon. The style of housing, the wide roads and grass verges are a really good example of the era, but it could really do with a landscaping feature, like a pond, don't you think?"

Paul had pounced on the innocent comment like a puppy tackling a large bone, and had seemed disproportionately overjoyed when he discovered she was an architect.

"So, what do you specialise in, then?" he'd said with a grin of admiration.

"I suppose I'm a bit of an expert on getting around the problems of dodgy ground, existing drains, old combined sewerage systems and the effects of the roots of nearby trees on building foundations, although I really prefer the landscaping and design side of things."

The slowly turning cogs of their respective professions had locked, perfectly connected, and then one had turned the other unmercifully as Paul had revealed he was the civil engineer on the new development site. His job, which he loved, and his obvious interest in hers, had become the entire focus of their conversation.

Despite the increasingly intimate atmosphere between them, Tammy felt he wasn't really interested in her. It was merely her career that had captured his undivided attention; a coincidental strand of connectivity between them that had given him an opening for animated conversation with a stranger. Still, she thought to herself, at least they had something in common and weren't sitting in an awkward silence.

Tammy drummed her fingertips on the arm of the sofa and then, not knowing what to do with her hand, fiddled with the stud earring in her ear.

"My father is a conservation officer."

"Really? How interesting ... "

"He works for the city council in York. He's into archaeology, too, but that's just a hobby. He's a geek, really. I'm an only child, so he's a bit overprotective. It drives me absolutely insane."

Tammy really didn't want to talk about her father, but she couldn't think of anything else to say that wasn't related to sewers and drains. She devoured Paul with her eyes. Everything about him was just slightly larger than life, strong and masculine. His hands were big, his legs long and his feet were massive. He was in a lot of ways the diametric opposite of her father, who was slightly built and dark-haired, whereas Paul's hair was lighter and his eyes the bluest of blue. Her father was tall, about the same height as Paul, but Alan's sensible head on his middle aged shoulders seemed too heavy for his thin frame, and it gave him a perpetual boyish appearance, which wasn't helped by his black-rimmed glasses and habit of continually running his fingers through his floppy hair, especially when nervous or unsure of himself. Tammy always thought he looked like an eccentric scientist, not a boring local government officer.

31

Paul leaned forwards, his legs spread wide as he rested his forearms on his knees and cupped his mug between his huge hands.

"My dad is in the building trade — he owns a builders' merchants."

"Is that why you went into civil engineering?"

"I suppose so. I'd always been interested in roads and bridges, that sort of stuff. I loved Lego and Meccano when I was a kid ..."

"I think I only drifted into architecture because of Dad's job," interrupted Tammy. "It's funny how your parents' occupations lead you into your career, isn't it? Doctors breed doctors and nurses; teachers breed teachers and lecturers ... and ..."

Tammy was burbling. She really didn't know what to talk about.

"And daddies with lots of money, a huge house, a top of the range Merc on the drive and only one daughter to dote on breed spoilt little slags," finished Paul with unexpected bitterness and dissonance in his voice. "Believe me. I know!"

Tammy's face fell. Surely he wasn't referring to her.

"I used to know one," he finished, lamely trying to extricate and distance himself from the clumsy comment.

Embarrassed by Paul's mistake, the fluttering in her tummy and slight breathlessness intensified. The unexpected physical attraction she felt for Paul was making her talk about silly things, like her father's job. She knew she was behaving like an awkward thirteen-year-old.

She was suddenly desperate for Paul to ask her why she was in Lyverton. She wanted to explain to him why she was so upset earlier in the evening. She needed to confide in him about her lost sister, her dead mother and her tragic father. She realised for the first time how lonely she had been for the past two years and, despite their easy conversation about work, her instincts told her Paul was suffering too. There was something in his life that was not quite right. But he didn't ask her any of these things. He wasn't interested. He didn't even want to know why she'd cried.

CHAPTER FIVE

Day Two
Tuesday, 26th May: 7.00 am

Tammy woke to the sound of a distant cuckoo. She slid out of bed and opened the old-fashioned French doors and stepped into the sunlight. Welcoming cool air brushed the tip of her nose and the balmy high-low call of the lone bird nearby beckoned to her, enticing her outside.

The roof of the pub kitchen below formed a small balcony, which had just enough room for a tiny table, two very old, folding metal chairs and several ancient clay plant pots filled with green foliage and early flowering summer bedding plants. She spread her arms wide, leaned on the rust-stained balcony rail and watched a car glide to a stop outside the village shop. A couple of newspaper boys shuffled out of the shop, laden with morning papers, hoisting heavy bags over their shoulders before climbing on their bikes and pedalling off furiously.

She could see quite a lot of the village from her vantage point, as the ground dropped away quite sharply from the high point of the Red Lion. Beyond the sprawling housing estate on the outskirts of the village, the undulating countryside rolled and dipped and then disappeared into an early morning haze.

Tammy wondered if the blue-grey splash of emerald edged water in the distance was the old quarries her father had remembered and had talked about in the past. She squinted, trying to make out the features of the landscape in the brightness of the sun, which sparkled enticingly on the distant rippling water, and she spotted two rows of tiny cottages at the water's edge. She shaded her eyes from the glare and shivered in the cool breeze, goose bumps visibly forming on her bare arms.

She turned her head and swept her eyes over the village in the opposite direction, and through a hotchpotch of buildings of various ages and colours she spied a tiny patch of mown grass and what looked like the top of a football goalpost. Could that be the playing field at the school where her sister was a teacher? And where was the Corner House in St Andrew's Lane, where, according to her father's list, Marian lived with her father, Tony Troutman, her mother's first husband? She would go there today, she decided. She would knock on the door and ask to speak to her. Quite what she was going to say, she hadn't worked out yet, but one thing she had deduced from her brief encounter in the post office, was that Marian Troutman seemed to be an approachable and perfectly ordinary middle-aged woman. It had been a stroke of luck that she had found her so quickly.

Her insides gave a tiny flip of trepidation as Lyverton's unique signature began to scribe itself somewhere deep inside her. The village was a living, breathing organism. It was as fresh and untainted as a newborn child and yet, at the same time, it frowned at her with eyes as wise and experienced as a scholar approaching retirement.

The old part of the village, through which the main road passed, included the Grade II listed ironstone Red Lion pub, the tea shop and some very pretty white, wafty-walled cottages with thatched roofs and colourful hanging baskets. The village had been added to in stages and had grown over the centuries, the most recent major addition being a cluster of smart, executive stone-built houses right on the edge of the village boundary, beyond the open plan, mid-twentieth-century housing estate, with its closely mown grass verges and mature silver birch trees swaying gently in the spring breeze. She turned her head. The church spire was very near to where Tammy stood on her balcony, rising proudly above rich foliage of yellows, greens and a splash of copper beech. The hands on the church clock told her it was still only just after seven.

"Hello. Did you hear the cuckoo?"

Tammy looked down into the pub car park, in the direction of a young girl's voice. The teenagers who, yesterday, had sat on the wall next to the post office and then waved to her from the pub's garden were standing just below her balcony, their fresh, young faces upturned.

"Yes," Tammy replied with a yawn. "It woke me up. Wasn't it lovely."

"We've been out cowslipping." The girl held up a bunch of yellow and blue flowers. "We found some bluebells too, in the spinney by the old quarry."

34

"Oh," Tammy said. "I don't think you are supposed to pick cowslips. Didn't you know? They are rare and protected by law."

The boy chuckled as if she had said something funny.

"Cowslips are supposed to be the keys of Heaven," the girl said. "The story is that St Peter dropped his keys and, where they fell, cowslips grew."

"You can make cowslip tea out of the flowers to cure rheumatism and gout," the boy added. "There are thousands of them around Fawsden Hall. They're not *rare*, missus."

"Do you like our village?" the girl asked.

"I think it's lovely — very pretty," Tammy replied. "Where do you both live?"

"Quarry Cottages," the boy said, pointing down the main road.

Tammy couldn't help herself smiling at them. They were just youngsters — clearly well mannered, but pushing the boundaries of parental constraints and stamping their own mark on the world by trying out a new type of grungy, weird fashion.

"I've got to go now — I can't stand out here any longer in my pyjamas. I need to go and get dressed," Tammy said.

"Bye," the children said together. "We'll perhaps see you later," the girl added with a wave.

Tammy stepped back into her room, leaving the French doors wide open. She yawned and her eyes focused on the antique oak dresser in her room, on which stood a tray containing an electric kettle and two china mugs decorated with snowdrops: her mother's favourite flowers. Tammy had planted some only last autumn in the place where they had scattered her ashes. It felt good to see the snowdrops on the mug. They represented a hint of familiarity in an unfamiliar place.

There was a rattle followed by a loud bang behind her, as a sudden swirling, cold breeze caught the open doors and they slammed shut. Tammy held her breath. It was still early and she didn't want to make a nuisance of herself by waking either Paul or the landlady.

***

In the adjoining room, Paul paused momentarily at the sound of slamming balcony doors.

She was up.

He finished adjusting his tie in the mirror and ran a comb through his thick flaxen hair before glancing at his watch. Then, on impulse, he decided to knock on her door and see if she needed anything. He couldn't remember everything he and Tammy had talked about last night, but he did know that almost three hours had passed by in a flash before she'd yawned, he'd glanced at his watch and they were both shocked to realise it was past one o'clock. The reticence and stilted reservation in her dark, haunted eyes had gradually disappeared as she had relaxed, to be replaced by a delectable gentleness and a flush of contentment on her cheeks as they had laughed and chatted about trivial, whimsical things. In the early hours of the morning, after they'd spent some time talking about their respective jobs, she'd even kicked off her sandals, drawn her feet up onto the sofa and hugged her knees under her fine, pixie-like chin as they'd talked about their hobbies and interests, long forgotten films they had seen and books they had read as children.

He opened his door, stepped across the landing and tapped hesitantly on Tammy's door. Her voice was muffled as she shouted a reply.

"Just a minute. I'll be there in a sec."

The door opened slightly and Tammy's surprised face peered out.

"Oh. Hello."

She opened the door wider, and self-consciously pulled her dressing gown belt tight, before running the fingertips of both hands through her tousled hair.

"I heard you moving about and wondered if you needed anything — I could fetch you a newspaper if you like."

"Oh ... thanks." Tammy rubbed her eyes and then ran her fingers through her hair again. "That's really thoughtful of you, but I was planning on going out today. I probably won't have time to read it."

"I wasn't sure if Cynthia had put any tea-making stuff in your room, either, but I see that she has. Good old Cynthia." As he spoke, Paul nodded towards the dresser in Tammy's room, with its kettle and identical snowdrop mugs on the tray.

"Thank you for being so kind to me last night," Tammy said, a

36

nervous laugh threatening to gatecrash her flustered voice.

She rubbed at a flush of redness on her neck and pulled her dressing gown belt tighter and tighter, before attempting to tame her tangled, unruly hair once again and hide an emerging red spot on her chin with her hand.

"It was nothing. Don't even think about it."

"It was totally out of character for me, breaking down like that. I'm usually so ... well ... controlled. I can't stand hysterical women who break down in tears all the time."

"Bloke trouble?"

"Oh no, nothing like that."

Paul smiled, pleased at her reply. "Which song was it that upset you?"

Tammy shrugged. "*Don't Go Breaking My Heart.* It came on the jukebox and took me completely by surprise. I didn't feel like crying and then all of a sudden, I couldn't stop myself."

"Oh, I know just what you mean. I hate that bloody jukebox. It churns up bad memories you would sooner forget and they are replayed over and over again. Makes you feel like Bill Murray in Groundhog Day. It gets you every time and there's just no escape, is there?" Paul said, leaning on the doorframe, with one hand in the trouser pocket of his suit, subconsciously jingling loose change.

Tammy rubbed again at her reddened neck. "I wish someone would invent a computer programme that could be plugged into the brain to erase bad memories like redundant, obsolete computer files."

"Oh yes, it would sell millions," Paul replied with a chuckle.

"They'd make a fortune," Tammy laughed. "But some memories are precious and music can be just fantastic when you actually want to remember happy times or a special someone."

Paul shook his head and rubbed his chin.

"Not for me, I'm afraid. That damned jukebox is lethal. I hate it. I just want to take a hammer to it most of the time, especially when people put on songs from last year."

Tammy frowned, intrigued. "Why?"

Paul looked at his watch. "Blimey, look at the time! I'll have to shoot off. Cynthia will have my breakfast ready by now and I have to be at work by eight. Enjoy your day, Tammy. I'll perhaps see you later."

And then, in a flash, he was gone.

***

Tammy shut the door and cringed as she caught a glimpse of herself in the mirror. She turned around to analyse her unwelcome reflection. She was an utter mess and her hair was so frizzed and tangled it made her look like Albert Einstein. Her breasts had completely disappeared into the thick folds of her dressing gown, which she was thankful she had pulled on just before Paul had tapped on her door. To top it all, a huge spot was emerging on her chin like an angry volcano.

She coughed and then squinted in the mirror against the reflected intensifying sun. She really did look quite unattractive when she screwed up her eyes like that — she must remember not to do it when Paul was around.

She sighed. Paul was much too successful and gorgeous to be interested in her; she needed to stop wishfully thinking about him and concentrate on the real reason she was there — her quest to find her family. She had already found Marian, so surely it couldn't be too difficult to find the rest of them in a small place like Lyverton?

***

After Tammy had dressed, for the second day running she found herself in the little tea shop, but this time she sat inside. By the time she'd showered and tamed her wayward hair, she had been too late for breakfast at the Red Lion. It was surprising how long it took to get ready when there were spots to conceal, eyebrows to pluck, fingernails to manicure, toenails to paint and people to avoid (especially those who might also be having breakfast downstairs before they rushed off to work).

"Mornin' miss."

Tammy turned her head to acknowledge an elderly gentleman who sat at a nearby table.

"Grand day again," he added.

Tammy smiled at him. "Yes, isn't it."

"Did you speak to Marian Troutman?" The elderly man shifted awkwardly in his seat and nodded towards the grinning waiter behind the counter, who was noisily sorting out cutlery behind a pile of folded snow-white napkins and red and white gingham tablecloths. "Young Daniel there tells me you're looking for her."

Tammy felt suddenly annoyed. Was nothing secret in a village?

"No, I haven't — not yet." She took a deep breath. "There's really no hurry."

The elderly man twisted around in his chair and leaned forwards to face her. He grimaced with the pain of arthritis in his hips. "What 'yer here for, m'duck? What's yer business in Lyverton?"

Groping for an explanation, Tammy lied, sending up an impromptu smokescreen.

"I'm a writer. I'm here to do some research into local history for a book I'm planning to write. It's a working holiday, really."

"What'yer writing about? Is it the fire?"

"The fire?" Curiosity beckoned and drew her further into the conversation.

"Just thought it might be the fire — what with Tony Troutman being involved and you wanting to speak to his daughter."

Tammy decided to throw him off track. She didn't want to attract too much attention to herself. It was obvious that Daniel, the waiter in the blue and white striped apron, had mentally noted every single name on her list and was in the process of spreading its contents around the village.

"I'm only writing about the history of the area and the archaeological features of the fields around Fawsden — you know, where the big development is going to be. Rather boring actually!" Tammy laughed self-consciously. It was false laugh and did little to convince the elderly gentleman.

"Umm ..." he said. "That's very interesting, m'duck."

"What fire was that, then?" Tammy enquired, curious.

"Just a bit of a fire in barns out Fawsden way. Two people got burned to death. The story was in all the papers. It's just that it involved Tony Troutman and I thought that might be why you were here. Oh, it doesn't matter — 'twas years ago, m'duck. Years an' years ago."

The elderly man shook open his morning paper and began to read, closing off the conversation. Tammy fell silent. Her father had said nothing about a fire, or about any sort of incident capable of making the news. Perhaps it had happened after he and Pippa had fled from the village.

"I've been talking to a couple of kids," said Tammy, making conversation. "They were out really early this morning. They said they live at Quarry Cottages. They look to be about thirteen or so. Do you know them?"

"Nah," the man said, shaking his head slightly as he continued reading his newspaper. "Can't say I know them — but we get all sorts of strangers through the village now they've started building out at Fawsden. Anyway, I can't see anyone living in Quarry Cottages — gone to rack and ruin, they have, over the years. They've just been sold for a quarter of a million quid, so I've heard. Some people have more money than sense, if you ask me."

"It's just that these children told me they had been picking cowslips, and cowslips are protected by law because they are so rare nowadays. I need to find these children and tell them it's illegal before they pick any more."

***

After she had eaten her breakfast, Tammy decided to visit the village churchyard on her way to The Corner House, where Marian Troutman lived. Traditionally, most quests for ancestral information began at churchyards, and it seemed as good a place as any for her to begin to discover her roots.

As she walked down Church Lane, the breeze rustled through tall, elegant silver birch trees. She met no one else: the lane was completely deserted and her only company was birdsong and the hum of the occasional car passing through the village on the main road.

Tammy looked over her shoulder. She had a powerful feeling she was being followed, but there was no one else in the lane. She glanced at people's homes as she walked towards the church. There were two or three rows of pretty thatched cottages and a couple of more

40

substantial, quite grand, houses linked together with outbuildings and barns. A sudden sense of urgency overtook her and the hairs on the back of her neck prickled as she heard a girl breathing heavily — almost panting — right behind her. She glanced over her shoulder again, alarmed. There was no one there, but she was sure she could still hear the heavy breathing of a young girl in her ear. It must have been the sound of the wind in the trees, she thought to herself with a sudden surge of fear as the sound faded away, but then almost immediately the same, warm feeling she had felt the night before washed through her body and made her feel serene and calm.

When she reached the church wall, she stopped and turned to face the churchyard, resting the palms of her hands on the rough, time-worn stone. After a minute or two she turned around and leaned on the wall, drinking in the picture postcard view of the old part of the village, with its pretty thatched cottages and tiny picket-fenced front gardens studded with bright jewels of early flowering summer shrubs. Hydrangeas, rhododendrons and pretty bushes laden with tiny pink flowers shed their perfumed petals like snowflakes over the narrow pavement and the breeze swirled them around and around in tiny eddies. She felt curiously light and timeless as she glanced up at an open bedroom window where curtains billowed gently. The sound of a newborn baby's cry drifted on the breeze, but it was so distant Tammy wondered if she had actually heard it or if it had been just her imagination.

Something in the air that morning was so perfect it felt as if she was being swept along in a different world. Was she always meant to be in Lyverton at that very moment? Right from the day she was conceived, was each minute and every second in her life pre-destined?

She shivered when she suddenly realised that there was not a single shred of evidence of the present day in Church Lane that morning. There were no parked cars or telephone boxes; no noisy electrical appliances or droning lawnmowers. The hum of traffic in the distance had faded right away. All she could hear was the sound of birdsong and the buzzing of insects, which harmonised perfectly with the faint smell of hawthorn and the fresh, light feel of a spring breeze on her face. She felt a prickle of fear on the back of her neck as the sound of the wind in the trees played games with her imagination. Something in the lane was spooky and odd. It could easily have been fifty, or even a hundred, years ago.

CHAPTER SIX

11.10 am

The funeral procession glided along the lane to St. Andrew's Church and the sombre tyres of the hearse crunched dramatically as it turned into the gravelled driveway before coming to a sedate stop. Relieved at the sight of a vehicle and people, Tammy watched from the corner of the churchyard where, for a few minutes, her eyes had been darting over various names on gravestones as she tried to push the sense of unease out of her mind.

A second car, presumably carrying the family of the deceased, ground to a stop a few feet behind. The car door opened and the driver slid out, before opening the rear door for the family mourners.

More people began to arrive, and a smart silver-grey 4 x 4 parked to the side of the funeral party. An elegant, mature lady swung her legs out of the passenger door and took the driver's arm with a beaming smile as she stood up, straightening her jacket with a refined, gloved hand.

Tammy's heart lurched with an unexpected, sudden déjà vu. Had she seen that smile before? She bit her lip and reluctantly dragged her eyes away; the woman had spotted her and she was near enough to recognise a certain curiosity in her eyes. Tammy was so preoccupied with staring at the funeral party, she didn't realise the vicar had just walked over to her, his hand extended.

"We're running a little late," he said, taking Tammy's hand and shaking it enthusiastically. "Would you like an order of service?"

Without waiting for an answer he thrust one into her hand and propelled her towards the funeral party before striding off to speak to the well-groomed mature woman who Tammy had thought seemed vaguely familiar.

Tammy stared at the order of service in her hand and then glanced up again. The elegant woman was standing next to a portly, middle-aged man in a dark grey suit. Courteous and polite, his well-trimmed greying moustache nestled comfortably on his upper lip as he took the lady's arm. The driver of the car opened the other passenger door and helped out an elderly gentleman. His black suit swung around his shrunken frame, and his trembling gnarled fingers folded tightly around his walking stick as he gripped the driver's arm with his other hand. He was very frail, but inexplicably Tammy felt he was once an athlete, and imagined him rubbing pungent liniment into his muscled calves before taking part in an important race.

A blonde-haired teenaged girl jumped out of the car behind the elderly man, followed by a harassed-looking attractive woman who was probably her mother, because they looked so similar.

"Come along everyone — we must hurry now — we're running late, I'm afraid." The anxious vicar walked behind Tammy, with his arms outstretched as if rounding up cattle. There was no choice: she had to step forwards. She turned around to try to escape, but other people were forming a queue behind her and Tammy was trapped, sandwiched between them and the family she had just watched arrive.

No one gave Tammy a second glance as she trundled into the church and resigned herself to having to attend the funeral of someone she didn't know. She was embarrassed, but thought it would be rude and disrespectful to the deceased person to just walk away. If she sat right at the back, she thought, she might get a chance to just slip out again, unnoticed.

There was room in a pew close to the back of the church, alongside a ruddy-faced, slightly dishevelled man with a huge, bulbous nose and heavy-lidded eyes. Tammy slid into the space at the end of the pew, leaving a considerate gap between them. She studied him out of the corner of her eye. A hard, brash character with sparse, grey hair that needed a good cut slicked over his balding head, he looked like an ageing rock star. The man's large stomach hung over the top of his trousers, his white shirt taut and strained at the buttonholes. With one hand on the pew in front he twisted around, laughing and joking with the mourners in the pew behind. Tammy could see pinpricks of sweat forming on his brow and his red jowls wobbled as he spoke in a broad Midlands accent.

"Shame about the ol' gal. Still she wuz a poor mess, weren't she, stooped right over nearly double like that. Talk about 'ere's me 'ead

44

and me bum's comin!"

He let out a much too loud guffaw, which echoed and attacked the dignity of respectful low murmuring voices and soft organ music playing inside the church.

"I wonder 'ow they shut the lid?"

The man was acting inappropriately. Tammy was shocked at his comment: it was almost as if he was enjoying himself. Heads at the front of the church turned to look at him, deprecating stares cutting through the shafts of sunlight from the stained glass windows. He continued to talk, still much too loudly.

"How old wuz she? Must've been crackin' on a bit. Good turnout from the village ain't there."

Tammy pretended to study her order of service as a well-spoken woman in the pew behind interrupted. Tammy glanced over her shoulder.

"She was ninety-six, Tony Troutman, as well you know! Show a bit of respect for her, will you? A grand woman was Alice Thompson — salt of the earth."

A flush of heat flooded into Tammy's face, her heart beating so fast she began to feel dizzy.

Tony Troutman: her mother's first husband. How on earth could Pippa have been married to such an obnoxious man. What strange fate had placed her outside the tea shop yesterday and in the church today? It was as if unseen hands of destiny had gripped her by the shoulders, propelled her into the church and pushed her down into the pew.

***

Marian Troutman had been worried all week about her father going to Alice Thompson's funeral. He didn't get out much, and, when he did venture out of the house, his behaviour was either inappropriate and loud, or detached and zombie-like. She knew no one in the village liked him — and she didn't much like him either. Although in a macabre kind of way she welcomed the sympathetic glances that were inevitably tossed her way whenever they ventured out together, the whispered comments behind hands and condemning stares embarrassed her.

45

She shifted awkwardly in her seat. In an effort to blend into the background and not draw attention to them both, she had chosen to wear a plain, black knee length dress, but she had lost weight recently and it hung from her shoulders, bunching shapelessly around her.

"Ssshhhh. Keep your voice down, Dad ... please?"

"All right, all right," Tony Troutman grumbled. "I was only sayin' ... don't get yer knickers in a twist."

Marian leaned forwards to pick up her handbag, suddenly remembering she hadn't switched off her mobile phone. An absence of make-up and her hair, tightly drawn back into a knot at the back of her head, made her appear haggard and drawn. She could really have done with her father being in one of his quiet, clammed-up moods today. Instead, he almost seemed over-excited — like a child about to go to a party.

The low drone of the organ music stopped abruptly, and the murmur of conversation in the church died out. There was a cough, a shuffle and then silence.

The congregation stood as the organ began to play again, heralding the arrival of the pall-bearers and the start of the funeral service. Marian glanced at the young woman who had just slid into the end of the pew beside her father. The woman turned her head and their eyes locked. Marian shot a half smile at the woman — a stranger. She supposed she was a distant relative of the Staverleys. They were a large family and it looked like they had turned out in force to give Alice Thompson a good send off.

Marian was completely unprepared for the woman's reaction. She had expected her smile to be returned, but instead she was met with a mesmerised gaze that could only be described as shock. There was a definite glimmer of recognition in the young woman's eyes, and it unnerved Marian that she could not place her. Perhaps she had once been a pupil? Yes, that would be it. She would have taught her in the past and didn't fully recognise her now she had grown up. She smiled again at the woman. Once again, her smile was not returned. She looked straight ahead and tried to calculate the young woman's likely age, mentally going through the names of red-haired little girls she had taught around twenty years ago.

Glancing sideways again, Marian noticed that the young woman's hand was trembling as she held her order of service. There was definitely something bothering her. With a lurch of the stomach she wondered if she had once shouted at her: could she once have pushed her too hard and undermined her confidence in some way? She hoped not. She would have hated to have left a scar so deep on a young mind that she was someone to be hated when they met again unexpectedly twenty years later.

***

Tammy was trembling so much it was forcing little gasps of air from her lungs as the funeral procession entered the church. Since her brief encounter with Marian Troutman in the post office queue, she had been thinking constantly about how she was going to introduce herself to her half-sister. But now her mother's other daughter had looked straight at her and smiled, Tammy felt physically knocked off balance as Marian's second, fleeting smile flooded her bloodstream with adrenaline. What on earth was she doing there, sitting in a church full of people she didn't know, just inches away from her long-lost sister, attending the funeral of a stranger called Alice Thompson?

The encounter in the post office yesterday had been different because Marian had not noticed her. Now she had, Tammy felt like a wild animal, trapped and confused with nowhere to run to avoid being captured by something so much bigger than her.

She tried to pull herself together and tell herself she was being stupid. It was just a glance and a welcoming smile. She had read too much into it. And anyway, she reasoned, she couldn't help getting caught up in the funeral. It had been something that couldn't be avoided.

Tammy began to calm down as Alice Thompson's close family members sat down in the front pew and the pall-bearers placed the coffin on its stand. The organ music came to an abrupt stop and the service began.

***

"I saw you in the church earlier," Cynthia, the pub landlady, said. "Did

47

you know Alice Thompson?"

Tammy shook her head, watching Cynthia cut up a homemade fruit cake into slices.

"No. I feel dreadful about it actually. I was just doing some research in the churchyard when the vicar thrust an order of service into my hand and ushered me in. It was a pure accident I happened to be there."

Cynthia threw her head back in an infectious chuckle, the knife in her hand waving dangerously through the air.

"I remember once I went to the wrong funeral at the crematorium in Fawsden. I got the time wrong, got there too late and, before I knew it, there I was, at the back of the wrong chapel with no chance of escape. After the service ended someone came up to me and made small talk."

Cynthia grimaced and gave an exaggerated shudder.

"Oh no! What did you say?" Tammy asked with a giggle.

"I made my excuses and just fled as quickly as I could. I overheard the embarrassed whisperings. *'Who on earth is that large Scottish lady who sat at the back – does anyone know her'.*"

"This is very nice," Tammy said, chuckling as she glanced around Cynthia's cosy kitchen. "Thank you for inviting me in."

Cynthia was the third person she had met in Lyverton who had made her feel welcome, and she had only been in the village for a little over twenty-four hours. The perfume Cynthia wore reminded her of magnolia and honeysuckle and was very similar to that her mother used to use. She was a very attractive lady for her age, Tammy thought to herself. Although a large woman, she was immaculately made-up with manicured bright red nails and coppery-blonde lacquered hair clipped up in a fashionably casual style. She noticed that Cynthia's earrings matched the heavy necklace that sparkled around her neck, and Tammy was suddenly conscious of her own, much too casual appearance and lack of jewellery. She felt dowdy in comparison to Cynthia and resolved to make more of an effort for dinner that evening, especially as Paul had said he might see her later.

"There were a lot of people at the church this morning," Tammy commented, making conversation.

Cynthia nodded in agreement.

"Alice was a lovely lady, very popular. She was a good age, though … late nineties, so I believe." She handed Tammy a slice of fruit cake on a china tea plate. "She had no family of her own, you know. She was orphaned as a child when her father was killed in action in the great war and then her mother died soon afterwards. The Staverley family took her in and she was brought up alongside the Reverend's other children at the vicarage. She then became a sort of matriarch for the whole village. Everyone loved Alice Thompson."

"So the local vicar gave her a home when she was orphaned?" Tammy said. "That was really good of him."

"Yes. The Reverend Edward Staverley. He lived to be a ripe old age, too — apparently he was the rector at the church for years. I remember his hundredth birthday party in the eighties, just after I came to live in the village. They had a marquee on the village green and everyone was invited. The parish council did a *This is Your Life* for him and it was absolutely fascinating."

She hesitated and then scratched the side of her nose, changing the subject. "Young Daniel tells me you're looking for Marian Troutman."

Tammy jumped visibly with shock. Did everyone now know why she was in Lyverton? On impulse, she decided to perpetuate the white lie she had told the old man in the tea shop that morning.

"I'm a writer, researching local history. My father gave me the names of some people he knew in the village years ago. He thought they might be able to help."

"How interesting! I can't believe I have a famous writer staying in my pub … och … that's just wonderful. What's your father's name? I might know him."

Tammy pushed her hair back and tucked it behind her ear. She knew Cynthia wouldn't remember her father's name. "Alan Hargreaves … but Marian and her father are on the list of people he remembers, that's all," she said, nervously fingering the stud in her ear.

Cynthia pursed her lips and gave a concerned shake of the head. Her voice dropped to a whisper.

"If you don't mind me saying, you don't look much like the type of lassie whose father would be associated with the likes of Tony

49

Troutman!" Cynthia wrinkled her nose in distaste. "How his poor wee daughter puts up with him I'll never know. He's almost a total recluse and sits watching television, drinking beer and smoking all day long, so I've heard." Cynthia sighed and shook her head again. "I think he's been suffering from depression for so long he's lost all sense of how to behave in public ... and he smells ... ugghh."

"Actually, I found myself sitting next to Tony Troutman and his daughter in the church this morning. He made a joke in a very loud voice about Alice Thompson and how bent over she was when she was alive. He wondered how they shut the coffin lid."

"No! How rude."

"A woman behind us ticked him off for his insensitivity, called him Tony Troutman and I nearly jumped out of my skin. I decided I wasn't going to approach them — not today anyway. Tony wasn't a friend of my father, by the way; just an acquaintance."

Cynthia reached out for a second slice of fruit cake, the golden bangles on her chubby wrist and the huge rings on her fingers catching the afternoon sun. Tammy thought that Cynthia could easily be everyone's mother. She closed her eyes momentarily. You didn't lie to a mother. But something stopped her revealing the real reason she was in Lyverton. She couldn't say anything about Marian Troutman yet. It was much too soon. She changed the subject.

"Cynthia. I spoke to some kids in the car park early this morning, and then again after the funeral service — young teenagers — about thirteen or fourteen I should think. They had been out picking cowslips and I told them they'd get in trouble. Cowslips are protected by law."

"Cowslips?" Cynthia replied with a frown. "The little monkeys — we ought to get in touch with the parish council to put something in the village newsletter. I knew there were some cowslips growing in the wild around here, but not that many. We can't have that ..."

"They were in the church at Alice Thompson's funeral, sitting near the front," Tammy said quickly. "You must have seen them. They hadn't made much of an effort to dress up — looked quite scruffy for a funeral, I thought."

Cynthia dabbed at her mouth with a folded serviette and frowned in puzzlement. "I can't think who they could be."

"They said they live in Quarry Cottages."

"Oh … I didn't realise people had actually moved in. Those old cottages went for a quarter of a million pounds, you know. They need lots of work doing to them — they've been empty for years, so I believe," Cynthia said. "Perhaps they are living in a caravan on the site or something."

"They both dress really weird — or perhaps it's just a new teenage craze. The boy was wearing a checked shirt, braces and baggy brown trousers and the girl had on a loose navy blue dress and black boots. They sat right near the front at the funeral."

Cynthia shook her head. "I don't think I saw them, hen."

Tammy continued. "They walked back down the lane just behind me after the funeral service, giggling and messing around with those big white flowers that grow in hedges. What's the proper name for them? They called them *Granny Pop Out of Beds*."

Cynthia puffed out her cheeks. "Bindweed flowers — or Morning Glory, as they are commonly known. They're the absolute devil to eradicate once they take hold in your garden. The root system can go down in the ground for about thirty feet, apparently."

"I think their mother must be some sort of herbalist," Tammy speculated. "Actually, I suppose they could even be Romany gypsies. They told me this morning that you can make cowslip tea out of the flowers to treat rheumatism and gout, and then, on the way back from the funeral service, the girl was screeching with laughter when she told me her mother once made a laxative out of the stems and roots of the bindweed flowers and someone drank too much of it, thinking it was parsnip wine. They really don't understand they mustn't pick the cowslips — they just laughed at me when I said they are rare and protected."

CHAPTER SEVEN

7:30 pm

The table was set for two with a triangular white plastic *reserved* marker sitting ominously in the centre. Tammy shot a quizzical look at Cynthia, who was busy behind the bar serving a customer. She smiled, gestured with a toss of her head and pointed towards the table in the alcove where she had sat the previous night, and where the *reserved* marker had been placed.

"I've put you with Paul. Is that all right?"

Tammy flushed a deep red. Cynthia was matchmaking: she just knew it. She hoped no one was going to put any old music on the jukebox; she didn't want a repeat of last night's embarrassing scene.

Tammy ordered a drink from the bar and realised that the barman was the young waiter, Daniel, from the tea shop.

"You get around a bit," she said. "Tea shop in the mornings and the pub in the evenings?"

Daniel grinned at her. "It's just summer jobs," he replied in his perfect, Eton English. "I'm at uni. Just finished my second year, actually. Did you speak to her yesterday? Old Trout ... Miss Troutman, I mean?"

Tammy shook her head and wanted to giggle at Marian's nickname. "Not yet."

"She's a great teacher. The best."

"Oh?"

Tammy wondered how such a dull and uninteresting person could possibly be animated enough to inspire her pupils and infuse them with enough motivation to learn.

"I told her you were looking for her," Daniel continued. "I bumped into her coming out of the church this morning, after Alice Thompson's funeral."

Tammy was horrified. The village was alive with gossip, and she appeared to be the main topic of conversation. She had always hated being in the limelight. She preferred to be the girl at the back who no

52

one remembered.

"But you don't even know my name!" Tammy remonstrated, unable to disguise the blind panic in her voice.

"I didn't yesterday, but I do now, because you are staying here, aren't you? It's Tamasyn Hargreaves, isn't it?"

Tammy gulped. Cynthia must have told him.

"Tammy. People call me Tammy."

She felt a hand touch her elbow.

"Hello, you."

She spun around and blushed, flustered. Paul was standing right behind her, grinning. Her heart thudded in surprise as she realised he was actually quite pleased to see her. She perhaps hadn't made too much of a fool of herself that morning after all?

"I think Cynthia has put us at the same table for dinner tonight. I hope you don't mind," Paul said.

Tammy shook her head and glanced up at the clock in the bar. She turned to face Paul, but her heart was beating so fast it made her feel momentarily light-headed and she forgot to smile at him.

"No, of course not. I just have to shoot off for a minute, though."

She dropped her head and rummaged in her bag, hiding her face behind her hair. "I don't mind at all as long as it's all right with you," she mumbled into her bag, exasperated at not being to find her mobile phone amongst at least six months' worth of detritus.

"I just have to go and make a telephone call to my dad … he's on his own. I need to check he's okay and let him know where I'm staying …"

Paul took her drink from Daniel's outstretched hand.

"… that's if I can find my phone in here …" Tammy mumbled as she began to back away.

"You go ahead and make your call. I'll take this over to our table for you."

Tammy knew he was watching her as, still rummaging in her bag, she hurried into the lobby and bumped down on an extremely old, rickety white wicker chair, almost disappearing into the plump, chintzy cushion. She pushed her wayward hair back with her hand and then tucked it behind her ear as she made her phone call, relieved to have escaped.

***

Paul leaned on the bar, watching Tammy as she clutched her phone to her ear.

"She's a smashing wee lassie, isn't she?" Cynthia said.

Paul gave an unconcerned shrug for Cynthia's benefit. "She's okay."

"You're about the same age ... both unattached ... both young ..."

Paul didn't answer.

"She's a writer, you know. She told me this afternoon."

Paul narrowed his eyes in puzzlement. "She didn't mention anything about being writer to me. She's an architect — she told me last night."

"Oh yes, she's definitely a writer. Local history, so I believe."

Paul shoved his hand in his trouser pocket, jingling the loose change.

"Probably a hobby ..." he began, but Cynthia interrupted.

"She's an attractive wee girl, but she doesn't realise how pretty she is. She just needs a man to tell her." Cynthia winked at him and cocked her head on one side. "She needs a strong, tall, handsome man just like you to breathe some romance into her life and then — you mark my words — she'll bloom like a magnificent rose on a summer's day."

Paul looked at his shoes, embarrassed at Cynthia's obvious matchmaking. Why couldn't people just leave him alone and stop trying to interfere in his life?

***

Tammy clutched the phone to her ear squinting in the amber evening sunlight. Her father answered straight away, before it had even rung properly.

"Hello, Dad. It's me."

"Tammy! I've been trying to ring you all day. Why didn't you answer your phone? How are you? Did you find somewhere to stay? How are things going? Have you spoken to Marian yet?"

Tammy avoided the bombardment of questions by telling Alan about her visit to the churchyard, and then made him laugh when she

54

mentioned accidentally attending the funeral.

The unanswered question about Marian lingered on the airwaves, and she smothered and killed it before it could escape by talking about Cynthia.

"The pub landlady is very nice, her name is Cynthia McLaughlin, do you remember her? She must have been here for some time, because she seems to know absolutely everyone in Lyverton."

"I think she must have taken over the pub after we left," Alan replied. "It was an elderly couple who owned it when I lived there. I don't think I know Cynthia. How old is she?"

"I don't know ... can't really tell. Probably about fifty ... ish ... give or take a few years. She's Scottish."

"You've got to remember, Tammy love, it's been over thirty years since I set foot in Lyverton."

Silence.

Neither of them knew what to say next.

The jukebox in the bar started to play and Tammy was relieved as Lady Gaga's Poker Face drifted through the pub. The irony of the song made her grimace as she imagined Alan's unsmiling face on the other end of the phone, and she realised she couldn't remember seeing him smile properly since her mother died.

"Whose funeral was it you got caught up in?"

"An elderly lady called Alice Thompson. Did you know her? She lived here all her life, so people say."

"Alice! She must have been getting on a bit. I remember her well. She lived in The House on the Hill right at the top of Church Lane with her companion, Lucy Staverley. Lucy ran the Church Boys' Brigade when I was a kid, and Alice used to be involved with the Brownies. Lucy had a sister, too — I think she might have been a missionary or something."

Tammy was thrilled her dad knew Alice Thompson and it somehow drew them closer together in a nice, controlled sort of way. She felt the threads of the past tightening and pulling her in. It was as if her roots were beginning to wriggle through soft, peaty Lyverton soil in an effort to anchor themselves in the village.

Inexplicably, she didn't want to talk to Alan about finding Marian.

The knowledge she had an older half-sister had been itching away at her for three, long years, ever since her parents had sat her down when it was clear that Pippa's cancer was terminal, and then tearfully told her about Marian Troutman. Now she was actually in Lyverton, scratching the itch, she was finding it was one of those type of itches that hurt when scratched. Tammy really wanted to talk instead about the two old ladies, Alice and Lucy. She was suddenly intrigued to find out more about them; especially now she had accidentally attended Alice's funeral.

"Do you think Lucy could be still alive?"

"I wouldn't have thought so. She was a bit older than Alice. Lucy had lots of brothers and sisters — there were always lots of Staverleys in the village."

Alan changed the subject. "You could knock on the door of my old house while you're in Lyverton. I know my parents don't live there now, but the people who do might know where they've gone."

"I need to find Marian first," Tammy said. "If my grandparents have moved right away from Northamptonshire, I'm not chasing off around half of England. I just want to concentrate on making contact with Marian before I do anything else."

Alan paused. He was disappointed and Tammy knew it, but she felt a tingle of annoyance. Surely it was *his* job to find his parents? *Her* quest was to fulfil her deathbed promise to her mother. Now all she needed to do was to pick the right moment to approach Marian.

"Did the old ladies always live in the House on the Hill?" Tammy asked.

"I think so — for as long as I can remember, anyhow. If Lucy was still alive she would have been at the funeral, though, wouldn't she?" Alan replied.

"I suppose so. I would think that Alice probably outlived her," Tammy said. "After all she was ninety-six, according to a woman in the church."

As she rang off, Tammy was conscious that she had deliberately held back telling her father about sitting next to Tony and Marian Troutman in the church. Why did she do that?

She looked at her watch. It was twenty past eight and Paul would be waiting to order his evening meal. Relieved that the music on the jukebox was more up-to-date tonight, she levered herself out of the wicker chair, ran her fingers through her hair and smoothed down her clothes before walking through to the lounge.

She stopped in her tracks at the door, her heart thudding wildly. Marian Troutman was sitting in her seat, talking to Paul.

***

It seemed like minutes that Tammy stood in the doorway, staring at her sister, but it could only have been a few seconds. It was obvious Paul had been uncomfortably waiting for her to reappear, because he spotted her straight away and stood up. Marian turned her head, and her eyes bored into Tammy as Paul smiled and she lip-read his: *'here she is'*. If she had wanted to make her escape a second ago, she certainly couldn't now they had seen her. She took a reluctant step forwards and felt like a frightened actress about to go on stage.

"Tamasyn ... Miss Hargreaves?"

Tammy glanced all around her, subconsciously seeking a bolthole. She blushed a crimson red and scrubbed her hand over her burning neck.

Marian Troutman stood up, pushed her chair back and extended her hand as Tammy reached the table.

"Hello."

"Hi ... I ..."

Tammy was lost for words as she took Marian's hand.

"I'm so pleased to meet you, Miss Hargreaves. I believe you've been looking for me?"

Tammy nodded and shook hands with Marian; warm skin on warm skin; her sister's skin. She was conscious that for the very first time in her life she had touched a relative who was not one of her parents. A tingle ran up her arm.

"I saw you in the church this morning at Alice Thompson's funeral." Marian said with enthusiasm. You were sitting beside us, weren't you, but then Daniel told me you had already gone by the time we left the church.

Tammy forced herself to throw a convivial smile into the air, and

57

glanced at her reflection in a Jack Daniels printed mirror behind her. Her hair was a mess because she must have been subconsciously twisting it around her finger while she was on the phone, and, even in the dull light, she could see the spot on her chin, which appeared to be getting bigger by the second.

Marian seemed animated, excited even, and her face and eyes were bright. It was as if she had mysteriously become much younger. She had changed into a completely different person.

"I'd be so happy to help you research your book. I've lived here all my life, you know."

"I would have spoken to you in the church but, well, it wasn't really the time or place …" Tammy's apologetic voice petered out. Was she really such an exciting topic of conversation in the village? Her throwaway comment this morning now seemed to be common knowledge. Villagers were now obviously fascinated by her presence, judging by the undulating sea of Chinese whisperers looking her way.

Tammy's eyes fell on Paul, who was looking at her and beaming. She noticed that, as well as the kindness in his clear, blue eyes when he smiled, he had a very attractive cleft in his chin. She closed her eyes momentarily in frustration. She'd told him she was an architect, which was the truth. Now he'd just discovered her white lie about being a writer, something she had conspicuously failed to mention last night. She realised Marian was still talking to her as Paul's gaze fell away and he went to fetch another chair.

"I hope you don't mind me seeking you out tonight," Marian said. "When I heard about your book I was so excited about it. I just love local history, don't you? I find it fascinating to learn about the people who've lived in the village throughout the ages."

Tammy was finding it very difficult not to stare at Marian, who didn't seem to have any idea of her discomfort.

Paul returned with her chair, but Tammy didn't sit down because she was still staring at Marian's face. Her eyes were dark like hers. The shape of their noses was identical, too. It was as if she was a student cramming in history dates just before an exam. Her mother's voice echoed in her head. *'It's rude to stare, Tammy.'* She tore her eyes away and pretended to search for something in her open, untidy handbag.

She could feel her neck burning even redder, and her palms were clammy. Her whole body was trembling inside. The stupid lie about writing a book was galloping away from her and she didn't know how to lasso it back.

She gave herself the luxury of another quick glance at her sister, and noticed Marian was wearing a smudge of eye shadow and a lick of mascara on her eyelashes. Her lips were brushed with a hint of lipstick and her dark brown hair, shot through with a few silvery strands, was loose. She looked smart and elegant in neat tailored trousers and a smart, fitted jacket. Tammy flinched, certain she could actually feel something tugging in the region of her navel, pulling her towards Marian in an imaginary umbilical cord that connected them both to the spirit of Pippa.

Tammy looked up at Paul as she felt his eyes on her. Marian stared at Tammy, beaming with the rare pleasure of being needed and useful for once in her life. Simultaneously, all three of them realised that they were still standing, but Paul was the first to move. He pushed his chair away and smoothed back his hair with a self-conscious hand.

"Put that away, Tammy. I'll get Marian a drink."

Tammy looked down. Her disconnected hand had stopped rummaging in her bag and her fingers had managed to clamp themselves around her purse, having taken on lives of their own.

"What would you like, Marian?" Paul reached into his back pocket for his wallet. "If you two want to share this table, I'm quite happy to sit somewhere else."

"No," Marian said, "please don't move on my account. After all, you'll probably be able to help Tamasyn, too. The more the merrier."

"I suppose I *could* be of some help," said Paul, "but I don't have any local connections. I grew up on the east coast in Norfolk. I do know a bit about the archaeological study on the new development site, though."

The three of them smiled at each other, the ice broken with the pickaxe of a forced conversation.

Daniel appeared at the table, a self-satisfied grin plastered all over his face. "Can I get you two ladies some drinks? They're on the house. Cynthia says it's not every day we have a famous author in the village, researching local history in her pub."

Tammy's heart sank.

"I'm not famous! Really, I'm not. And I've already got a drink, thanks."

Lost for words she picked up a menu and studied it as intently as if it miraculously contained instructions on how to introduce yourself to a long-lost sister. She couldn't look at anyone. She really wished she'd not mentioned the writer story to the old man in the tea shop that morning. The spur of the moment smoke screen for the real reason behind her visit had obviously crept around the entire village and multiplied like Virginia creeper entombing an old building.

"I'm starving," she muttered, and then looked up at Marian. "Will you eat with us Miss Troutman? That's if Paul doesn't mind."

"Only if you're sure I'm not intruding — and please call me Marian, or Maz if you like."

"Of course I don't mind," Paul interjected much too quickly.

"Feel free, then." Tammy laughed nervously with a toss of her head. "Paul and I are both staying here, and Cynthia has sat us together at this table. We're not ... well ... erm ..." Her voice tailed off; again she didn't know what to say. "We didn't plan to eat together tonight, did we, Paul? So no, it doesn't matter if we all eat together and have a little chat. I appreciate you taking the time to seek me out, I really do."

Tammy looked down into her lap and rubbed her forehead with a shaky hand. The words had come tumbling out — far too many and all wrong. Paul would think she hadn't wanted to share a table with him.

"A bottle of wine then?" Daniel enquired. He had been standing beside the table, patiently waiting for them to order.

It was a thankful distraction.

CHAPTER EIGHT

9.30 pm

Marian Troutman had been looking forward to meeting the young writer all afternoon. It wasn't often that a reason to dress up and go out socially presented itself to her quite so eloquently. She had been astonished when young Daniel had stopped her in the street after Alice Thompson's funeral, told her that there was a famous writer in the village and she was right at the top of her list to interview for research purposes. He'd been quite insistent really. *'She'll be in the Red Lion around eight o'clock if you want to pop in,'* he had said. Being needed by someone who wasn't, alternately, a thorn in her side and a millstone round her neck was actually quite uplifting and refreshing. In any case, it would be lovely to be herself for a change instead of just *Miss* to a class of eight year olds, and *our Marian* to her father.

Now, an hour later, she wasn't quite so sure. During the main course of the meal, as they had chatted about the Lyverton village design statement, the emerging parish plan and the pros and cons of the new urban extension outside Fawsden, she had wondered if she had done the right thing in accepting the invitation; by the time dessert arrived she had felt mildly uneasy, and now, as she sipped her coffee, she felt she was definitely intruding. Daniel had conveniently forgotten to mention that Tammy would be dining with the disturbingly handsome young civil engineer who was also staying at the pub. Now, Paul was frowning and making a great show of inspecting the wine list when they still had half a bottle on the table. He was obviously frustrated she was still there.

"Let me buy you both another bottle of red," Marian said, pinning a convivial smile on her face, trying to make the best of an awkward situation. "And then I really must get back home."

Paul raised his eyebrows at Tammy. "Okay with you?"

"Fine. Thank you, Marian."

"How did you know Alice Thompson?" Marian said to Tammy, trying to make conversation as she tried to quickly finish off her glass

61

of wine.

"I didn't know her from Adam," Tammy replied with a grimace. "I was only looking around the churchyard at the gravestones when the vicar ushered me into the church and it felt a bit disrespectful to refuse to go in."

Marian chuckled. "I thought you might have been a relative of the Staverleys when you sat down beside us. It wasn't until afterwards, when Daniel stopped me in the street, I found out you were a writer and wanted to speak to me. Everyone in church wondered who you were."

"Like I said a while ago, it's just a hobby ..." Tammy said apologetically with a withering look at Paul.

"The vicar asked me this afternoon if I could get your autograph for his collection — and he wondered if you would sign a copy of your book for him," Marian said.

"I'm not well known. Really I'm not!"

Marian smiled at her. Tammy was being very coy about her writing. She even seemed embarrassed. Still, it must be hard to admit to being a writer, she thought to herself. People were quick to jump to conclusions about writers being either wild, eccentric, alcoholics or perpetually nervous recluses.

"Cynthia says Alice Thompson was a really popular woman: she must have had lots of friends, there were so many people at her funeral," Tammy said.

Marian noticed that Tammy was speaking much too quickly, the words tripping over themselves as they tumbled out. She wished the poor girl would just relax. She was a nervous wreck.

"She was a village legend," she replied as she felt another pang of unease. Paul was running his finger around the collar of his shirt and fidgeting in his chair and Tammy was spinning her wine glass round and round the table by its stem. In a flash of sudden understanding she knew what was going on. Why hadn't she realised it before? The tension she was feeling was sexual tension between the two of them. She decided to leave them to it as soon as she politely could.

"What did Alice used to do for a living?" Tammy said as she tore her eyes away from Paul and smiled at Marian.

"Alice was a nurse at the hospital in Fawsden — a children's nurse. She was a lovely, gentle, quiet lady. She'd never say a bad word about anyone. She was a great friend of ours and I've known her all my life. Her companion, Lucy Staverley, was the music teacher at the big school in Fawsden up until the early seventies. She actually taught me when I went there."

"Really?" Tammy said. "What was *she* like?"

"Enthusiastic to the point of eccentricity," Marian replied. "You wouldn't believe how many strands of jangling beads she wound around her neck and the wild, bad perms she used to have, which made her hair unbelievably frizzy. When she conducted the choir in church, her bushy eyebrows used to go up and down in time with the baton, and, I don't know why, but her petticoat always managed to peep out under the hem of her frumpy frocks.

"In contrast, Alice Thompson was quiet, unassuming and homely, but I don't think she was ever overshadowed by Lucy's extrovert personality. They complemented each other perfectly."

"Cynthia told me Alice was orphaned as a child. Did she have any other family? asked Tammy."

Marian shook her head and took a sip of red wine.

"No. She was an only child and never married. Neither of them did. But Lucy's family made up for it. They treated her as an aunt and even called her *Aunt Alice*."

"It's really the end of an era, then, isn't it?" Tammy said.

Marian nodded. "It is. Everyone in the village loved the *ladies* as they used to call them. What about you? Where do you live?"

Tammy took a large gulp of wine and answered too quickly.

"I live with my father in Yorkshire. My mother died two years ago. I was on the point of moving out into a flat with two of my friends when I was twenty-four, but then Mum was diagnosed with cancer and I felt I ought to stay at home and help Dad look after her. Then she died, and now I'm desperate to leave home — I'm much too old to be still living with my father."

Tammy coughed and spluttered, grabbing her wine glass again before swigging back another large mouthful. Too late, she had realised her gaffe and Marian didn't know whether to be offended or giggle at the remark. She was nearly fifty and still lived with *her* father.

"Husband? Boyfriend?" Marian speculated with raised eyebrows, trying not to seem offended by Tammy's remark.

Tammy shook her head vigorously and coughed even more.

"No."

Marian almost gave up. She didn't know what it was she was doing wrong, but the poor girl seemed to be most uncomfortable in her presence. She glanced to one side at Paul. She had been right about the sexual tension. He couldn't have disguised his obvious pleasure at Tammy's last remark even if he had pulled a brown paper bag over his head.

"Where do *you* live, Paul?" Marian asked.

"Here," he said with a theatrical flourish of his hand. "Right here is where I lay my hat."

"No wife … partner … girlfriend?"

"Nope."

"Oh."

Paul's clipped answer made Marian feel uneasy, even though Tammy was obviously quite pleased.

"We're all three of us free spirits, then, aren't we?" she said, much too brightly.

Paul didn't answer and neither did Tammy. They were still looking at each other. Tammy looked down at her hands and fiddled with what looked like a wedding ring, but on the wrong finger. Marian felt her discomfort: Tammy reminded her of a frightened bird, beating its wings against the hard wires of a steel cage, hopelessly trapped by her and Paul.

Marian changed the subject with a little dry cough.

I was thinking earlier — the Parish Council has a wealth of information about the village, Tamasyn … Tammy … if you are interested? We have parish records dating back to the beginning of the last century, census details and, of course, there are the minutes."

"That would be very useful," said Tammy with a sage nod of her head. "Very, very useful."

***

"You're on the parish council, aren't you, Marian?" Cynthia shouted over the din of multiple conversations, the chinking of glasses and the music on the jukebox. Paul looked over his shoulder, relieved at the change of conversational focus, but annoyed that Cynthia had quite obviously been eavesdropping little snippets of their conversation from her vantage point behind the bar a few feet away. He wished Cynthia would just get on with her job and Marian would clear off and leave him alone with Tammy. The evening was turning out to be a complete disaster.

"Yes, I am. I've been on it for about ten years now," Marian replied.

Cynthia waddled over and interrupted the conversation. "I think you might need to get something put in the parish newsletter about people picking cowslips. Tammy said some children had been picking them this morning, didn't you Tammy. They are supposed to be protected, aren't they?"

"Oh my word ... that's terrible. Yes, I shall ..."

Paul's attention waned as the conversation continued. He wasn't in the least bit interested and hoped Cynthia wasn't about to begin a long, boring conversation about wild flowers and then launch into her usual, vivid description of how to make home made sloe gin so strong it nearly blew your head off. She kept in her sideboard for special occasions, along with a vintage bottle of Johnnie Walker Blue Label that must have been worth a fortune. Tammy gave a little hiccup and her eyes seemed to lose focus, just for a second. He bit his lip, killing the chuckle that rose into his chest. He knew the wine was going to her head.

"We could all meet up tomorrow, if you like?" Marian said enthusiastically.

"I thought you were a teacher, don't you need to be in school?" Paul said, hardly bothering to remain polite. If she didn't go soon, the whole evening would be wasted and he would lose his chance to be alone with Tammy.

Marian shook her head. "Not this week, it's the Whitsun break — well Spring break, as they call it now. I don't go back until next week."

"I'd appreciate that Marian. It's very, very good of you to give up your time," Tammy said, her hands taking on a life of their own.

Paul grinned and his eyes crinkled at the edges in amusement. It was as if her hands were trying to escape from her wrists as she concentrated on fiddling with a beer mat, tearing off tiny pieces. Marian was obviously making her feel uncomfortable.

"How about ten o'clock tomorrow morning at the tea shop over coffee?" Marian suggested. "My treat."

Tammy looked up and forced a smile. "Thank you," she said. "That would be lovely."

"I can't, I'm afraid," Paul said before giving an exaggerated yawn, which he hoped would give a subtle hint to Marian. "I have to go to work." He shot a quizzical glance at Tammy, who had just bitten her bottom lip so hard it had left a mark. Was it that blasted woman, Marian Troutman, barging in on them and overwhelming Tammy with questions, or could it be he, himself, who was making her so jittery?

He'd never understand women, even if he lived to be a hundred years-old.

***

The wine was loosening her tongue and Tammy knew she should stop drinking. She shut her eyes and withdrew for a few moments into the dark world behind her closed eyelids. Her physical attraction for Paul and the proximity of her long-lost sister, who was completely oblivious to everything that was going on, had merged into a compelling desire to gulp down as much alcohol as she could so that she could escape from the inescapable, despite knowing that she needed to be in full control of her wits (and tongue). The wine was injecting her with a kind of life-blood, making an unbearable situation bearable.

Tammy opened her eyes and glanced across the bar towards Cynthia. She was wobbling; laughing; smiling; listening. Cynthia gave her a private little wink, which Tammy returned with a wonky smile.

Suddenly, Tammy knew intuitively that a complex kind of symbiosis was in play. The atmosphere in the Red Lion might have been tense with unfamiliarity, but the four of them were feeding off each other, grasping wildly at a peculiar type of spiritual affinity. It was as if the village was gradually snaking its way around them all, drawing

66

them into its coils, but paradoxically not for the purpose of crushing the life out of them, but rather to gather them together to bring nourishment and richness to its community.

Tammy closed her eyes again, her imagination unleashed, running free as the wine dulled her physical senses.

***

"You two just sit right there," said Cynthia. "Don't go away. I'll lock up and then we'll have a little nightcap."

Paul exhaled in a sigh of relief that Marian had left at long last. Tammy had drunk far too much wine, though. It had, at first, been a good thing because it had chased away some of her nerves, but she was now paying for it. She could hardly keep her eyes open, and Paul knew she'd have a bad hangover in the morning. Sighing, he resigned himself to writing off the evening. Marian might have gone, but now Cynthia was intent on joining them.

"Marian didn't drive home, did she?" Cynthia said.

"No, she left her car in the car park and walked," Paul replied.

"Good. She really let her hair down, for once? I've never seen her smile and laugh so much. She's such a sad lady — the poor woman leads a dreadful life with that father of hers."

"Could I have a coffee, pleashe, do you think?" Tammy slurred. "Any more alcohol will jusht about finish me off."

Paul chuckled. Tammy's voice sounded endearingly quirky.

"Och, hen! It'll help you get a good night's sleep it will. Just have a wee dram or a spot of brandy and then I'll get you a nice, strong coffee."

Tammy nodded. "Okay, brandy, then ... but jusht a tiny, tiny little bit." She threw a wide grin at Paul as she cocked her head on one side, narrowed her eyes and indicated with her thumb and forefinger just how small an amount she wanted. She hiccupped and put her hand over her mouth. "It's all this cure pountry air. Itsh making me so tired ..."

Paul's stomach lurched. Stripped of her inhibitions, Tammy was the loveliest woman he had ever met — it was as if every sexual feeling he had experienced in his life had rolled themselves up into a fireball in his abdomen. On the one hand he felt he had known her all his life, and on the other he knew he would never tire of watching her eyes when she laughed or marvel at the way she expressed herself so well with her hands as she talked.

He wondered if he should slip his arm around her. She appeared to be sliding sideways towards him and looked as if she might fall off her chair. What had happened to her in her life to leave her suspended as if in a time bubble? Emotionally, she was immature, almost childlike, unable to handle unexpected situations, like Marian Troutman turning up out of the blue and barging in on their evening. Yet behind her outward innocence lay an iron rod of steel-grey determination right down the length of her backbone. He could see she was entirely focused on her research for her book, and despite her outward fragility, underneath he sensed she was strong, resolute and, he thought, probably almost indestructible.

But something was wrong. It gnawed and niggled in the back of his mind. Why the hell hadn't she told him about being a writer?

***

Tammy was worried about the nightcap. She tried to focus her eyes on the empty wine bottles on the table. Were there three? Or four? She blinked and then gave up. Perhaps there were only two.

The Red Lion was empty, apart from herself, Paul and Cynthia. She didn't know what time it was and she really didn't care.

Something wriggled and fidgeted in her mind, and she forgot what it was for a moment. Oh yes, She was not an aspiring author, was she? And Marian was not just a nice, kind lady she had just met, she was her older half-sister. Everything converged in Tammy's confused mind and got in the way. Her mother's death, her father's grief and the huge question mark that hung in the air over both her past and her future was getting all muddled up in her head with strong feelings for a man she'd only just met. It felt like a jungle of tangled creepers and vines that she would never be able to fight her way through to the other side. In contrast, the accidentally attended funeral and the interesting story of Alice Thompson and the Staverley family beckoned enticingly, drawing her away from the need to hack through the dark forest of confusion in her own life and her death-bed promise to her mother.

Tammy watched through disconnected eyes as Cynthia returned from locking up the pub, disappeared behind the bar and bent down. She straightened up, rattling brandy glasses on the bar. Tammy blinked, trying to keep her eyes in focus.

She opened her mouth to tell Paul and Cynthia that the reason she was so drunk was because Marian was really her long-lost sister, and she had promised her mother on her deathbed that she would come and find her and tell her that Pippa had always loved her, but then she pressed her lips together so the words couldn't escape. She screwed her eyes shut, too. If she shut her eyes, she wouldn't speak. If she opened them, she knew her tongue would start to waggle and she would start blabbing about Marian. Her mouth would start opening and shutting and the words would come bursting out all on their own.

"Och. The poor wee hen is tired out."

The jingle of Cynthia's jewellery rang in Tammy's ears like clanging church bells. The tray rattled on the table. She slid sideways a little more, but couldn't muster up the inclination to straighten herself up.

Tammy's stomach did a little drunken flip as her eyelids fluttered open. Paul looked as if he was about to put his arm around her. He didn't do it: he hesitated too long, but Tammy knew he wanted to.

Cynthia settled herself down, wriggling her ample backside into the wooden chair with a tuneful tinkle of her jewellery. She leaned forwards, cradling her brandy glass. Her rings made a slight clink on the glass and her bracelet fell back halfway up her arm.

"I've got a bit of a story for your book. Not ancient history, but history all the same."

Tammy struggled to focus her eyes on Cynthia's face and gave a distorted grin as words escaped her lips.

"Oh. How interesting."

"It's about Marian's father ... Tony Troutman."

Cynthia leaned back in her chair, taking a sip of her brandy and raised her eyebrows conspiratorially.

Cynthia somehow slid right out of focus. Tammy turned her head. She must try to concentrate. Cynthia, now back in her line of vision, was wobbling both up and down and side to side at the same time. It made Tammy feel slightly sick, and so she closed her eyes again.

"I wasn't living in the village when something happened to put Lyverton on the map," Cynthia said. "It was years ago, but folks still talk about it, even now."

"Was it a fire?" Tammy managed to say as she opened her eyes again. "An old man in the tea shop mentioned it this morning. He said it made the national newspapers." She was making a huge effort to speak coherently, but she was struggling. Everything seemed distant and echoey. She felt the back of her chair slide away. This time she did feel an arm around her shoulder. It was so warm and cosy, Tammy couldn't resist the urge to slip further into the welcoming comfort and rest her head for a while. Oh dear, her head had fallen on Paul's chest. It did feel lovely and warm. Oh well. It wasn't her fault they gave her too much wine.

"Awww ... poor wee hen. Such a pretty young lassie."

Cynthia's voice fell to a whisper. "The little lamb's worn out. I'll tell her the story tomorrow."

Tammy was still listening. Her ears were not drunk.

"Did you know about Marian Troutman's father, Paul?"

Paul's voice vibrated through his chest into Tammy's ear as he replied. "I know there was some sort of scandal. You can't live in a village for nearly a year and not listen to the gossip."

As Tammy's heart fluttered, her abdomen tingled with excitement at the lovely feelings that rippled through her as if a pebble had just been dropped in her pond of desire, because Paul had put his arm around her. She heard Cynthia's bracelets jangle, then a slight slurp of brandy. The glass rattled on the table like a thousand crashing cymbals as she put it down.

"They say ..." Cynthia said to Paul in a whispered, theatrical voice, "... that Tony Troutman got away with murder."

CHAPTER NINE

The moment Tammy opened her eyes on her third day in Lyverton, her gaze fell on her mother's charm bracelet on the bedside cabinet. The bird in the cage was sharply focused in her field of vision, as if it was shouting out to her not to forget that she was the cuckoo in the Lyverton nest. The second thing she saw — after she had sat up in bed, running both hands through her tousled hair and wondering if she had brought headache pills with her for her hangover — was a folded sheet of paper under her door.

She slid out of bed and picked up the note.

'On Monday you left me holding soggy tissues. Last night you fell asleep on me and dribbled on me in a most unladylike manner. Despite all this I'd love to have dinner with you tonight. I promise I'll bring a clean shirt, just in case, and we will go somewhere very posh, very quiet (with no jukebox) and very far away from Marian Troutman.'

Underneath Paul had written his mobile phone number. She felt a flip of excited anticipation in her tummy and savoured it. She wouldn't text him just yet, but she would — later on — after she had met up with Marian Troutman and revealed her true identity. She didn't want to seem *too* keen. It wouldn't hurt Paul to be kept waiting for a text message in reply to his note. She felt like a little girl saving the last unopened present of Christmas until Boxing Day as she showered and dressed, ready for her meeting with her long-lost sister. This unexpected, exciting distraction from the difficult day that lay ahead of her would carry her through the awkward moments, unpalatable truths and painful emotions that would inevitably transpire after she had turned Marian Troutman's life completely upside down.

***

The only reason she had lied to the old man about being a writer was because she was worried about people discovering the real reason for her visit to Lyverton. Even so, as she waited for Marian inside the tea shop, it seemed to her that every time a little white lie was repeated it grew stronger and bigger. The entire village now thought she was a famous writer and she had only succeeded in drawing more attention to herself because it seemed everyone who passed by the window waved at her with a big, cheery smile.

She glanced at her watch and her stomach churned with nerves. How, and when, was she going to tell Marian that she was really her sister? Tammy rehearsed some words in her aching head, but nothing seemed appropriate. Perhaps it would be better to get to know her a little better first, and then tell her.

Daniel appeared.

"Do you want to order anything?"

Tammy thought about it, but a faint wave of nausea changed her mind. She most definitely couldn't face food.

"No. I'm meeting Marian Troutman at ten o'clock. I think I'll wait. She'll probably want to order something, too."

Daniel reached into his apron pocket.

"I thought you might like to read this."

He shoved a village newsletter into Tammy's hand.

"When you've finished with it would you mind autographing it and letting me have it back?"

Tammy blushed a deep crimson red with embarrassment.

"I'm not famous or anything."

"No, but you will be soon, won't you?" Daniel said confidently. "Once you've written about our village, you'll be a local celebrity."

Marian was late.

Tammy looked at her watch: it was ten past ten. She made up her mind to wait until half past ten, and then go, should Marian fail to arrive. She glanced out of the window and didn't know whether she was dismayed or relieved to see that she had just pulled up outside in a blue Nissan Micra, almost knocking over the two, grungy teenagers who had to jump out of the way of her car.

Marian Troutman looked nothing like the woman she had stood

72

behind in the post office on Monday, or the woman at the funeral yesterday, or even the lady she had shared dinner with last night. She climbed out of her car and her loose, white, cotton shirt billowed in the breeze as she opened up the boot and tugged out a cardboard box. Her hair had been coloured and cut into choppy, fashionable layers, more becoming to her age than the straight bob she had worn previously. The vibrant, chestnut brown colour had lifted the dowdiness and pallor from her face and seemed to have taken at least ten years from her appearance. As she hoisted the box into her arms and walked across the patio towards the shop, Tammy thought she looked just like Lynda Bellingham from Loose Women on the television.

Tammy stood up to hold the door open for her. She was intrigued. What was in the box?

***

"Thanks, Tammy. It's a bit heavier than I thought."

Marian looked down at Tammy's legs as she struggled through the door with the box and noticed that they were wearing identical clothing; blue denim jeans and a white shirt (although Tammy's was more tightly fitting than hers). The coincidence of their identical clothing and hung in the blank space between them, unspoken but not unnoticed.

When she had first heard about the writer in the village, researching local history, she just knew she *had* to become involved. For years she had been gradually becoming more and more depressed with life. She was forty-nine years-old and had achieved nothing. She had no children (and no prospect of any now the childbearing years had trickled through her fingers). She had no direction in her life and, she had to admit, very little to live for. The anger, embarrassment and hurt when her mother had abandoned her and fled from the village had burned deep into her heart; it had gouged wide scars that had taken years to heal; it had swept all vestiges of youthfulness from her and it had taken her a very long time to come to terms with the dreadful scandal it had left in its wake.

Today, though, Marian was happy. For some strange reason, she

73

felt as if her life was about to take a turn for the better. She was important to someone. She was wanted for herself and her extensive local knowledge, and for once, not a skivvy for her father or about to be pounced upon by anxious parents of eight-year-old children.

"I'm really sorry I'm late," she said, "but I rang the hairdresser this morning and managed to get an early appointment. Just as I was coming out of the salon, I was stopped by Lucy Staverley's great niece, Sophie. Her family wanted you to have this box, because they've heard you're writing a book about the village. So I popped round and collected it for you."

"What is it?"

Marian dumped the ancient cardboard box on a red gingham tablecloth, almost knocking aside a glass vase filled with fake water and red rosebuds. "This," she said, "came from the House on the Hill. They've started to clear the place, and it's stuff that belonged to Alice Thompson. I haven't had time to look at it, but Sophie says there are some old magazines from the nineteen fifties and sixties, some vintage church pamphlets, parish newsletters, photographs and personal letters and suchlike dating back nearly a hundred years."

"What about Alice's family? Don't they want them?" Tammy asked.

Marian shook her head. "Alice had no family of her own. Not even distant relatives. She was an only child. The story was that her parents ran away together as children and completely lost contact with their families, so she didn't ever know if she had any cousins or aunties and uncles. Sophie's mother said that we might as well have this box of memorabilia for our research — it would only have to be thrown out if not."

Marian picked up a large, old brown envelope from the box and peered inside the flap. It was stuffed with yellowy-edged letters tied into bundles with pink cotton tape. A flush of optimism flooded into her veins. It felt so good to have something else to occupy her mind, other than her class of generally well-behaved children and her recalcitrant, difficult father. She caught sight of herself in the reflection in the window, and, for a split second didn't recognise the friendly-looking lady who stared back at her. She smiled, glad she had decided to have her hair done, and wondered why she hadn't changed her style

74

years ago.

Daniel loped over, drying his hands on a tea towel. He had been listening.

"I know Sophie Staverley really well," he said to Tammy. "I was with her yesterday and she said she'd love to help with your research." He raised his eyebrows. "I bet she'd be down here like a shot if I texted her."

"Marvellous," Marian gushed as she become even more instilled with enthusiasm. She clasped her hands together. "Isn't this amazing? Now, where's your notebook, Tammy? We'll order coffee and something to eat and get started on this lot while Daniel texts Sophie."

***

As Tammy lifted the contents of Alice's box onto the tablecloth, the dreadful nervousness she had felt moments earlier at the prospect of telling Marian she was really her half-sister disappeared without trace as she had a sudden flash of inspirational excitement. She could research Alice Thompson's life story and try to discover why her parents had ran away together. She could find out about Lucy Staverley's sister, Emily, who Cynthia thought might have been a missionary, then she could have a shot at writing about it all. She could turn the ugly lie into a self-fulfilling prophecy. As soon as they were alone she would reveal to Marian she was really her sister, but in the meantime she would just act out the role of the writer everyone thought she was. Her difficult task would just have to wait.

Half an hour later, Tammy was engrossed in one of the women's magazines from the box. It was dated July 1960 and contained a journal by the Hesitant Housewife.

"Hey, look at this, Marian. It's absolutely hilarious!"

"What's that?"

Marian shuffled around the table and looked over Tammy's shoulder.

"The Hesitant Housewife?" she said cocking her head on one side, chuckling out loud. "Oh look – she only used to vacuum half way up the stairs to fool her long suffering husband into thinking she had spent the entire day cleaning, and then eat chocolate and drink wine in the afternoons while she listened to the radio or watched TV."

Tammy giggled. "I bet that was frowned on in those days."

"Hello."

A young woman's voice interrupted their laughter and Tammy looked up to see Daniel standing beside a very slim, pretty young woman with long, straight blonde hair that contrasted with her fashionable black-rimmed glasses. He was grinning as usual. Tammy shoved the magazine to one side and stood up with a scrape of the chair, taking the young woman's extended hand lightly in hers.

"Miss Hargreaves — meet Sophie Staverley. Sophie, meet *the* Tamasyn Hargreaves — writer for the stars."

"Wow," Sophie said. "A real life ghost writer! Who do you write for? Or are you not allowed to say?"

Tammy wanted to fling her arms around Daniel and give him a huge hug. She might have been mildly annoyed at him for gossiping and promulgating her white lie, but he had just presented her with the perfect cover. A ghost writer — why hadn't she thought of that? Tammy didn't need to actually confirm it or deny it. She just beamed at Sophie and Daniel and tapped the side of her nose before pressing a forefinger to her lips.

"Oooohhh," Sophie said, wide-eyed with admiration. "Is it someone from the X Factor?"

***

Marjorie, the owner of the tea shop, beamed with pleasure, her plump cheeks shiny, echoing the cheerfulness of the bright, flowery apron she wore as she buttered a plate of toasted tea cakes. She was overjoyed to be sharing in the discovery of the memorabilia contained within the contents of Alice's box, and she soon forgot that she was supposed to be making a living out of the tea shop. Every time someone offered to pay, she dismissed it with a wave of her hand.

"It's on the house. This is social, not *business*! Daniel, go and fill up that coffee pot again," she would say periodically throughout the morning.

Tammy felt a wriggle of sprouting Lyverton roots at Marjorie's generosity; they were gradually gaining hold, growing in strength. She felt she belonged. For the first time in her life she felt real and solid — her own person instead of her parents' pampered possession.

Marian suddenly spoke over the incessant chatter and laughter. She banged a teaspoon on the table to get everyone's attention.

"Let's have a little bit of order here, we're getting nowhere!"

Everyone stopped talking.

"We're not really making any progress, are we? We need to be more organised if we are going to do this properly and help Tammy get lots of information for her book."

Tammy began to giggle. Daniel looked at her and chuckled too, a devilish look creeping across his face.

"Yes Miss," he said, and bowed royally and slowly, throwing Tammy an exaggerated wink.

Marian started to laugh. Tammy watched, spellbound, as the laughter visibly stripped years away from her face: it touched her cheeks with a happy flush and her eyes crinkled at the corners. She wiped the moisture away with a forefinger. Their identical gazes locked and Tammy felt something fizzle, sparkle and crackle in the air. She felt a slight draught, as if someone had just exhaled close to her cheek. Inhaling sharply in surprise, she caught the merest hint of the fragrance of a familiar soap.

Marian's hearty laugh dissolved into a wide, happy smile. Tammy looked on in amazement as she touched the side of her face with her fingertips. Had she just felt the same draught on *her* cheek?

Tammy's nose prickled and tears of happiness welled in her eyes. She wiped them away with the back of her hand; no one took any notice because everyone thought they were tears of laughter.

"Isn't this just the best day ever?" Marian said, looking at Tammy.

Tammy smiled and blinked the tears away. Her mother's presence was so strong, she felt as if she could just turn around and Pippa would be standing right behind her.

"It most certainly is. I haven't enjoyed myself so much in ages," Tammy responded.

Marian turned to Daniel and Sophie and waggled her finger at them, feigning a strict teacher look.

"Now — you two chatterboxes at the back — just keep it down, will you? Or else you can expect a week's worth of playtime detention."

Spontaneously, Daniel stepped forwards and wrapped his long arm around Marian in an affectionate hug.

"You need to get out more, Miss Troutman. If you don't mind me saying so."

***

There were no shops in the village apart from the post office, which doubled up as a corner shop, and a small supermarket on the housing estate on Fawsden Road. Tammy needed something special to wear because, having lugged Alice's box up the stairs to her room with Cynthia's help, she had just texted Paul and accepted his invitation for dinner. They were, apparently, booked for a table for two at eight o'clock at The Gamekeeper's Lodge in Little Somerton.

"I haven't got a single thing to wear," she whined to Cynthia, who tried hard to act surprised at the news that Paul and Tammy had a date. "I wasn't expecting to go to any posh restaurants while I was here. I thought I would be tramping around churchyards and talking to elderly people verging on the point of senility for the next fortnight."

"What you need my girl, is a *Little Black Dress* ..." Cynthia began with a waggle of a plump, authoritative forefinger.

"I'll have to go into town, but I really wanted to go through the photographs in Alice's box this afternoon, and make a start on the old letters."

Cynthia raised her eyebrows. She could see straight through Tammy's smokescreen of contrived indifference. "Och ... I don't see what the problem is. Shall we both have just a teeny, tiny little shopping trip? We'll find something in Fawsden, I'm sure."

Tammy gave a false groan — she didn't want Cynthia to think she was *too* enthusiastic about her date with Paul — but she was pleased at Cynthia's offer of an afternoon's shopping.

"Let me fix us both a sandwich for lunch, and then we'll get going — that's if you want me to come with you? I don't want to intrude."

Tammy very much wanted Cynthia to go with her. She'd never much liked shopping for clothes on her own. Pippa had been indifferent about her own appearance, uninterested in clothes and so Tammy had grown up unsure of what suited her and, more importantly, what colours to avoid because of her striking, red hair.

"Yes, please," Tammy replied. "I'd like that."

CHAPTER TEN

Cynthia and Tammy chatted almost non-stop in the car on the way to Fawsden. They discussed the new development site, summer bedding plants for the pub garden and the smart new tea shop at a nearby garden centre and how they hoped it didn't take trade away from Marjorie's quaint little cafe in the village.

Tammy looked sideways at Cynthia. "How long have you had the Red Lion?"

"We bought the place in the early eighties. It was a bit run-down, but Rabbie and I did it up."

"Who's Rabbie?"

"He was my husband. He died of a heart attack ten years ago."

"Oh, I'm sorry … I didn't realise."

"We came down from Glasgow. We'd never been much on having children, and so we decided to put our hearts and souls into building up a business in a village pub in the heart of England. Rabbie had an older sister who lived in Corby, so it was nice for him to live close by. The Red Lion fitted the bill for us in every way. We were very happy, you know, my Rabbie and me. We had nearly eighteen, perfect years of complete heaven in Lyverton. If only he hadn't gone and died on me …"

Cynthia's voice wavered and petered out. She fell silent. After a couple of minutes, out of the corner of her eye, Tammy noticed that Cynthia's hand was trembling as she rested it on her huge bosom, over her heart. Her head fell forwards, her usual upright posture slumped and her double chin quivered. Despite her bright, glitzy, glamorous appearance and cheerful personality, Tammy could see Cynthia was a very lonely, sad woman.

"Do you have any parents or brothers and sisters?"

Cynthia shook her head.

"Other relatives?"

She shook her head again and tried to speak, but the words caught like a blunt saw in her throat and she gave up. She cleared her throat and looked to the left, out of the window, her flushed face turned away. Tammy sensed Cynthia was crying.

Tammy spotted a parking sign up ahead and looked for the lay-by. She pulled over and stopped the car, turning off the engine. The silence assumed an intruding, almost human, presence as Cynthia gazed out of the window, still not looking at her.

"Cynthia. I know how it feels to be alone in life. I do understand. Really I do."

"How?" Cynthia's voice was nasal and she dabbed at her nose with the back of her hand before biting hard on the side of her forefinger with a loud sniff. "You've got your family back in Yorkshire ... you're not alone."

Tammy leaned over her and opened the glove compartment. She extracted a pocket pack of tissues.

"Here," she said. "Have these."

Cynthia's hands trembled as her red fingernails pulled open the cellophane and she extracted a tissue. She dabbed at her eyes carefully, so as not to ruin her eye make-up and then blew her nose.

A few seconds later, she fixed a watery smile on her face. She stared out of the driver's side window, beyond Tammy, and locked her gaze on distant fields. "I'm such a sentimental old fool. You'd think that almost ten years after burying my Rabbie, I'd be able to speak about him without blubbering, wouldn't you?" She sighed. "It wasn't that we didn't *want* children. We just couldn't have them — my fault, not his. If only I could have given my Rabbie just one child, I wouldn't be so lonely now."

"My mum died, too." The words were out of Tammy's mouth before she could stop them.

"Och! I'm so sorry. How long ago?"

"Two years. She had cancer."

Cynthia sniffed, shifted in her seat and wound her arms around Tammy in a maternal hug. "You poor little lamb."

Tammy couldn't cry. The tears that so readily came on Monday night while she was listening to old songs on the pub jukebox were still there, buried deep, but they wouldn't flow because taboo, unsaid

81

words were blocking their way. But it felt as if her unspoken words were bleeding into Cynthia's tears like watercolours on a still-wet painting and leaking uncontrollably from her lips.

"My dad is sucking the life out of me, Cynthia. He's so lost without my mother. He just can't come to terms with losing her and he's dragging me down with him. I've just *had* to get away for a bit. That's why I came to Lyverton. I so badly want to leave home … get right away … but I feel selfish and ungrateful …"

Tammy's guilty words faded into a heavy silence. Cynthia stroked her hand with what she didn't know was a loving, motherly touch. She was nothing like Pippa, and yet, to Tammy, being with Cynthia was like being with her mother.

"Och, you poor wee lassie; so young to be left without a mother. That's terribly tragic. Why Lyverton, though?"

"To find my roots, I suppose."

"I don't understand …" Cynthia puckered her brow. Tammy knew she was trying to piece things together. "So you have family in Lyverton? Is that why you are writing the book?"

Tammy shrugged her shoulders. "Not really. Well, yes, I suppose it is. My parents both lived here once. My dad grew up here."

Tammy knew she was saying too much, but Cynthia seemed so wise and her heart so warm and big, she felt an almost uncontrollable urge to confide in her.

"Cynthia? Do you think it's possible to be loved more than anything, and to be someone's entire world, and yet still be incredibly lonely?"

Cynthia mulled Tammy's words over in her mind. She began to nod, but then the nod turned into a shake of the head.

"No, I don't think so. Being truly loved by someone makes you feel you feel secure. It's the purest thing in the world, is love. Everyone needs to be needed. Your dad obviously loves you very much, hen. He'll get through his grief in time — but he'll always shed a tear now and then, like I did just now. You must hang in there for him. It's still early days. Two years is not that long ago and you're all he's got."

Tammy sighed. Two years might not seem long when you were fifty, but when you were twenty-seven, stifled, suffocated and trapped

82

it almost seemed like a lifetime.

"You can be surrounded by people and still be lonely though," Cynthia added. "I know that's true — look at me. I'm never alone. I have a lovely life. I have plenty of friends in the village, I keep busy — too busy sometimes. But you are lucky, Tammy, you have someone who *loves* you. I don't."

Tammy gave a frustrated sigh. "I know I'm just being stupid. I sometimes feel as if he is almost … well …" Tammy's voice faded. She couldn't voice the words to Cynthia that Alan was squeezing the love out of her so that she couldn't feel anything for him any more and almost hated him. It felt so churlish to say it when Cynthia had no one to love her. She pulled her hand away from Cynthia's and gripped the steering wheel for a few seconds before starting the engine again.

"It's just that he relies on me. It's like he's an old man, and he's only fifty."

Cynthia sniffed, dabbed at her nose with the tissue and smiled, her sparkle returning as they resumed their journey. "Come on, lassie. Let's hit the shops."

***

Tammy's dress was not black. She had bought a dress in a bright, teal green colour, which suited her red hair and pale colouring. Standing in front of the full-length mirror in her room, Tammy wondered if she would be overdressed for her date with Paul. Cynthia was one serious shopper: it was no wonder she always looked so glamorous.

Tammy had bought a complete new outfit: some irresistible, impossibly high heels she just had to have; a matching handbag and dainty shrug top in dark brown, soft mohair, shot through with a fine, turquoise thread she wasn't quite sure about. *'You don't want to catch a chill,'* Cynthia had said. *'There can still be a nip in the air in the evenings.'* Tammy had wanted to laugh; Cynthia had sounded so much like Pippa.

She fingered a new necklace around her neck and the matching set of silver, brown and turquoise bangles (a treat from Cynthia) fell down her forearm. She smiled at herself in the mirror as Cynthia tapped on her door.

83

"Well?" Cynthia enquired in a muffled voice from outside Tammy's room. "How does it look?"

"Come in. The door's open."

Cynthia stood in the doorway, beaming. Her chubby, bejewelled hands flew up and she cupped her face. Her mouth formed into a silent 'O' as she gave an excited little squeal.

"You look stunning, hen," she gasped, "absolutely beautiful."

Cynthia's enthusiasm was infectious and Tammy did a little twirl, finishing in the exaggerated pose of a supermodel.

"Oh my word. That colour is so you! What are you going to do with your hair?"

Tammy whirled around again, laughing. She couldn't remember the last time she had felt so happy. Cynthia stepped forwards into the room and shut the door behind her. Tammy piled up her hair on top of her head and held it there. Cynthia shook her head.

"No. You need to wear it down. You've got such beautiful hair and you're young enough to carry it off."

Tammy stood with her elbow raised, clutching her wayward frizz to the back of her head. She wrinkled her nose.

"It's such a pain to wear down — it sort of goes all fluffy round my face after a couple of hours. It's so fine and curly."

"Ummm. Does it straighten out into spirals if you do it properly?"

Tammy puffed air out of her cheeks in a gesture of reluctance.

"It does, but it's such a faff. My mum used to tame it for me, but I haven't bothered since she died."

Cynthia looked at her watch. "We've got time. Just about."

"Okay then. But don't make me look like a ten year old with ringlets."

"I won't, hen. You'll look sophisticated and elegant. I won't make you look like Bonnie Langford ... I promise."

Cynthia disappeared into her flat and then returned with various fearsome looking electrical implements, a salon-type hairdryer and an armful of assorted hair products.

Once Tammy had showered and washed her hair, Cynthia set to work, drying and then curling a section at a time.

"So how long has Paul been staying here?" It was a question

Tammy already knew the answer to, but she asked it anyway. Last night, while in her state of semi-consciousness and slumped on Paul's chest, he had commented that you couldn't live in a village for nearly a year and not become aware of village gossip. But it was an opener, and Tammy hoped that Cynthia would tell her more about Paul.

"Och, it's got to be nigh on a year now. I've grown really fond of him. Such a nice boy, you know. He's the strong, silent and reliable type. I hardly know he's here."

"Where does he live — I mean, where does he come from? Where does he go home to? He must go home sometimes."

Cynthia shook her head.

"Not that I know of. He told me his parents live on the east coast, but if he's gone home to visit, I haven't realised. He didn't even go home at Christmas. He stayed here and helped me out in the pub and then, after the pub closed on Christmas day, I cooked us both a lovely, traditional dinner, and we watched the Queen's speech together."

"What's his last name?"

Cynthia's reflection in the mirror frowned and she cocked her head to one side. She placed her hands either side of Tammy's head and forced it straight.

"Keep your head still. You'll end up with a burnt ear if you're not careful. It's Pepper. And Paul is his middle name. His first name is Nicholas, but he's known as Paul. His mail comes addressed to Mr N P Pepper."

Tammy tried not to fix her gaze on the unwelcome, developing spot on her chin while she mulled the name over in her mind. Cynthia worked busily, twisting her hair into shiny spirals. Nicholas. Nick. He was much more like a Paul than a Nick. Why did he use his middle name? There was something significant about the name *Pepper* too, but it was stuck too far back in her childhood memories and she couldn't for the life of her think what it was.

Tammy touched her chin. The spot was definitely going to be a problem. It was just so typical — by that evening it would be as fiery as a volcano ready to erupt.

CHAPTER ELEVEN

His knock on Tammy's door was tentative. Paul gulped and swallowed. It was really important to him that he made a good first impression tonight, but nothing could have prepared him for how gorgeous she looked as she opened the door. He tried to think of something witty to say, but his brain seized up, mesmerised by Tammy's transformation.

"Hello."

Paul opened his mouth and then shut it again, like a floundering fish. The Adam's apple in his throat bobbed and jumped as he swallowed. Too late, he realised he was empty-handed. He should have bought her some flowers or something. Or was that just being silly and old fashioned? Then he managed to get some words out, but they were disappointing and inadequate.

"Hello you! Are you ready to roll then?"

He looked at his watch, his shoulders tense and stiff. The corner of his left eye twitched and his eyelids blinked rapidly. His gaze drifted upwards to Tammy's face. God … she was absolutely gorgeous! Her hair, vibrant and alive, had been tamed and coaxed elegantly into gentle spirals. Her startling, brown eyes were framed perfectly by her pretty, lightly freckled face. Her skin was alabaster smooth with just the subtlest of makeup. Tammy turned and grabbed her handbag from the bed and then shut the door behind her. He needed to pay her a tasteful compliment. It would be remiss of him not to, that much he *did* know.

"You smell really nice."

He cringed. What a stupid thing to say? He'd meant to say *look* nice, but the right word had somehow withered in his head as he'd breathed in the sexy, light smell of her perfume. He was so out of practice; he'd forgotten how to behave in the presence of an attractive woman.

He was slightly behind Tammy as they made their way along the narrow landing to the top of the stairs. She turned, looked over her shoulder and grinned.

"Thanks. Have you got some tissues on you — and what about that spare shirt in case I get drunk again and dribble?"

Paul's stiff shoulders dropped, and he laughed as he relaxed slightly.

"For one thing I'm not planning on making you cry — and for another I hope I'm not going to bore you to death so that you fall asleep on me again."

The ice broken, they decided to have a drink in the bar before they left for the restaurant.

"Usual table?" Daniel enquired.

"We're eating out tonight, but we're having a drink before we go."

"I know. I'll bring your drinks over to you," Daniel replied.

They sat down at the table in the alcove. Paul wondered what he should say. He supposed he ought to pay her another compliment. He felt awkward and inexperienced. Hell. He *was* awkward and inexperienced!

"You look really nice tonight, Tammy."

"So do you."

Paul took a deep breath. He had something he absolutely must say, and didn't quite know how to phrase it.

"Tammy. Before we go out tonight you need to know something about me. It's not bad or anything. It's just that I don't want you to find out from anyone else — like Cynthia or Daniel."

"Oh?"

Paul looked up as their drinks arrived and Daniel shot them his usual grin.

"Awww," he said. "Didn't we have a great time this morning, Tammy? Have you had a chance to have another look through Alice's old letters and photos?"

"No," Tammy replied. "I wanted to, but then I went shopping with Cynthia instead this afternoon."

Paul's slightly disconcerted expression turned to amusement and he laughed out loud.

"Shopping? With Cynthia? I bet that was fun."

***

Did she not *always* smell nice? It had been such an odd thing to say, it made Tammy worry that perhaps she had bad breath, or perhaps she really ought not to walk around in her socks after taking off her trainers. Paul seemed to appreciate her efforts tonight though. He'd hardly taken his eyes off her.

It was a shame he'd had a haircut. Tammy had liked the little curly bits that rested on the top of his collar and the sticky-up bit that wouldn't lie flat on top of his head — and now they had gone. She needn't have worried about being overdressed. Paul's level of formality, or informality, was similar to hers. His black shirt looked as if it might have been new and he wore it open necked. Just one button undone, thank goodness, and no gold chain or other kind of necklace around his neck — something Tammy hated. There was the tiniest nick on his chin where he'd cut himself with his razor and a flicker of amusement crossed her face as she realised that it must be quite difficult to shave a clefted chin.

Nick. That was his first name, not Paul, according to Cynthia. Tammy wondered just what it was Paul had wanted to tell her about himself before Daniel had arrived with their drinks. Did he have some horrible dark secret in his past?

"So you've got some of Alice Thompson's old letters?" Paul said.

"The Staverleys have given me a box of her belongings," Tammy replied. "But I'll tell you all about it later."

Tammy deliberately didn't look at Daniel. She wanted him to go away and leave them alone because she was impatient to hear Paul's confession about himself. She groaned inwardly. She hoped he wasn't married because that would be the end of everything before it had even started. Daniel was walking away but Cynthia was bearing down on them, making a bee-line for their table.

"Helloooo," she said giving Tammy a surreptitious little wink, which she was sure Paul noticed. She bit her lip and looked down at her hands.

"I hear you two girls have been out this afternoon. I hope you didn't cause too much havoc in the shops in Fawsden," Paul said with a laugh.

Cynthia thumped Paul's shoulder affectionately. "If going on a date

88

is what it takes to make you have a haircut, then bring it on!"

It was public. Paul and Tammy going out to dinner was a *date*.

Nerves began to flutter in Tammy's stomach and the events of the three days she'd spent in Lyverton flashed before her like a sequence of video clips. What the hell was she doing? She had been plucking up the courage to come to Lyverton for two, long years and now she was actually here it appeared she was going right off the track of her quest to find her sister by researching another, unrelated, family's history and going out on a dinner date with a man she had only just met. And, to top it all, he had dropped a significant, loaded comment into the conversation about *wanting to tell her something about himself*, and then left her wondering what it could be.

***

As ladylike and elegantly as she could, Tammy slid into Paul's smart, almost new black Honda Civic. He was holding the passenger door open for her and she sensed he was staring at her legs.

"Right then," Paul said.

He shut the door and walked around to the driver's side. He settled in next to Tammy and started the engine. Suddenly Tammy felt nervous. She decided to tell Paul about Alice's box to calm herself down. Just as she was about to speak, she spotted the odd cowslip-picking youngsters sitting on the pub wall a few yards away from Paul's car. They were squinting in the evening sunlight, eating crisps, waving and smiling at her. She waved back. They looked so happy. Tammy had thought they were brother and sister, but something about them that evening told her they were just a very young couple: best friends about to fall in love for the first time in their lives.

"I had a lovely morning with Marian," said Tammy, as Paul reversed the car. "She brought a box of Alice's belongings with her that Lucy Staverley's family had given her to pass onto me. It was full of old photographs, letters and magazines they thought might be useful for my book."

"That's brilliant. Will it be of any use?"

"Oh, yes. I've decided to shift my focus a bit. I'm going to concentrate on Lucy Staverley and Alice Thompson's stories and their family trees as background for my book. Marian tells me that the two ladies were real village characters. Lucy died a few years ago ... she was ninety-two, apparently, and a wacky, eccentric music teacher whose eyebrows went up and down with the baton as she conducted the church choir."

"Paul laughed. It seems as if it was fate you ended up at Alice's funeral."

Tammy shook her head. "No, not fate: nothing like that. It's *because* I accidentally ended up at Alice's funeral that I've decided to write about their lives. Don't you think it's a great idea? It's sort of beginning at the end. The final link in the chain, squaring the circle, that sort of thing. It will make a fabulous story."

Paul glanced sideways. "You creative types get me all flummoxed. I'm just a black and white sort of guy. Tell it like it is, that's me. Drains, bridges and roads. You can't get more straightforward and boring than that, can you?"

Tammy gave a cynical little laugh. Paul most definitely was *not* straightforward and boring. "Still," she went on. "Alice *was* almost a centenarian. Did you know her parents ran away together as children? That alone will add a fantastic twist to the story, if I can get to the bottom of it."

"She was a nice old girl, was Alice Thompson. I did some work for her just a couple of months back, at the House on the Hill. She had a problem with the drainage and I sorted it out for her. She was very frail — had a job walking — but she still lived independently with the help of the Staverley family."

"That's what is so intriguing about her," Tammy said enthusiastically. "Marian told me that Alice had no family at all. She was an only child and never married. Neither did Lucy Staverley, but her great nieces and nephews took care of her right up until the end. It's so kind of the Staverleys to give me the box for my research."

Paul gave a little frown. "It'll be fascinating to research a total stranger's family history, but I'd bet on it taking longer than the next two weeks — we're already at Wednesday and you're only here until a week on Saturday."

Tammy knew Paul must have been talking to Cynthia. She was

certain she hadn't told him how long she was planning to stay in Lyverton. Still, a week on Saturday was ages away yet. Her heart sank when she thought about going back to Yorkshire. Back home. Back to work.

"Oh God," Tammy said suddenly, bending down to grab her handbag. "I've forgotten to ring my dad!"

"Do it now, then." Paul tossed a quizzical look at her disproportionate state of panic. "That's if you want to. Or leave it until we get to the restaurant if you like. I don't mind."

Tammy decided to make a brief call. She opened her smart new handbag, trying not to think about how much it had cost: it was nice not to have to rummage around for her mobile phone for a change.

"Hello, Dad."

"Tammy! How's things. Have you had a good day?"

"I've had a lovely day. This morning I had breakfast in the tea shop with some local people I've met, and acquired a box full of bits and bobs that belonged to Alice Thompson. I'll tell you about it when I've got more time. This afternoon I went shopping in Fawsden with the landlady of the Red Lion, and tonight I'm going out to dinner with a new friend."

Silence.

"Dad?"

"Yes?"

"Are you okay?" Tammy frowned at the lack of response.

"Who are you going out to dinner with, Tamasyn?"

"His name's Paul, and he's lodging at the Red Lion. He's a civil engineer and he's working on the new development site."

"Oh ... well ... you be careful, won't you."

Silence.

"Listen, Dad. I can't really talk much right now. We're in the car on our way to the restaurant. I'll ring you in the morning, before you leave for the office. I promise."

"Okay. Speak to you then. Have a nice time, Tammy. And ... oh ... you will take care, won't you? You hear such horror stories about young girls out on their own ..."

"Dad!" Tammy interrupted defensively. "I'm twenty-seven years-

91

old and I really don't think Paul is about to chop me up, leaving my body parts all over the countryside. He's been living here for nearly a year and Cynthia knows him well."

Paul exploded into stifled laughter beside her. Tammy smirked at him as she said a final goodnight to Alan and bent down to drop her phone back into her bag.

"I'm twenty-eight," said Paul with a flick of his head and a wink. "Well, I shall be on Friday, anyway — it's my birthday. I'm clearly much more sensible and grown-up than you."

After twenty minutes or so of gentle teasing, flirting and idle chit-chat, Paul swung the car into the restaurant car park. Tammy's eyes widened. The Gamekeeper's Lodge was very grand, with immaculately tended gardens, colourful hanging baskets and outside ornamental lighting. It was still light outside, and the setting sun bathed the golden stone in an almost orangey glow as tyres crunched on gravel and then stopped.

***

Although he had been grateful for the light-hearted car journey, which had soothed away all traces of his nervousness like waves lapping gently on a Caribbean beach, Paul had really meant to plunge in feet first and tell Tammy about the not-so-small matter of Claire in the car on the way to The Gamekeeper's Lodge. Once they had arrived, the moment had been lost. Now, having enjoyed easy conversation and good food, Paul knew he couldn't put off the inevitable much longer. If the jukebox had upset Tammy on Monday evening, last night it had stirred up all the murky residue and unfinished business in his life when it had been playing songs from last year. As Tammy and Marian sat chatting over dinner he'd been quiet and reflective, the music from last summer transporting him back in time to the day he'd packed his bags and left Claire for good. He'd gone to sleep with all the murkiness he'd left behind in Norfolk swirling around inside his head, and had woken up filled with an unwelcome certainty that he couldn't begin to take things further with Tammy until she knew about Claire.

"So come on then … back at the Red Lion you said you had something to tell me about yourself that you didn't want me to find out from anyone else."

This was it. Just as he was mustering up the courage to tell Tammy about Claire, she'd asked the question herself.

"Ah ... er ... yes." Paul looked down at his hands, twiddled his thumbs and coughed. He almost backtracked. He almost didn't tell her, but then he knew he had to — it most definitely had to be done.

"Go on then."

"I hope you won't think any less of me, but I made a decision in the heat of the moment when I came to Lyverton. Now it's sort of run away with me."

"Oh, what was that?"

"My name is really Nick. Nicholas. When I arrived in Lyverton, I was so determined that no one would be able to find me, I decided to use my middle name."

"Is that all?"

"Yes." said Paul. He hesitated, shifted in his seat and then gave another nervous cough. "Well, no, not really. It was just that I wanted to tell you I wasn't really Paul before we ... we ... er ..."

Paul rubbed his neck. What the heck was the right phrase? Dated? No they were already on a date. Slept together? No! Tammy most definitely wasn't the type of girl who was likely to be into one-night-stands. Started a relationship? No, that was even worse. She'd think he expected her to jump into bed with him straight away once they arrived back to the Red Lion after their meal — not that he'd have any objection to that. In fact the thought of it was actually quite distracting. He took another swig of wine. This was more awkward than he'd imagined. Tammy was the first girl he'd been seriously attracted to since the split with Claire, and he was completely out of touch.

"Get to know each other a bit better?" Tammy queried, raising her eyebrows.

"Yes. That's just what I mean — before we get to know each other better."

Tammy sucked her bottom lip under her top teeth and fiddled with her earring thoughtfully. She smiled and the smile flooded into her eyes with a flirty twinkle.

93

"It's not really *that* big a deal, is it? Lots of people use their middle name. But why didn't you want to be traced to Lyverton? You're not married, are you?"

"No. I'm not married. I've just cut myself off from my family because of something that happened to me last year. I've carved out my own life now — a life I don't want them to interfere with. But the thing is, it's left me in limbo. I don't know how to unsay some of the things I said in the heat of the moment and begin to make amends without having to turn back into Nick. I'm Paul, now, and I want to stay that way. I'm a bit of an idiot really, aren't I? Cynthia says I'm burying my head in the sand and need to get myself sorted out."

"What happened to make you fall out with your family?"

"I really didn't mean to sever myself off so completely, but I needed to get away from them — it was all too claustrophobic — and so I applied for jobs as far away as I could."

"Why?"

Paul put his head in his hands in frustration and then pushed his newly cut hair back with both hands.

"Cynthia knows all about it. I told her quite soon after I arrived in Lyverton. She's fantastic, you know. She has dispensed many words of wisdom, which I promptly ignore. I've just bumbled along without doing anything about it. But I know she's right. I've got to face things one day. Anyway Tammy, you're honoured. You are about to become the second person in Lyverton to know why I won't go home, not even to visit."

Paul's hand hesitated, trembling slightly over the bottle of red wine on the table. He picked it up and poured himself an inch or so in the bottom of his glass, and then filled Tammy's. He cradled his glass in his hands, swirling it around and around, and then traced the rim with his thumbs. Tammy placed her hands either side of his in a comforting gesture, but he just flinched, hesitated, looked her straight in the eye and then leaned back, pulling his hands away from the glass. She had to let go.

His eyes were naked and embarrassed, but he was hiding nothing. He grimaced and looked up at the corner of the room so he didn't have to look at Tammy. "Until just over a year ago, I thought my life

94

was set. I was engaged to a girl called Claire. We'd been together ever since we were eighteen and started uni together. We were already a big part of each other's families, because she became my sister's best friend, and I worked with her father. Six weeks away, we were, just six weeks from our wedding day, when ..."

Paul stopped short and bowed his head. He couldn't bring himself to tell Tammy what had happened to him. He was afraid she'd think he was less of a man for running away and not facing up to his problems. His Adam's apple bobbed as he swallowed the words, and his eye twitched.

"What happened?"

Paul's embarrassment couldn't be restrained, and as he looked back into Tammy's eyes it turned to hard, icy anger. "She stole them from me, and they bloody well let her do it! They couldn't have thought much of me, could they? And I was their only son for goodness sake!"

"Stole them?"

"Yes. So I got this job in Fawsden on the development site, and then just sodding well left them all to it. And I've never gone back. Good riddance to the lot of them."

Paul was breathing heavily. It had to be done. Tammy had to know. He couldn't start another relationship with anyone until he'd sorted out his head. But the story was tumbling over and over itself in the wrong order and he could see she was confused. He realised he had missed out the most important part.

"Hang on ... what do you mean by *stole them*. Who do you mean? And what happened with the wedding?"

"She got pregnant."

"Claire? Who did she steal, though? I really don't know what you mean?"

Paul's exposed and uncloaked eyes glistened and he put his head in his hands. He buried his face so his voice became muffled. "Claire was my whole world — my life. She got pregnant just a few weeks before we were due to get married."

"Why was that so bad? You were getting married anyway. I really don't understand."

Paul looked up at Tammy. Ten months of repressed emotion had made his eyelashes moist. Mortified with embarrassment, he viciously kicked out a brick in the imaginary wall that had surrounded his heart for the last year.

"Because, Tammy, it wasn't mine!" he blurted out.

***

The car pulled into the Red Lion car park. The date had gone horribly wrong. Paul hadn't uttered a single word in the car all the way back, other than to repeat several times that he was sorry for ruining the evening. When they had left the restaurant in a hurry because he was so upset, Tammy had slipped her hand into his and squeezed it. He had squeezed it back and then let go quickly, before shielding his eyes from an imaginary sun. He had put his head down and looked away as he opened the car door for her.

Although acutely embarrassed because he had very nearly broken down when he had told her about Claire, Tammy felt even more drawn towards him. There was something touching, human and real about Paul. He judged himself harshly, believing he had ran away from his problems, but Tammy could see that he had actually been quite brave and decisive in the actions he had taken. He just needed to take some time out to mend things with his family and tie up a few loose ends of his old life in Norfolk and then he could begin to live his life again.

He switched off the engine and hesitated, thumping the heel of his hand a couple of times on the steering wheel as if venting his frustration with himself before he opened the car door. They slipped, unnoticed, through the main entrance of the Red Lion and made their way in silence through the old wooden door in the corner of the lobby. It opened with a creak and they climbed the stairs to their rooms and then walked, one behind the other, to the end of the landing.

"Look," Tammy said softly. "Come into my room and I'll make us both a coffee." She remembered the hand squeeze in the car park at The Gamekeeper's Lodge and took his hand again. This time he didn't pull it away. He let her lead him into her room. It was a warm night and so Tammy opened the French doors onto her little balcony. Noise flooded into the room as some customers below left the pub.

96

Laughter, the slamming of car doors and intermittent sounds from the bar when people left the front doors open were both intrusive and yet welcome because the noise removed the need for conversation between them.

Paul spoke anyway. "I'm so sorry. I've really mucked things up, haven't I? God knows what you must think of me — I've totally ruined the evening."

"Of course you haven't. It was a terrible thing to happen to you. I can't even begin to imagine how you must have felt. I don't blame you at all for wanting to get away from Claire. What she did to you was diabolical."

He sighed. "I've kept it bottled up all this time. I was so angry, but I wouldn't allow myself to get upset. Stiff upper lip, and all that. I suppose it had to come out sometime, though."

They both sat down on the balcony. Paul reached out to Tammy, took her hand and cradled it between both of his, smiling as the anger left his eyes. His palms were warm and her heart began to beat faster at the sudden, surprising realisation that witnessing Paul's raw emotion had been, for her, one of the most sensual moments of her life. It might have been uncomfortable and embarrassing at the time, but she could see now that the power of his attraction for her had been strong enough to break through a year-long wall of silence. She forgot about the coffee. They didn't move, but just looked at each other without speaking for a few seconds, before Paul sighed again and pressed his lips together. His eyes flickered upwards to the star-studded, clear sky in a philosophical gaze.

"It's just life, Tammy. I don't suppose I'm the first bloke to be made a complete mug of."

"Why do you think Claire has stolen your family from you, though? I don't really understand that bit," Tammy asked.

"She had a one-night-stand. She slept with a stranger and got caught out."

"How did you find out?"

Paul shook his head slightly. "She came clean about it. She told me just three weeks before our wedding day. *'I've just found out I'm pregnant,'* she said. *'I made a dreadful mistake on my hen weekend three weeks ago and I don't think it's possible the baby can be yours.'* She begged me to forgive her and offered to get an abortion straight away. I suppose I should be grateful she just didn't let me think the bastard kid was mine."

Tammy pieced together a picture in her head and realised what must have happened. Paul's family had forgiven Claire and cast *him* out of the family because he couldn't forgive her, too. It was tragic. How on earth could they have expected him to go through with his marriage, knowing his bride was pregnant by another man? Even if she'd had an abortion, the betrayal and infidelity was still there and always would be.

"I take it she still sees your parents, then?"

Paul nodded. "*Much* more than that, she's only gone and moved in with them. When we were planning our wedding, her parents were in the process of moving to Spain where her dad has some business interests. They continued with their plans and once they'd gone abroad she gradually stole my life from under me. They wanted her to move out there with them and start a new life, but she wouldn't. She somehow became my parents' daughter and shoved me right out. We had some awful rows because my dad said he wouldn't — couldn't — turn his back on someone who had become like a daughter to him just because of one mistake. Mum just cried, and cried and cried. Split the family right up, it did. It was like gradually peeling segments from a sour orange. So I left. I couldn't stand it any more. She just elbowed me right out of my own life."

"*Did* she have a termination?"

"No. That was the reason we split up. I *was* actually going to forgive her, and I made all the arrangements for her at a private clinic — she was only in the very early stages of pregnancy and it was a simple procedure. It only took about three days to arrange and it would have all been over, with Claire fully recovered, by our wedding day. Her mother went with her on the day, but Claire broke down in tears in the clinic car park. Claire rang me but my dad answered the call because I'd just left for work. He jumped in his car and drove to the clinic to find Claire and her mother both sobbing their hearts out. It turned out Claire couldn't bring herself to go through with terminating the pregnancy. She felt she would be murdering her unborn child. My dad just brought them both back home, rang me, and by the time I got there my parents had completely taken her side and pledged their support for her. I said I couldn't go through with the marriage knowing she was having another man's baby and, between them all, they somehow managed to make me feel like an axe murderer."

Tammy was speechless. Surely they must have understood that in the circumstances Paul couldn't have been expected to go ahead and marry Claire.

"I'm a right idiot, aren't I? I don't know why I don't just go back to visit them, tell Claire, *'hey, I am so over you now, have a nice life,'* and just get on with things. So what if people call me by my middle name. I haven't committed a crime, have I?"

"Exactly," said Tammy. "I think you're being daft worrying about calling yourself Paul, although I have to say I can't imagine you as Nick."

She realised her hands were still encased within his as he gently pulled her towards him. She found herself sliding onto his lap. She nuzzled her head into the crook of his neck and felt the light, electric touch of his lips on the top of her head.

"I'm okay now, Tammy," he breathed into her hair. "I'm sorry for ruining the evening. Perhaps tomorrow night we can try again. Can we, do you think?"

Tammy's insides were jumping and fizzing like an Alka Seltzer in a glass of water. She was so attracted to Paul she didn't trust herself. Okay, he had some baggage to get rid of, but then again, so did she — in the form of a long-lost sister, a possessive and clingy father and a dodgy scandal he had left behind in Lyverton over thirty years ago. She and Paul had both somehow ended up in the village to sort out the tangled and twisted mess of their respective lives. Did she dare hope that destiny had brought them together?

She lifted her head slightly, brushed her lips across his cheek in a light kiss and closed her eyes. His big, strong, sexy forearms closed around her waist and she wrapped hers around his neck. The warm, evening breeze blew gently across the balcony and the scent of hawthorn blossom curled around them, silently and timelessly.

Across the road, concealed in the shadows of an untamed copper beech hedge, the teenagers stood gazing at the scene of love's first kiss. Had anyone passed by at that moment, they would have blended with shifting shadows and the whispers of a spring evening blowing delicate kisses through rich, mahogany leaves.

The youth gently drew the girl into his arms. "Come on Jessie, my lovely. It's time for us to go now," he said. "It's done. We have to leave."

"What will happen to us now, Harry? I'm so frightened."

"Don't be," said Harry. "I'll take care of you — just like I always did."

CHAPTER TWELVE

Day Four
Thursday, 28th May: 4.30 am

Tammy woke early, just as it was getting light. She couldn't get back to sleep and on the spur of the moment she decided to write Paul a note, thanking him for dinner last night. It would be much more personal than a text message. She didn't want him to go off to work thinking the entire evening had been a disaster, and, in any case, the soft, but oh-so-delectable kiss on the balcony had made her bold. Just one, brief, sensual brushing of their lips had left her so excited for her future she couldn't sleep.

Not her father's future, but her future. How on earth was she going to handle it? Her dad was alone in the world and his future was inevitably caught up in her future. He would just have to grow up, come to terms with the loss of her mother and swallow his pride. If he wanted to try for reconciliation with his aged parents, he'd have to do it himself. It really was nothing to do with her.

Suddenly something else occurred to her. Could her mother have acted out the role of *his* mother, too, in a weird kind of Oedipus-type relationship? She raised her eyebrows. She had not thought of that before. Perhaps that could be the strangeness she had always detected in her parents' outwardly perfect marriage.

Tammy started to write on her notepad, conscious of her usually untidy handwriting.

'Paul,

Thank you so much for the lovely evening. I enjoyed the meal and the good company. I'm very much looking forward to seeing you later on. Try not to worry too much about Norfolk. You've done nothing wrong. At least you didn't need to change into that spare shirt!
Tammy x'

She mulled over the words. They were not very creative. She

scratched her cheek with a pensive forefinger. It would do, she supposed. Ordinarily, to practically everyone else in her life she would put *love Tammy*. But putting *love* might frighten him away. It was much too big a word to use just yet. After all, they had only shared one kiss.

Before she could change her mind, she ripped the note off the pad, tiptoed out of her room, crept across the landing and shoved it under Paul's door — right the way under so that she couldn't change her mind and retrieve it. She was wide awake and it was only half past four.

She crawled back into bed and sat, cross-legged, in the light of the bedside lamp. She wonder what it was really like to be a writer and decided to scribble a few sentences about her time in Lyverton so far, just to see how it felt. She wrote one very inadequate sentence about the ghostly moment when she had looked in her rear view mirror in the car as she had approached the village on Monday morning, and saw her mother's eyes reflected back at her. She read it back to herself: it sounded childish and very much like the beginning of an awkward essay or memoir, and she realised writing about Alice Thompson and Lucy Staverley was going to be much harder than she had first thought.

Monday morning! It seemed like months away, and today was only Thursday. And last week seemed like another lifetime entirely. She chewed the end of her biro. What she needed was a thesaurus and a dictionary. She wondered if the post office would stock them. No, not the post office; that would really blow her cover. A writer would never embark on a research expedition without the well-thumbed tools of her trade. She would have to nip into Fawsden, where she was anonymous.

Tammy's eyes fell on Alice's box beside the dresser. She uncrossed her legs, slid out of bed and pulled out the tatty brown envelope that contained the bundle of old letters. She shivered and reached out to tug her dressing gown off the chair where she had discarded it earlier. Her make-up bag, which had been left unzipped, clattered to the floor. The noise echoed around the room and she held her breath. She really must be quiet, she thought to herself. She couldn't go waking up everyone with her clumsiness and insomnia.

Sitting on her bed in the faraway, silent world of magic that exists between midnight and dawn, Tammy teased at a knot of faded pink cotton tape with her fingernails and untied one of the bundles of letters. They were from someone called Harry Thompson and at the top of each letter he had addressed 'my dear Jessie'. They were Alice's parents, obviously.

Tammy quickly became engrossed in the letters, imagining the terrors Harry had faced as a young man sent to fight in the Great War. They were in chronological order and it was heartbreaking to sense Jessie's terror through her written words, wondering if she was ever going to see her husband again. Harry mentioned *my dearest Alice* in every letter. It was clear Alice's parents had doted on her.

The majority of the letters were from Harry to Jessie, but then Tammy came across a very grubby letter that had been written from Jessie to Harry. It was a long letter. Tammy propped her head on her hand, as she settled down to read it.

> *5, Quarry Cottages,*
> *Lyverton,*
> *Nr. Fawsden,*
> *Northamptonshire.*
> *March 31st, 1918*

"Quarry Cottages!"

Tammy was so surprised she said the words out loud. Her heart began to thump in her chest. Was this one coincidence too far? She glanced around the room as fear tingled through her body, half expecting to see ghostly teenage images materialise before her. She didn't dare to think about the spooky thoughts that were rapping on her brain, waiting to be let in. She almost gave into a terrified urge to snap off her bedside light, shut her eyes tight and dive under the duvet to escape from the frightening shadows that seemed to loom at her from every corner of the room. Trembling, she continued reading, despite herself.

To my dearest beloved Harry,

103

Today is Easter Sunday, and we have just returned from Church. Alice looked very pretty in her new, white dress, but I must say it was a real job to iron, with all the tucks in the bodice and gathered tiers in the skirt. She is such a good girl, Harry. We have truly been blessed.

The twins continue to light up all our lives. They are so close to each other. They are both still fair-haired, although Lucy-Joy is the taller of the two by a good two inches. Emily-Rose is quieter and more studious. She follows the Reverend around like a little puppy, whilst Lucy-Joy learns to play the piano in the drawing room. She is very, very good at it. We think she might take examinations soon. I am so proud of her Harry (and, of course it goes without saying that I am proud of quiet, angelic little Emily-Rose, too).

I still go to the vicarage every day and help Mrs Staverley with all the children. I collect the younger ones and take them to school for her. Alice and Philip can't wait to go to school, too. Every morning Alice trots down the lane to the school, holding either Emily's or Lucy's hand. Then I walk Alice and Philip back to the vicarage and they play, either in the garden or in the playroom, while I help Mrs Staverley with the daily chores. Alice is growing up into such a bright, happy little girl, Harry. She is always laughing and giggling with the twins and Philip.

I love them all so much. They keep me going through the dark, long nights Alice and I are alone in the cottage, missing you dreadfully and wondering constantly if you are keeping yourself safe from the German bullets and bombs.

I have a funny story about the children to tell you.

Last week, they were playing in the meadow when they found a four-leafed clover and a dead blackbird. They brought the blackbird home, wrapped in Emily's handkerchief. The Reverend suggested they might like to bury it in the garden at the vicarage and say a prayer.

We dug a little hole under the apple tree. The girls did not want to touch the dead bird, and so Andrew held it. The Reverend asked him to say the prayer and the children all put their hands together and shut their eyes. Andrew made up a touching little prayer and then he made us all laugh when he finished it off with 'in the name of the Father, and the Son, and into the hole thou goest'.

We couldn't help giggling our heads off as Andrew dropped the dead bird into the hole. Even the Reverend found it funny. Andrew can be so amusing at times. He's a real comedian. The little mound is still there, under the apple tree, only the children have decorated it with all manner of tiny sparkling trinkets and beads hanging off a little dead twig to mark the spot.

The children wanted me to send you the four-leafed clover for luck, so I have enclosed it with this letter.

My dearest Harry. I love you so much and cannot wait for you to come home to us all. There is not a day goes past when I don't thank the Lord for our good fortune in becoming part of the wonderful Staverley family.

She is happy, Harry. Our Angel is so, so happy. As long as we can always remain a part of her life, we will be contented, won't we?

Please take good care of yourself. Come back to me soon, I miss you with all my heart.

With all my love, and may God be with you, always.
Your dearest Jessie xxx

Tammy remained still for a few moments and shut her eyes after she finished reading Jessie's letter. The vision of the children finding the four-leafed clover and the dead blackbird, and the little boy, Andrew, saying a funny prayer over its grave was so vivid it was like a film playing behind her closed eyelids. She inhaled and imagined the smell of the meadow and newly mown grass, and felt the chill of a cold, but sunny day in 1918 and, inexplicably, the feel of sticky, jam-covered little fingers on hers as she imagined Jessie holding the children's hands. She opened her eyes and re-read the letter, furrowing her brow in puzzlement. It was a really odd thing to say *'as long as we can remain part of her life'*. Why wouldn't Alice remain a part of Jessie and Harry's lives? She supposed it was the uncertainty of war. That would be it. Jessie was terrified Harry wouldn't live to see Alice grow up.

The rush of terror that she might actually have been conversing with ghosts in the village had receded somewhat. Was it just a big coincidence? If she took a walk down to Quarry Cottages she would most likely find either gypsies, or the new owners of the cottages, and they would be the cowslip-picking children's parents.

Tammy turned to the next letter in the pile. It was another one from Harry to Jessie, and she noticed how, in each letter Harry sent to his wife, he ended it with a prayer. He must have been a very religious man.

She unfolded the next letter. Out of it dropped an exquisite gold locket on a chain. It was incongruous — like finding an orange in a

105

bag full of apples. Why on earth would anyone keep a locket hidden within the folds of a letter? She held it in the palm of her hand and ran her fingertip over the delicate embossed filigree pattern. Tammy turned it over in her hand and noticed the hallmark. It was proper gold.

She wriggled her fingernail under the tiny catch: it was old, tarnished and fragile. Expecting to see heart shaped, tiny photographs of a young Harry and Jessie, she was surprised to find, nestled inside the cavity where, usually, lovers unite in a sepia marriage, a tiny folded piece of yellowy tissue paper. She unfolded the paper: it was discoloured and brittle and Tammy knew it would disintegrate if she wasn't careful. Inside the paper nestled a small golden curl of fine hair, tied in the centre by a piece of cotton.

Tammy shivered, suddenly cold. Instinctively she knew that the locket harboured a secret. Was it a secret lover? The locket had been deliberately hidden away. People only hid things from those with whom they shared their lives because they represented something they didn't want them to discover. Tammy remembered that Sophie Staverley had told her that Alice had given away all her most precious, personal belongings before she died. Had Alice forgotten about the locket? Tammy shook her head. She wouldn't have forgotten. The locket belonged somewhere else entirely and there had been no one worthy of becoming its new owner.

Tammy turned her attention to the letter in which the locket had been hidden, unfolding it carefully. Puzzled, she could see it wasn't a letter, after all. It was a crude but detailed pencil drawing of some sort of strange contraption. She turned the drawing around in her hand a full 360 degrees, but she couldn't work out what it was.

She replaced the lock of hair in the tissue paper, re-folded it carefully into the locket and then snapped it shut before placing it on her bedside cabinet.

Suddenly tired, Tammy lay down and closed her eyes. She tried to imagine Harry and Jessie Thompson living on the outskirts of the village at Quarry Cottages with their little girl, Alice. What sort of life did they lead? What did Harry do for a living before he was called up for active service? Her heart sank as she remembered Marian had told her that Alice had been an orphan. Did he survive the Great War in the trenches and return to the village before he died? Were they ever reunited after Jessie had written her letter to Harry on Easter Sunday in 1918? Tammy sighed. There was so much to find out.

She sat up again, picked up the locket from her bedside cabinet and turned it over in her hand, feeling the weight of it, and then ran her thumb over the filigree pattern. She could feel raw emotion flowing through it; it was as if gentle, loving hands were reaching out to her across time. It really was quite beautiful. She wondered if she should give it back. *No* an inner voice screamed out in her head. *It's yours. It was in the box so it's yours.*

***

Tammy slept in. She hadn't intended to, but it was just after nine o'clock before she woke. The gold locket was still clutched in her hand, under her chin, and as she opened her palm there was a red, almost heart-shaped imprint where she had clutched it tightly in her sleep.

She realised she had forgotten to ring her father, as she had promised last night. He'd be in his office now, probably panicking because she hadn't rung him, thinking obsessive, dark thoughts about Paul having murdered her and thrown her body in the Grand Union Canal. She leaned over and grabbed her phone. There was a text from Alan.

'Hi, Petal. I suppose you are sleeping in after your wild night out. I'll ring you sometime this morning, if I have time. Dad xxx'

Tammy smiled at the unabbreviated words and perfect punctuation in the text. As she put her phone down, she noticed another unopened text. It was from Paul. She jumped out of bed, her tummy giving excited, little somersaults.

'Hi Tammy. Thanks for the note. I'll ring you this afternoon. (I've got your mobile number from when you texted me yesterday.) Love Paul xxx'

Love. He had written *love*. With three kisses!

***

Standing in PC World in Fawsden, Tammy was flummoxed. The smarmy sales assistant was bothering her, trying to sell her a laptop computer. She didn't want another laptop: she already had one at home (although, to tell the truth, it was quite old and she could do with a new one). She wanted a dinky little netbook computer she could slip into her handbag. She wanted to look Marian straight in the eye that afternoon when, as previously arranged yesterday morning, they met up at the school where the parish council's records were stored. She could tell Marian she had decided to splash out, and that all writers were buying netbooks nowadays.

"No," she said firmly to the perspiring sales assistant as she twitched her nose at the sight of wet patches under his arms and the faint smell of sweat. "I want one of these — a blue one please."

"Yes but ... they've not got a massive hard drive."

No, Tammy thought to herself. *But you obviously have, and I'm not changing my mind.*

"You'd be much better off with a new laptop. How about this one? It's on special offer this week. I'll throw in a free laptop bag, too."

"No." she said as assertively as she could. "I'll have this blue netbook, please. And a case to go with it."

"This is so much better value."

Tammy shook her head.

The sales assistant sighed and Tammy knew he was thinking about his lost commission.

Tammy walked out of the shop with her computer, a case and a new optical mouse and tried not to think about the credit card bill that would fall through her letterbox in Yorkshire in a couple of weeks time. Still, she had saved money really. With this little piece of technical wizardry in her handbag, she wouldn't need a bulky thesaurus or dictionary because she could access them online, as well as begin typing her story.

All she had to do now was to find a greetings card shop and buy Paul a birthday card for Friday. She smiled. He was just a few months older than her. It was a much more normal gap than the eighteen years between her parents' ages.

CHAPTER THIRTEEN

11.30 am

Paul sat in his portable office in Fawsden East Urban Extension, drumming his fingers on his desk, looking out of the window at a bulldozer rumbling noisily back and forth, shifting a pile of earth.

"So what are you going to do, then? *Are* you going to Norfolk tomorrow? You need to make up your mind."

Paul's grey haired PA stared at him over the top of her glasses. If he was intending to take annual leave tomorrow, there was a meeting with the local authority that would need to be rearranged.

"I think I'll go. The weather's good and I haven't seen my parents for months. And it's my birthday — it'll be a nice surprise for my mum."

"Righty-ho. I'll ring round and rearrange your meeting, then, should I?"

"Yep. If you could, please."

Paul stood up, and leaned on his desk in a resolute, determined pose. He had always known he would have to face up to his cancelled wedding, the single mother who was once his pregnant bride-to-be and his estranged parents one day. And not only that, he was fast developing strong feelings for Tammy, and he just had to draw a line under his old life before he could even think about someone new.

***

Driving along the main street in Lyverton on her way back from Fawsden, Tammy passed a war memorial. Faded wreaths of artificial poppies were propped untidily around its base, still in place from Remembrance Sunday six months ago because no one had the heart to take them away. Impulsively, she stopped the car and clambered out.

Harry Thompson.

She scanned the list of names until she got to the letter 'T'.

He was there.

Tammy's heart sank in genuine sadness as she reached up and

110

traced her finger over the indentations in the stone that represented all that was left of poor Harry.

Harold Leigh Thompson 1896-1918.

Tears formed behind Tammy's eyelids; she was almost crying. He'd been so young and full of optimism. He had been an honest young man who was devoted to his young wife and little daughter. How could God let such a good person die and leave behind a wife and child? He'd loved his Jessie so much. He'd always put *'With All My Love Forever'* followed by three kisses in his letters. She tried to imagine what he'd looked like. Was he tall or short? Dark or fair-haired? She instinctively knew that he would have been an up-and-coming pillar of the Lyverton community. It was so unfair. He shouldn't have been allowed to die. There was no God. There couldn't possibly be. Her inner voice kicked in: *but he wasn't the only one, there were thousands of others whose lives were wasted, just like Harry's.*

***

Back at the Red Lion, Tammy could hear Cynthia singing along to her radio in the pub kitchen, and so she wandered through to tell her that it was Paul's birthday tomorrow.

"Hi lovely — how did your date go? I've been wondering all morning."

"It was very nice."

Cynthia raised her eyebrows. "And ...?"

"And what?"

"Did you — well — get on? Did you kiss him? Are you seeing him again?"

"Cynthia McLaughlin! You are soft, sloppy romantic. I bet you read all sorts of sentimental claptrap in those romantic quick reads and women's magazines you put in the foyer."

"Don't knock it," Cynthia replied with a laugh. "Love makes the world go round. Everyone needs to escape from the world in a little bit of romance."

111

Tammy wouldn't kiss and tell, but Cynthia was satisfied with the silence. She couldn't erase the smile from her face. She bent down and opened the oven to bring out a tray of freshly baked scones. The warm smell curled around the stark stainless-steel functional kitchen and Tammy almost forgot about her new computer because the smell was so homely she felt like a little girl again.

"Go through," Cynthia said, gesturing at a doorway from the kitchen that led to a cosy staff room.

Tammy sank down at the wooden table and withdrew the box containing her purchase out of a plastic carrier bag.

"I bought a tiny netbook computer today. I've been meaning to get one, and it'll help with my writing."

"My, oh my! That's smart."

"It'll be really handy."

"Mmmm ... it'll need all manner of thingamajigs and gizmos installing on it before you can use it, though," Cynthia said.

The electric kettle rattled and hissed as it began to come to the boil and Cynthia set out two pansy-decorated china cups and saucers, a matching bowl of sugar and a jug of milk. She then added a plate containing two hot scones and a tub of butter on the table and looked over Tammy's shoulder as she studied the instructions for setting up her new computer.

"Oo-er. What you need is a man."

Tammy quickly changed the subject. "Cynthia. You really must add all these little treats onto my bill. We had cake the other day. And now tea and freshly baked scones."

Cynthia feigned a horrified look and spread the fingers of one ring laden hand over her chest.

"Tammy, my dear. Despite my Scottish roots, I do *not* charge my friends when I invite them into my kitchen for elevenses!"

She bumped down heavily on the chair opposite Tammy and looked at her watch. "Well, twelveses — I'm a little late."

The scones were delicious and Tammy realised how hungry she was. In her enthusiasm to get to Fawsden that morning, she had forgotten to eat breakfast. Tammy spoke through a mouthful of scone.

"Before I went out this morning, I read some of the letters in

Alice's box."

"Did you?" Cynthia leaned forwards, interested. "How exciting."

"They were the letters Alice's father sent to her mother when he was at Ypres in the trenches. It's so sad. He died in the Great War, Cynthia. He was only twenty-two. His name is on the war memorial in the High Street. He sounded like such a lovely man from his letters."

Cynthia pouted her lips in sympathy, tutted and shook her head.

"How very tragic. What was Alice's mother's name?"

"Jessie."

"What a pretty name. I wonder what she looked like? Are there any photographs in the box?"

"There are quite a lot of loose photos in an envelope, but I haven't had time to go through them yet."

Cynthia tossed her head towards the door. "Fetch them. We'll have a little browse now. I could do with a little prevarication before I start work on my accounts."

Tammy looked at her watch.

"That's if you've got time," Cynthia added. "When is it you're meeting Marian Troutman at the school?"

"Not till two."

Tammy stood up with her palms flat on the table, pushing back her chair. She laughed out loud. "How on earth did you know I'd arranged to meet Marian this afternoon? Have you seen Paul?"

Cynthia rubbed the back of her neck with a guilty hand.

"No. He'd gone before I got up this morning. It was Daniel."

That explained it. Although Daniel was not the archetypical village gossip, he *was* one nonetheless.

"I'm beginning to think it's Daniel I should be asking about local history around here. He knows everything about everyone, where they're going, where they've been and, it wouldn't surprise me if he could tell you when everyone's birthday is too!"

"He can. And he does. He's like a human computer is Daniel," Cynthia replied.

Tammy laughed. "He's just so nosey — and he is such a gossip."

"Go on then," reminded Cynthia. "Go and get the photos, or we won't have time to look at them before you have to go out and meet

113

Marian Troutman."

The photos. Tammy had forgotten about them while they were talking about Daniel. She ran up the stairs to find the tatty, brown envelope stuffed with bundles of sepia and black and white photos. As she was about to rush out of the door, her eyes fell on the locket on her bedside cabinet. On impulse, she put the envelope down on her bed, picked up the locket and fastened it around her neck.

She stood for a few seconds, gazing into her reflection in the mirror. Again, it seemed like days ago that Cynthia had done her hair for her, yet it was only less than twenty-four hours ago. Tammy grasped the locket between her fingers and shivered slightly at stray thoughts of the odd coincidence of the modern day teenagers living in the same cottages as Harry and Jessie.

She turned away from the mirror, picked up the envelope and ran back down the stairs to the pub kitchen.

"Here they are. And look what I found in the box."

Tammy fingered the locket around her neck and Cynthia's eyes widened.

"That's lovely, absolutely beautiful. What a find. Is it gold?"

"I think so. Do you think I should give it back?"

"They gave you the box didn't they?"

Tammy nodded, sucking her bottom lip under her top teeth.

"Well then, it's yours, isn't it? They must have gone through the contents before they gave it to a perfect stranger."

For some reason, Tammy didn't want to tell Cynthia about the golden curl of hair inside the locket.

Cynthia emptied the photographs out onto the kitchen table, and Tammy began to rummage through them, curious and impatient to find one of Harry and Jessie. Her eyes fell onto one particular photograph; it was partially obscured by others, but it was clear it was a professionally taken family portrait, mounted onto thick, cream embossed card and underneath was written in copperplate script.

'The Staverley family. June 1913'

Tammy pulled out the photograph from the pile. Simultaneously,

114

Cynthia found one that had taken her eye.

A clerical-collared vicar stood proudly in the centre of the photograph Tammy was holding. Nestled in the crook of one of his arms was a newborn baby, wrapped in a trailing, delicate white lace shawl. The vicar's wife sat on a chair in front of him with a wide-eyed toddler on her lap. Two small girls stood either side of her. They were of similar height and looked to be twins, although they were not identical. Tammy remembered Jessie's letter to Harry, where she had referred to *'the twins continuing to light up all their lives'*. The vicar had his other arm around the shoulders of a young girl, who stood upright with a big beaming smile that reached out to Tammy through time. Subconsciously, Tammy smiled back at the girl, who must have been the eldest daughter. A boy of about eleven or twelve stood ramrod straight with his arms pinned to his side in a wooden pose on the other side of his father, the eldest son, no doubt. Two younger boys sat cross-legged at their mother's feet. The family scene was set in a beautiful cottage garden beside a gnarled apple tree, and despite its faded and time-worn dog-eared state, Tammy imagined she could feel the warmth of the lovely family spreading into her hand as she gazed at the picture.

"This is a picture of the Staverley family," Tammy exclaimed. "The vicar and his wife had eight children and look, here are the twins. Jessie referred to them in her letter to Harry."

"There's something written on the back." Cynthia stared at Tammy's face with a quizzical frown and her gaze slowly slid back to the photograph in her hand. Tammy turned over the family portrait to read the writing on the reverse.

"Oh look! It's the names of the family, with the ages of all the children."

Tammy read them out one by one.

"The Reverend Edward Staverley
Mrs. Hannah Staverley
Polly-Anne Staverley, aged 13
Edward John Staverley, aged 10
Henry George Staverley, aged 8

Andrew Thomas Staverley, aged 6
Emily-Rose and Lucy-Joy Staverley, aged 3 (the birthday girls)
Matthew Paul Staverley, aged 18 months
Philip Ronald Staverley, aged 3 weeks."

"I didn't realise Lucy and her sister, Emily, were twins," Cynthia said absentmindedly. "Tammy, you *did* say your parents came from the village didn't you? I haven't imagined it?"

Tammy's heart thudded and she clutched her locket nervously. Had Cynthia worked out who she really was?

"My parents lived here for a while as children. My father's parents came from Hertfordshire, originally, and my mother's parents both died before I was born. My mother was an only child."

"Are you sure?"

"Yes."

Tammy was not lying to Cynthia. Not this time. Her grandparents really did come from Hertfordshire, and they hadn't lived in the village for some time. Alan knew his parents had left at least twenty years ago, but hadn't managed to trace their whereabouts. She had done some research on her family history before she had decided to come to Lyverton and knew that Marian Troutman was possibly her only living relative in the village.

Cynthia gave her a strange, wide-eyed look and handed her a photograph without saying anything. It was another family portrait, mounted on embossed cream card. It was taken in the same cottage garden as the Staverley family photograph, beside the same apple tree. Underneath, was written:

> *The Thompson family. June 1913*
> *Harry, Jessie and Alice Thompson*

Tammy gasped in horror. Her hand flew up to her mouth, where her jaw was hanging so loose in surprise she looked like a gargoyle carved in stone on an old church.

The people in the photograph were unmistakably the young couple she had spoken to in the village. They were older in the photograph,

116

but it was definitely them. But that wasn't the most shocking thing. Tammy could actually *be* Jessie. Jessie could be her. They looked so similar — like twin sisters — even down to the heart-shaped locket around Jessie's neck.

"Oh my God!"

Tammy threw the photograph back onto the table, recoiling in terror. She clutched her face in her hands and a cold shudder shook right through her body as hundreds of icy cold fingers gripped her. She felt sick and faint as blood rushed in her ears. Grasping the locket round her neck, she yanked it hard. The chain broke and she flung it across the room. Her heart thudded painfully and the colour drained from her face.

"I *can't* be related to her," she gasped. "It's impossible ..."

"What about your mum? Was she born around here? I know it's a huge coincidence, but *could* you be a relative?"

"It's her, Cynthia. It's her!"

"Who?"

"It's Jessie. Remember the teenagers I've been talking to ... the children I've been seeing everywhere ... the kids who have been picking cowslips. I said she looked familiar, didn't I? That was because she looked like me at thirteen or so. Don't you remember, I asked you about them? They seemed real, Cynthia. Real, solid flesh-and-blood people. Remember the cowslips? And the Granny Pop Out of Beds they were messing about with after Alice's funeral?"

Cynthia's hand flew up to her mouth in horrified surprise.

"I can't believe I've been seeing and speaking to ghosts," Tammy continued, and gulped with fright. "Are they haunting me, do you think?"

"Tammy ... listen ... calm down. *Could* you be related to her?"

"No — at least I don't think so! I'm not sure exactly where my mother's family originated from, but I was always told it was Hertfordshire. It definitely wasn't here."

Cynthia frowned. "It might just be an odd coincidence. They say everyone has a double." She picked up the photograph and stared at it closely. She shook her head in disbelief and looked from the photograph to Tammy's face and then back again. "It's just a similarity,

117

Tammy. You're not identical. It's your hair, that's all. And you *are* at a sort of crossroads in your life, aren't you? It could be stress — they say stress does peculiar things to you — I've heard it can even make you see things that aren't there."

"I saw them, Cynthia," Tammy said with obstinate certainty. "Harry looks different only because he is older and has a moustache in the photograph, but I'm sure it's him. Anyway, Paul saw them too — we both did. It was last night as we drove off on our date. They were sitting on the pub wall and they waved to us."

CHAPTER FOURTEEN

2.00 pm

Marian was already waiting for Tammy in the school car park. She was leaning up against a low wall beside her Micra as Tammy's silver Audi TT drew up next to her.

Tammy clambered out of the car rather indelicately, before depositing the contents of her old handbag on the car park as she grabbed the strap and the handbag turned itself over. Marian smiled. The young writer was so clumsy and she always seemed to be in various stages of flustered disorganisation.

"Hello Tammy, how are you?"

"Fine, thanks. You? Sorry I'm a few minutes late. Cynthia and I lost track of time looking through some of the old photos and letters in Alice's box. I'll be with you in a minute." Tammy stuffed everything back in her bag, but still didn't close the zip before hoisting it over her shoulder.

"Oh, yes, I'm fine Tammy." She smiled warmly, held up a bunch of keys and rattled them. "The school's empty today, apart from Davey, the caretaker. I expect he'll be milling around somewhere."

"It's really good of you to give up your time for me," Tammy said breathlessly.

"That's all right," Marian replied. "To be honest with you, I wish I had a bit more time to spend with you this week, but I'm going to stay with my Auntie Joan in Leicestershire later today — I'll be back on Sunday, though, if we need to look up anything else."

"Whereabouts in Leicestershire does your auntie live?"

"Just outside Market Harborough. I'm her only niece, so I visit her as much as I can, and I always go to stay for a couple of days in the school holidays."

As Marian unlocked the front door, the unmistakable familiar smell hit the back of her nose and she instantly relaxed; she was back in her comfort zone, in school, away from her father.

119

***

Tammy's heart flipped in anticipation. She was intrigued by the existence of an Auntie Joan. Dare she hope that this auntie would turn out to be on Pippa's side of the family and therefore her auntie, too?

After Cynthia had brought her back down to earth earlier, she had realised that her mind must have been playing tricks on her when they had found the photograph of Harry, Jessie and Alice. They had come to the conclusion that, somehow, her accidental attendance at the funeral and the contents of Alice's box had planted strange thoughts in her mixed-up mind. She was merely suffering from some sort of delayed stress following her mother's death, and surely she must have caught a glimpse of the photograph when she had been going through the box in Marjorie's tea shop yesterday morning. It would be easy to disprove the ghost theory, too, Cynthia had said. All it would take would be a visit to the new family or the gypsies who had recently moved onto the Quarry Cottages site, or even to make some discreet enquiries about them. But the logical explanations didn't stop fear throbbing in her head like a whining child tugging on its mother's skirt.

Marian looked old again today. Tammy noticed she was dressed like an elderly lady in a flowery dress that wouldn't look out of place on someone in their seventies, but on Marian at forty-nine, made her look frumpish. A cardigan was slung casually around her shoulders – navy blue with brass buttons. Bobbly with age, it was covered in white dog hairs. She wore no make-up and her newly styled hair was lank and flat around her face. This was her sister, but the huge age difference and the lost years between them seemed as impenetrable as a brick wall. Marian was one side, Tammy the other.

As Marian unlocked the parish council's cabinets, Tammy decided to pull herself together. She was going to cast all thoughts of Harry and Jessie out of her mind, concentrate on telling Marian that she was really her sister and finally fulfil her mother's last wish. While they were alone in the school, it was an ideal opportunity. Researching the family tree of someone else's family would just have to wait.

Tammy formulated a plan in her head as Marian, with her back to her, sorted through files in the cabinet. They would sit down at the staff room table and she would tell her that she had something

120

important to discuss. She gulped, trying to prepare herself for the difficult task that lay before her. She knew hardly anything about Marian Troutman, but she didn't strike her as the type of woman who could ignore a letter written straight from the heart.

"Tammy?"

"Yes?"

Marian turned around to face Tammy, clutching a bundle of old files to her chest.

"I have a story for you, if you would like me to tell it."

"Oh? What's that?"

"You know what they say — truth is stranger than fiction. I thought about writing this myself, but I'm no writer. I'm just a boring primary school teacher who leads a dull life. No one will find me in the least bit interesting."

"Go ahead," Tammy said, sitting down at the staff room table, relieved that probably the most difficult task in her life could be put off for a few minutes longer. "We're not in any hurry, are we?"

"No. I'm not if you're not. It's just I thought you might be able to use my story, fictionalise it and send it to a magazine or something. It might give other people hope."

Tammy forced a bright smile. "Okay. Do I need my new netbook computer?"

Marian gave a shrug of her shoulders. Tammy imagined they carried a huge weight, and it wasn't the ancient navy cardigan draped around them that gave them the hunched appearance.

"Last year I kept dreaming about my mother. I haven't seen her, or heard from her, for over thirty years now."

"Go on," Tammy said, her face falling with apprehension.

"We had a spiritualist visit the village and I went along, just out of curiosity really. You know, the type of thing you see on the television and think what a load of old bollocks it is?"

Tammy bit her top lip and tried not to laugh, despite the knotted feeling in her stomach. *Bollocks* was probably at the limit of Marian's vocabulary of swear words. She couldn't ever imagine her using anything worse.

"I was bored, sitting at the back on my own, wishing I hadn't wasted a fiver on a ticket, when the spiritualist asked if anyone knew a 'Phil' who had passed over last year."

"And did you?"

The hair prickled on the back of Tammy's neck, just like it had in the tea shop when they had been laughing and joking whilst going through Alice's box.

"Do you believe in the paranormal, Tammy?"

Tammy puffed air into her top lip and scratched her forehead pensively. "No, not especially. I think the mind is a strange thing though. I don't think it can be trusted sometimes — especially when you're stressed or upset."

Last week, her denial would have been forthright and resolute, but now, after her recent experiences in Lyverton, Tammy had an uneasy feeling that she might have to revise her opinion on such things.

"Do you believe in God, then?" said Marian.

"I'm not a churchgoer. I haven't really given it much thought but I think there is something more to this life than meets the eye. Whether that's God, or not, I don't really know. What happened then, Marian? Did you see a ghost or something?"

Tammy couldn't look directly at Marian's face. She couldn't stop herself from thinking about the discovery of the locket, the Thompson family photograph and her extraordinary likeness to Jessie. And now, on top of all that, her long-lost sister was about to talk about her own weird experience. She just couldn't cope with it all any more. The day was turning out to be a series of odd coincidences and Tammy wished she could press *rewind* and go back three hours to just before she decided to stop at the war memorial to find Harry Thompson's name.

"No. I haven't ever seen a ghost," said Marian. "To tell the truth, I don't believe in the afterlife and the paranormal. I only went out of curiosity and, to be honest, I don't get out that much. It was just somewhere to go."

Tammy was relieved and didn't realise she had been holding her breath. She breathed out. "What happened then?"

"The spiritualist just said the usual stuff, like Phil loved someone in the audience very much — that sort of thing. Then she said Phil was a woman, not a man, and *'it's the smell of soap you can smell in your dreams'*."

122

Marian rubbed at her eye. "I was stunned and riveted to my seat, but hugely embarrassed. There aren't many people in the village who remember my mother, let alone that she was called Phyllis, or Phyll for short, but even so I felt sure people would recognise the name and look around over their shoulders to see if I was there. I went bright pink and just slipped out of the door as soon as I could. I didn't put my hand up. But you see, Tammy, the spiritualist was right, I *had* been dreaming about my mother, there *was* a smell of soap, and when I bought some of the soap my mother used to buy it was exactly the same smell. Surely, Tammy, even though my mother has obviously forgotten about me and hasn't ever wanted to contact me, someone would let me know if she was dead? That's if the spiritualist was right and she *is* dead."

Tammy took a deep breath again, trying to find the right words to tell Marian she was her sister. It was an ideal time. She would begin by reaching across the table, taking her sister's hands in hers and just tell her the truth. She would say, yes, their mother was there with them right at that very moment, bringing them together from the afterlife because, somehow, Alan's letter hadn't reached her. She would tell her that she, herself, *had* reached her and that their mother's last words were to ask Tammy to find her and tell her that she had always loved her. It would be a consolation after the initial shock. It would be okay, it really would. From Tammy's side of the wall, her mother's name had been Pippa, not Phyllis. Tammy didn't know she had once been a Phyllis. It was yet another secret; another life; another mother. Tammy suddenly realised that she had never actually seen Pippa's birth certificate, or her parents' marriage certificate or even the death certificate, after her death. Alan had squirreled everything away, protecting her from this other life: this other mother. She tried not to tremble too much. She was going to do it ... she was ... after a count of three. One ... two ...

"'Ello m'duck. What yer doin' ere?"

***

The deep male voice punched through the tense atmosphere from the direction of the staff room door. Marian nearly jumped out of her skin

123

as Tammy spun around in her chair, and then leapt to her feet, startled.

"I thought I heard voices. Can't keep away from the place, can you Mazza."

"No, I'm afraid not, Davey. Who else do you think would keep a check on you to make sure you're not skiving, slumped in the Head's office reading the Daily Mirror!"

Davey winked at Marian, smiled at Tammy as she sank back down in her chair and then shuffled over to the table, wiping his hands on the front of his jeans. He held out his hand.

"Pleased to meet you, miss. You must be Tamasyn Hargreaves. A famous writer, so I've heard."

Tammy stood up again and shook his hand. Marian noticed that her eyes were wide with fright and the smile on her face was rigid and fixed. She hadn't meant to scare her with the paranormal story. She'd only known her for a couple of days, but it was clear to Marian that Tamasyn Hargreaves was a very anxious, jumpy, young woman. She couldn't help liking her, though. There was something rather lovely about her that Marian couldn't quite put her finger on.

"I couldn't help overhearing your conversation. Have you had some news about your mum, Mazza, after all these years … did I hear that she's *dead*?"

"Davey is an old friend of mine," Marian said by way of an introduction. "We were at school together; known each other all our lives, haven't we Davey?"

"We certainly have."

Marian glanced at Tammy. She got the distinct impression she was relieved at the distraction of Davey's unscheduled appearance. She sank back down at the table. She really shouldn't have told Tammy the spooky story about her absent mother and the experience with the spiritualist. The poor girl was trembling with fright, despite her vehement denial of belief in the afterlife.

Davey found a tin of biscuits and opened it with a clatter. He extracted a couple of Hobnobs, offered the tin around and then sat down at the table.

"What's this about your mum, then, Maz?"

"Nothing really. I … I just heard from a friend that she might have died. There's nothing definite though. I was just telling Tammy ..."

Marian's voice tailed off. Davey had obviously heard the last few words she had uttered before he stuck his head around the door. He was quite persistent, though, and it was obvious he was determined to expose the roots of the overheard conversation.

"Didn't they tell you, then? How did you find out? I know she was your mother, Mazza, but let's face facts. It's no real loss, is it? How could she have just taken off with a young lad and abandoned you like that? Everyone thought what she did was unforgivable, and no one blamed you for being so angry and hurt. Even so, you would have thought she'd have made some sort of contact with you over the last thirty years. After all, you *were* her only child."

***

Tammy tried to calm herself down. None of this could possibly be a coincidence. This was something else entirely. There was no escape from hearing all these bad things about her mother. Pippa had been two different mothers with two different lives, rotating before her like a spinning coin, tossed high into the air, sunlight reflecting off her lives in all directions. Heads/Tails: Phyllis/Pippa. Tammy didn't fit into this life in Lyverton where her half-sister and a stranger were talking about her mother's other life in this other place; this other time. She didn't even come into the equation.

Davey chuckled. "Remember your eighteenth, Mazza?"

Marian rolled her eyes.

"Do I remember my party! How could I ever forget."

Marian panned her eyes to look at Tammy, who realised with shock that Davey's presence had brightened her. Her sister was like a chameleon, only she changed not by colour or hue, but by age and years.

"My father, Tammy, used to be a bit of a character in his younger days. When I was eighteen he really surpassed himself."

"This is really funny," Dave interrupted through a mouthful of biscuit. He chuckled in Tammy's direction. "It wasn't funny for Mazza at the time ... but she got over it."

Marian continued. "Way back in the seventies it was pretty unusual

125

in the village to celebrate an eighteenth birthday in such glamour and style, but my dad — well, Tammy, I can tell you, it was like Dallas in Lyverton. Anyone would have thought he was an oil baron. God knows how much it all cost."

Marian's eyes were twinkling. The years were falling away even further. She was travelling back through time right in front of Tammy's eyes as she remembered her mother in the life that didn't include her.

"My father bought me a brand new red Mini Clubman for my eighteenth birthday. I was ecstatic. Even though my parents were indecently wealthy at the time and could afford it, to have a brand new car at eighteen was practically unheard of amongst the village teenagers."

The news that Pippa had once been wealthy came as a complete and sudden shock to Tammy. She hadn't been well off when she was Pippa. In fact, Tammy knew her parents had struggled financially and Pippa had to work full time in a residential care home right up until she became ill and died.

"Spoilt to death, was Mazza," Davey teased. "Big house, a huge marquee in the garden for her birthday, a pony. You name it, Maz had it."

"Really?" Tammy said, gazing at the white dog hairs that were smothered over Marian's old cardigan and the faded cotton print dress. "Lucky old you."

"If she *was* spoilt rotten, it certainly didn't show, though." Davey shot a fond, admiring glance at Marian. "She was a smashing girl was Maz ... still is."

"So what happened at the party?" Tammy said.

Marian continued.

"My dad hired a marquee for the garden. Practically everyone we knew in the village was at my party and the alcohol was flowing, mainly down his own throat I have to say. He was absolutely slaughtered by the time the evening came."

Tammy laughed. "Isn't that just typical of parents, they're like big kids really, aren't they?"

Marian giggled. "He certainly was that night. It was my dad who

126

caused all the trouble, not my friends. My party was a disaster from beginning to end. Dad picked a fight with the chap next door, who'd complained about the loud music. He threw up in the rose bushes and then, in his drunken state, pee'd in the pond in full view of my extremely well brought up friend."

Tammy laughed along with Marian and Davey, and tried to imagine the Tony Troutman she had studied briefly in the church on Tuesday urinating in a pond, throwing up in rose bushes and picking a fight with his neighbour.

Davey wrinkled his nose. "She was a stuck up bitch. Alexandra something-or-other — posh name. She only went and called the police and complained because Marian's dad had exposed himself in front of her."

"No! Really? That was a bit extreme, wasn't it?"

Marian shot a private glance at Davey under her eyelashes and continued with the story. "Alexandra De Montpelier was probably the most eligible girl within a fifty mile radius. Her parents were rich and distantly related to royalty. I think she's now a beautician to B-list film stars no one's ever heard of. Anyway, she ran home, pretending to be horrified. Then half an hour later Dad was carted away by the police, arrested for indecent exposure and drunkenness. My mother was mortified."

"That was the night you finally got it together with Alan Fielding, wasn't it?" Davey grinned, shifting from side to side in his chair. "When I tootled up the lane to the old quarries to rescue you, there you were, sitting in the driver's seat of your car absolutely furious because Alan had just confiscated your keys."

"Yes. That's right," Marian said, lowering her voice and looking straight at Tammy as she confided in her. Her voice fell to a conspiratorial whisper. "I wasn't *that* drunk. I'd fancied Alan Fielding for years — I couldn't believe I'd finally got him. Then afterwards we had an argument about my car keys, and when Davey turned up, Alan stormed off back to the village, together with my keys."

Marian looked down at her hands, her face flushed and bright, and the chameleon added a few years to her appearance as a rush of bitterness flooded into her.

"But the thing was, Tammy, Alan Fielding was also the bloke who ran off with my mother, never to be seen again. He broke my heart into a thousand pieces and turned my lovely mother against me. Can you imagine that, Tammy? Your boyfriend running off with your mother? It was absolutely horrific, I can tell you."

A mobile phone rang, its shrill tone snapping the taut threads of tension in the air. Tammy jumped up, feeling sick and dizzy with relief and practically ran outside into the school corridor to answer it, grateful for the chance to escape.

Fielding had been her father's name before her parents changed it to *Hargreaves*. She had always known that her parents changed their names, ever since she found her father's birth certificate in a drawer when she was ten and they had told her the story of how they ran away together, conveniently leaving out the fact that she had an older sister.

CHAPTER FIFTEEN

7.00 pm

Tammy sank down on her bed and clutched her head in her hands. She was confused about so many things; she didn't know what she was going to say to her father when she rang him. How on earth would she be able to keep the anger out of her voice? He had lied to her. He hadn't told her he had a *relationship* with Marian. He had only ever said she was his old school friend.

She flicked open her phone. Best get it over with there and then.

Alan answered.

"Hello, poppet. Have you had a nice day? Did you have a good time last night?"

"Lovely. I'm having a drink with Paul later. I need to get ready, so I can't be long on the phone."

"Where are you?"

"In my room, why?"

"Just wondered."

"How are you then?"

"So-so. I'm missing you, though. The house seems really empty without you chattering away, singing in the shower and one of your CDs playing in the lounge …"

Tammy interrupted him. "Dad. I have to ask you a question and I want a straight answer. No bullshit, okay?" She narrowed her eyes in determination. She'd find out the truth. He wouldn't be able to lie his way out of this one.

"What?"

"I have to know the truth, Dad. Did you ever have a relationship with Marian Troutman?"

Silence.

The rotating coin of her mother's separate lives stopped mid-air. It suspended itself in time like an insect caught in amber.

"I take it you've spoken to her, then." Alan's voice was low and shaky.

129

"No, I haven't. I found out from someone else." Tammy cringed and pulled a face into her mobile phone. It was only a half-lie because she hadn't spoken to Marian about being her sister. She'd been within a split hair of telling her, and would definitely have done so, had Davey not interrupted them when he did. "Well, did you? I have to know, Dad. You owe me that much."

"No."

"Don't lie to me Dad!" Tammy yelled down her mobile phone, almost losing control. She swiped an angry hand across her eyes, brushing away tears of disgust for her father and sympathy for Marian.

"Well ... yes ... I did, for a very, very short time, though. Just a few weeks, it was. Who on earth told you?"

Tammy ignored the question. "Sex? Did you have sex with her?"

"No!"

Tammy's eyes narrowed. "The truth, Dad!"

"Well ... yes," Alan whispered. "But only a few times. Who told you, Tammy?"

"And then you dumped her for Mum!" Tammy gulped down a wave of nausea.

"No ... well, yes, I suppose I did. But it wasn't like that. I always loved your mother. You know I did."

"What about poor Marian? Didn't you know what it would do to her?"

"Yes. I ... we ... knew." Alan's eventual honesty in his whispered reply curled out of Tammy's phone and wrapped itself around her throat. She gulped again, and her heart thumped painfully.

"We couldn't help our love, Tammy. It was perfect, and you know it. We were soul-mates: two sides of the same coin, your mother and I, until death parted us."

Tammy gasped at her father's coin analogy. This kept happening, time after time. She imagined something, and then someone else mentioned it to her. Surely there were too many coincidences. There was most definitely something weird going on in Lyverton.

"Look Tammy, I'll tell you about it — right now, if you like. It was the night of Marian's eighteenth birthday that I finally realised how much I loved your mother. It had all gone wrong. Her father had got steaming drunk, had a fight with his next door neighbour and then been arrested for indecent exposure and Marian had stormed off like a formula one driver in her car. She hadn't long passed her driving test and she'd been drinking Cherry Bs all afternoon. I was petrified she'd crash her car. I knew where she'd gone: I knew she'd be at the old quarries, so I went after her. When I found her, it just sort of happened. Tammy, I swear I'm telling you the truth ..."

"Go on, then," Tammy interrupted in a clipped voice. "Tell me."

"She came on to me at the quarries. She was upset and crying about her ruined party, so I comforted her. Hell, Tammy, we had been friends for ages. We were both only teenagers, for goodness sake. One thing just led to another. You know how it is."

Tammy wanted Alan to fast-forward. She didn't want to have to think about her half-sister and her dad having sex in the back of a steamed up red Mini Clubman.

"What happened afterwards?"

"Mazza really shouldn't have been driving because she was very drunk, so I confiscated her keys at the quarry. By that time my mate, Davey, had arrived. He'd been out looking for her too. We had a bit of an argument over the keys and so I took them off her so she couldn't drive. When I got back to the party, your mother was busy, clearing away. Everyone had gone home, embarrassed, after Tony Troutman had been arrested, and so Pippa was alone. I stayed back to help her. Also, I wanted to wait for Davey to walk back with Mazza. I was confused about what had just happened and I was upset, too."

Tammy was spellbound. She had heard all about the disastrous story from Marian and Davey's point of view only that afternoon, and now she was listening to it from her father's point of view, and possibly about to hear it from her mother's point of view, too. It was bizarre.

"Are you still there, Tammy?"

"Yes. Go on." Tammy said in a shaky voice.

"Anyway, your mother and I cleared up the mess in silence. She didn't cry or get angry or anything — not then, anyhow. Her eyes just sort of glazed over as she methodically went around the house and garden with a black plastic sack, gathering rubbish. I watched her,

131

wombling around the garden from the kitchen sink where I was washing up. I remember the music was still playing on a cassette player in the kitchen. Pippa appeared at the back door just as Bill Withers' hit *Lovely Day* started to play. I'll never forget the lyrics as long as I live Tammy, I can tell you. It was at that exact moment that I realised just how much I loved Pippa. And I did love her Tammy, for all the rest of her life. I loved her so much and you know that."

Tammy imagined Alan, closing his watery eyes on the other end of the phone in Yorkshire, as an army of bittersweet memories accompanied him down memory lane. The intense emotion he was so obviously feeling, made her hold her breath. In her mind's eye, his eyes were still closed, his head was on one side, and he was sat with the phone clamped to the side of his head, resting his elbow on the dining table.

Tammy flinched as Alan began to sing *Lovely Day* softly down the phone, so that she could listen to the lyrics.

Evanescence stirred inside Tammy like glitter in a glass dome at Christmastime. She closed her eyes and the hairs on the back of her neck prickled again. It was the first time she had heard her father sing since her mother had died. His voice was trembly and unaccustomed, having been silent for so long. The shiver started in her legs and moved up her body until she was quivering and her teeth were almost chattering. The sound of her father singing to her down the phone was transporting her back in time. She was right there at her sister's eighteenth birthday party in 1978. She could see a younger Pippa with her black plastic sack; she could smell the aroma of stale food and alcohol; she could hear the sounds of the birds as they went to sleep in the twilight. She was there, smelling the warm, evening air of midsummer. She could see her father at nineteen — tall, thin, hippy-like — and his shoulder length hair blew in the breeze as he stood at the kitchen sink in his flared jeans and huge collared shirt, watching her beautiful, timeless mother out of the kitchen window, bending down, picking up rubbish and empty beer cans from the garden.

Alan's singing continued, his voice soft and shaky. They were there, together, frozen in time watching her mother and listening to Bill Withers.

Alan stopped singing and the suspended coin in Tammy's imagination started to spin again. She opened her eyes and was momentarily surprised to find herself in her room in the Red Lion and not in an imaginary Lyverton garden in 1978. Alan cleared his throat down the phone. His voice grated as he spoke.

"Only it wasn't, was it, Tammy? It wasn't a lovely day for your mother. It was a horrible day. I'll never forget the sight of my lovely Pippa, framed in the kitchen doorway, her lovely red hair straggly with perspiration, holding a black sack of rubbish and bursting out laughing at the irony of the lyrics. She was always like that, Tammy. She was so bright and sunny: she never, ever let things get her down, no matter how bad the situation. Well, I started to laugh too. Your mother's laughter was so infectious, as you know. She dropped the sack on the floor, put her hands on her hips and shook her head at the satire of the words. I went over to the cassette player to turn it off. *'No,'* she said to me. *'Leave it on, Alan.'* The giggling became real side-splitting laughter as my hand hovered above the stop button on the cassette player. We just couldn't tear our eyes away from each other. I don't know how long we stood there, with tears of laughter running down our faces, but the magic was broken when Maz returned home with my mate, Davey."

"Was she all right? Poor Marian!"

"No. She was heartbroken, and absolutely furious when she walked into the kitchen and your mother and I were laughing hysterically. *'How could you,'* she yelled as she turned her back on us and ran up the stairs two at a time. *'How could you laugh like that when my birthday's been completely ruined!'*."

***

Tammy thumped her huge handbag down on the table.

"I'm sorry I'm so late. I was talking to my dad on the phone and then I forgot the time."

"That's okay,"

Paul got up to get Tammy a drink from the bar. "Vodka and Coke?"

Tammy nodded. "Yes, please."

Tammy sat down. She was still furious with her dad for what he had done to poor Marian. Had her parents not realised how she must have felt? And then they'd left her, abandoned and vulnerable at only eighteen. Her sister was the saddest person she had ever met and it was all their fault.

Paul returned with her drink.

"Thanks for phoning me this afternoon. It got me out of an embarrassing situation with Marian Troutman," Tammy said.

"How? What's up?"

"We went to the school to look at the parish council's records, but the caretaker was an old friend of hers and they sat in the staff room reminiscing all afternoon about their teenage years. I couldn't wait to get away. I felt as if I was intruding on something. I was so relieved when my mobile phone rang at three o'clock and it was you. I made an excuse — said I needed to make an urgent phone call — and just left them to it in the school staff room. We didn't get any research done at all. Now, she's going off to visit her auntie in Market Harborough in Leicestershire and won't be back until Sunday, so I don't know if I shall ever get to go through the parish records now."

***

Paul loved listening to Tammy talk. He loved her Yorkshire accent and the way her words tumbled around playfully with her expressive hands. He had to admit to himself though, he found it a bit strange when Tammy asked him to describe the kids who had sat on the pub wall and waved to them as they had set off for the Gamekeeper's Lodge last night.

"So you definitely saw them, too?" she said, gleefully.

Paul nodded, confused. "I thought you knew them ..."

Tammy laughed, interrupting him. "No, I don't. I spoke to them a couple of times on Tuesday, that's all. They seem to have made friends with me. You're going to laugh your head off at this, Paul — I really thought they were ghosts!"

Paul exploded into laughter. "Why? I know they look a bit strange, but that's just teenagers for you, isn't it?"

Tammy shrugged her shoulders and rolled her eyes. "I really think

I'm going barmy. Hang on a mo. I'll just fetch a photo to show you, and you'll see what I mean."

A couple of minutes later, Paul held the photograph of Harry, Jessie and Alice Thompson in his hand. He looked up at Tammy and then back at the photo, his heart thumping in his chest at the incredible resemblance.

"Well?"

He rubbed his chin with his hand. "Hmmm. She *does* look like you, Tammy, but I think it's because your hair is the same. She's much smaller than you are. But I think you're right about the similarity to the kids in the car park. You can see it, even though they are older in the photograph. It's uncanny …"

He saw Tammy shiver. He shivered too, as he gave her back the photograph.

"We'll probably see them around again," he said. "We can talk to them and find out more. They aren't ghosts Tammy. They are definitely real kids. It's just a coincidence they look so similar."

Paul reached across the table and gently took her hands in his.

"I'm really sorry about last night Tammy. I don't know what came over me."

"It's okay, Paul. I understand. It doesn't matter."

Paul thought about telling Tammy that he'd taken a day off work and planned a birthday visit to his parents the next day, but then decided against it. He didn't want to talk about Norfolk. It would only spoil things when he was finally getting to know the incredibly gorgeous Tamasyn Hargreaves.

***

Tammy hoped Paul would ask her into his room for coffee. The evening had been relaxed and comfortable. Paul swept his key card into the lock. He turned to face her and their eyes blended into each other's. He held out his arms and she moved willingly into them. She closed her eyes as his lips found hers. The kiss was mind blowing, sexy, deep and Tammy never, ever wanted it to end. He broke away and hugged her tightly, pressing her into him. They were both breathing heavily.

Paul released her gently and held her by the shoulders, gazing straight into her eyes. It was a look of longing; of deep desire. She knew he wanted her. But then his voice became abrupt. He shut his eyes momentarily and then focused them on a point somewhere over her shoulder.

"Good night, Tammy. I really can't do this — not yet. Shall we go out somewhere again tomorrow night, that's if you'd like to? Perhaps to a club — MBs in Northampton, I think. We can have some fun."

Tammy nodded and mumbled a confused acceptance.

Paul turned on his heels, gave an exaggerated sigh and pushed his door wide open with a frustrated hand. He turned to face her again, a plastic smile masking his real feelings.

"Good night, Tammy."

Safe in her room, Tammy was confused and bitterly disappointed. He didn't want her after all. She had got it all wrong.

CHAPTER SIXTEEN

Day Five
Friday, 29th May: 5.00 am

It was not the sight of a silver canary charm or a gold locket that filled Tammy's waking moments on Friday morning. It was the sound of her mobile phone. It invaded a deep sleep and, at first, she thought she was dreaming, then she realised it actually *was* her phone ringing.

She jumped out of bed in a daze and grabbed her handbag. Damn. She couldn't find the blasted thing. It was in there, somewhere. She rummaged around and in desperation up-ended her handbag onto the bed. Her phone tumbled out with a various assortment of combs, lipsticks, pieces of paper, used tissues, keys and old credit card bills, but just as she scooped it up, it stopped ringing.

"Damn. Damn. Damn," Tammy muttered to herself.

She flipped open the cover and was surprised to see that she had a missed call from Paul. She was expecting to see her dad's name, or any other name in her phonebook, except Paul's, on the display. She hit the green button to call him back.

"Paul? Did you just ring me?"

"Yes. I know it's stupidly early — but I really do need to talk to you. Can I come in?"

Tammy swore her heart stopped as she cast her eyes around her room. It was a diabolical mess. She had discarded her clothes where they fell last night, after Paul had kissed her passionately and then turned his back on her. Her coffee mug was unwashed, and the top of the dresser cluttered and messy. Her make-up bag was empty, the contents scattered on various surfaces around the room, and there were a couple of empty cans on the floor.

"Yes, of course you can," she said before she could change her mind. As she spoke she was dashing around, shoving dirty clothes, underwear, magazines and the empty cans into her suitcase.

Tammy knew she was shameless, but she didn't care. She caught a glimpse of her reflection in the mirror and winced at the mountainous unconcealed spot on her chin. She tried not to think about it: she wanted Paul and she wanted him right then, spotty chin or not.

There was an immediate tap on her door. She stood up, her silent phone still clutched to her ear. She opened the door a little, peering through the crack, acutely conscious of her appearance.

"Thanks." Paul said as he slid around the door to avoid pushing it open further. He was wearing a t-shirt and boxer shorts and his thighs and calves, Tammy noticed blissfully, were every bit as sexy and attractive as his forearms.

She glanced at her travel clock and realised that it was only just after five o'clock. She caught another glimpse of herself in the mirror. Her strappy pyjamas were really quite revealing. Still, five am or not, Paul was in her room and probably about to jump into her bed. Things were most definitely looking up, and with a bit of luck he would be so busy ravishing her, preferably more than once, he wouldn't even notice the spot on her chin. She'd give him the best birthday present he'd ever had in his life. She'd make sure he always remembered waking up on the morning of his twenty-eighth birthday.

***

Paul plucked the silent phone from Tammy's ear with an accommodating smile. She obviously had no idea how funny she looked, standing there with her disconnected mobile phone clamped to her head, the straps of her pyjamas falling off her shoulders halfway down her arms and her tousled hair tumbling into her sleepy eyes.

"Is anything wrong?" she said, breathlessly.

The fond smile slid from his face and it became serious. "Yes everything. Everything is wrong."

"What? Why?"

Tammy slid her arms around his waist and he was suddenly acutely aware they were both only wearing nightclothes, with only a millimetre of thin fabric between their naked bodies.

He hugged her to him tightly and the breath caught in his throat as his body quickly stirred in response. He pushed her away gently and held her by the shoulders momentarily closing his eyes in frustration.

"Tammy. I know I've got an awful cheek asking you this when

138

you're on holiday, but could you come to Norfolk with me today? Just for the day. We'll be back tonight."

"Of course I will," Tammy said, much too quickly.

Paul sighed in relief. Everything suddenly became as clear as the glorious early morning sunshine flooding in through the crack in the closed curtains. He would clean the muddied waters of his life in Norfolk and then he could come back to Lyverton with a clear conscience. Only then could he take their relationship one step further. In any case, he didn't want to rush things with Tammy: she was far too much of a nice girl to jump into bed with him just yet. She most definitely wouldn't be into impromptu early morning sex with someone she had only just met. Oh no, he thought to himself, Tamasyn Hargreaves was the type of woman who needed to be wooed and cherished before sliding beneath the sheets with anyone.

***

Just before seven o'clock they left a note for Cynthia to tell her they would both be out for the day.

"You should ring your parents first," Tammy said. "What if they're not there and it's a wasted journey?"

"Dad doesn't work on a Friday. He works on Saturdays instead. If they're out, we'll just have a day by the sea. It's not far; just a couple of hours away. I don't want to ring first and pre-warn them. I just want to sort things out once and for all, and then get on with my life."

"Do you think *she'll* be there?"

Paul gave a cynical laugh. "Oh yes. She'll be there all right. My dad rented out the granny annexe on the side of our house to her. That was the final straw. I just couldn't bear to speak to them after that, Tammy. I'm sure my mother didn't want it though. She tried to change Dad's mind when I gave them the ultimatum last June. It was either her or me. They chose her, so I left. Simple as that. And now she's living with them."

"For what it's worth, Paul, I don't blame you for leaving. Claire betrayed you, but you are the one who has ended up paying the price. I think you are doing the right thing by facing up to things with your parents, though."

Paul shot her a sideways glance. "When I left, Dad said he thought that, given time, I could come to terms with it." He shook his head as he focused on the road ahead. "I couldn't bring up another bloke's kid."

"Paul. If I'm going to meet your parents, can you tell me a bit about them?"

"Well. Dad is fifty-five. He manages a builders' merchants in Norwich. He's just a regular bloke, really. He likes a pint on a Sunday lunchtime, the odd flutter on the horses on a Saturday and he's into the usual stuff — snooker, golf, his garden and his greenhouse, that sort of thing. Mum is about fifty-three and works part-time in an accountancy office. She's always busy with housework and it really annoys me how she hurries around, picking up things that are left on the floor and tidying up after my sister. She doesn't get much time to herself. She likes cooking and baking and up until last year she let my dad think he wore the trousers in the family, when really she was the boss and always had been."

"Your sister? What's she like?"

"Lois is twenty-five. She's tall, like me, but she thinks she needs to lose weight and is always on a diet. She's all right in small doses, is Lois. But she's far too loud and noisy for my liking. She laughs all the time and has too many friends: giggling, immature females who fill the house with complicated conversations about women's dress sizes, bitchy gossip about celebrities and they leave chocolate cake crumbs and empty wine bottles all over the place."

Tammy grinned to herself as Paul negotiated a particularly tricky roundabout, the authoritative voice of the sat-nav giving him directions from the dashboard. She had lots of friends like Lois. They gave her the confidence she lacked by being brought up as an only child. She sounded really nice.

"She's never got on with my dad, though," said Paul. "She can't stand him and he can't stand her. I always got the impression he was disappointed in her — embarrassed even. I think he is completely out of order, if you want my opinion. He openly criticises her and puts her down in front of people because she didn't go to university and has ended up as a hairdresser. He somehow thinks she is a failure and has

140

let him down."

"That's awful," Tammy interjected.

"And Claire is Lois's best friend," Paul added once they were back on the motorway. "That's half the trouble."

"What about Claire? What's she like."

Paul turned his head towards Tammy and she detected a shield of bitterness cloud his eyes. He sighed and bit his lower lip.

"We got together when we were eighteen and were rock solid. She's a vet."

"A vet?"

Tammy was not expecting to hear that Claire was a vet. She couldn't square the woman in her imagination with being a vet.

"Yeah — loves animals, does Claire, and she's so clever, too. She did really well at uni. She got a first."

"Why doesn't she get her own place?" Tammy said, wondering what Claire looked like. "Vets earn loads of money. She could afford to buy a place for her and her baby, surely."

"I suppose she will eventually," Paul replied. "She's still on maternity leave, though. The baby was born in November last year."

"What did she have?"

"I dunno. Didn't ask. I haven't spoken to Mum and Dad since Christmas."

"Didn't they tell you?"

Paul gave another cynical laugh. "Hell, no! Christmas was when they told me that Claire was staying with them for a few months, renting out the annexe. I just slammed the phone down on them. They tried to ring me several times after that, but I was seething and wouldn't answer. I even changed my mobile number so they couldn't contact me. They tried a few times at work, but my PA always answers the phone and so I managed to avoid them. I sent an e-mail to Dad to tell him not to try and contact me any more because I wouldn't answer them."

"Haven't you even spoken to your sister?"

"Nope. I don't think she lives at home now, anyway. She was about to move into a flat with her mates around the time I left. She had a huge row with my dad — it was nothing but rows at that time, mainly because of me — and he told her to get out of his sight. So she did."

Tammy was beginning to wish she hadn't agreed to go to Norfolk with Paul. She resolved to make herself scarce if things got too heavy; she could go into town and do some shopping on her already battered credit card. She tried to remember what she did last Friday, back in Yorkshire. It seemed like years away. Who would have thought that just one week later she would be on the road to the Norfolk coast, sitting beside a man she had only known for four days, zooming towards a family confrontation with people she had never met? Who would have thought she would have attended a funeral, been on a dinner date, found a gold locket and been given a box of old magazines, letters and photographs?

She pushed to the back of her mind a disturbing thought of her father and half-sister writhing half naked on the back seat of a red Mini Clubman, and then grew pensive as she stared out of the window at the countryside rushing past, thinking about Marian's disastrous eighteenth birthday party, her mother as an attractive thirty-eight year old picking up rubbish to the lyrics of *Lovely Day* and the strange, coincidental moments she had experienced since she set foot in Lyverton.

Pippa's age when she had run off with her father suddenly hit her like a thunderbolt. Thirty-eight. Just eleven years older than herself. If she was honest, she found Daniel, the waiter in the tea shop, quite attractive, and he was only nineteen. The age difference suddenly didn't seem so huge. Did big age gaps really matter? Or was it just self-righteous busy bodies who made them matter? Tammy's thoughts then wandered to Marian and how she was like a chameleon, changing her appearance and age in a strange type of time warp. Had her parents done that to her? Had she *really* been unable to move on with her life, even after all these years?

"Are you okay?" Paul asked, turning his head. "If you're having second thoughts about all this I can take you back to Lyverton. I shouldn't have asked you to come. I feel dreadful now, putting on you like this."

"No, I'm all right. I just need to open the window," Tammy said, fumbling around looking for the electric switch. "Feel a bit sick."

"I'll put the air con on. It's more comfortable than opening a window."

Paul flicked on the radio in the car, as well as the air conditioning. On Monday night, as she had sat in the bar in the Red Lion, the jukebox in the corner had been like a robotic archaeologist, turning over and examining in detail the precious artefacts in its hand. It had teased golden jewels of memories out of Tammy's earth, and then it had held them up to the world for everyone to see. It had left her churned up and exposed. Today, the radio in Paul's car was having the opposite effect. Calming and normal, she could listen to the music without emotion. The tracks on Radio One were up-to-date, but the songs that were playing, some of them so new her brain had yet to learn the rhythms and tunes, were injecting a curious mix of apprehension and optimism through her veins so that her soul would remember precisely how she felt this week. She felt she belonged somewhere — real, alive and welcome, despite the strange things that had happened to her. Was the music creating such strong memories that, one day when she was much older, would she turn on Radio Two and listen to those songs as golden oldies and when the tunes were played, would she remember the mixed emotions she had felt as she travelled to Norfolk to meet Paul's family on his twenty-eighth birthday?

"Hey, I've just had an idea. Shall we stop for a while and have some breakfast? It might make you feel better to have something inside your stomach."

Paul's voice was too cheerful. Tammy could see he was feeling guilty about asking her to go with him. He had mistaken her queasiness and silence while she listened to the radio for second thoughts. She could tell by the way he twiddled his thumbs as he held the steering wheel, and, when she turned her head to look at him, there was that slight twitch in his cheek, just at the corner of his eye.

***

Their breakfast balanced precariously on a single tray in Paul's big hands, they made their way to a sunny table by the window in the service station restaurant so that he could keep an eye on his car while

143

they were eating. Tammy trailed behind with two mugs of coffee. They sat down and Paul put Tammy's breakfast in front of her.

"So", he said. "You know all about me — just about everything there is to know actually. So what about you, Tammy? What's your story?"

Tammy took a sip of her coffee and then sighed.

"Okay. Firstly, I'm not a writer — never was, and never could be. It's far harder than you think."

"I know that," Paul replied with a shrug and a smile. "I knew right from the start."

"How?"

"Because on Monday night, when I rescued you from the jukebox and we sat in my room talking until the early hours, you told me you were an architect, and we chatted about, if I recall rightly, conservation areas, design and access statements, tree roots, drains, planning committees and dodgy local councillors. Not very writerly was it! Then you told me about your hobbies: painting, drawing, swimming and reading. You never once mentioned writing."

He laughed, but then he noticed her eyes brightening with embarrassed tears, and he felt dreadful for teasing her. He put his hand over hers.

"Sorry, I shouldn't have laughed. Why did you say you were a writer, then?"

"I'm not naturally deceitful, Paul."

"I know. I was just teasing."

"The thing is, I have a parent problem, too. Pretending I was a writer was all tied up with that."

"I know that as well," Paul mumbled through a mouthful of egg and bacon. He gestured with his head toward her plate. "You'd better eat that before it gets cold."

"You're not taking me seriously, are you?"

"I am. I will. It's just that I do know how things run away with you. It was probably just a stupid throwaway comment about being a writer, and now the whole village wants to be a part of it. I know what Daniel is like — he's a right gossip. He's been telling everyone about you."

144

Tammy sighed and shook her head. "I don't know where to start, Paul. I don't know where the beginning is."

"How about starting twenty-seven years ago?"

Tammy smiled, grateful for the prompt.

"My mum's name was Pippa. She's dead now, as you already know, and my dad's name is Alan. My parents' marriage was unusual in two ways. The first thing was that there was a huge age gap. In 1978 when they got together, Dad was just nineteen and Mum was thirty-eight. The second thing was that they both turned their backs on their families for good, and so I grew up as an only child with no relatives."

Paul gave an understanding nod of his head. "That's why your dad is so protective of you. No wonder. You're all he's got left."

"I loved my mum so much," Tammy said simply.

"I know you did. It was obvious on Monday night when you cried at the musical memories on the jukebox."

"When my mother was dying — on her death bed — she was desperate to get in touch with her other daughter, who she had abandoned and left behind when she had ran away with Dad, and so he wrote a letter to her. Even though he sent the letter recorded delivery, there was no reply. I didn't even know I had a sister until Mum was diagnosed with cancer, although they *had* mentioned to me that they both originated from Lyverton. I've always wanted to come to Lyverton, ever since I was a little girl and they used to tell me all about it."

"That's so sad. You would have thought your older sister could have put her differences aside when she knew your mum was going to die. Have you managed to find her yet?"

Tammy bit her lip and nodded.

"Who is it?"

Tammy shook her head, unable to get the words out, but Paul sensed she wanted to tell him. She would tell him, when she was ready. He wouldn't question her any more, though. He'd let her collect her thoughts for a bit.

They ate their breakfast in silence. The gap between telling him about her parents and their unusual marriage and going just one, single baby step further and telling him who was her half-sister was long and

145

wide and the other side seemed miles away.

A good minute or two passed while they both finished their breakfast. Paul put down his knife and fork with a clatter, raised his eyebrows and stared straight at Tammy.

"Well?" he said, cocking his head on one side.

Tammy closed her eyes momentarily. "Marian Troutman is my half-sister."

She blinked rapidly two or three times.

"What? Bloody hell Tammy ..."

"She doesn't know yet. I was right on the brink of telling her yesterday afternoon when we were alone at the school, but then the caretaker wandered into the staff room and they started talking about their teenage years. It was horrible to have to listen about my mum's other life and my dad as a nineteen year old. I was so relieved when you rang me on my mobile and I managed to escape."

"Bloody hell, I can't believe this, Tammy. On Tuesday night when she turned up at the pub unexpectedly, did you know then? And how on earth did you manage to stay calm?"

"I wasn't! I was a blubbering wreck!"

"I wish I'd known. I wouldn't have agreed to having dinner with you both." Paul shook his head. "I've got you all wrong, Tammy. I knew you weren't a writer, but I was convinced you'd come to the village to escape from a bad relationship. I imagined you'd just broken up with your boyfriend or something and had jumped in your car and headed for Lyverton because it was where your parents had lived years ago. I thought you needed to go somewhere anonymously to lick your wounds, like a frightened puppy, hiding under a chair."

Paul scratched the back of his head and puffed out his cheeks, exhaling slowly. "Cynthia thinks you're the long-lost daughter of Alice Thompson's love child. She's convinced you are in the village because of Alice's death, chasing an inheritance."

"Oh, Paul, everything else I've told you is true. I'm nothing to do with Alice. There is no connection at all. I can't possibly be related to her. I really *did* accidentally attend her funeral on Tuesday."

Paul grabbed both her hands.

"Tammy, I believe you, one hundred per cent. I told Cynthia as

146

much this morning just before we left."

"Cynthia," Tammy said with regret in her voice. "I've lied to Cynthia. It feels like I've lied to my mother!"

Paul laughed. "I know just what you mean."

His face clouded over with concern and he rubbed the back of Tammy's hands with his thumbs.

"Tammy, what the hell is your dad thinking of, sending you back to Lyverton to do his dirty work for him?"

"He didn't send me. I wanted to come. I had to come. I promised my mum on her deathbed that I would find Marian. Then Dad thought I could perhaps search for my grandparents. They don't know I exist either."

"Tammy. Look at it this way. It's his problem. His past. He should have paved the way for you with Marian. You have always had an absolute right to know her. He shouldn't have let you come in cold. He's left you so exposed."

"Yes. But he's frightened. Frightened of losing me."

"Is he a man, or a mouse?"

"He's lost, Paul. He's like a little boy with no friends since Mum died."

"He's a grown man, Tammy, with a smashing daughter who always had a right to know her family, and he and your mother have denied you that. Wouldn't you think that fact, alone, would be enough motivation for him to overcome his fear, swallow his pride and do the best thing for her? He's no better than *my* father, putting Lois down all the time because she wasn't academic and wasn't the type of daughter he imagined himself having; trying to make her into something she wasn't and never could be."

***

Paul was firing truths at her in a bizarre type of Russian roulette. She tensed her body, waiting for the one with the lethal bullet.

"And how could your mother let you grow up without giving you at least the chance to know your sister and your family? How could she Tammy? I was despicable — like stealing your birthright from you."

147

Paul's face was a picture of incredulous rage as he fired the last bullet — the one that no one had dared to fire before. The truth that had been eating away at Tammy's insides for three years since she had discovered that she had a sister in Lyverton and grandparents who had once lived there. The truth that had left her hollow, filled only with the weight of her mother's untimely death and her father's grief.

The lethal bullet flashed past Tammy's eyes, leaving its trail of truth in its path. She had been like a precious jewel in the palms of their hands. A bright diamond to be kept hidden away; a possession. A delicious secret to be cooed over, petted and stroked while she slept, cocooned in the bubble of their secret life, shielded from the outside. But Tammy was a living, breathing person in her own right. A child could only be a child for as many years as could be counted on fingers before the fingers ran out and the child needed space to grow. A child needed more than its parents, it needed a life of its own, carved out bit by bit with its own hands. Had she been someone different, not a submissive, quiet, innocent child-woman who always did as she was told and soaked up the copious amount of parental love like a sponge, frightened of the world outside the bubble, they would have lost her when she hit sixteen or so in a spectacular explosion of pushed boundaries and defiant independence.

As Tammy sat, completely deflated by Paul's last bullet, she didn't crumple to the ground. She knew, at that moment, she *was* strong. She would get through the muddy knowledge that her parents had made huge mistakes and hadn't been perfect after all. She was at a pivotal point in her life, spinning like a plate on a stick, but she'd fall without breaking, because she was stronger than that and, in any case, Paul was there, right with her, ready to catch her if she fell.

CHAPTER SEVENTEEN

9.30 am

Paul looked down. Tammy was clenching his hand so tightly the skin on his fingers was going white.

Her parents had been so wrong to keep her from her birthright. Every child had a right to know its parents, brothers, sisters, aunts, uncles and grandparents. It was just stirring up trouble to keep a child away from its family. The time would inevitably come when that child would become an adult and do as Tammy had done. They would break away to seek out their family for themselves. Now, in some strange, twisted destiny, he was going back to his carelessly discarded family, just as she was about to find hers. It was bizarre — as if they had both been spinning around in space and had gravitated together to help each other repair their respective shattered families.

After a few minutes of silence, Tammy spoke in a clear, level voice, echoing Paul's thoughts.

"I need us to make a pact, Paul. Today is about you, your family and confronting the awful situation you've been running away from for the past year. I'll be there for you every single step of the way. I'll do my best to be strong for you and I'll speak for you if I have to. Then, once we are back in Lyverton I need you to be beside me when I tell Marian she is really my sister and when I confess to everyone that I'm not really a writer. I need you Paul, as much as you need me. We both have huge tasks ahead of us, but we can help each other through them."

There were no more words to be said. Paul knew that if what he felt for Tammy was fledgling love, then it would just have to wait. Their families had to come first.

They had parked in the driveway. Paul had wanted to park about a hundred yards away, but Tammy had said no, he needed to be assertive and strong and not creep back like a dog with its tail between its legs.

He took an audible deep breath and exhaled slowly.

"Remember I'm Nick here," he said as he opened his car door.

149

"I'm only Paul in Lyverton." He had one hand on the steering wheel with one leg out of the driver's door so that he was looking at Tammy over his shoulder. Their gazes locked in mutual determination.

"Come on then," she said with more confidence than Paul knew she was feeling as she opened the passenger door.

Paul hesitated at the front door of the house. "Should I knock, or do I use my key?"

"The key; this is your home. Lyverton is your lodgings."

Paul opened the door and gestured for Tammy to go in first. The hallway was bigger than it looked from the outside. The beige carpet was fuzzed over with black dog hairs and dust had gathered in the spindles and balustrades on the stairs. On the wall, various family photographs smiled a welcome, gathering a fine layer of dust over the tops of the frames.

Paul shut the door behind him. "Hello? Anyone home?" he called out.

An excited whine and a squeaky bark emanated from behind the lounge door.

"Zak. Barney!"

Paul threw open the door. A whirlwind of black, clumsy paws, flapping ears and thumping, wagging tails tumbled into the hallway.

"Tammy, these are our Labs."

The assault of pink, wet tongues, explosive sneezes, thumping of tails and nuzzles by huge wet noses, made Tammy giggle. The Labradors were barking, but the excited yaps were of pleasure rather than an indignant protection of their home against a stranger.

"You didn't tell me you had dogs!"

Paul was crouching down hugging the excited black Labradors. "There's no one here, Tammy. The dogs usually have a free run of the house when someone's here."

"Oh, I just love dogs. We have a spaniel — Max. He's my best friend," said Tammy.

Once Paul had let the dogs out into the garden through the back door, he joined her in the lounge. His initial euphoria at returning home had turned to a worried frown.

"What?" said Tammy. "What's the matter?"

150

Paul swept his hand through the air.

"This. It's an utter mess – the carpets haven't been vacuumed for ages, there's dust and dog hairs everywhere, dirty washing up in the sink, tea stains on the worktops in the kitchen.' He shook his head. 'I just can't believe it."

***

Tammy's heart went out to Paul's mother. She knew it was the home of a woman who couldn't be bothered; someone who did the bare minimum and nothing more. She remembered Paul's comment in the car that his mother had been obsessively house-proud and spent all her time cleaning up after his sister. This was the home of the same woman whose family had exploded apart because of a few minutes of drunken stupidity. Paul's mother was in mourning — her aimless existence lived out in a ritual of working, eating and sleeping. It was perfectly obvious to Tammy that the poor woman was grieving for her lost son and most probably her lost daughter, too.

"She's just depressed, Paul. She'll be all right now you've come back."

"Should we wait? Or should we go out for a bit? I bet they've gone shopping or something."

Before Tammy could answer him, she heard the soft click of a door opening. Intuitively, Tammy knew which door had opened. She had noticed the doorway at the foot of the stairs when they had grappled with the excited dogs in the hallway.

A string of baby babble and a simultaneous female voice uttering just one word cut through the air.

"Nick?"

Paul stood up, apprehension burned into his face like a ritual branding. He turned to face the doorway, his legs slightly apart. He looked like a man trying to keep his balance on a bobbing boat in a stormy sea as he thrust his hands into his pockets, squaring up for the inevitable confrontation.

"Claire," he breathed. His voice was little more than a whisper, more to himself than in reply.

"Happy birthday, Nick."

She was not what Tammy expected. She didn't look like a woman who had slept with another man just weeks before her wedding. The baby in her arms blew a loud raspberry and craned its neck around to stare at them with huge brown eyes. It was a boy.

***

Paul reeled backwards as a powerful, new emotion trickled into his veins and made his heart race. He wasn't expecting the sight of Claire's baby to affect him in quite the way it did. The little boy blew a raspberry at him and then rammed his fist into his gummy mouth, smiling broadly as he perched on Claire's slightly plump, denim-clad hip. It was a direct, unconditional, innocent smile, without even a hint of condemnation or disapproval. The baby took his fist out of his mouth and grabbed at his mother's red sweatshirt, leaving a trail of saliva down the front. Paul felt something tug painfully in his chest. Nothing that had happened was the baby's fault. He suddenly felt incredibly sad for the child: he had no father to tumble with on newly mown grass, or to hold his hand as he looked for crabs in rock-pools on the beach, or to teach him how to skim pebbles across waves in the sea. It was an unfamiliar, new feeling and he stepped backwards, surprised at its intensity.

Claire's voice was clipped as she stared at Tammy.

"Aren't you going to introduce us, Nick?"

"Claire, this is Tammy. Tammy, this is my … my ex, Claire."

"Have you finally come home?" Claire shifted the baby onto her other hip.

Paul evaded the question. "I've come to see Mum and Dad and Lois."

"Oh." Claire swallowed. Her voice wavered and her eyes brightened "This is Lewis, my son."

"I gathered that."

"He's six months ..."

"So I understand."

"Rosemary and Keith have gone to the supermarket. They should be back soon. Do you want me to text them?"

Paul shook his head.

"Isn't he gorgeous? I called him *Lewis* after Lois, because she's been fantastic — a true friend. Did you know I live here now?"

"Yes," Paul said darkly. "That's why I don't."

The tears were welling in Claire's eyes and were about to spill over her lower eyelids. She sniffed. "Would you like a cup of tea, or something?"

"If I want one, I'll get it myself."

"Tammy?" she asked.

"If she wants one, I'll make it. It's my home, not yours."

"Don't be like that, Nick ..."

"Like what?"

"That! We were as good as married. You loved me once ..."

"Yes," said Paul. "I did ... until ..." Paul gestured towards baby Lewis with his head.

Claire sank into one of the armchairs in the lounge and sat her little boy on the floor between her feet. She looked up at Paul. "Your poor mum is a wreck. When you turned your back on us all and stormed off like that, it broke her heart. I know I messed up." She turned to address Tammy. "It was just one mistake and I was totally up-front and honest about it. We could have worked things out — we really could have done if he hadn't just gone off like that."

Paul closed his eyes and tried not to shout at Claire as fury and betrayal tingled in his arms and legs. He clenched his fists by his side, deliberately digging his fingernails into the palms of his hands so that the pain would distract him from his anger. He hated feeling angry. He was a peaceful sort of chap generally, but if just thinking about Claire was hard, seeing her in the flesh had flooded his veins with almost a year's worth of repressed rage. He took a deep breath and forced himself to speak rationally.

"You forgot something, Claire. It wasn't me who did anything wrong. It was you who dropped her knickers for some loser, then played the sympathy card when she got found out."

"I didn't forget ... I know what I did was diabolical ... Rosemary and Keith ... they've been so good to me. But I didn't mean to drive you away, Nick. I said I was sorry a thousand times. You know that!"

"How dare you wriggle your way into *my* family and take over like

153

this. It's insane, Claire!"

"But was you who left, Nick …"

"I had no choice, did I? I couldn't bring up another man's child. How could you expect me to …"

"Did I ever ask you to? I might not have been able to force myself to have an abortion, but I was seriously thinking about adoption. You wouldn't even discuss it …"

A deep, gruff, voice interrupted from the hallway.

"No, she didn't, Nicholas, did she? She never asked you to bring up another man's son. You didn't give her a chance to put things right."

***

Paul didn't move his head, but in the lounge doorway a tall, gaunt man, the owner of the deep voice, was standing holding two supermarket bags. He was glaring at Paul. Tammy was shocked. He should have been welcoming his son back with open arms, not speaking to him like that. He was siding with Claire. She just couldn't believe it. In all the commotion of raised voices, no one had heard him come in.

Baby Lewis began to wail, turning his head from one adult to another in an uncertain panic at the tension in the atmosphere. Claire picked him up and settled him on her knee.

"Nicholas? Oh God, thank you! Thank you!"

The woman's voice that drifted into the lounge from the hallway was bursting with unrestrained joy. In contrast to her husband, Rosemary Pepper couldn't disguise the surprised happiness at her son's unscheduled return to the family. It seemed strange to Tammy to hear them call Paul *'Nicholas'*, or *'Nick'*, but she realised it was a sad reflection of the terrible situation in which he had found himself. He had been living his Lyverton life in parallel to his family in Norfolk, changing his name in a heart-breaking but futile effort to get away from this terrible situation. Unresolved, it would keep them all forever apart into infinity unless they could build bridges across the deep chasm.

Paul's father stood to one side to let his wife into the lounge, shaking his head from side to side.

"If you haven't come back to put things right with Claire, then I'm

154

not sure you should have come back at all," he said in a sharp voice, without looking at anyone. Hesitating briefly, not knowing which way to turn, he strode into the kitchen with the bags, but Tammy noticed the brightness in his tired eyes and knew that his abrupt manner was just a front for his confused emotions.

"Nick ... oh Nick ...Happy birthday, darling!" His mother flung her arms around Paul's neck and he hugged her tightly to him. "I've been thinking about you all day — and now here you are." She pulled away and ran both her hands over his face and through his hair, as if checking him over to make sure he was all right.

"I've missed you, Mum." Paul's voice was thick and emotional. "I'm sorry I didn't keep in touch ... I ... I've been working."

Paul pulled away and looked in Tammy's direction.

"Mum, this is Tammy ... Tamasyn Hargreaves. She's a friend of mine. Tammy, this is my mum, Rosemary, and my dad, Keith ... er ... I think he's just putting the shopping away."

Paul's voice faded, ashamed and annoyed by his father's apparent rudeness towards Tammy.

Paul's father stepped briskly back into the room and patted down an imaginary object in front of him as, embarrassed, he realised he had forgotten it was his son's birthday.

"Happy Birthday, Nick." Paul's father shoved his hands deep in his pockets before immediately taking them out again and wiping them on the front of his jumper. He had tears in his eyes that were completely incongruous with his earlier inappropriate comments and angry manner. He extended his hand to Tammy politely. She stood up and fixed a smile on her face as she shook his hand.

Rosemary smiled broadly at Tammy. A big, welcoming, happy smile as she flung her arms around her and Tammy heard a soft whisper as Rosemary's head brushed against her ear.

"Thank you. Thank you for bringing him back to me."

Tammy glanced across the homecoming scene towards Claire. She expected to feel a certain smugness — a satisfaction that Claire was finally getting her just desserts for what she had done. She was not a part of Paul's family. Tammy was merely an observer, but she was far, far worse. She was an impostor; a Cuckoo Claire. But Tammy was

155

surprised to find that she didn't feel smug or hate her at all. She just felt pity for her and her baby. She might have been stupid, but she was really just as much a victim as Paul. She was only trying to do the best for her child and give him the nicest possible home until she could get back to work after her maternity leave and afford a place of her own.

CHAPTER EIGHTEEN

Tammy was not entirely sure how she happened to be pushing a smiling, happy six-month-old baby in a pushchair aimlessly around unknown streets in a small Norfolk town. Tammy Hargreaves, the girl who made excuses when asked to hold her friends' babies and said she couldn't ever imagine having children of her own. Tammy Hargreaves, the girl who (if truth be told) was scared of babies and children and the power they held over their parents' lives.

She stared at baby Lewis in the buggy as they walked along. He kept turning his head to gaze at her with soft, trusting brown eyes. Little Lewis, an innocent child being cared for by Tammy, the lost child of innocence, while both of them floundered in a sea of uncertainty. Tammy replayed the awkward scene she had just left behind in her head as she walked along.

"Claire," Rosemary Pepper had said in a clear, level voice not twenty minutes ago. "I'm afraid I must ask you to leave us alone to discuss this. This is family business between Nicholas, myself and his father."

Claire had looked shocked to the core, and almost lost for words. She'd turned to Keith Pepper for moral support.

"Keith," she said. "I *am* family, aren't I? Doesn't Lewis call you Grandad? And after all, I do live here."

"No," Rosemary Pepper screamed before her husband could open his mouth. "*You* call Keith *Grandad*. Oh, and unless it's escaped your notice, Lewis can't yet talk!"

"Rosie." Paul's father had said. "Calm down, for goodness sake. I don't know what's come over you. I think perhaps, on balance, Claire should stay."

Rosemary Pepper had then jumped up off the sofa and squared up to Keith and Claire. Her tone had been one of measured hysteria as she'd stood, steadfast and unmoveable with her hands on her hips. The words were well practised, as if she'd been rehearsing them over and over in her head for months.

"Claire. I have something to say and it's been a long time coming. Nicholas is *my* son. You are *not* my daughter and never will be, despite what my misguided husband thinks. Will you please leave my living room and let us talk to our son — alone!"

Paul had been at breaking point as he sat on the sofa beside Tammy. "We shouldn't have come," he had muttered to her under his breath. "Let's go back. I've tried, Tammy. I've tried. It's no good. I can't stand all these arguments — nothing's changed."

Tammy had suddenly found an inner strength she didn't know she possessed and taken charge.

"Claire," she had said as she stood up and looked straight at her. "Why don't we take little Lewis out of here and let Paul and his family have some space."

Three jaws had fallen open. Three brows had furrowed into a frown simultaneously. Three voices had spoken in a perfect chorus.

"Paul?"

Then three pairs of eyes had stared at Paul, who had mumbled that, in Lyverton, he always used his middle name.

"But why?" his mum had whispered. "Why, Nick?"

Paul's voice had been thick with months of heavy, repressed emotion escaping in just a few loaded words. "Because I don't want to be Nick any more," he'd bellowed. "Because I can't bear to be the bloke whose wife-to-be shagged a stranger, got pregnant and then turned my family against me when I couldn't bring up the bastard child as my own!"

"Oh, Nicholas," Rosemary Pepper had whispered, as tears had begun to roll down her face. "I'm sorry. We're sorry. Please don't be so angry with us. We've made some dreadful mistakes. But it'll be all right. We'll sort it out. Don't leave us again. Please?"

Claire had collapsed like a crushed meringue as Tammy had lifted Lewis from her lap. She'd put her arms right over her head and begun to cry, her chest heaving with huge sobs. Tammy had settled Lewis on her hip, taken Claire gently by the arm and then led her out of the room, shutting the door behind them.

They had gone into Claire's little annexe through the doorway in

158

the hall and Tammy had made her a cup of tea. Lewis had started to cry, loud frightened wails escaping from his little chest and massive, fat tears rolling down his chubby cheeks. While Claire sobbed her heart out on the sofa, Tammy had offered to take him out for a little walk so she could have some space, too.

Now twenty minutes later, Tammy found herself in charge of a pushchair containing a six-month-old bewildered baby, and she had no idea where she was going. She had no nappies for Lewis so she couldn't go far. He gave her a wide-eyed smile and shoved his fingers in his mouth, sucking them furiously. There was a seat just up ahead that overlooked a tiny green space bordered by bushes. Tammy sat down and unstrapped Lewis from his pushchair.

He settled easily into her lap and fixed his eyes on a group of starlings, pecking worms in a shady, moist spot a few yards away. He raised his chubby hand, waved excitedly in the direction of the birds and babbled, looking round at Tammy with a trusting, beaming smile.

"Well, little boy," said Tammy, stroking his soft, downy head. "I wonder where we'll end up? Where are we going in our lives? Are we just ships that pass in the night or will our paths ever cross again?"

***

They were going out to lunch at The Village Inn in West Runton. With Lewis none the worse for his excursion with a clueless childminder, Paul's father had made the suggestion. Claire was included in the invitation and Tammy's heart sank.

His mother shot Paul a look of maternal understanding and then put her foot down.

"No," she said, glaring at her husband. "How can I get to know Nick's new girlfriend with Claire around."

Paul had hardly said a word since Tammy came back to the house from her walk with Lewis (although he had squeezed her hand and mouthed a silent *'thank you'* to her) but even so, she needed him to be a bit more talkative.

"All right then," Keith capitulated, and with undisguised annoyance, added, "I'll just pop through to the annexe and tell her. Poor girl will feel dreadful at being left out of Nick's birthday

159

celebration."

Tammy had had enough of lies that week, and so she resolved to be honest about their relationship with Rosemary Pepper. "Paul and I are not ... well ... seeing each other, we're just friends."

"He's not Paul, he's Nick."

Rosemary's annoyance was quashed by an exaggerated sigh from Paul. "Look, Mum. I don't want to be known as Nick any more. I haven't been Nick since last June."

"We're just friends," Tammy reasserted, hoping that there was no hint of disappointment in her voice.

"For the moment. Things might change," Paul muttered as he smiled at Tammy and grabbed her hand. She squeezed it back in a mutual understanding.

Rosemary's eyes glistened. "I hope so ...um ... Paul ... I really hope so. I just want you to be happy. That's all I have ever wanted, but — well, you know what your father's like. He gets a bee in his bonnet. Even Lois doesn't come round much now, and she seems to be cooling things a bit with Claire, too. Everything has just fallen to bits ..."

"I know ... Mum, I know. Try not to worry. We'll sort things out."

While Paul and his mother made small talk, Tammy thought it was touching that she had decided to call him *Paul*. It bode well for the future. They were actually listening to him now.

Rosemary looked at her watch several times in the ten minutes or so that Keith was in the annexe with Claire.

"Where's Lois living now?" Paul said uncomfortably.

"Oh, not far. She's got a flat in town. She's on holiday at the moment. She's in Magaluf with some friends, but she'll be back on Monday. We hardly see her since she moved out, though ..."

Tammy was disappointed. She was looking forward to meeting Lois.

"I think Tammy and I will get going now. We'll go on ahead and find a table — shall we sit outside?" asked Paul, as Rosemary looked again at her watch.

"Oh, yes," agreed Rosemary. "If we sit in the garden we can take the dogs, have a nice pub lunch outside in the sunshine and then go

160

for a walk along the beach later."

***

Once Paul and Tammy were alone in the car he finally relaxed. "Phew," he said. "That was awful. What on earth do you think is going on with my dad and Claire? It's unnatural."

Tammy shook her head. "I don't know, but I think it might be something to do with your sister. Perhaps Claire is the daughter he would like to have, rather than the one he's got?"

Paul nodded. "I'd never looked at it quite like that, but yes, I think you could be right."

Tammy knew she needed to tread carefully. She felt as if she was picking her way through a field of landmines. It would only take one careless comment and Paul would blow up, turn the car around and zoom back to Lyverton, never to return.

"Thanks again for coming with me, Tammy. I couldn't do this without you."

"That's okay. Your mum is lovely, by the way."

"She is. She's just the best."

They were driving slowly down a narrow, single track road, and Tammy felt a childish rush of excitement when she realised she could see the sea. It was hazy and the horizon was fuzzy where the grey blue smudge disappeared into the sky.

"Dad still can't understand why I left," Paul said as they bumped along on the uneven surface. "And Mum's changed. She's really bitter, and it's not like her at all."

"I'm not surprised — poor Rosemary," Tammy sympathised. "I feel so sorry for her. Still, perhaps you coming back will help them all come to terms with what's happened."

The track opened out into a wider road and the bumpiness gave way to a smooth tarmac surface. Before long, they arrived in the pub car park. They made their way through a rose-covered archway, which opened out into a huge, walled garden with lots of picnic benches and tables nestling under parasols. They chose one at the edge of the garden that was well away from its neighbours, secluded and shaded. It was still early for lunch, and only a few of the outdoor tables were

161

occupied.

"No alcohol for me," Tammy said with a grimace as she remembered how drunk she had been on Tuesday night. "Not today."

"Okay. Coke?"

Tammy nodded. "Thanks."

When Paul returned with the drinks he didn't want to talk about his parents or Claire. He avoided the subject as he squinted against the sun.

"I think you should tell your dad you've met Marian. When you ring him tonight you should definitely tell him. And then, as soon as she gets back from visiting her aunt, you should tell her that you are her sister. You shouldn't delay it any longer."

Tammy trailed her finger down the condensation on the cold glass in front of her, deep in thought.

"I don't know what to do, Paul. Part of me feels it's all wrong. Perhaps it will never feel like the right time to tell Marian the truth."

"And do you know why you feel like that?"

"Why?" Tammy looked up at Paul, as he slid on a pair of sunglasses.

"Because it's not your job to tell her — it's your dad's."

***

Tammy awoke from a deep sleep. Exhausted after their trip to Norfolk, she had only meant to shut her eyes for a few minutes when they'd arrived back at the Red Lion just before six. At least tonight's telephone conversation with Alan would be easy. She could tell him all about her trip to the seaside.

She sat up on her bed and reached for her phone.

"Hello, love," Alan said in a cheerful voice.

"Hi Dad. How are you?"

"Fine. What have you been up to? Any progress?"

"I've been to Norfolk with Paul."

"Oh, that's nice. Well, it was a lovely day for it."

"We went to a place called West Runton on the coast for lunch and sat outside in the gardens of a lovely village pub. Then we walked along the beach with his dogs. I had an amazing day."

162

"That sounds great."

"It was. I really enjoyed it."

Tammy was telling the truth. Once Paul's father had relaxed, and after a prickly moment when Rosemary had announced that any mention of Claire was to be banned for the entire afternoon, and that if either Paul or his father mentioned her, she would chop off their ears, Tammy could see the broken relationship between Paul and his parents being rebuilt, brick by wonky, imperfect brick. Paul had held her hand tightly for the duration of the walk, and she had remained largely silent, enjoying listening to him telling his parents about his job, his new friends and colleagues and speaking so fondly of Cynthia — it was obvious the two of them had built up a special bond while he had been staying in Lyverton.

Alan was listening to Tammy, but she got the feeling he was impatient for her to finish telling him about her day out. She babbled on, keen to avoid picking up any threads of last night's conversation when they had talked about Marian's disastrous birthday party.

Tammy paused momentarily, giving Alan the chance to interrupt. It was like a missile exploding in the midst of their polite conversation.

"Tammy. You have to find Marian now, introduce yourself and tell her something important."

"What? It's not that easy ..."

Tammy frowned, remembering Paul's words when he had said he thought it was Alan's job to speak to Marian first.

"I want you to tell her that I have a bundle of unsent cards and letters from your mother waiting here for her. There must easily be a hundred of them, Tammy. There's over twenty years' worth — a whole boxful. I found them hidden in the bottom of the wardrobe after she died."

Tammy gritted her teeth. The unpalatable words had to be said. "I think *you* should approach her, Dad. Not me! It's just too hard. I can't just go up to her and say *'hi, by the way I am your sister'* can I? Anyway, she's gone to visit her auntie and won't be back here until Sunday. You should swallow your pride, come back to Lyverton at the weekend and just tell her the truth."

Alan wasn't listening.

163

"Marian should know she was always loved. She was never, ever, forgotten by Pippa. Not for one, single minute. And, Tammy, you *must* tell her that. You have to tell her how much Pippa loved her."

Tammy gulped with the hurt of it. Secrets ... and then more secrets. All of them were going on behind her back while she was growing up. She was twenty-four years-old before she knew she even had a sister, and yet her mother had been covertly buying cards, writing letters and yearning for another daughter living another life in another part of the country and had never told her. This was not her responsibility. She couldn't do it. She wouldn't do it.

"I can't tell her that, Dad!"

"You must."

"I can't! It's all too personal and patronising. It's like rubbing it in and saying I was there to be loved by Mum when she wasn't ..."

"Tamasyn!"

Tammy knew he was exasperated with her.

"The entire purpose of your visit to Lyverton is to find Marian, and perhaps find out where my parents went when they left the village ..."

"I know," Tammy interrupted, "but I'm having such a nice time now I'm here! It's a real holiday and I'm enjoying myself so much I don't want to spoil it."

Alan wasn't listening.

"... tell her I always cared about her, too, and I'm sorry we both hurt her so much. Tell her that in any other circumstances things could have been very different ..."

"No, Dad! I won't," Tammy yelled, interrupting him again. "Sorry. End of story."

"Tamasyn ..."

"If you want to say that to her, you'll have to do it yourself!"

"You know I can't do that," shouted Alan. "Don't yell at me Tammy, you know how it is. I can't ever go back to Lyverton — I just can't."

"Why?"

"You know why!"

"Dad, answer me this ... what's actually stopping you? And come to think of it, what was *ever* stopping both of you getting up off your

164

cowardly backsides, jumping in the car and coming to Lyverton to sort things out with Marian? You're absolutely pathetic, Dad! Nothing will bring Mum back, and if you don't face up to that, then you might as well be dead yourself!"

"Tammy. Listen to me. You know why I can't go back there. Tony Troutman will kill me if I go back — for sure."

"Dad — get real. No he won't. For goodness sake, Tony Troutman is an old man now. He's to be pitied, not feared." Tammy just managed to stop herself before repeating Paul's sentiments earlier that day when he'd said: *'is he a man, or a mouse?'*

Alan sighed in angry frustration on the end of the phone. Tammy set her jaw in a defiant pout. "I've got to go, Dad. I'm meeting Paul for a drink in the bar in a few minutes. Bye."

Tammy pressed the red button on her phone and cut Alan off, her face burning with fury. The parent-child roles were transposing. She was becoming the adult and he was turning into the child.

But had her father *always* been the child?

CHAPTER NINETEEN

On Saturday morning, once again it was noise that woke Tammy. Huge, loud plops and splatters rained monotonously on her French doors and in the distance she could hear an intermittent rumble of thunder. The weather matched her mood. She turned onto her stomach and buried her face.

Paul had gone.

Last night, after her phone call to her father, she had sauntered into his room. He had left his door ajar for her. On his bed was an open red sports bag into which he was hastily stuffing some clothes.

"I'm going back," he'd said, forcing himself to look up at her.

"Oh," she had replied inadequately. "When?"

"Now."

He'd stood up, walked over to her and had given her a hug and a peck on the cheek. It was an innocent enough moment but Tammy had straight away sensed a change in him and within just a few thumping heartbeats she had realised she was beginning to lose him.

"It's just for the weekend," he said.

Tammy had shrugged her shoulders and tried to act unconcerned, even though her body felt as if it was about to turn inside out. Her voice sounded strange and disconnected in her head.

"I'll see you on Monday then — that's if I'm still here."

"Okay. I just need to sort things out with Claire. I ... I ..."

"It's what you should do," she had said quickly, even though she had wanted to shout at him that he shouldn't go back so soon.

Paul had nodded, and she had noticed that his eye had begun to twitch furiously. "See you then ... you will still be here, won't you?" he said.

"Probably."

She sighed, biting her lip painfully. "I'll still be here."

"Bye then. I'll be back on Sunday night. I'll text you. We'll meet up for a drink, if you like."

"Okay. Bye."

She had stepped forwards and given him a peck on the cheek before turning around and fleeing back into her room.

Tammy lifted her pillow over her head to drown out the sound of the rain and hide from the truth. He obviously still loved Claire and despite his resolute insistence that he could never bring up another man's child, that was probably exactly what he would end up doing. He would be a fantastic father. Claire would welcome him back with open arms. Who wouldn't? He was young, successful, gorgeous and there was no one else like him in the whole world. Tammy squeezed her eyes shut. She was sure Paul and Claire would live a long and happy life, have two children of their own and in fifty years' time on their golden wedding anniversary Claire would say: *'I wonder what happened to that red-haired girl who came back to Norfolk with you. What was her name? Can you remember, Nick?'*

By then, Paul would be a crooked and stooped old man. He wouldn't even be Paul any more, because he'd have morphed back into being Nick long ago, his brief existence as Paul all but forgotten. His gorgeous eyes would be clouded with cataracts, his eyebrows white and bushy and his memory would be failing him. Old songs would be playing in the background — the same songs and tunes that had been playing on the radio in the car yesterday. The tunes would churn up ancient memories and he'd have a flicker of a happy recollection of a bright, sunny twenty-eighth birthday and a walk along the beach with a female companion, but he wouldn't be able to recall her name. He'd scratch his age-spot-splattered bald head and say: *'I don't know what happened to her and I can't remember her name, but if it wasn't for her we'd probably never have got back together.'* And then baby Lewis (distinguished and grey-haired himself by then) would say: *'didn't she take me for a walk in my buggy?'*

Tammy would be the forgotten one. Their friendship had been as brief as the flash of a shooting star in a vast, night sky. Nothing more. He wouldn't even remember her name. She had wanted to fling her arms around him, to tell him she loved him — and wanted to be forever by his side. Paul and Tammy. Tammy and Paul. Only they weren't Tammy and Paul, were they. They never had been and never

167

would be, because was going back to *her*.

Cuckoo Claire.

Tammy turned onto her side and tried to get back to sleep, but her blocked up nose, puffy eyes and the loud crashes of thunder outside were all preventing her from closing the curtains on her brief encounter with Paul, the horrible vision of him with Claire in the future, and the sickeningly happy life they would lead from today onwards. Despite the short time they had known each other, he was the only man she had ever loved and now he had gone.

***

"Thanks, but I'm not hungry," Tammy called out to Cynthia after she had tapped on her door.

"Och, Tammy, you must eat."

Cynthia's voice was concerned and motherly. There was a pause and a shuffle outside her door. Tammy knew Cynthia was thinking: wondering how she could coax her both out of her room and her dark mood.

"Look. Listen to me, hen. I spoke to him last night, just before he left. He has to come back here, Tammy. He'll have to go to work on Monday. I know it's hard for you, but it's for the best that he goes back home and gets things sorted out, one way or another. I've been telling him that for months."

Tammy's heart lifted, just a little. She hadn't thought about him having to go to work next week.

"Okay. I'll just get dressed and then I'll come down."

"I'm standing here in curlers and a pink dressing gown," Cynthia confessed from the other side of the door. "It doesn't really matter ... just hop across the landing to my flat. You don't have to go downstairs for breakfast, you can have some with me. You can get dressed later."

Tammy slid out of bed, shuffled across the room and opened the door.

Cynthia gave her a broad smile, raised a plump finger and brushed a lock of hair away from Tammy's puffy eyes, and she felt like a child again. She could smell Cynthia's soap and shampoo and it was warm and comforting. She still belonged. She still felt as if her future was in

168

Lyverton, only now it would be a life without Paul. She couldn't even think about going home to Yorkshire next weekend.

Tammy deliberately avoided looking in the mirror. She knew she must look a frightful mess because she'd not combed her hair. The spot on her chin had also now turned into a big scab because she had not been able to resist popping it. Still, she thought, it didn't really matter now. She couldn't care less if she sprouted a dozen more big, red spots on her chin. She stepped outside her room onto the landing wearing just her pyjamas. She couldn't be bothered to find her dressing gown. Come to think of it she didn't feel as if she could be bothered to do much at all, because the horrible sick feeling of despair in her stomach overwhelmed any enthusiasm for the day ahead. She flicked her door onto the latch so that she could get back in, and dragged her feet as she shuffled barefoot along the landing behind Cynthia.

Cynthia waved her in the direction of the white, squidgy, leather sofa in her opulently furnished flat and picked up a TV remote control from a huge smoked glass coffee table, on which sat an elaborate arrangement of fresh star lilies and pink and cream roses. The huge screen on the wall burst into life with the familiar tune of BBC news.

"Coffee? Toast?"

"I don't mind. Anything."

Tammy's eyes widened as she cast her eyes around Cynthia's amazing home.

Cynthia shouted from the kitchen. "I know it's hard for you, hen. I know how fond you are of him, but sometimes ... well ..." Cynthia's voice faded away as she struggled to find the right words to comfort her.

Tammy knew Paul would come back physically because he would have to, but after a weekend with Claire he would change back into Nick. The wedding would be rearranged and everyone would say what a wonderful man he was to forgive Claire and take on another man's child as his own.

Tammy's voice sounded weak inside her head when she spoke. She was half hoping Cynthia couldn't hear.

"I know I've not known him long, but I'm really fond of him."

"What did you say, hen?"

169

"I'm really fond of him."

"Och, I know. It's such a shame."

"We had such a lovely day yesterday with his parents, but he didn't get a chance to speak to Claire properly. I suppose that's why he's gone straight back."

Cynthia reappeared in the kitchen doorway, drying her hands on a tea towel. Tammy wondered how on earth she managed to look so glamorous all the time. Even with big curlers in her hair, a pink dressing gown and black and white zebra-striped slippers, she exuded a certain elegance, despite her size and lack of make-up.

"You've been crying, haven't you."

Tammy nodded. "A bit."

Cynthia padded over to the sofa and sat down next to her.

"Do you believe in love at first sight, Cynthia?"

"Come here," said Cynthia as she put her arm around Tammy. "Of course I do. Everyone knows it's true."

The just-showered smell of soap, shampoo and the comforting hug made Tammy feel grimy and stale. Her feelings for Paul, her newly-found sister, Alice's box and the story of poor Harry and Jessie were all whirling around in her head with grief for her mother, her father's desolation and the shocking revelation that he once had sex with her half-sister, which had now driven a huge rift between them. And now, on top of it all, she had lost Paul. She should never have agreed to go to Norfolk with him — in an effort to do the right thing and offer her support she had only succeeded in leading him along the rocky pathway back to Claire. It had been like kicking herself in the teeth. She needed a shower. That might make her feel better.

She sniffed and rubbed her red-rimmed eyes. "You would have been a fantastic mother, Cynthia."

"Och, no … I wasn't cut out to be a mother."

"Just take it from me." Tammy smiled at her through bleary eyes. "I'm an expert on mothers. I had a good one."

Cynthia was fast becoming Tammy's best friend, and she hated lying to her. "Can I talk to you after we've had our breakfast, if you have time? Only I have a confession to make to you — several, actually."

170

"Of course I have time, lassie. I've got all day once Daniel comes in." Cynthia clasped her hands either side of her face in horror. "Oh. Daniel — that's just reminded me."

She stood up, waddled over to her sideboard and extracted a slip of paper from a drawer.

"I almost forgot. Daniel gave me this for you last night. It's a note from Sophie Staverley."

"Sophie? I wonder what she wants?"

Tammy unfolded the unsealed note.

'Hi Tammy. Tomorrow afternoon (Saturday) I am going into Fawsden with my mum to visit my great-grandad, Philip Staverley. He lives in a residential care home. He was very excited when he heard that you were researching local history and thinks he might be able to help. He's really old but my grandma says he's got all his buttons on. My mum says you would be most welcome to come with us and she will pick you up from the pub about 2.00 pm. Please can you ring me on this number and let me know if you are coming.
Love Sophie'

"I don't know what to do." Tammy said as she passed Cynthia the note so that she could read it for herself.

"Why? It's a golden opportunity to find out more about Alice Thompson and her runaway parents. Who knows what you might discover. There might even be a logical explanation for your similarity to Alice's mother — you might find out some deep, dark secrets about your ancestors."

Tammy remembered the conversation with Paul in the Little Chef on the way to Norfolk, when he had told her that Cynthia was convinced she was in Lyverton because of Alice's death, and was really a long-lost relative looking to claim her inheritance.

"Cynthia, one of the things I have to tell you is that I really didn't know Alice Thompson. Honestly, I ended up at her funeral on Tuesday by a complete accident. I've never clapped eyes on her and I'd never even heard of her until someone behind me in church said her name. I'm in Lyverton for another reason — something else entirely."

Tammy was surprised Cynthia didn't look shocked, just

171

disappointed.

"On Tuesday morning, in Marjorie's tea shop, I told a little white lie to an old man about why I was visiting Lyverton and now everyone thinks I'm a famous writer. Well — I'm not. I've never written a creative word in my entire life, apart from when I was at school."

Cynthia patted Tammy's hand. "Let me just go and get us that coffee and toast and then you can tell me all about it."

***

Back in her room in the shower, Tammy was relieved she had told Cynthia about the lie. She had sympathised, and said that young Daniel had a lot to answer for, spreading it about like that. She had also told Cynthia that she was really searching for her family, but she had stopped short, though, at telling her that Marian Troutman was the sister she had come to Lyverton to find. Tammy already felt guilty that Paul knew this before Marian. It would be very wrong of her to tell Cynthia before she'd had a chance to speak to Marian herself when she got back from visiting her aunt tomorrow.

Cynthia really was a Mother Earth. Tammy couldn't help likening her to the mythical Gaia, dispensing words of maternal wisdom to all the lost, young people who drifted through her bed and breakfast rooms, setting them back on the road to their future when they'd fallen by the wayside or had a big problem to resolve.

Tammy sighed as stinging, hot water cascaded down her back. After the glorious weather of the previous week, it was a horrible day and the receding thunderstorm had cast a grey, damp blanket over Lyverton. She felt very down, but had decided to take Cynthia's advice to go to Fawsden to visit Philip Staverley so that she could take her mind off Paul. She had to admit to herself: she felt a tingle of excitement about meeting the baby cradled in Reverend Staverley's arms in the photograph. She was desperate to find out more about Harry and Jessie Thompson's story and find out why they had run away together. Then, provided the rain cleared, she could take a brisk walk to Quarry Cottages just outside the village, and satisfy herself that the cowslip-picking youngsters lived there with their family in the chaotic midst of an expensive renovation project, and weren't really

172

ghosts.

There was really no harm in letting people think she was a writer because lots of people wrote as a hobby. People took up a new hobby all the time. *'Are you telling me that if I decide to take up photography as a hobby, I can't call myself a photographer?'* Cynthia had said convincingly to Tammy not half an hour ago. *'Writers write. Photographers take photographs. Dressmakers make dresses. Simple isn't it? I can't see you've done anything wrong, Tammy.'*

Tammy shut her eyes as the hot water cascaded down her back. It felt good; healing and relaxing. Her white lie was suddenly not a lie any more. She *was* a writer. As of that moment, Tamasyn Hargreaves was a writer because she was going to write about Harry, Jessie and Alice Thompson and the Staverley family.

CHAPTER TWENTY

Day Six
Saturday, 30th May: 9.00 am

Paul stroked the ears of one of the Labradors with his big hand, deep in thought. His father had gone to work, and Claire had left him alone to talk to his mother over breakfast. It felt good to be home; his mother was wearing her usual old, blue patterned dressing gown, drinking tea out of a familiar mug, a towel twisted around her head. In some ways it felt he had never been away.

Rosemary Pepper looked down at her slippered feet. "I'm sorry about the mess in the house. I just haven't been able to muster up enthusiasm for anything since you left us, Lois moved out and our family fell apart."

"Mum, what exactly is going on between Dad and Claire?"

Rosemary didn't look up. "It's not what you think it is. It's because Lois won't talk to him any more. It's driving me insane — I've nearly left him, you know, several times. He's completely irrational."

Paul shook his head. He couldn't begin to imagine how his poor sister felt — being replaced by her best friend who was now living with her parents, practically as a daughter.

"It was just a temporary arrangement. It was only meant to be for a few weeks until she could find herself a flat with the baby, but now she seems to have rooted herself here with Lewis." Rosemary gave a long, weary sigh. "I don't know where it will all end up. The worry of it all will just about finish me off."

"It's okay, Mum. I'll sort it all out. It's my problem," Paul said, feeling acutely responsible for all the trouble in his family. "I'll talk to him."

"Don't do this just for me," Rosemary said, shaking her head, "or because of your father. "If you get back with Claire, you have to be sure it's what *you* really want ..."

"I'm not. It *is* what I want."

"Do you still love her?"

Paul pursed his lips, shook his head slightly and sighed. "I don't know — I might be able to again, one day, I suppose. I did love her, until ..." His voice faded. He still couldn't fully face the hurt. It was much too painful. Hell, he couldn't even bring himself to talk about it. There was a child to consider now, though, and baby Lewis radiated everything that he had once loved about Claire. The unwanted, faceless mass of human cells he had despised last year had materialised into something beautiful and innocent. Yesterday, the first time he had gazed at Lewis, perched on Claire's hip, blowing raspberries, he had felt a painful tug at his tangled heartstrings. Lewis needed a father and it was something not to be messed with — a human responsibility, even though it wasn't his to bear. Lewis deserved a father. None of this was his fault. Paul had never been so certain about anything before in his life, but he wasn't so certain about loving Claire again.

"We've done a terrible thing to you. We drove you away. I don't know how to begin to say sorry for what we've done," Rosemary said with a slight wobble in her voice.

Paul smiled at her. "I'm back now. That's all that matters, Mum."

Rosemary looked down at her feet as silent tears began to trickle down her face.

"It was the emotional detachment — you could have gone to the other side of the world, but you'd still have been my son. I felt as if you were dead. Your father didn't understand. He just got angrier and angrier and blamed you, when it wasn't even remotely your fault. And then when Lois left under a cloud, too, and you wouldn't answer your phone to me, and your father said you had told him not to e-mail you again — well — my life just wasn't worth living."

Paul sighed. "Don't cry, Mum. Please? I'm sorry. I shouldn't have cut myself off like that."

Rosemary dried her eyes on a tea towel. "I really don't think you should do it," she said, sniffing, searching for a tissue in the pocket of her dressing gown. "I don't think you and Claire should get back together."

"Why?"

"Because you don't love her."

Paul didn't protest.

"Tammy's a smashing girl. She loves you. Do you realise that?"

"You can't know that, Mum," Paul exclaimed. "You only met her for a few hours yesterday."

"A mother knows these things. It's maternal instinct. I tell you, Nick, Tammy loves you. She's the one for you. End of story," interrupted Rosemary with a confident shrug of her shoulders as if underlining the conviction in her voice.

Paul shook his head. He couldn't believe that his mother could possibly know what, or who, was right for him, especially after just a few hours of knowing Tammy.

"Do *you* love Tammy?"

Paul bit his lip and screwed his eyes shut. He swallowed a lump in his throat, but it only made a huge gulp escape from his chest. Then another that was embarrassingly like a sob ... and another ... then another. Then he felt his mother's arms pulling him towards her and the sweet smell of maternal love smashed through his solid dam of carefully-constructed repressed emotion as if it was mere tissue paper, and ten months' worth of tears gushed out of his eyes and nose. He tried to pull away, embarrassed. What was he? Grown men didn't sob and wail like babies. He wasn't a man. Men didn't cry — even when the woman they had once loved more than anything in the world jumped into bed with another man without even a backward glance and got themselves pregnant. Real men didn't cry. It was just too embarrassing for words. He had to get away.

Rosemary tightened her hold on him and he resisted, trying to push her away. "Let me go, Mum. I'm all right."

"No, I won't. No one's here. No one knows," whispered Rosemary in a voice that washed a soothing balm around his troubled mind like a cleansing antiseptic.

Paul relaxed in her arms. She would never tell. The embarrassing secret of crying into his mother's breasts was safe. Only the two of them would know. He suddenly loved his mother very much, and the knowledge of it made him cry even more because he knew, now, just how much he had hurt her.

"You must ring her, you know, Rosemary whispered through her own tears."

"I can't. I've let her down ..."

"Please, for me?"

176

"I've only known her since last Monday."

"So? What has that got to do with anything?" Rosemary released her hold on Paul, picked up his mobile phone from the kitchen table and dragged him by his arm to the lounge door. "I'll make sure you're not disturbed, or overheard."

Paul nodded as he took a deep breath and regained his composure. His mother was right. Tammy deserved more than a polite, curt goodbye. He should never have taken her out on a date when he was still in limbo about Claire.

***

As Tammy was about to turn off the shower, dry off and dress, her mobile phone rang. She jumped out of the cubicle, quickly wrapped a white bath sheet around her and twisted another towel around her head. She almost tripped as she hurried across the room to grab her mobile phone from her bedside cabinet. The display read *Paul*. Her heart began to beat so fast she could feel it in her throat.

"Hello."

"Hello Tammy. Are you okay?" Paul's voice sounded odd and croaky.

"Yes ... I've just got out of the shower. I'm naked and dripping wet." Tammy mentally kicked herself at the stupid reply. Paul would think she was trying to come onto him. She tried to make her voice business-like by pretending she was at work, talking to a client.

"What can I do for you?"

"I just thought I'd ring — see how you are — have a chat?"

"Oh, I'm fine. I'm going out later with Sophie Staverley to meet her great-grandad. He's the youngest of the Reverend Staverley's children in the photograph I found in Alice's box." Tammy forced a nervous laugh. "Well, actually he's now ninety-six and living in a residential care home in Fawsden."

Paul laughed softly and the sound of his breath down the phone made her tummy tingle.

"I just wanted to say how grateful I am to you for coming back to Norfolk with me yesterday, Tammy."

"So you said last night."

177

"Yes, but I really, really appreciate it. You're an amazing girl ..."

Tammy interrupted. She didn't want him to say that some other bloke would be very lucky to have her. She didn't want to hear it. "A screwed up, clumsy red-head, more like," she muttered and then mentally kicked herself for sounding so flippant.

Questions were dancing around inside Tammy's head like heated popcorn. It was no good, she'd just have to be direct and ask him about his intentions with Claire.

"What are you going to do about Claire?"

"I don't know."

The honesty vibrated in Tammy's ear, but she had to ask the question.

"Are you going to forgive her?"

"Possibly ... no ... probably. Oh, I don't know. I really can't say until I can speak to her without being angry. All I do know is that I have to find out if I can, and then take things from there."

"What about Lewis?"

"It's not his fault, Tammy. He didn't ask to be born. He deserves a good life. He deserves to have a proper dad."

Tammy closed her eyes and suddenly understood. He would be a fantastic father. He didn't love Claire any more, but she could never compete with Paul's vicarious paternal instinct.

"I wish you the best of luck, Paul, I really do." Hopelessness swirled around in Tammy's stomach and she felt sick again. Paul was at a crossroads in his life. Tomorrow he would be *Nick* again; Claire's Nick.

"Shall I see you tomorrow? I'll be back in the afternoon," Paul asked her.

Tammy nodded, forgetting to reply; forgetting she was actually on the phone.

"Shall I? You won't be gone or anything, will you?"

"No," she replied in a small voice. "I'll still be here."

"Good."

Silence.

Neither of them hung up. She could hear him breathing. Her office-voice and clipped manner was fading fast and was being replaced by a gut-wrenching, physical ache because she knew she had lost him forever, even though he had never been hers to lose.

Paul spoke first.

"Tammy. I can't stay estranged from my family and you have helped me realise that. I should never have gone to Lyverton. I should have stayed here and faced up to things. I'm so worried about my mum and I miss my sister. But it's not just that; God only knows what's going on inside my dad's head, and if getting my family back has to include Claire then really there'll be no choice. How on earth can I let little Lewis down? He's the real victim in all this ..."

Paul hesitated, his voice lowering to almost a whisper. Again Tammy nodded and forgot to speak.

"... but I want you to know that I could very, very easily love you Tammy. It would be the easiest thing in the world. In different circumstances, in a different life."

His voice wavered and finally cracked. Emotion ebbed and flowed across the airwaves between them.

"But the world is not always easy, is it Tammy? You of all people know that. Life is rarely perfect. We can't always have what we want. We have to take a chance on what's on offer and turn it into something we can live with ..."

Paul's voice broke up completely and he spluttered down the phone, trying to regain his composure. Tammy heard him take a breath to say something else, but then his breath transformed into a gulp.

"Take care, Paul," she whispered, cutting him short because she just couldn't bear to hear any more of his words. "I'll be thinking about you. I'll still be here when you get back. We'll talk ..."

"Don't hang up. Please, Tammy, don't hang up just yet." Paul's voice was urgent and desperate.

"Okay."

Tammy closed her eyes. "Paul?"

"Yes?"

"Thank you for being so honest with me. You've been such a gentleman, too."

"That's all right: it didn't enter my head to take advantage of you when you're so vulnerable. It wouldn't have been right. Well, that's not to say I wouldn't have wanted to, but I couldn't do that to you, Tammy. You're too nice."

Tears were rolling down Tammy's face. She sniffed and heard Paul sniff too. The phone crackled slightly.

"Are you crying?" she asked softly.

There was a moment of hesitation. "No, I'm fine … really …"

Tammy knew he was, despite his denial.

He sniffed again, and then she heard the same catch of breath in his voice as she had noticed yesterday morning when they had hugged each other, wearing just their nightclothes. A naked sob escaped from his throat into Tammy's ear and the helplessness in her heart was roughly elbowed out by a different, primal eroticism. Hearing a big, strong man like Paul cry because he loved her was the most arousing sound she had ever heard in her life.

"I'm sorry, Tammy."

"I know," she said, breathless at the exquisite, new feelings flowing through her veins.

"Can … can I just say this once, so that I can have the memory of it for the rest of my life?"

"What?" Tammy brushed the back of her hand over her wet cheeks. She knew what he was going to say.

"Then tomorrow, and afterwards, neither us will mention it. We won't have to because we'll have already said the words and they won't be necessary any more."

"What?"

"I love you Tammy: with all my heart. I really do."

"I love you too," she whispered.

Then suddenly he was gone and the dialling tone buzzed in her ear like static electricity in an off-line television channel. The picture had gone. There was nothing left. He would marry Claire, for sure. His mind was made up and the lamb slaughtered when he had pressed the red button on his phone and cut her off. It was all about Lewis, but Tammy couldn't resent an innocent child for taking Paul away from her. In an odd, maternal kind of way she kind of understood why he had put the little boy first. He was a man — a real, rock-solid man

180

with a huge heart. He was tough and dependable, strong enough to put his own feelings aside for the sake of a child who had no father. But she had been wrong about one thing. He'd never forget her name when Claire said to him: *'I wonder what happened to that red-haired girl who came back with you that day, what was her name? Can you remember, Nick?'*

'Tammy', he'd say. *'Tamasyn Hargreaves.'* Then his eyes would light up behind his cataracts and, just for a second or two, he would be Paul again and his eyes would swim with a lifetime of tears and unsaid words of love for a woman he had only known for four days.

CHAPTER TWENTY-ONE

2.00 pm

Sophie's mother looked so young, she could easily be mistaken for her sister.

"Hi, Tammy," she said, tucking her long, blonde hair behind her ear. "Pleased to meet you."

"Thanks for this," Tammy said, shaking out her umbrella before she clambered into the back of the Range Rover, inhaling the distinctive, steamy smell of wet clothing. "It's very good of you to take me to see Mr Staverley."

"That's all right. He's really looking forward to it."

Once Tammy had settled on the back seat, she decided to ask Sophie about her family.

"So, it must be your grandad who is Philip Staverley's son, Sophie?"

"That's right. If I have a baby soon and Great Gramps is still around, we'll be five generations and get our photo in the local newspaper."

Tammy bit her lip, trying not to laugh. Sophie's mother's face had contorted into a grimace. The highly tuned strings of a mother-daughter relationship when the child is no longer a child but not quite a fully-fledged adult were evidently being eloquently played.

"Not while you're still at university," she mumbled.

The windscreen wipers hummed rhythmically as Sophie turned her head to look at Tammy, rolled her eyes and then shot her mother a self-satisfied smirk.

"Thank you for Alice's box. It was most thoughtful of you," Tammy said to Sophie's mother.

"That's all right. It would only have ended up being chucked out. Alice wasn't a relative. She just lived with Great Aunt Lucy."

"I know, I've been hearing about the *ladies*. They were legendary, weren't they?" Tammy said.

"They were. I don't know too much about the Staverley family history, though," Sophie's mother admitted. "Your best bet, besides

Gramps, will be Noah — he's my father-in-law — he might remember something useful and I'm sure Philip's niece, Wendy, will be willing to help, too."

"Whose daughter is Wendy?" Tammy asked. "I found a family photograph in Alice's box, and on the back are the names of all the children."

"I'm not sure, but Gramps will know. Wendy's getting on a bit herself now; must be in her late seventies, I should think."

Before long the Range Rover pulled into a small car park. It was still raining and so they hurried to the main entrance so as not to get too wet.

Philip was sitting in the lounge waiting for them. He levered himself up with trembling, gnarled hands clutching the wooden arms of his chair. He stood up slowly, as straight as his advanced years would allow. He had obviously made an effort to look smart for his important visitor. He straightened his tie and checked the brass buttons on his navy blue blazer before extending a hand towards Tammy in greeting.

"Pleased to meet you, Miss Hargreaves, I'm sure."

Tammy shook his bony, veined hand and recognised him from Tuesday's funeral. He was the old man she had watched struggling to get out of the silver Range Rover. If she had felt a strange, arcane moment of connectivity when she first saw him from her vantage point in the corner of the churchyard — when she had imagined him as an athlete in his younger days — the feeling wasn't evident now. She didn't know Philip Staverley and never had done.

Tammy's voice was bright and friendly. "Hello, Mr Staverley. I saw you on Tuesday. I was at Alice Thompson's funeral, too."

"Oh yes," he replied, in the rasping, croaky voice of old age. "We knew each other all our lives, you know. Practically grew up together, we did. Shall we sit at the table, and Sophie will make us some tea?" He gestured towards the corner of the room.

They walked slowly over to a small dining table. Sophie and her mother disappeared, promising to return not only with tea, but cakes as well.

Once Philip had settled himself into his chair, Tammy opened her bag. "I've got some photographs I thought you might like to see."

She placed the family portraits of the Staverley and Thompson families on the table in front of Philip, and then pointed to the tiny baby in the Reverend Staverley's arms. "According to the list of names on the back, that's you!"

"Oh yes. I remember this photograph. I used to have one myself. I think my son, Noah, has it now. We had some copies made, as I recall."

He picked up the photograph and held it in his trembling hand, pointing out various family members. His voice was pensive and wistful as he remembered each of his brothers and sisters in turn, telling Tammy a little about each of them.

"That's Polly." He pointed to the girl who was standing next to the Reverend Staverley. "She was my big sister and Wendy's mother. You know my niece Wendy, don't you? She was at the funeral on Tuesday."

"No. I've never met Wendy, but I would love to speak to her."

He gave Tammy the photograph. "I'm the only one left now," he said with watery, opaque eyes. "They've all gone except me."

"Were you the youngest? I mean, I know you were then, when the photograph was taken, but were there any more Staverley children after you?"

Philip shook his head and chuckled. "No. I was always the baby of the family, and now look at me." He pulled himself up in his seat and squared his shoulders. "I'm ninety-six next week and still going strong. I put it down to keeping myself fit. Do you know, Miss Hargreaves, I was at the Olympics in 1932 in Los Angeles? I was in the rowing team. We didn't get a medal, but I was very proud to serve my country."

Tammy gulped. There it was again — the strange sixth sense she seemed to possess in Lyverton. She had imagined Philip as an athlete the first time she had seen him at Alice's funeral. She tried to put it to the back of her mind and concentrate on the task in hand.

"Do you remember Harry and Jessie Thompson?"

"Oh yes, of course I remember them." He picked up the Thompson family photograph, stroking the surface of the image with a trembling hand.

"Aunt Jessie was a lovely, gentle woman. Oh, it was so, so sad

184

when she passed away. I remember she used to come up to the vicarage every single day and help my mother look after us younger children. Then, when I was twelve, she died suddenly of the scarlet fever and her daughter, Alice, came to live with us permanently because she was an orphan. She was twelve too. We were the same age."

Tammy was captivated and felt a sudden, intense pang of regret that she had never met Alice Thompson. She imagined her, sitting at that very table when she visited her lifelong friend in the care home, probably just a few weeks ago, sharing tea and cake on a Saturday afternoon. She would watch television and reminisce with Philip about the good old days and put the world to rights. For no particular reason, the traffic sign that warned of elderly people crossing the road sprang to mind, where the hunched over lady was being helped along by an equally frail man using a walking stick. Tammy imagined Philip and Alice as being like that: childhood friends and companions into old age.

Philip shook his head, lifted his glasses and wiped a tear away from his eye with a white handkerchief.

"I don't know what I am going to do without her." He cleared his throat and his eyes lit up, the moment of sadness gone as he looked over Tammy's shoulder. "Here comes my little Sophie, bless her. She's the light of my life."

"Fondant fancies?" Sophie said as she rattled a plate of cakes on the table. "Great-Gramps's favourites."

"Oh yes. My favourites. You're a good girl."

They began to talk about the photographs, and Philip patiently pointed out all the family members again for the benefit of Sophie's mother, who hadn't seen them. Sophie, however, *had* seen the photographs before. Through a mouthful of her third cake she spluttered that she remembered looking at them at her grandparents' house when she was a little girl.

"Granny and Grandad have these. They've got loads of old photographs. When I was little I used to look at them with Dad."

"What's your dad's name?" Tammy asked.

Philip replied for Sophie, proud to tell Tammy that her father, his grandson, was called Andrew after his brother who had been killed in action in the Second World War. "Do you know, Miss Hargreaves, we are four generations. There's me, Noah, Andrew and Sophie. Not bad going, eh?"

"No," Tammy agreed, feeling a pang of sadness for Philip's brother, Andrew, the little comedian who had been mentioned in Jessie's letter to Harry.

"They said she died of a broken heart," said Philip, changing the subject quite abruptly.

"Who died of a broken heart?" Sophie asked.

"Aunt Jessie — Alice's mother. Her heart gave out when she contracted scarlet fever. She had never really got over losing Uncle Harry. He was a proper hero who died in the Great War. He was awarded a posthumous medal for his outstanding bravery. I do vaguely remember him, but Alice and I were only five years-old when the news came through that he'd given his life for King and country."

"Is that the medal you gave to me last week?" Sophie asked her mother, who nodded with a smile.

Philip leaned forwards and squinted at Tammy.

"You look like Jessie, you know. Are you sure you're not a relative of hers?"

Tammy shook her head. "No, I come from Yorkshire. It's probably my hair isn't it? It looks just like Jessie's in the photograph, all fluffy and curly around my face."

Sophie picked up the Thompson family portrait and shared it with her mother. They leaned into each other. Two identical pairs of eyes stared at the image and then simultaneously looked up at Tammy, who flushed with embarrassment.

Sophie wrinkled her nose. "You do look just like Jessie, but I think you're right, Tammy, it's the hair. You're much taller than her. Look, she's really tiny at the side of Harry. Oh my God, he was amazingly good-looking, wasn't he? Really hot."

"Was Harry related to the Staverleys, then?" said Tammy, smiling at Sophie's comment.

"Oh no, definitely not," replied Philip. "You obviously don't know the story about Alice's parents do you, Miss Hargreaves … about how

186

Harry saved one of the twin's lives?"

Tammy looked at the back of the photograph. "Lucy-Joy and Emily-Rose."

Philip had a captive audience. He nodded in confirmation.

"The story was that Harry and Jessie had run away from home and turned up at my father's vicarage on the day the twins were born. One of them was a bonny lass of a proper weight and size. The other one was a runty little thing. She was sickly and weak, and not expected to survive. Oh, no, it was impossible the baby could live, the midwife apparently said."

Philip paused for a moment to extract his handkerchief from his pocket. He lifted his glasses and wiped his leaky eyes and then his mouth, which had started to dribble.

"Did you know that your Auntie Wendy was named after her?" he asked Sophie.

"Who?"

"My mother's sister: the midwife. My Aunt Gwendoline."

"They did that a lot in the olden days, didn't they?" Sophie mused. "Named babies after family members, I mean."

"It was a mark of respect. If you ask me, that's what's missing in today's society — respect for elders and good old family values," Philip said with a shake of his head. "Families used to look after each other and stay together in one place."

"What happened then?" Tammy was keen to hear the story about the twins.

"Aunt Gwendoline had, apparently, written off the tiny twin at birth because she was so small and wasn't breathing. She weighed not much more than two pounds or so. Can you imagine that — in those days when there was no technology to keep tiny babies alive?"

"What do you mean by *turned up*," said Tammy. "You said that Harry and Jessie *turned up*."

"The story was that as my father was pacing the floor, distraught about the tiny twin that was not expected to live, Harry and Jessie just turned up at the door, completely out of the blue. It was on midsummer's day in 1910. They had run away together, but Jessie was ill and they desperately needed help."

187

"What was the matter with Jessie?" Sophie asked.

"I don't know. I don't think I ever knew. I wasn't even born then. I didn't come along until three years later. I'm telling you this story second-hand."

"So how did Harry save the tiny twin's life?" Sophie's mother asked.

"My father always said it was a miracle and God had answered his prayers that day. Harry Thompson was a gamekeeper's apprentice and knew how to make an incubator box — you know, for hatching eggs? Things were grim. My baby sister was dying because she was so tiny."

Tammy recalled the diagram that had been folded around the gold locket in Alice's box.

"Did Harry make an incubator for the baby?"

Philip bit his top lip and rolled his eyes upwards, trying to remember. "I remember my father showing me a homemade contraption in the barn when I was a little boy. I think Harry must have designed it himself. My father said Harry had saved some motherless puppies in the same contraption. You remember such things when you are a boy. In those days, us boys learned about making and repairing things and little girls learned about how to look after a house and cook meals for a family."

Philip stopped talking and looked at Tammy through narrowed eyes. "Aren't you going to write any of this down?"

"Oh, yes."

Tammy rummaged in her bag. "I'm so fascinated by the story I nearly forgot."

"Where was I?"

"The puppies," Sophie reminded him. "You were going to tell us about the puppies."

"No I wasn't! I don't know anything about the puppies. I was going to tell you about Harry Thompson, wasn't I?"

Sophie's mother didn't believe the story. Tammy could tell by the way she arched her eyebrows and shook her head, ever so slightly. "I find it hard to believe that a fourteen year-old boy hand-reared a *baby*?" she said.

"Not on his own, silly. He just made the contraption to keep her

188

warm," retorted Philip.

Sophie's mother shrugged. She was not convinced. "Which twin was saved by Harry's incubator? Was is Lucy or was it Emily?"

"I don't know. Like I said, I wasn't even born. I can't for the life of me remember which one it was."

"Did Emily-Rose ever have any children?" Tammy asked.

"Oh no, the twins were both spinsters, as was Alice. The three of them were all very clever. They were much cleverer than us boys. Emily went to university and qualified as a doctor. She was also very devout — a really religious woman. She eventually became a missionary, working for years in Africa and then later went on to India."

Philip shifted his weight in his chair and grimaced at the pain of his arthritic hips.

"Lucy was the flamboyant, feisty one, always singing and dancing — oh my word, Miss Hargreaves, you should have heard her play the piano. She was so gifted. Heavenly it was, hearing her play. And sing — just like a songbird. Beautiful, her voice was."

"Where did Emily live?" Tammy asked.

"She lived with Alice and Lucy, of course, when she was at home. The three of them lived together in the House on the Hill."

***

It was after five o'clock when Sophie's mother dropped Tammy off at the Red Lion. The rain had stopped and the sun was trying to break through, and so Tammy decided to go out for a walk to see if she could find the Corner House in St Andrew's Lane. She was intrigued to put a setting to the scene of Marian's disastrous eighteenth birthday party and to see where her mother had lived in her other life.

Tammy ran her hand over the lichen-covered stone wall bordering the churchyard and the age and roughness under her hand reminded her of the strange, eerie feeling of urgency she had felt on Tuesday, when she had paused to soak up the picture postcard scene of the cottages and houses just before Alice Thompson's funeral. Her eyes fell on the mound of the newly dug grave covered in funeral flowers. She felt instant guilt. On Tuesday, in her haste to get away from Alice's funeral service, she hadn't lingered to join mourners at the graveside to pay her respects to the woman whose life story was packaged up in a cardboard box back in her room at the Red Lion. Although Tammy had never known Alice, now she was researching her family history it seemed bad-mannered to pass by her grave without stopping for a few moments.

Tammy squatted down onto her heels at the foot of the grave to read some of the cards on the flowers.

'Age is just a number, with much love from your best friend, Ruth, and all the family xxx.'

She imagined Alice befriending a younger woman and the special times they shared, reaching out in friendship across the generation gap.

There were numerous cards referring to *Aunt Alice*. She may have had no family of her own, but if they referred to her as an aunt when she was no relation to them, she must have been loved by so many people. Tammy shook her head and smiled at another card:

'I never knew my mother, but you have been like a mother to me. Love from Peggy x.'

As Tammy read the cards she resolved to buy flowers in Alice's memory before she went home to Yorkshire. After all, they were connected in some small way. Tammy suddenly felt a huge sense of loss. She wished she could have known this lovely old lady. If she'd been like a mother to someone who wasn't her daughter, she could easily have been like a grandmother to Tammy and now it was all too late. If she had come to Lyverton just a few months ago, she might have had the chance to get to know her. A sudden thought struck her: was *she* destined to live out her life like Alice's? Would she be all alone, too, with no siblings (because Marian wouldn't want to know her). Would she grow old with no relatives, because one day, her father would die and she would be an orphan, just like poor Alice? After her death, would a total stranger stand at her grave and mourn her empty life, too?

"She wasn't lonely, you know."

A male voice drifted on the cool breeze. Tammy lifted her head and turned around to see who had spoken to her.

"Although for the last few years she lived alone, she was never lonely. She had so many friends, you see."

The vicar was smiling at her from the side entrance to the church, a few yards away from Alice's grave. "She was very much loved."

"Oh, hello," said Tammy. "I was just looking at the flowers; aren't they beautiful."

Once again, someone had voiced her thoughts. Tammy felt slightly unnerved, and the company of the vicar was welcome.

"I'm sorry about Tuesday," the vicar said, banging the church door and locking it with a huge black key. He walked over to join Tammy at Alice's graveside. "I didn't realise you weren't part of the funeral party when I directed you into the church. I was trying to get everyone in and seated because we were already late, and I had an appointment afterwards."

Tammy laughed. "That's all right. If I hadn't attended her funeral, I wouldn't have ended up with a box of her belongings as research material for my book."

"How interesting!"

Tammy hadn't just lied to a vicar. She really was going to write the story. She *was* a writer (well, she would be once she had started to write). She told the vicar how she was going to tell the life story of the Staverley and Thompson families as background for the local history of the village, and how it would be a good base on which to build a picture of life in Lyverton over the last hundred years.

"What a fantastic idea! May I help you? I'd be most honoured. I haven't lived here for very long, just a couple of years actually. But I can be of assistance with church records and suchlike, can't I?"

"Oh … thank you. Would you happen to know if Emily and Lucy Staverley are buried in this churchyard?"

"I don't know. Shall we look?"

Tammy and the vicar walked up and down the rows of gravestones. The birds were tweeting and twittering loudly, relieved at the sun breaking through in a brightening sky after a day of rainy greyness and gloom; the sun felt warm on her back and her new-found imagination was working overtime as she invented life stories in her head for the people for whom all that remained of their lives was a carved name on a gravestone. They paused at a grave tucked away in dark, damp corner of the churchyard. It had a plain, unembellished headstone.

'Here lie the remains of two unknown souls
21.9.1978 '

"What's the story behind this grave?" Tammy asked.

"Ah — I was curious about that one, too. Apparently, two bodies were found after a fire in some barns between Lyverton and Fawsden. A man called Tony Troutman was the prime suspect initially, so I was told, but police apparently let him go. Then forensic tests were carried out and the police said the bones had been there for a long time, concealed in the barns when the fire started. The identity of the victims was never proved beyond doubt because they were so badly burned, although there was lots of speculation they were the bodies of the fifth Earl of Fawsden and his daughter-in-law, who apparently disappeared off the face of the earth in the 1960s."

Tammy nodded in agreement. "I heard about the fire on Tuesday. An elderly man in the tea shop mentioned it and said Tony Troutman was involved in some way."

"Well, you know what it's like in villages. One exciting incident provides gossip for at least fifty years," the vicar said with a chuckle.

They moved along to the next row. Tammy's eyes fell on a grave right on the edge of the churchyard, beneath a tree.

'Jessica Mary Thompson
Devoted wife of the late Harold Leigh Thompson
Loving mother of Alice Mary
21.7.1896 to 11.3.1925 '

"Oh look. It's Jessie, Alice's mother," said Tammy as a shiver started in the region of her left buttock and then travelled down her leg and up into her shoulders. It ended as a buzzing noise in her ears. She had died on 11th March — Tammy's birthday — another coincidence.

Tammy managed to speak. "Harold died in the first world war. He's on the war memorial in the High Street."

"My, you have been busy." The vicar tutted and shook his head. "Poor Alice, losing her father in the war and then her mum."

"She was only twelve, apparently. The Reverend Staverley and his wife took her in, according to Philip, the youngest of the Staverley children. He's still alive. I visited him this afternoon and he told me the story. He told me about their childhood and how Alice's father, Harry, saved the life of one of his baby twin sisters by making a contraption based on a design for an incubator for pheasant eggs."

"How very interesting, fascinating, in fact. Do you have time for afternoon tea, Miss Hargreaves? We can sit and chat in my garden, enjoy the sunshine and be more comfortable than standing in a graveyard."

"That would be nice," said Tammy. "It's very kind of you. I'd like that."

They walked out of the churchyard, across the crunching gravel driveway and the vicar pointed to his house across the road. Tammy's heart pounded with what she could only have described as excitement. Her eyes were misty with emotional tears of joy. What on earth was happening to her?

They walked around the house to the back door, but Tammy's eyes were drawn to the huge oak front door, the heavy iron black-painted knocker and the front doorstep, worn concave by the feet of time. The vicar's kitchen was modern, but in her mind's eye she saw it as it might have looked a hundred years ago, when Harry and Jessie turned up at the vicarage on midsummer's day in 1910. She imagined the tiny, newborn baby girl, clinging onto life; fighting to survive alongside her stronger, robust sister. She tried to picture a teenaged Harry, desperate to do anything he could to help the vicar's tiny baby survive.

The compulsion Tammy felt to go inside the house was almost unbearable, but the vicar's wife greeted them at the back door, thrilled that her husband had invited the writer for late afternoon tea.

"Let's sit in the conservatory," she said. "Do you mind if I join you? I can't miss the opportunity to chat to a real, live writer."

The garden of the vicarage was glorious; a tapestry of early summer colour that flooded into the open patio doors. Tammy peered inside the house again. In her imagination she was opening doors, running excitedly from room to room. This house had a strong, beating heart and blood flowing through its veins. Tammy could hear it and she could feel it. She turned her head to soak up the gems of colour in the vicar's garden, and her ears rang with the sounds of early summer. She breathed in the heady smells of wet honeysuckle, hawthorn and rhododendron and the clean smell of grass, washed into a vibrant green by the earlier thunderstorm.

Tammy's eyes fell on two gnarled, old apple trees at the bottom of the garden, and she imagined the Staverleys and Thompsons, having their family photographs taken, laughing and happy in the summer sun. She could almost hear the cry of three-week old Philip, cradled in his proud father's arms, and Polly, the eldest daughter, ordering everyone into their positions for the photograph while her cheeky younger brothers made silly faces for the photographer.

Tammy took a deep breath. This was not déjà vu. This was much more than that. This was her destiny; her fate; her home. This was where she had always belonged.

CHAPTER TWENTY-TWO

Day Seven
Sunday, 31st May: 8.30 am

Tammy woke up feeling apprehensive for the second day in a row.

Last night she'd had another awful argument with her father on the phone. She really didn't know what was happening to her: she had only been in Lyverton for a week and already she was turning into a different person. She never, ever argued with her father. In fact, she couldn't even remember the last time she disagreed with anyone. She was a quiet, submissive woman who hated arguments and would go to any lengths to avoid them. But in Lyverton she was strong, confident and spoke her mind. The village had done that to her — it was as if Lyverton was somehow the loud-hailer through which she could make herself heard. It was the direct antithesis of her dull, unimaginative home in Yorkshire, which, in contrast, gagged and stifled her feelings, rendering her sterile.

After Paul's sad phone call that morning, Tammy had needed to feel Alan's paternal love down the phone as a sort of macabre consolation prize, telling her how much he loved and missed her. But the sympathy she craved hadn't been forthcoming.

"Tammy," he had said firmly when she had told him Paul had gone back to his fiancée, "you only knew him for less than a week. You'd only been out on one date. You can hardly say he was the love of your life, can you? Pull yourself together, girl, for goodness sake. Don't be so silly."

Alan had then changed the subject and asked for news about Marian. He had been like a ravenous wolf, saliva dripping from its chin: ready to pounce on her every word and devour it up, before spitting out the bones. "Have you made contact with Marian yet," he had growled at her down the phone. "Time's running out. Have you forgotten what you're there for?"

Tammy had felt an intense annoyance. He was trying to control her life again, even though he was over two hundred miles away.

"I told you last night," Tammy had retorted. "Don't you ever listen? She's gone to visit her auntie and won't be back until tomorrow. Anyway, I don't really want to talk about Marian. I've just been dumped and could do with some sympathy."

Her father had not thought much of her little excursion to visit Philip Staverley, either.

"You don't even know them, Tammy! The Staverleys are nothing to do with us. You should be concentrating on trying to find your grandparents, and yet you've not made one single enquiry about them yet, have you? Someone in the village will know where they moved to. You're just faffing around with someone else's family tree when you should be concentrating on your own!"

"No! I haven't made any enquiries about them," Tammy had yelled down the phone. "And why the hell should I, they didn't ever try to find me did they?"

Alan had bellowed a reply at her, and Tammy had been taken aback; her father hardly ever shouted at her. "They didn't know you existed! How could they have tried to find you when they didn't even know you'd been born."

"And whose fault is that?" Tammy had screamed back. "What are you, Dad, a man or a mouse? It wasn't up to me to tell them they had a grandchild, was it? And while we are on the subject, it is not for me to tell Marian she has a sister.'

Tammy had burst into angry tears then; defeated and hurt.

Alan had been upset, too. He was sorry for shouting. He'd lost his temper because he was going out of his mind with the worry of it all. After they had both calmed down, he had told Tammy that he thought the mysterious Auntie Joan in Market Harborough might be Tony Troutman's sister. She definitely wasn't a relative of Pippa's. They had reached an uneasy truce before they had ended their phone call, but they both knew things were changing between them. It was as if the gently undulating, smooth snows of winter were melting away to leave hard, sharp rocky peaks in their relationship.

***

"Helloo," said Cynthia in her broad Scottish accent.

Tammy stared at Cynthia and immediately felt dowdy and plain in her business-like jacket and trousers. She had dabbed on some make up and was trying to look happy, despite the row with her father and the constant sick, heavy feeling in her stomach that was the loss of Paul.

Cynthia looked stunning, her golden hair regally piled on top of her head, contrasting perfectly with her black and purple outfit. Cynthia always looked immaculate and her smiles were infectious. They made Tammy want to smile and be happy. Cynthia was meant to be larger than life; she tried to imagine her slim, and couldn't.

"Do I look all right for church, Cynthia? I haven't really got anything else to wear other than this jacket and trousers – apart from my new dress, of course," Tammy said, feeling like a slice of plain Madeira cake at the side of a cream-topped luxurious black forest gateaux.

"You look lovely — but why don't you wear your new dress? It'll brighten you up, and would be just perfect with that jacket."

Tammy had only agreed to go to church with Cynthia to take her mind off Paul and the argument with her father, but now she was glad she was going somewhere — anywhere, even church — instead of sitting moping inside her room. She decided to slip back to change into her dress.

"That colour does suit you. I was right wasn't I?" Cynthia said when Tammy returned. Tammy smiled and admitted that yes, the richness of the green colour had lifted her mood.

"Well. How did it go with old Philip Staverley then? Did you get any more information?" Cynthia asked as they set off.

"It was fascinating. Did you know that Alice's father, Harry, saved the life of one of the Staverley twins by making her an incubator and caring for her night and day?"

"Really?" Cynthia was puffing slightly with unaccustomed exertion. She was having some difficulty keeping up with Tammy, who slowed down a little.

"It's a great story," Cynthia said with enthusiasm after Tammy had told her about the twins. "It will be fascinating for people to read. Which twin was the tiny one, Emily-Rose or Lucy-Joy?"

"No one seems to know, and it is *so* frustrating! I'm going to try and find out. Philip has a niece, Wendy. He says she might know. Apparently, Emily lived with Alice and Lucy, too, although she used to spend lots of time abroad."

"Oh, yes. I remember her, now. She used to only come home every couple of years. She was a delicate, gentle, bird-like woman. Always on the go, as I recall. I remember seeing her at village cricket matches, church fetes and fund-raising events a few times just after I came to Lyverton. She was always busy selling Alice and Lucy's home-made jam and preserves to raise money for the church."

"She was a missionary," Tammy said.

"Yes, she was. I remember reading an article about her. She was quite famous in her younger years. Apparently, in India, young girls were sometimes dedicated to the gods and forced into prostitution to earn money for the priests. She founded a sanctuary for those young girls and saved hundreds of them. She used to dye her skin and wear traditional Indian clothes when she was out there so that the poor wee girls would trust her."

"When did Emily die? Can you remember?"

"It was a good few years ago, now. They had a special service of thanksgiving for her in the Parish Church in Fawsden. Oh, Tammy, it was so moving. At the service, the congregation was told a story about how she walked for over fifty miles in the most dreadful heat to save one little girl — only eleven years-old — that she had heard had been forced into prostitution. There wasn't much money and she only had enough for one journey, so she walked for three days on hot, dusty roads so that she could save the child and bring her back to the sanctuary in comfort and safety."

Cynthia changed the subject, looking sideways at Tammy with admiration. "Your mum must have been very proud of you, hen."

"She was lovely, Cynthia. She was a proper mum. Not that my dad isn't a proper dad, though. He's fantastic too, and I know I'm so lucky to have him. It's just that I wish he'd let go a bit, and remember I'm grown up now."

"And mebbe grow up a bit himself?"

"Yes."

198

Tammy thought about it. Cynthia was right: Even though he was almost fifty years-old, her dad most definitely needed to begin living his own life and make his own decisions. It was almost too painful to face, but away from him, Tammy realised that Pippa had been the one to set the direction of their lives. When they'd married, she'd become his wife and mother all rolled into one.

Cynthia nodded. "I feel for your father, I really do. I know just what it feels like to lose your soul-mate. It's a massive, uphill struggle to get over it and carve a life for yourself, alone. Don't be too hard on him, Tammy. You're all he's got, and he sounds like such a lovely man."

"I know, but Cynthia, I really don't want to go back to Yorkshire. I want to find another job, maybe in Fawsden, and live here in the village."

"No! That's not the answer to your problems. Your dad will be devastated if you move such a long way away from him. Don't do anything hasty, hen. What about the recession? There's no guarantee you'll easily find another job. You just need to have a good old heart-to-heart and it'll clear the air and make you both feel better about things."

***

Cynthia and Tammy were already sitting down when Marian arrived breathlessly at the church, having just returned from visiting her aunt.

"Do you mind if I sit with you?" she asked, without waiting for an answer before she sat down.

Marian had been disappointed when Davey had gate-crashed her afternoon with Tammy. She had been thinking a lot about her mother since their conversation, and the silly episode with the spiritualist had somehow been put into perspective. She was ashamed to admit it, but she had probably been taken in and duped into believing her mother was dead. That morning, she had woken early to the sound of the birds singing in her Auntie Joan's garden in the Leicestershire countryside. She had made up her mind there and then. She was going to try hard to find her mother.

"Hello, Marian," said Cynthia, leaning forwards in greeting. "You

199

look very smart today."

"I just felt like dressing up. It's a lovely morning, I've had a nice, relaxing couple of days with my aunt and I feel really happy today; glad to be alive, that sort of thing. I can't for the life of me think why, because I'm back at school tomorrow!"

Cynthia groaned in sympathy. "I don't envy you," she said. "The little blighters can be so rude nowadays, can't they? I bet you have your work cut out."

Marian laughed. "They call me *Old Trout* you know. A couple of my pupils are second generation and their parents called me *Old Trout*, too."

Tammy smiled at her. "I'm so sorry I had to shoot off on Thursday. I had a phone call that I needed to attend to."

"That's all right. It was my fault for going off at a tangent and telling you silly stories about dodgy spiritualists and my disastrous birthday party when I should have been concentrating on the parish council's records."

The organ started to play the first few bars of *All Things Bright and Beautiful*. They stood up and Marian began to sing with enthusiasm. It was, after all, a happy, singing kind of day, because today, she was going to begin her search for her mother.

***

At first, Tammy was embarrassed about singing, but Cynthia and Marian on either side of her soon put paid to that. They were loud, hearty and unselfconscious and so Tammy decided to shake off her awkwardness and join in. She was soon enjoying herself. Since Pippa had died, Tammy had forgotten how to sing.

The hymn ended and the vicar launched into his sermon. Tammy looked at Cynthia, who dabbed a solitary tear from the corner of her eye and smiled back at her. She glanced to her other side and Marian was staring intently at the vicar delivering his sermon, which was about the importance of family life and being part of a community. She was pensive and thoughtful, taking it all in. She might have been dark-haired and Tammy's senior by over twenty years, but, as they sat together in church, it was obvious they did have some physical similarities. Tammy felt guilty. She really ought to stop prevaricating by researching a complete stranger's family tree. She absolutely *must* reveal the truth to Marian today.

After a few parish announcements and some prayers, the congregation rose to sing the next hymn.

'Immortal, invisible, God only wise ...' sang the congregation, slightly out of time with the organist.

Tammy didn't know the words to the hymn, and so was reading from the hymn book as she sang, but all the strange things that had happened to her since she had been in Lyverton were streaming through her head with the significance of the words. Was this her fate or destiny or was it something completely different? Had something brought her to Lyverton to resolve the mysteries of the past? Tammy felt as if she held a huge, white ball of knowledge in her arms that was too big for her to hold without dropping it. There was something more to this world: much, much more. Whether it was God or not, she didn't know, but at that moment Tammy knew that this undiscovered thing was real and true. She was in Lyverton for a reason and she knew without any doubt that it was something to do with Alice Thompson and absolutely nothing to do with finding her sister.

'We blossom and flourish as leaves on the tree,
And wither and perish - but naught changeth Thee.'

Harry and Jessie blossomed like leaves on a tree, thought Tammy. They withered and perished, but nothing had changed since they had first arrived in Lyverton nearly a hundred years ago. The blackbirds were still singing, the cuckoos calling, the hawthorn still blossomed and wafted its pungent smell on the spring breeze, just the same as ever, and the sun was shining down on the village, exactly as it had on midsummer's day in 1910 when they turned up at the vicarage asking for help because Jessie was ill.

As the hymn ended, Tammy knew something wonderful was cradling her in its palm, bringing her home to Lyverton. She was not a lost child of her parents' secrets, after all. She had a place in the world, and it was right here in this village. Her eyes filled inexplicably with tears of happiness and the words on the page became blurry. As the congregation sat down again she glanced sideways at her sister's hands. They were hands that had shaped and formed from a disparate bundle of cells fifty years ago in the same womb that had created her. She breathed in a delicate smell of a distant perfume and felt the breeze from the open door on her face. Her mother's soul was infused within them. Harry, Jessie and Alice seemed strangely a part of her, too. They might not have been related to Tammy by blood, but nevertheless they were claiming her for their own now she had come to Lyverton.

***

As they walked out of the church, Tammy slipped her arm through Cynthia's. Cynthia grabbed Marian's arm on the other side and the three of them crunched, arm in arm, along the gravel pathway. "That was grand, wasn't it," Cynthia enthused.

"Do you go to church in Yorkshire, Tammy?" Marian asked.

"No," replied Tammy.

"I go every week," Marian stated, "almost without fail …"

Tammy looked at Marian, but didn't say anything. She suddenly felt like a heathen; hugely inferior to her devout, elder sister. She was obviously a paragon of virtue. A do-gooder; a pillar of the Lyverton community, and she would find it hard to live up to her.

"… but it's only so I can get away from my dad on a Sunday morning," Marian added with a conspiratorial giggle.

The bubble burst as Marian's halo slipped, and they both leaned forwards and grinned at each other around Cynthia.

Marian put her finger to her lips and nodded towards the vicar, his black cassock and white surplice billowing around his legs as he enthusiastically shook hands and greeted members of his congregation.

"Sssshh … don't say anything in front of the vicar," she continued. "I hate Sunday mornings when I can't get out of the house. It's just cooking and cleaning and nursing my dad's inevitable hangover for him. I'd much rather sing my heart out in church instead of creeping around the house with him in a foul mood."

Tammy laughed out loud. Marian was like a brilliant butterfly and a dull, brown moth, all at the same time. She could light up the world in an instant with a carefree smile and then, just moments later, cast gloom and depression on those who surrounded her. She was both fascinating and boring; and she was like a mother and sister rolled into one.

"Hello, Miss Hargreaves ... Cynthia ... Marian. How nice to see you all."

"Loved the sermon," Cynthia said.

The vicar was clutching his prayer book. He opened it up, extracted a sheet of paper and handed it to Tammy with a smile.

"Here you are. After our chat yesterday afternoon I went through the church records. These are the dates of birth, weddings, baptisms and deaths of all the Staverleys and Thompsons for you. I thought it would save you some time and I could give it to Cynthia this morning to pass on to you. It's lovely to see you here. I hope you enjoyed the service."

"That's really kind of you, Reverend. Thank you very much."

Tammy took the sheet of paper. The vicar had taken the time on the busiest day of his week to help her research. It was incredibly good of him. The vicar turned to shake someone else's hand. Cynthia seized the moment and made a suggestion.

"I've got a great idea, you two. Why don't we all get together in my flat this afternoon and have another look through the photographs in Alice's box. Now we have the church records it should be quite easy to put names to faces."

"I'm up for it. How about you, Marian?" Tammy agreed.

"Oh, definitely. I'd like that. It's nice to get out of the house on a Sunday afternoon, instead of listening to old black and white war films blaring out on the TV."

After saying goodbye to Marian and agreeing to meet in Cynthia's flat at four o'clock, Cynthia and Tammy walked idly back to the Red Lion. Tammy was quiet, toying with the idea of confiding in Cynthia about Marian being her half-sister and telling her the story of how her father and mother ran away together over thirty years ago. She decided against it: she absolutely *must* speak to Marian first — and it had to be today. She had been in the village for a week now, and each time she had been about to speak to her, something had happened to thwart her good intentions. Had Davey not interrupted on Thursday, she would have done it then. It had been an ideal time at the school, when they had been alone. Then Marian had gone to visit her auntie and the opportunity had not arisen again until today. Perhaps she could ask her into her room after they had gone through the old photographs? Yes, she thought to herself. That was what she would do.

"What time did Paul say he'd be back?" Tammy asked Cynthia.

"Late afternoon."

"Oh right."

Tammy gave a loud sigh. The horrible, helpless, sick feeling flooded back into her stomach. He was with Claire and there was nothing she could do about it, other than try to take her mind off the hopeless situation.

"Paul's mum and dad were really nice to me on Friday," Tammy said, causing the knife in her tummy to give a masochistic twist. "I felt sorry for his mother though. I could tell she's been badly affected by him leaving home and Claire taking his place, she was so angry and resentful."

"Poor woman, he should never have cut himself off from them, and I've been telling him that for months. The betrayal was in the relationship between Paul and Claire, not Claire and Paul's parents. It sounds to me like Paul's father got his priorities all wrong, and that's what has caused all the trouble, more than the break-up and cancelled wedding."

Tammy knew Cynthia was right. She was so wise in such things. "Do you know what the first thing was that Rosemary said to me?"

"What? Tell me."

"She said: *'Thank you for bringing him back to me'*, and then she gave me a hug. I didn't know the woman from Adam, and she gave me a hug."

"She'll be so angry with Claire," said Cynthia. "But you can be angry with people and not stop loving them or caring about them. And there is the poor little baby to consider, too. Even so, I think Paul's parents made a bad error of judgement letting her move in with them. They seem to have forgotten that Paul is their son in their eagerness to do the best for Claire's innocent bairn. They've taken on a responsibility that wasn't theirs to shoulder."

They turned the corner and Tammy subconsciously glanced into the pub car park at the space where Paul's black Honda Civic was usually parked. It was there.

"Paul's back already!" she almost shouted, unable to disguise the joy in her voice.

CHAPTER TWENTY-THREE

12.00 noon

"You'll absolutely love it here, Claire, just as much as I do. It's a great place to bring up a child."

Tammy let her hand fall to her side, stunned. She had been about to knock on the door when she heard Claire's muffled voice from inside his room. This was worse than ever. Cuckoo Claire was in her territory now. Paul had obviously brought her back to Lyverton, and she was claiming that tiny piece of him that was Tammy's. Couldn't she even spare a teeny, tiny bit of him?

Tammy let herself into her room as quietly as she could and tiptoed over to her French windows. She unlocked the doors and slipped outside onto her roof terrace, shutting Paul and Claire out of earshot and out of her life.

After a few minutes of silent despair, Tammy took the vicar's list out of her bag and studied it. She absolutely must get Paul out of her head. His life was nothing to do with her now.

Emily-Rose and Lucy-Joy Staverley were baptised on the 21st June 1910, the day of their birth. This was to be expected, though, as one of the twins was not expected to live.

Harold Leigh Thompson and Jessica Mary Smith were married at the church on 24th August 1912. Harry was seventeen and Jessie just sixteen. Alice was born the following year, the same year as Philip. Tammy felt happy they were married so young. If they'd waited until they were older, they wouldn't have had so much time together before Harry died in the war. She wondered about their story. Why had they both run away from their families? Perhaps that was what Lyverton did to people — spat them out, ate them back up and then regurgitated them later, over and over again through time.

Tammy was hungry, but there was no way she was going to risk bumping into Paul and Claire on the landing or on the stairs. She crept back inside and tensed at the dull sound of the television in Paul's room through the dividing wall. She found herself a can of drink, a few sweets and a family sized bag of Kettle Chips (to which she was hopelessly addicted). That would have to do. It wasn't much of a Sunday lunch, but at least she wouldn't starve. She also had plenty of tea, milk and a few tiny, complimentary packets of biscuits. Tammy placed her stash of food on the patio table on the roof terrace and then went back inside to lug out Alice's box.

There. She was set for the afternoon. She still had on her best clothes, but she decided against getting changed. She would make too much noise, clattering around in the wardrobe, and Paul would know she was in her room. She didn't want that. She wanted to keep well out of his way. Tammy tiptoed back into her room to fetch her mobile phone: she couldn't have it ringing out and alerting anyone to the fact she was there.

Tammy had intended to read the rest of Harry's letters to Jessie to divert her mind away from the difficult task she faced later on when she confronted Marian, but instead she found herself spending a pleasurable afternoon with the old magazines. She was soon absorbed in the chaotic life of Margaret Regent, the Hesitant Housewife. She laughed, almost out loud, when she wrote that she'd removed the labels and lids of cheap shop-bought jam and replaced them with hand-written labels and neat gingham tops cut with pinking shears, so that she could enter the jam-making competition at the Women's Institute. She'd been absolutely certain that it was the worst jam she had ever tasted and wouldn't stand a chance of winning. Instead, she spent the precious time she should have been jam-making eating chocolate in the autumn sunshine and sitting in a deckchair reading her favourite book. But her jam had won the competition, and she'd felt terrible and so she'd guiltily baked four cakes for the cake stall at the village hall the following week, spending twice as much time baking as she'd saved by buying the jam.

Tammy giggled uncontrollably at the antics of Sally and Susie, the Hesitant Housewife's twin daughters, and her ongoing battles with her mother-in-law, which were thought out and planned like wartime operations.

Tammy chuckled at the corny short stories and clipped, curt replies to hilariously twee women's problems in *Clara's Confidential*. She imagined Pippa reading the magazines as a young housewife and couldn't equate the 1960s housewife to the mother she knew.

There were thirty-eight magazines in the box. Tammy was puzzled. Why had Alice kept them? She piled them onto the patio table and flicked through them one by one, making notes of the weekly articles and the names of the fiction writers. She ended up with six common denominators:

The Hesitant Housewife
Clara's Confidential Page
The Recipe
The Knitting Pattern
The Travel Article
The Mothers' Good Manners Guide

Tammy wondered if Alice could have been a part-time magazine columnist, but then discounted this. She was a full-time children's nurse and would have been unlikely to have the time to write regularly. In the end she shrugged to herself. It might just be a pile of old magazines. They might have just been shoved in the box and then the photographs and letters piled on top of them. Still, they had entertained Tammy and taken her mind right off Paul. She looked at her watch. It was a quarter to three. She had just over an hour before she met Marian and Cynthia.

Tammy decided to make herself a cup of tea and set up some spreadsheets on her new computer, so that they could catalogue the old photographs and form a basic database of the Staverleys and Thompsons and their dates of birth, marriage and deaths.

She opened the French doors carefully with a soft click and listened for a few moments. The room next door was silent, the television had been switched off and her heart sank at the thought of what might be going on behind Paul's closed door. She really must get over him, she couldn't creep around like a stalker for the rest of her time in Lyverton. She filled the kettle and plugged it in as quietly as she could. While it was coming to the boil, she connected the computer to the mains to charge up the battery and spread out the various instruction leaflets on her bed.

***

"Can I help you with that?"

Paul had been listening out all afternoon for Tammy. He had not been able to shake yesterday morning's intimate telephone conversation with her out of his head. It was as if it had left an itch in his heart that couldn't be scratched until he spoke to her face-to-face. As soon as he had heard the sound of her door opening, he'd leapt up from his bed, where Claire was dozing and he was quietly reading a construction magazine.

Tammy was backing out of her room holding Alice's box, balancing her new computer on top of the contents. She held it steady with her chin.

"Umm ... thanks," she mumbled. "But I've managed to set it up by myself. I noticed you were back. I'm just taking Alice's box along to Cynthia's flat. We're going to go through the old photos and letters."

Paul lifted the box from her arms and breathed in the light, fruity smell that he hadn't realised until that moment, was Tammy. He wondered what perfume she wore, or which shower gel or shampoo she used. He needed to be able to remember the fragrance. Their eyes met briefly. She was wearing the same dress she had worn on their date, and his stomach flipped and lurched with jealousy. He couldn't bear to think that some other bloke might, one day, lift that dress over her head and run his fingertips over her long, slender, naked body.

He looked away as their hands brushed. She plucked the computer from the top of the box and tucked it under her arm.

"Thanks. Did you get things sorted?"

"Yes. Kind of." He couldn't look at her. He couldn't look anywhere but at a brown envelope balanced on top of Alice's box.

"Hello, Tammy."

Paul looked up. Claire was standing in his doorway. He noticed Tammy's eyes brush lightly over her, lingering on Claire's bare feet and then dissolving into something that Paul thought might be despair at the sight of Claire's tousled and tangled dark hair. He felt awful, absolutely dreadful. He'd hurt Tammy so much.

"Hi," Tammy said, too brightly. "Did you have a nice day yesterday, Claire? It was dreadful weather here, thunderstorms, lightning, hail, the lot. What was it like in Norfolk?"

"Much the same."

"How's that little boy of yours. He's such a sweetie."

"He's fine. He's with Keith and Rosemary; they are giving me a bit of a break. I'm here for the week with Nick."

Paul cringed. He would never, ever get used to being called Nick again.

**

Tammy's heart almost disappeared into her flip-flops. She could visualise the second week of her holiday rolling out before her eyes. Paul would have to go to work. Claire would declare herself her buddy for the entire week and she would be lumbered with her, gushing about how wonderful her Nick was. Her Nick. Tammy's Paul. They would be off to Fawsden on a macabre shopping trip, browsing bridalwear shops, and then Claire would drag her round hundreds of boring estate agents, looking at huge four-bedroom properties with a double garage and enough room to build a conservatory. She would constantly talk about her Nick, how much in love they were and what a wonderful father he would be to Lewis. She would lean forwards over lunch and whisper confidentially that they wanted a baby as soon as possible after their wedding — a little brother or sister for Lewis — to cement their relationship. Tammy would even have to listen to the gory details of the one-night stand and how she was drunk and couldn't remember anything about it. She would have to hear over and over again how sorry Claire was for how much she had hurt him and how marvellous her Nick was to forgive her.

"Does Cynthia know Claire's here?" Tammy said, rather ungraciously, without looking at Claire.

"Not yet."

"Oh. Do you want me to tell her for you?"

"No. I'll pop along to the flat later, if that's okay with you."

Tammy shook her head as if unconcerned. "Feel free," she said. "Marian's coming round, too."

"Have you — you know — told her yet?"

Tammy answered quickly. She didn't want Claire knowing her business.

"No, not yet. She's been away since Thursday night visiting her auntie. She didn't get back until this morning. I'm going to do it later on in my room. About six, I thought."

"Oh, right. If you need some moral support, just give me a knock."

Tammy grimaced, looking up at Paul under her eyelashes, trying to stop herself looking into his eyes.

"Are you okay?"

She shrugged and looked down, summoning up every bit of bravado she could muster. She jerked up her head to look at Paul with a beaming smile. "Of course I am — why wouldn't I be? I'm having a fantastic holiday."

Her words formed themselves into a fog in the air between them. Out of the corner of her eye Tammy could see Claire hovering in the background. She was tight-lipped and silent. Tammy knew she wouldn't make eye contact and neither would she. Claire smoothed her tousled hair flat with her hand and then straightened her t-shirt, pulling it down over her hips. Without looking directly at her, Tammy detected just a tiny shimmer in Claire's eyes before she disappeared back into Paul's room.

"I'll pop in to see Cynthia in a bit." Paul's voice was flat, dull and resigned. "Tell her I'll be there about five."

"Okay. See you then."

They walked the few steps to Cynthia's front door. Tammy tapped it gently.

"Come in, Tammy. It's open."

Tammy opened the door and lifted Alice's box from Paul's arms. She watched him return to his room, his shoulders hunched over with the weight of another man's responsibility. She knew Paul and Claire still had a long way to go, but in a strange, masochistic kind of way she actually wanted them to make it. One mistake should not be enough to swipe aside a ten year, happy relationship. A quick five minute, alcohol-fuelled fumble should not be enough to ruin lives. And four-and-a-bit days couldn't possibly be long enough to fall in love with someone. Not properly. Her four-and-a-bit days did not equate to the ten years of love that Paul and Claire had shared. The equation just did not equate.

CHAPTER TWENTY-FOUR

4.00 pm

Cynthia was obviously a big fan of Elton John, because Tammy had heard it playing in her flat before. The lyrics of *Daniel* drifted out onto the landing and she remembered her mother once telling her that the song was about a Vietnam veteran who lost his sight. Her mother had liked Elton John, too.

Marian was already there, and she jumped up to help Tammy with the box and her computer. All three women were still wearing their smart church clothes.

Tammy's mind wandered into the future again. If she decided to dig up her roots in Yorkshire and transplant them in Lyverton, Cynthia would proudly take her and Marian under her wing, and they would all be great friends. Paul and Claire would settle in the village and their children would call her *Auntie Cynthia*. She would stop feeling the pangs of longing for Paul and would eventually be able to chat to him outside the supermarket without feeling like her insides were going to fall out. He would sit in his car with the driver's window open, with three children arguing and fighting in the back, and they would have a cordial, polite, mutually respectful chat about local council planning committees and sewers while Claire popped into the supermarket for milk, bread and a bottle of wine … and quite possibly a jar of chocolate spread and a can of squirty cream, having planned an early night.

Tammy gave herself a mental slap on the wrist. She really must stop thinking about Paul and Claire. It was none of her business now.

"You're quiet," Marian said with a concerned, furrowed brow as she shut the door. "Are you okay, Tammy?"

"I'm fine. Just a bit tired."

"She's not fine," said Cynthia. "What she needs is girl-time, with absolutely no men allowed."

"Paul?" said Marian.

Tammy rolled her eyes and then nodded. "He's just got back with

212

his fiancée," she replied, stressing the word *fiancée*.

Marian threw Tammy a cheesy grin. She really was quite old, even though she was her sister. The years between them crumbled away into a deep generation-wide gorge.

"I have to agree with your taste in men, Tammy. Paul is undiluted, raw manliness," Marian said with a lascivious glint in her dark eyes.

In a split second Marian closed the age gap with an infectious chuckle. She was a woman in her twenties again. She was Marian the chameleon; genetically modified to change age from nearly-a-pensioner to twenty-something in less than half a second.

"Now then," said Cynthia. She waggled her pudgy finger at Tammy and her bracelets jingled on her wrist. "Keep your head on, lassie. Keep your head on and just play it cool."

"Yes, but *she's* here, Cynthia. She's only gone and come back with him!" Tammy whined.

"I didn't even know Paul had a girlfriend, let alone a *fiancée*." Marian said, looking peeved on Tammy's behalf. "What's her name?"

"It's Claire. Cuckoo Claire. They split up, but they're back together again."

Cynthia laughed at Tammy's alliterative nickname for Claire. "She's here in Lyverton?"

Tammy tossed her head sideways in answer. "Along the corridor. In his room."

Cynthia tutted. "Well, hen. There's plenty more fish in the sea you know. There's plenty more apples on the tree, too, just ripe for the picking, and they don't all end up stewed and mushed-up in an apple tart."

Tammy smirked. Cynthia had never publicly passed judgement on Claire before, but her comment had come within a whisker of contrite condemnation of her infidelity.

***

"Alice Thompson told me once about how her mother ran away from home when she was only thirteen," said Marian as she picked up and studied the family photograph of Harry, Jessie and Alice.

"Philip Staverley told me the same thing yesterday. I wonder why

213

she ran away?" said Tammy. "He said that Harry and Jessie turned up at the vicarage on the same day his twin sisters were born — midsummer's day in 1910. I wonder if that was on the actual day they ran away, or if they had been on the run for a while? I wonder what they ran away from. And why go to the vicarage?"

"For sanctuary — for help," Cynthia speculated. "It makes sense if Jessie was ill."

Tammy pulled out the Staverley family photograph from the box and pointed out the twins to Marian. "Look — there's Lucy-Joy and her sister, Emily-Rose. It was taken in 1913 on their third birthday."

"My mother used to be an auxiliary nurse on the children's ward at Fawsden General Hospital and Alice Thompson was a senior nurse on the same ward," Marian explained. "They worked together for years. Alice was practically a grandmother to me. She told me all about her parents, Harry and Jessie. She said that although she was an only child, she was always out and about in the village, getting up to mischief with the Staverley twins. I used to be fascinated with her stories of village life in the olden days.

Tammy took a deep breath in amazement at the newly discovered connection between her mother and Alice Thompson. So she *hadn't* been a complete stranger at Alice's funeral, after all. Her mother had known her well in her other life. She hesitated. Was this the right time to tell Marian? Should she make an excuse to Cynthia and ask Marian to pop along to her room for a few minutes? She exhaled. This was it. The time was right. Exactly right.

Marian continued. "Lucy's sister, Polly, was Jessie's best friend. Polly once told Alice that Jessie had grown up at Fawsden Hall, where her parents worked, but ran away when she was thirteen because she was terrified of one of the Earl's sons. He was always threatening to slit her throat in her bed while she was asleep and then, one day, she woke up in the early hours of the morning to find him blind drunk, standing on her bed, straddled over her, waving a curved ceremonial sword over her head. She couldn't scream or cry out, because he threatened to kill her if she did. She managed to scramble out of bed and escape. It was later that day she and Harry decided to run away together. Polly once told Alice that she thought her mother might have been sexually abused by the Earl's son."

"Cynthia," said Tammy, desperate to cut into the conversation and carve an opportunity to disappear along to her room with Marian. "Do you mind if ..."

"Poor Jessie!" exclaimed Cynthia, interrupting Tammy. "That's absolutely shocking. She must have been terrified, but why did he do it? He must have been a wicked man to do that to a child."

"Everyone thought she was lying about how frightened she was of the Earl's son," Marian went on. "He used to be really nice to her in front of other people. He was colourful, flamboyant and liked the ladies, but he used to make suggestive comments and then threaten her if she told anyone. Alice always said her father was the only one who understood how terrified Jessie felt. Harry was the gamekeeper's apprentice when they ran away, but the old fellow who was in charge was going to retire and Harry would have eventually been promoted into his job. Alice always said her father made a huge sacrifice to run away with her mother to protect her from the earl's son. He gave up his whole life for her"

Tammy sighed in frustration. The right moment to tell Marian had been snatched away from her yet again. Still, she thought, there would be another opportunity later on in the afternoon once they had sorted through the box.

"Jessie's father was furious with Harry, and tracked them down," Marian went on. "He arrived at the vicarage one day later that summer, and there was an awful row when he found out Jessie was living under the same roof as Harry. He caused no end of trouble for the Reverend Staverley, even though the vicar and his wife hadn't done anything wrong. It was quite usual in those days for fourteen-year-olds to find work, and by then, Jessie and Harry were both employed at the vicarage — Harry tended the garden and the church grounds and Jessie helped out with the children. They both lived-in at the vicarage and then, as soon as Jessie was sixteen, the vicar married them in the church and they rented a tiny cottage not far away. Alice told me once that her mother never went back to Fawsden Hall because she was far too frightened of the Earl's son, and, in any case, her parents had washed their hands of her and refused to speak to her again, because she had brought shame on them."

"This is absolutely fascinating," said Tammy as she found her notebook and a pen and scribbled down some notes about Harry and Jessie's story. "It's lovely that things worked out for them in the end. Were they *ever* reconciled with their families?"

Marian shook her head. "No. According to Alice, her parents could never forgive their families for not believing Jessie about the terrible things that had happened to her. And she was far too scared to ever go back to the Hall, even to visit. The Staverleys became their family, and it was just as well they did because Alice lost her father in the First World War and then her mother died young too. She was left an orphan."

Marian shut her eyes for a few moments, before continuing. "When I was a teenager, I used to love listening to Alice's stories. She was such a lovely woman, Tammy. I wish you could have known her."

***

They had barely started cataloguing the photographs, and recording details on Tammy's computer, when there was a tap on the door.

"Yes?" Cynthia called.

"It's me."

"Come on in, laddie."

Paul stepped into Cynthia's lounge, running his fingers through his hair. He shut the door behind him.

"Let's all have a wee dram, shall we?" Cynthia suggested as she waddled over to her sideboard, from which she extracted a bottle of Johnnie Walker Blue Label. Tammy's eyes widened. She knew it was really expensive.

"I keep this one for special occasions. Anyone else up for a wee dram?"

Tammy shook her head. "I'm more of a Chardonnay girl. I'm not keen on whisky."

"Me neither," Marian agreed.

Cynthia threw up her hands in horror. "Sassenachs! The pair of youse."

Paul laughed. "Looks like it's just you 'n' me, Cynthia."

216

Cynthia shook her head as she poured out two small measures and placed one of them on the table in front of Paul, who sat down next to Tammy. She still hadn't looked at him properly, and was pretending to concentrate on her spreadsheet on the computer. He leaned in towards her, looking at the screen.

"What are you doing?"

"Cataloguing the old photographs — some of them have names and dates written on the back, and some don't. We're trying to identify who is in what photograph, where it was taken and when it was taken, that sort of thing."

Tammy heard the jangle of Cynthia's bracelets and a bottle of chilled white wine and two outsized wine glasses plonked themselves miraculously on the table in front of her. Cynthia filled them to the brim — one for Tammy and one for Marian.

"Are we celebrating something?" Marian said, arching her eyebrows. She let her gaze drift from Tammy to Paul.

"Most certainly we are." Cynthia said, raising her glass. "We're celebrating Paul finally getting up off his backside and sorting out his life back in Norfolk, are we not?"

"Cheers." Tammy raised her glass and took a gulp. The cynicism in Cynthia's voice was almost indiscernible, but Tammy could tell she was not convinced Paul had done the right thing.

"Cheers."

"I need to ask you a favour," Paul said to Cynthia. He scratched the side of his neck and it left a red mark.

"Oh?"

"Claire's come back with me. I wondered if she could stay in my room for the next week. I'll obviously pay for her. It's just that we are hoping to buy a house in the village and she's never been here before."

Cynthia gave a dismissive wave of her hand. "Fine by me," she said. "What about work?"

"I'm going to take a week's annual leave."

"And can I just ask, seeing as I have been your surrogate mum for the last year, are you happy about this?"

Cynthia's forthright words hit a curtain of silence.

Tammy couldn't see Paul's eyes. But she could see the top of his cheek, just at the corner of his left eye. It was twitching. He took a sip of his whisky and his Adam's apple bobbed as he swallowed. Then it bobbed again, and again.

"I could do with a bit of a break," he said. "And the room's quite big really. We can make do, as long as you're okay with it."

Cynthia stared at Paul. It was a long, hard look and he was forced to look away. He dropped his head and gazed into his whisky as he swirled it around and around in the glass without drinking it.

Tammy didn't know why she did it when she was feeling just the opposite: not loud and bouncy at all. She jumped up with her glass in one hand and rootled around in Alice's box with the other, swaying in time with the music in the background.

"Hey, you have just *got* to read these articles about the Hesitant Housewife. They're absolutely brilliant."

Paul stared at her with a strange look in his eyes and Tammy beamed at him. "I've been reading magazines from the 1960s all afternoon," she told him. "How sad is that?"

Tammy just caught the dying ember of a knowing look between Marian and Cynthia and there was a heavy moment of nothingness, when no one spoke. Then Elton John's *Sacrifice* broke through on the CD player, almost rudely.

"I love this track," Marian said dreamily. "It's absolutely beautiful, don't you think?"

"1990, I think," Cynthia said wistfully. "Rabbie and I went on a Mediterranean cruise. Oh, it was glorious. Beautiful. Magical."

Cynthia reminisced about the places they had visited and the people they had met on their holiday, but Tammy was listening to the lyrics: she stood very still looking straight into Paul's eyes, cradling her wine glass. Paul gulped, but didn't look away. They held the gaze, both conscious of the significance of the lyrics.

"I'd love to go on a cruise," Marian said with a whimsical look in her eyes. "Perhaps one day …"

Tammy's breath caught in her throat as her heart pounded. She wanted to scream at Paul: *Don't do it. Don't sacrifice your life. It's so wrong. All wrong.* But the words stayed stuck firmly in a lump in her throat, despite the effects of the wine washing around them, loosening them,

218

like a gentle wave washing the sand from around rocks.

The moment between them was interrupted by another tap on the door.

"I suppose that's Claire," Paul muttered. "She'll be wondering where I've got to."

"Helloooo?" called Cynthia.

"It's me," said Daniel's muffled voice. "Is Tammy in there with you?"

"Och, yes. Come on in, laddie. Come on in."

The door opened, but Tammy was still standing up with her back to it, swigging back great gulps of wine, her eyes locked with Paul's. Out of the corner of her eye, she saw Marian glance up at the door as *Sacrifice* faded into silence.

Tammy watched every bit of colour drain from Marian's face as her eyes widened and then become fixated and glazed. She spun around as, simultaneously, Daniel said: "Tammy, you've got a visitor."

Tammy's mouth opened but no words came out. She forgot she was holding a glass of wine, and it almost slipped through her fingers and crashed to the floor, but she tightened her grip just in time and it merely wobbled, splashing a few drops onto the carpet.

The hairs on the back of her neck prickled and her insides flipped over and over. Her bladder almost released itself with dismay. An old magazine dropped to the floor and the next track on the Elton John CD burst into life.

'Don't go breaking my heart ...'

Somehow Tammy managed to sit back down on her chair just before her legs liquefied. Her heart thumped huge amounts of blood around her head and with each beat the doorway wobbled slightly in her field of vision.

"Dad?"

***

Alan took a step backwards, almost stumbling over his own feet. His jaw set itself rigid over his heaving chest as he ran his fingers through his floppy hair three times in rapid succession.

She'd deceived him. His quiet, gentle Tammy had betrayed him,

219

lied to him and now she had tossed him aside for Marian Troutman. All the time he had been going out of his mind with worry in Yorkshire, Tammy had been swanning around in Lyverton, building a cosy relationship with Marian and all these other people he didn't know. He had been right. He'd known he had no choice but to come back to Lyverton as soon as Tammy had slammed the phone down on him last night, but he was too late: he had already lost her. The village was coiling around him like a giant anaconda snake, squeezing the breath out of him, just like he had always known it would. Now it had Tammy in its sights. It was about to strike, open its jaws wide and devour his precious daughter forever.

Marian Troutman wasn't a wizened up, dowdy spinster as Tammy had described her. Granted, she was no longer the girl he had left behind, but she was smartly dressed and remained a very attractive woman. Tammy had lied to him about that, too. He stared at Marian in amazement and took another step back but there was nowhere to go and his heel hit the wooden skirting board on the other side of the landing. He laid his palms flat against the wall to steady himself, but the coils of the snake were tightening even more, squeezing and crushing the breath from his lungs.

"Oh my God, it's Alan!" he heard Marian say.

***

Was it really Alan, back in Lyverton after all these years, or were her eyes playing tricks on her? Marian blinked and he was gone, but she could hear footsteps clunking down the stairs, then the sound of the latch and finally the door banged shut, and she knew it was him.

'Dad.' The word was still resounding in her ears like the clang of a church bell. Tammy had said 'Dad.'

A powerful floodlight switched on inside her head. It illuminated a dark corner of ignorance in intense brightness. It revealed the savage truth in sharp silhouette against the shadowy background of her existence for the last thirty years.

"Oh my God, it's Alan," said a voice that sounded like her own.

***

It was a mere twitch on the big hand of time, but the spinning coin of Pippa's life had finally rattled onto the floor. Tammy and Marian's lives had changed forever.

Paul held Tammy's hands and she gripped them like a lifeline and hung on tightly. The swirling vortex of her parents' secrets was sucking her down, down, down. She shut her eyes and her chest heaved; she was drowning, gasping for air in the vacuum. Then she heard a voice pulling her back. *'Oh my God, it's Alan.'*

Tammy forced open her eyelids and blinked through the swirling waters of the vortex into a hazy brightness. She couldn't breathe: it felt as if the air around her was devoid of oxygen. The voice continued, echoey and distant in her ears. *'They had a child together? My mother — and him — how could they? She only went and had another baby — by him!'*

Tammy's eyes focused and the buzzing noise in her ears faded to leave her face burning with embarrassment.

"She's hyperventilated," said Cynthia. "I knew she was swigging back that wine too fast. Where on earth has her father gone? Did someone put a rocket up his arse? Daniel. Go after him. Fetch him back. Anyone would think he'd just burst in on his daughter in the middle of an afternoon of wicked depravity — not just enjoying a wee dram with friends."

Tammy heard Cynthia tut loudly, swear very rudely under her breath and mutter, "I know Tammy said he was possessive, but this just takes the biscuit."

Suddenly, Tammy's head buzzed and her face began to burn. Everything went momentarily black and when the light flooded in again, she was cradled in Paul's warm arms and he was brushing the hair back from her hot, flushed face. She must explain to Marian, tell her she was sorry and she didn't mean for it to happen like this.

"I'm so, so sorry, Marian. I didn't know he was coming ..."

"Oh my giddy aunt!" she heard Cynthia say, and Tammy knew that the spinning coin had well and truly rattled to rest on the floor, newly-minted and shiny, for everyone to see.

"I was going to tell you this afternoon. I really was. I'm so sorry ..."

***

Marian stumbled into Cynthia's kitchen and leaned over the sink, Tammy's voice swiping through her heart like a machete cutting through tangled jungle creepers. *'I was going to tell you this afternoon. I really was. I'm so sorry ...'* She couldn't stay in the room with everyone's eyes on her. She didn't want to hear an explanation. She felt so sick she was gulping and gagging as she turned on the tap and ran her hands under cold water before clamping them over her face, shaking her head from side to side in denial. Was Tammy really her sister? Her mother's other daughter? She'd never forgive her mother for this. Never, ever, as long as she lived.

"Marian?"

She heard a slight jangle of jewellery as Cynthia stepped beside her and slid an arm around her shoulder.

Marian pulled her hands away from her face. Cynthia handed her a tissue and she dabbed it over her eyes and then patted at her wet face with a trembling hand. She shook her head.

"I apparently have a sister ..."

Cynthia smiled nervously. "It appears so. But I'm confused. Tammy's father can't possibly be *your* father — he's far too young."

"Tammy's father — Alan — ran off with my mother in 1978. He used to be my boyfriend ..."

Cynthia's eyes widened in amazement.

"Your boyfriend ran off with your mother?"

Marian nodded. "And they obviously had a baby together. I had absolutely no idea about Tammy."

After a few minutes of whispered conversation in the kitchen, Cynthia and Marian returned to the living room, Cynthia's chubby arm around her shoulder in a gesture of friendship, support and protection. Marian stood still for a while, blinking back tears as she watched Paul cradle Tammy in his arms. She felt a slight tug in the region of her abdomen. It wasn't Tammy's fault. She hadn't asked to be born.

"My sister," whispered Marian at the sight of Tammy, vulnerable and almost child-like. The scene melted through her initial anger as easily as a hot knife through butter and her heart fluttered with an enormous, glorious realisation that she wasn't alone in the world, after all.

222

"My little sister."

***

Tammy gulped and her head cleared with welcome relief as the words flooded into her ears.

'My little sister.'

Someone shoved a tissue into her hand and she held it over her tightly shut eyes. Just like on the first night in Lyverton, she felt someone's hand pulling at hers. Only this time it wasn't Paul's. It was Marian's. Her eyes were bright, sparkling like sunlight on broken glass and Tammy couldn't begin to describe the tapestry of mixed emotions embroidered on her sister's face.

Marian's silent tears spilled over her eyelashes. She was crouched down on her heels, staring at Tammy like a mother gazing at her newborn child. Tammy shifted to sit properly in her chair and then, in one perfectly synchronised action, their arms were round each other and they were hugging and crying into each other's hair. It felt so good that Marian was accepting her and not turning her back on her.

Tammy heard Paul speak.

"At least this way you didn't have to tell her yourself. It'll all turn out fine in the end. Don't worry. Daniel's gone after him. He'll be back in a minute. It was just the shock of seeing you with Marian."

Marian wiped her eyes on the back of her hand. "I knew there was something familiar about you when I first saw you in church on Tuesday morning at Alice Thompson's funeral. I thought you might have once been a pupil of mine."

"I'm sorry it had to happen like this," Tammy said finally. "I've been trying to tell you all week, but I kept getting interrupted by people just as I was on the point of telling you."

"It doesn't matter," Marian said, breathless and flushed. "I understand. Where is she? Where's Mum? Is she with Alan? When can I see her?"

Tammy took a deep breath.

"I'm really sorry, but she's dead, Marian. She died two years ago of cancer. We sent you a letter."

"No! Oh no!"

223

Cynthia pulled another tissue out of a box with a flourish and handed it to Marian, patting her shoulder with a sympathetic hand. Tammy felt overwhelmed with sadness for Marian's lost years. Pippa had been such a good mother to her, and she had obviously been a good mother to Marian before she completely messed up and abandoned her for Alan.

"How did she die?"

"Cancer. Multiple Myeloma. It's terminal, but some people are lucky and manage to have a reasonable quality of life for a good few years after diagnosis. Mum wasn't so lucky. She suffered terribly and it was all so quick. Just fifteen weeks from the first sign that anything was wrong."

Tammy let Marian take it all in. She felt so sad that her sister would never see their mother again.

Marian sniffed. "It's like I told you on Thursday afternoon, I think I knew in my heart. Two years ago I began to dream about her, and smell her soap in my dreams."

"It was her dying wish that she could be with you for just one last time. I promised her on her deathbed I would come and find you. She wanted me to tell you she always loved you. Marian … I smell her soap too."

"Do you? Really! Do you?"

Cynthia motioned to Paul and whispered the words so as not to intrude on Tammy and Marian's private moments. "Let's leave them alone for a while. Come on into the kitchen."

Paul patted Tammy on the shoulder and reluctantly left the room with Cynthia.

"I thought you'd turn me away and not want anything to do with me," said Tammy.

"Why would I do that? Nothing is your fault, is it? Children are the innocent victims of their parents' mistakes. I see it every day in my job. For about five years after Mum ran off with him, I swear I would have killed them both had I seen them in the street. Then something happened to me to make me understand and, after that, all I wanted to do was find her."

"What happened?"

Marian leaned forwards to push a lock of Tammy's fluffy hair away from her eyes. People seemed compelled to do that, as if they thought Tammy's hair bothered her but she was so used to her unmanageable hair, she didn't even notice it in front of her eyes.

"I met someone very special," Marian said fondly. "I loved him so much. We shared ten, magical years together before I lost him."

"What was his name?"

"Lloyd. He was the head teacher at the school before he retired. After he had left the school we realised that the easy companionship we had shared was really love. We moved in together. He had separated from his wife a few years before his retirement, but they had never divorced. When he died suddenly without making a will she inherited the house, and so I had to move back into the Corner House with Dad, but that's all ancient history now."

"I'm sorry …"

Tammy didn't know what else to say to her, but she sensed Marian needed to tell her more about Lloyd to temper the intensity of the pain of discovering their mother was dead.

"It was inevitable that I'd lose him one day, but we had hoped to share few more years together. What I'm trying to say, Tammy, is that he was over thirty years older than me. He was sixty-two when we got together. I was just about your age — in my late twenties. It made the nineteen years between Mum and Alan seem like nothing at all!"

Finally, Tammy understood why Marian was like a chameleon. She was truly ageless at almost fifty. She could be thirty: she could be seventy. That Sunday afternoon she stood at a pivotal point in her life. She could either begin to live from that moment onwards or she could begin to die. Marian could easily grab her future with both hands and the constantly sweeping hands of time would slow and stop, ready to reverse back over the last thirty years and brush away the dirty cobwebs of the past.

"He was the love of my life, Tammy."

Tammy nodded and understood. The pieces of Marian's life jigsaw were slowly falling into place.

But she still wondered what happened to the letter.

CHAPTER TWENTY-FIVE

Day Eight
Monday, 1st June: 12:10 am

Tammy didn't actually wake up on Monday. She didn't wake up, because she hadn't gone to sleep.

Alan was still missing. How could she sleep when her father was missing? All she'd heard from him was a single text and she was worried.

> *'I can see that you have found your sister and embarked on a new life. It is a pity you could not find it in you to share that information with me before I made such a fool of myself.'*

There was no *Love from Dad.* No kisses.

It was a long text by Alan's standards. He had never managed to master the art of texting. (Tammy allowed herself a cynical smile: he'd once accidentally called predictive texting *'protective sexting'* and she and Pippa had howled with laughter at his slip of the tongue.) She imagined him sitting in his car, parked by the side of the road in the countryside somewhere. It would have taken him ages to compile the text message. He would have had plenty of time to change his mind, turn the car around and come back to Lyverton and sort things out. Had Paul been right? Was he really a mouse and not a man? A man would have stood squarely in the doorway and faced up to his past. Paul was a real man, but he just needed to take a step back and follow Paul's heart, not Nick's head. She shivered as she remembered his warm arms encircling her and the secret, shared look as *Sacrifice* played on the CD player just before her father had spectacularly arrived on the scene.

Her stomach churned with worry. Not only had her father gone missing, but Paul and Cynthia, in some kind of weird, secret conspiracy, had gone off, too. As darkness fell, they had taken Paul's car and driven back to her address in Yorkshire to see if her father had gone home. He hadn't; it had been a complete waste of time and fuel and they were now on their way back to Lyverton. Tammy did think about ringing her father's friends, Brenda and Colin, but everyone had agreed it would have been a bad idea. Brenda would only worry herself half to death, and in any case, if Alan had turned up at her house in an agitated state, Brenda would have rung Tammy straight away. Tammy knew that for certain.

Tammy had wanted to go with them to Yorkshire, too, but they had said no: it would be far better for them to go alone, because her father didn't know them. Alan was a gentleman; a polite, pleasant kind of chap and not the sort of bloke to shut the door in anyone's face and they could explain the situation to him, in an unbiased, rational way. In any case, someone had to stay in Lyverton, in case Alan came back to the Red Lion. Someone needed to keep Claire company, too. Tammy had been annoyed at that. She had thought it was a bit of a cheek to ask her to faff around with Claire when she and Marian could have done with some private time together. And another thing, Cuckoo Claire hadn't looked particularly happy, but she damned well ought to be. She'd got him back, hadn't she? What more did she want? What a mess. How could everything go so horribly wrong in such a short space of time?

After Paul and Cynthia had left for Yorkshire, Marian and Tammy stayed in Cynthia's flat for a while, listening to old CDs and catching up on Marian's last thirty years and Tammy's entire lifetime. Alan and Pippa might have made a bad parental judgement, Marian had said, but babies weren't pushed out of their mother's wombs clutching instruction manuals in their little hands. That had made Tammy laugh. They had both laughed, but then they had made a solemn promise to each other not to let all the troubles of the past get in the way of their future as sisters.

Four hours later they had both felt guilty about Claire, sitting alone and abandoned in Paul's room. Together, they had ventured along the landing and knocked on Paul's door to ask her if she wanted to come down into the pub with them and have something to eat.

Now, just after midnight, Tammy didn't actually hate Claire any more: she had been supportive and sympathetic. She hated to admit it to herself, but in almost any other circumstances, Tammy knew she and Claire could be good friends.

Tammy had toyed with the idea of ringing the police to report Alan missing, but Claire and Marian thought they would just laugh at her. After all, her father was a grown man. If he wanted to take off in a huff he was perfectly entitled to do so.

As soon as the text message from Alan had come through, Tammy had texted him back. She kept trying his number constantly, but he had switched his phone off: he hadn't read her text, and he wouldn't even receive it until he switched it back on again.

***

Marian and Tammy sat, cross-legged, on Tammy's bed, sharing the remains of the bag of Kettle Chips. Claire sat on the floor, browsing through Alice's photographs and old letters. Marian rubbed her eyes and then yawned, just before the bleep of her mobile phone made Tammy jump. She leapt off the bed and snatched it up, flicking open the cover with an anxious, fumbling hand.

It was from Paul. She didn't know whether she was disappointed or elated.

'We are about half way back. Tired - so stopped at a motorway café. Having kip in car. Have you heard anything yet? Love Paul xxx'

"It's Paul. They've stopped for a while because he's so tired," she announced.

Claire sighed and rubbed her bleary eyes. She yawned and then stretched. Too late, Tammy realised Claire, sitting beside her, had also read the text message. She quickly flipped the cover over the screen. Paul really shouldn't have put three xxx at the end of the text.

"I might try to get some sleep, then, if you don't mind. But I'll leave the door on the latch. Just come in if there's any news about your dad." Claire stood up and just one glance at her eyes told Tammy she *had* seen the kisses at the end of the text. The tingle inside Tammy's tummy turned to guilt as she felt Claire's pain.

"Okay," Tammy replied as she flicked open the cover on the phone

228

again, and sent Paul a quick text back to tell him there was still no news from Alan and to make sure he had a proper sleep before driving again.

Tammy turned to look at Marian. "What about you? You have to be in school tomorrow. You ought to get some sleep, too."

Marian shook her head. "I'll stay here with you, if that's all right. I don't want to leave you alone. In any case I need to be here when Alan comes back, just for a quick word to let him know I'm not still angry with him."

Tammy chuckled inwardly at the irony. Over thirty years had passed since Marian and Alan had uttered their final, scathing words in their last blazing argument. She was curious to hear what they would have to say to each other. Then a feeling of dread wrapped itself around her like a wet blanket. That was if he ever came back.

Once Claire had gone back to Paul's room, Marian and Tammy decided to try and catch a couple of hours sleep. Tammy undressed and slipped into her pyjamas. She realised she had been wearing her new dress all day: it was crumpled and grubby, and so she pulled her suitcase out from under the bed and stuffed it straight inside, instead of putting it back in the wardrobe.

"That colour really suits you," said Marian.

"Thanks. It's new. I wouldn't have chosen it for myself, but I went shopping with Cynthia for something to wear last Wednesday, when Paul and I went out to dinner at The Gamekeeper's Lodge at Little Somerton. Do you know it?"

Marian's eyes widened. "Blimey — he pushed the boat out didn't he? It costs a fortune for a meal at The Gamekeeper's Lodge." She paused before continuing. "What's this Paul and Nick thing? Why do you call him Paul and Claire calls him Nick?"

"It's a long story." Tammy clambered into bed; her head felt like a washing machine with something hard rattling around inside and she didn't really want to churn over the whole sorry tale right then. "I'll tell you sometime."

Marian pulled the duvet over Tammy, like a mother would, and then she brushed her hair away from her eyes.

"Tell me about Paul tomorrow," she said. "You need to get some

229

sleep."

Tammy lifted the duvet and shifted to one side of the bed, moving one of her two pillows to the other side. Marian hesitated and then slid in beside Tammy, fully clothed. They lay still and silent for a few seconds, facing each other in semi-darkness. The curtains had not been pulled together properly, and an orangey glow from street lights outside fought its way through the gap.

"I can't describe how happy and sad I am, all at the same time," Marian whispered, her eyes bright and shiny. "I can't believe I actually have a sister. I haven't been this happy since Lloyd died, nor so sad since Mum left. It's such a huge roller-coaster of mixed emotions, it's making me feel dizzy."

"I wish I could have met Lloyd," Tammy said in a hushed voice. "You must have loved him very much if the age gap thing was of no consequence to you."

"I did. The years between us meant nothing. They were never an issue."

"Marian. Did you ever love my dad?"

Marian hesitated. Tammy knew she had asked a difficult question that her sister didn't know how to answer.

***

Marian shut her eyes momentarily, remembering the intensity of the exquisite feelings of Alan's bare skin on hers and how she had adored him for years, ever since she had been fifteen. The memory of the time they had finally made incredible love in the back of her new red Mini Clubman was one of her most precious memories. She wouldn't have missed the few weeks that followed for the world. Those sacred weeks had belonged to her, even though, with hindsight, she knew Alan had been hopelessly in love with her mother. She regretted ever mentioning it to Tammy on Thursday in the staff room: had she not laughed and joked with Davey, Tammy would never, ever have known about her and Alan, because they would both have kept their secret hidden and buried to protect her.

"Yes, I did — once. I adored him from about the age of fifteen until it all went disastrously wrong. I loved him but he didn't love me,

230

Tammy. He cared deeply about me, but that's different. It wasn't until I discovered the awful truth about him and Mum that everything fell into place. He was very honest and told me he'd always loved my mother and there had never been anyone else for him." She shook her head, remembering the turmoil and scandal.

"I was devastated, but it wasn't until I met Lloyd that I finally understood."

"Why didn't you try to find us?" Tammy asked.

"I did."

"Did you?"

"I tried for years to find Mum." Marian replied. "Lloyd helped me to go through telephone directories, but it was so hard. Then, in the mid-90s, as soon as I could get my hands on a computer with the internet, I searched in earnest. I really thought I'd find her. I even telephoned random people called Alan Fielding all over the country, asking them if they'd ever lived in Northamptonshire. There were no Phyllis Troutmans at all. It was as if they both had disappeared from the face of the earth, and it did cross my mind more than once that they might have changed their names."

"They changed their names as soon as they got to Yorkshire," Tammy explained. "Did you and Lloyd live in Lyverton?" she asked, changing the subject.

"No. We lived in Lloyd's house in Fawsden. I was desperate to have his baby, but he didn't want more children because he already had four with his estranged wife, although they were all grown-up by the time we got together. I used to dream about a little girl with strawberry blonde curly hair. She'd be giggling, with ice-cream on her face; then in another dream she'd be sitting on my lap and I'd be reading her a Peter Rabbit story. Sometimes I'd be putting sticking plasters on her skinned knees, soothing her when she cried or combing the tangles out of her hair. Then my dreams of her turned into a physical ache, but it was the one thing Lloyd felt he couldn't give me. Then, out of the blue, when I was in my thirties he changed his mind all of a sudden. He said he'd been thinking about it and he couldn't bear to imagine me, all alone, when he'd gone. All his life he'd held strict beliefs about a child being brought up by two parents who were married to each other. He had

231

been devastated when his marriage failed, but I think he finally realised how desperately I wanted a baby, and he set aside his high morals for my sake. We tried for a baby for about six months and nothing happened. Then I got pregnant and we were both ecstatic. I don't think I have ever felt such happiness in my life as I did then."

"What happened?"

"Lloyd started divorce proceedings so that we could get married. Then I had a miscarriage at four months. It *was* a little girl, they said. We were both inconsolable. Then, just a few weeks later, Lloyd had a heart attack and died suddenly. I thought my world had ended. I just wanted to die, too."

"Oh, Marian ..."

"I had no choice but to go home to The Corner House, because Lloyd hadn't made a will and his estranged wife inherited his house, even though he had already given her his share in their old home. My dad, Tony, had always been a bit of a loner, but he became a complete recluse after Mum went off with Alan. As if all the kerfuffle with being accused of indecent exposure at my birthday party wasn't enough, a few weeks later he had been arrested on suspicion of murder when two bodies were found in a burnt-out barn near Fawsden. He was quickly eliminated from the police enquiries, but it all left its mark on him. In the aftermath of everything that happened with Mum and Alan, he became angry, lonely and bitter. Then, in 1987 when I went to live with Lloyd, he turned to drink and let himself go, big time. Eventually, his business failed and we only just managed to save The Corner House from being repossessed by the skin of our teeth. I'd neglected him so badly while I was with Lloyd. It's something I feel quite ashamed about, actually. So I went back home and tried to get him sorted out. It occupied my mind, I suppose, after Lloyd's death. It gave me a purpose in life. Only now, Tammy, I'm stuck there and can't escape and spread my own wings again. I can't move out, because I own the house now and I pay the mortgage. I can't just throw him out, can I?"

"Couldn't he move out into a flat or something, if you own the house?"

"It's his home — I couldn't be that cruel. In any case, he's a sad old man now. He's got no savings, because he almost went bankrupt when his business failed. Over the years Dad's lost all his social skills. Mind you, he didn't have that many to lose in the first place, and he says inappropriate things all the time because he doesn't know how to behave any more."

Marian fell silent, thinking back to last Tuesday at Alice Thompson's funeral. She could have crawled under the pew in the church with embarrassment when Tony had said about Alice being bent over nearly double in her final years, and he'd wondered how they'd shut the coffin lid in such a loud voice everyone could hear.

"What does Alan do now, Tammy? Where does he work?"

"He's a conservation officer ..."

Marian burst out laughing. "I'm not surprised — that is such an appropriate job for him. He used to go on about trying to save the world before anyone knew it needed saving! Is he still into fossils, Roman architecture and old churches?"

"Yep," said Tammy. "He likes nothing better than moseying around old ruins, and staring aimlessly at churches and cathedrals. That's when he's not crunching his way through pebbly beaches looking for fossils in cliffs, or involved in archaeological digs."

"And does he still have that habit of writing in capital letters all the time?"

"He most certainly does — and he can't use a mobile phone or send text messages to save his life."

They laughed out loud.

"He's been a brilliant father, though," said Tammy, feeling suddenly ashamed for her recent, obsessive thoughts about having to get away from him. "I haven't got the same problems as you have. They're different problems. He is a very caring person and would do anything for anyone. He has worked so hard, too, to progress in his career. He studied all the time I was growing up so that he could give us a decent life. He's honest and conscientious and all my friends think he's great. He's so over-protective of me since Mum died, though. I feel as if he is suffocating me. He rings me at work at least twice every day — it's so embarrassing — and I constantly feel like a ten-year-old. He's hard working, got a good job at the City Council, no nasty or messy habits that I know of and I actually don't mind living with him. But that's not the point, is it? I want my own flat now — my own life. When I finished university five years ago, I went back to live with my parents. I had a reasonably well-paid job, but wanted to save for a deposit on a flat so it made sense to live at home for a few months while I was saving. Then, just as I was about to start looking for a place of my own, Mum got cancer. I couldn't leave then, could I? Then when she died, I had to stay with Dad for a while. I couldn't have left him on his own straight away. Then, when I began to think about putting down my deposit on a flat, that's when the trouble started. I told him around six months ago that I wanted to move out and he just couldn't understand why I would want to leave him. I feel trapped, Marian. I needed to fulfil Mum's dying wish to find you, and I just *have* to know who I really am before I can move on with my life."

"Oh Tammy. Isn't it strange that we are both trapped living with our fathers? I do have my own separate space in our house, though. I can't bear to sit with him all the time, so I've made a tiny sitting room upstairs. It's little things that niggle me; having to do everything, like shopping, cleaning and cooking. He just sits on his backside all day long, drinking beer, smoking and watching old films on television. I tell you, Tammy, it's like The Royale Family round our house. Some days he doesn't even get dressed. He slobs around in the same tracksuit bottoms and t-shirt he's slept in, watching endless repeats of old TV programmes and black and white films. I'm so relieved to get out of the house and go to work, some days I stay in the staff room until about eight o'clock at night, working, because I don't want to go home. On Sundays, I always go to church, but to tell you the truth, I'm not really that religious. Like I said to you outside the church earlier, I only go there to get out of the house on Sunday mornings and sing my heart out in some kind of macabre release from it all. I sit and listen to the sermon, take it all in, and then I come out feeling all refreshed and happy and ready to face the week ahead. It does lift my spirits, granted. But it's not right, though, is it? To go to church just to get away from your drunken bum of a dad."

They smiled at each other in the semi-darkness.

"Actually, I feel quite tired now," Marian yawned. She sank down

234

onto the pillow.

"Me too," Tammy said, "but before we try and get some sleep, let's make a date to spend some time together."

"When?"

"How about in two weeks, when Dad's calmed down and my holiday is over, let's meet up half way between here and Yorkshire, perhaps on the Lincolnshire coast somewhere, and spend Sunday together, just the two of us. We'll eat chips and ice-cream on the beach."

"I'd really like that, Tammy. I'll look forward to it."

CHAPTER TWENTY-SIX

3.00 am

Tammy lay awake, staring at shadows, worrying about Alan. She shut her eyes. Where the heck had he gone? He had disappeared like this once before, about six months after Pippa had died. Tammy had gone shopping with a friend one Saturday afternoon and when they had come home, laden with shopping bags and giggling, Alan had glared at her. She hadn't known what she'd done wrong. He'd stalked off into the garden and had been really quite rude to her friend, which was uncharacteristic because usually Alan was polite and proper to the extreme. When her friend had gone home, he'd shouted at Tammy. *'How dare you come home, laughing and giggling like that when your mother's just died. It's not on Tammy, not on.'*

Tammy had apologised, but then she'd said: *'I was feeling happy for the first time today, and you've gone and spoilt it. I miss her too, but nothing's going to bring her back, so we just have to get on with life.'*

The television had been on in the corner of the room; it was tuned in to an oldies music channel and Tammy had picked up the remote control and switched channels. He'd lost his temper then, grabbed it off her and jabbed it back onto the golden oldies channel again. He'd paced up and down the living room, ranting and raving about how Tammy had no respect for Pippa's memory, before storming out of the front door and jumping into his car. Too late, Tammy realised that *Close to You* by The Carpenters was just coming to an end, and she must have cut it off, mid-song, when she had changed channels. It had been one of her parents' special songs. She'd glanced at the television screen and, in the video, the musicians were swaying in time to the music on a giant Y, O and U in a rude sort of prodding at her father's happy memories of her mother. She had rushed to the front door, yanked it open and yelled at him as he sat, gripping the steering wheel, glaring at her. *'I understand, Dad. I'm sorry. You shouldn't keep listening to all these old songs, it's not doing you any good. You're living in the past when we've both got to face the future.'*

236

Then she had noticed the tears and had seen the savagery of the huge sobs that had escaped. He had started the car engine, and she had just caught a muffled: *'What do you know about it Tammy? What do you know about the pain of losing your wife?'*

He'd reversed out of the driveway and driven off like a maniac. Tammy had ran round to Colin and Brenda's house to see if he'd gone there. They had driven around and around looking for him, but in the end Brenda had convinced her he'd be back when he had got it all out of his system, so Tammy had gone home to wait for him. He was missing for four hours, and when he came back he was puffy-eyed and dishevelled. Tammy had put her arms around him and he'd clung to her, apologising for losing his temper. *'I went to Ilkley Moor,'* he'd said, *'to get my head straight. I don't want to go on, Tammy. I can't face life without her.'*

Afterwards, Tammy had made him visit the doctor and he'd been given some tablets to help him through the grief. After that, he had stopped watching old music channels on the television and had packed away Pippa's CDs. He hadn't even listened to the radio in the kitchen any more, and Tammy knew it was because when it was playing, he was on edge, thinking an old song would burst into life, lever up memories of their time together and then the remembered songs would make him lose his head again. Until then, Tammy had not realised how much she would miss music playing in the house. It had been so much a part of her parents' lives that when Alan had decided to banish it, it was as if he had erased all memories of her mother for her, too.

Tammy opened her eyes. Marian was fast asleep on her stomach with her mouth open slightly, breathing evenly. Her hand rested lightly on Tammy's shoulder and if there had been anyone else in the room, they would have thought it was a protective, maternal hand that lay there. Tammy knew differently though. Her sister's hand had been subconsciously placed on her in the same way her spaniel fell asleep with its head on her foot so that it would wake up if she moved. Now Marian had found her, she didn't want to lose her and it made Tammy feel secure and yet apprehensive at the same time.

Tammy dozed, but it wasn't proper sleep and silly, whimsical thoughts began to stream through her mind. The quirky thoughts turned into a waking dream — she knew she was dreaming, but her mind played out the scene anyway, like watching a film on the television. She opened her eyes and tried to turn her head, but it wouldn't move. She lifted her hand and waved it in front of her field of vision in the dull light, but oddly, her hand wasn't there. She tried to speak to Marian beside her, but no sound came out. Panicking, she closed her eyes again. Then, in a brilliant, panoramic vision behind her closed eyelids, she saw an old fashioned shiny, dark blue car pulling into the sweeping, gravelled driveway of a mansion and the sound of the crunching tyres brought a group of children, dressed in what looked like Victorian clothing, running to the car. *'What have you got this time, Master Frederick. Which bird have you brought back from Africa,'* they babbled, excited.

A chauffeur strode around to the front passenger door and lifted out a bird cage, before opening the rear door for the passenger. The bird in the cage was pure white. Its crested head twisted from side to side, surveying its new surroundings. Its eyes were hard and predatory, and its beak and clawed feet pink, completely devoid of pigment.

'Is it a white magpie?' The children were shouting excitedly as they crowded around the chauffeur, who was holding the cage. Tammy was curious and stepped forwards to join them. *'Is it a white jackdaw? Is it a dove?'*

The male passenger alighted from the car and stared straight at Tammy as he said: *'It's a cuckoo. A rare, pure white albino Jacobin cuckoo from Kenya. Jessie, do you want to look, too?'*

Tammy opened her eyes with a start. She could see the orangey glow of the street light in the room, but she still couldn't move. The vision had been odd and yet strangely fascinating — nothing like this had ever happened to her before. Marian was still sleeping: she could feel her hand resting on her shoulder. She tried to fight a terrifying feeling of falling before the vision overcame her once again and her strange dream resumed.

She was now stroking a horse at a stable door; she could smell the aroma of its rancid, steamy breath as it snorted in pleasure when she patted its neck. A collection of brightly-coloured, exotic birds in

238

various cages were twittering, tweeting and whistling in a cacophony of birdsong at the back of the stable, and she wanted to go in to look at them. Footsteps crunched on the cinder path behind her and she turned around: *'Would you like to see my birds, Jessie?'* She felt uneasy. Just lately, Master Frederick always bent down to put his face close to hers when he spoke to her, and his breath smelt of cigars and whisky, which made her feel sick. She felt a hand on her bottom and stiffened as she felt probing fingers snake their way between her buttocks. She thought about running away, but then realised in a flash of horror, there was nowhere to run because the master's leery, slobbery, drunken friend was blocking her way, his hand slowly rubbing at his crotch through his trousers.

The smell of whisky-tainted, cigar breath intensified and she felt two or three blasts of rapid hot breath on her cheek as the master's hand left her backside and ran its way up her back. Suddenly, she lurched forwards as she was pushed heavily from behind. She fell to the ground on her face, her arms and legs flailing in the hay and horse manure. The two men were laughing at her: deep, guttural, lurid laughs. She screamed as she tried to get up, but a huge nicotine-stained hand clamped itself over her mouth and nose from behind. She couldn't breathe. She was suffocating, turning her head, this way and that, trying to gasp in some air and at the same time scream out for help.

Her dress was yanked up over her head and her underwear tugged off with a rough hand. She heard her knicker elastic ripping; it cut painfully into her hip as she tried to pull her dress down to cover herself. When she felt a warm hardness brush against her inner thigh, the feel of it made her want to be sick and she gagged as bile rose in her throat. Kicking out with all her might she managed to scream, slither out from underneath the master and scramble up, but he caught hold of her foot and she fell heavily onto a bird cage, which crashed to the ground, the bottom of the cage breaking away. A bird fluttered out, its strong white wings brushing against her face as it flapped around the stable.

A horse reared up and whinnied, its front hoof just missing her as it thudded down just inches from her head. Filled with terror, she

239

watched as the bird escaped and flew away into the fields and the master roared in anger. A single white feather drifted on the breeze and settled onto the hay as she screamed. One of the men shouted *'shut up you bitch'* and a few pulsating heartbeats later something hit her on the back of her head and everything went red and sparkly before turning black.

Tammy jumped with a start as she returned to full consciousness, her heart pounding with terror in her throat as she opened her eyes.

She had been raped. Tammy knew without any doubt that, in her dream, she had been Jessie Thompson a hundred years ago, and she had been brutally raped in the stables by 'the master' whose name was Frederick.

Wide awake and rational again, Tammy reasoned with herself. Surely it had just been stress that had made her think she was paralysed and see odd things in the twilight between wakefulness and sleep. She had dreamed about a white cuckoo because she had Paul on her mind and couldn't help thinking of Claire as *Cuckoo Claire* because she had been living in Paul's home with Paul's parents and had shoved him out of the nest. She had Jessie Thompson on her brain because of the photograph in Alice's box, Marian's story about how Jessie and Harry had run away from Fawsden Hall, and her uncanny resemblance to Jessie. Then she remembered her imagined sightings of Harry and Jessie in present day Lyverton — but no, the children were just regular everyday teenagers experimenting with a new, different fashion. That would be the most logical explanation. She lifted her hand and it moved easily. She had just been imagining things. She was so stressed about everything, it was almost driving her insane.

Then fear overcame her again and her heart began to pound as the truth prickled on the back of her neck. Nothing was logical. Not one single thing was normal. In fact, everything was most definitely paranormal.

What on earth was happening to her?

***

Tammy watched the new day break through a chink in the curtains. She was exhausted. Frightened of the horrible paralysed feeling and bad dream of Jessie's rape, she daren't go to sleep, jerking awake with a start every time she dozed off.

Marian stirred and then sat up.

"Morning," Tammy said.

"What time is it?"

"I don't know. Probably about four-thirty ... five."

"I'll make some tea, shall I?" Marian suggested. "Is there any news?"

"No."

Marian slipped out of bed and tucked the duvet back around Tammy before putting the kettle on. She bustled about, rinsing out used snowdrop mugs in the bathroom, and Tammy realised that, actually, age-wise they could be mother and daughter.

Marian set the clean mugs down on the tray and turned to face her. "Mum loved snowdrops."

"I planted some under the oak tree where we scattered her ashes," Tammy replied. "They came up for the first time this year. We must go together and lay flowers ..."

"She used to grow them in little pots on our kitchen windowsill," Marian interrupted wistfully.

"Yes, I remember, she did that in our house, too. She planted daffodils, tulips and grape hyacinths in the borders in the garden ..."

Marian nodded and smiled, memories flooding back. "Did she make daisy chains with you?"

"Oh yes. Great long ones that stretched half way round the garden ..."

"And did she put a buttercup under your chin to see if you liked butter?"

"And let you run around barefoot in dewy grass?"

"Did she make toast for you after school?"

"With best butter and a half-and-half ..."

"A half-and-half! Mum's concoction of a weak coffee with half milk and half water," Marian reminisced with a smile, caressing the mug in her hand. She looked down at Tammy and they stared into each other's eyes without speaking.

The rattling sound of the almost-boiled kettle cut through the air, intruding on the moment, their eyes bright with the happy memories of their shared mother. Tammy sat up in bed.

"I loved her so much, you know." Marian said tearfully.

"So did I," Tammy replied, the atmosphere in the room becoming heavy with the question playing on her lips. Tammy knew what she was going to say. Within only a few minutes of meeting Marian last Tuesday night, she had suspected that she hadn't deliberately ignored Alan's letter. She understood, now, that the sadness that curled around Marian and followed her like some kind of mocking demon wasn't just because of her pitiful, reclusive father, it was a hybrid of grief for her lost baby daughter and the unrelenting self-deprecating pain of rejection by her mother.

"Why did she abandon me, Tammy?"

"She didn't ..."

"She never contacted me — not once. Was I that bad?"

Tammy wished there was an easier way of saying it, but Marian had to know.

"She did, Marian. I never knew this before, but last week, on the phone, Dad told me that, after she left, she wrote to you all the time, begging you to forgive her. Dad said she was inconsolable when she got no response, so then she just kept on writing cards and letters and storing them in a box in her wardrobe ready for you to open one day. There are hundreds of them. Look. I can see it wasn't your fault. Don't beat yourself up ..."

Tammy felt a sudden overwhelming guilt for the love Pippa had poured into her. She felt like a huge, fat cat, the one that always got the cream. Her poor, abandoned sister had been the skinny, scrawny one, denied even basic sustenance, just managing to survive on the scraps life threw at her now and again.

"I knew nothing about all this, Marian. I didn't even know I had a sister until three years ago ..."

"I can't believe they didn't tell you about me," Marian said, shaking her head. "How could they just pretend I didn't exist?" A look of horror crossed her face. "My father! He must have intercepted my letters and birthday cards after Mum left. It's the only explanation."

Tammy knew her words would hurt but she had to say them

242

anyway.

"We sent you a letter to tell you Mum was dying. Dad posted it using recorded delivery because he had to know that you'd received it. He begged you to come to her, because Mum's biggest fear in her last days was that she'd die without seeing you again."

Marian's hands flew up to her face. "And did it get signed for?" she asked through trembling fingers, shaking her head as if she already knew the answer.

Tammy nodded. "Someone signed for it."

"It must have been Dad."

Marian let her hands fall away from her face. Her mouth distorted but nothing came out. She was still shaking her head slowly from side to side.

Tammy continued. "That's the reason I've come to Lyverton. Just a few minutes before Mum passed away she made me promise that I'd come and find you and tell you that she always loved you. I put it off, again and again because I was too scared to travel all this way on my own and worried about how to tell you that you had a sister when you were so much older than me. Then, two weeks ago, coincidentally on the day Alice Thompson passed away, a sudden, overwhelming compulsion came over me. I just knew that I couldn't move on in my own life until I had fulfilled my promise to Mum. I took two weeks' holiday from work, and — well — here I am."

"Oh Tammy. I'm sorry. I just don't know what to say. I should have been there. I should have been by her side when she died, held her hand and let her know I had forgiven her."

Marian's face crumpled as old wounds opened up inside her. "I'd have dropped everything and just gone to her. I would, believe me. I loved her. She was everything to me. But I always thought she didn't care …"

Marian's whole body began to tremble and her voice sounded as if it was darting about, chasing shadows in her mind, the words tumbling over and over themselves as she tried to order them through her confusion.

"He hoards things: piles of stuff all over the house. He won't let me touch them. He has terrible rages if I go near his things. I'll kill

243

him, Tammy. I will … I will … I swear …"

Tammy felt as if she had unleashed a tiger. Marian began pacing up and down the room, her arms thrown around herself in self-restraint. "He had the telephone taken out after mum left. Now I know why. I hate him … hate him! How could he do this to me?"

Tammy thought about Tony Troutman, the too-loud man in the church who'd joked about poor Alice. The man with his shirt buttons popping over his huge stomach, his purple, bulbous nose and spider-like broken veins covering his face like a Virginia creeper; he must be such a selfish, hard-hearted man to deny his only daughter the love of her mother for more than thirty years. Tammy felt angry for her sister: cheated for herself.

Marian sank down onto the bed, her hands clamped over her face. The grief she felt for her mother's untimely death was beginning to spill over the edges of her anger. Tammy knelt up on the bed and put her arms around her sister: she was dishevelled, her clothes crumpled and her hair a tangled mess. Her bony shoulders heaved as she said over and over again. "Why, why, why did he do it to me?"

After a while Marian's tears subsided and Tammy passed her a tissue before sliding off the bed. She didn't speak because she just didn't know what she could say to make things better for her sister. She took Marian's hand and sat down on the bed beside her. She brushed the hair out of Marian's eyes. They were both mother and sister to each other, despite the age gap between them.

CHAPTER TWENTY-SEVEN

9.00 am

Just as the sun was beginning to gain in strength, sparkling like fairy dust on the water of the distant old quarries, the mobile phone beeped twice. Tammy had a text.

'Feel much better now. Will see you at the Red Lion in about 20 mins. Love Dad xxx'

"Is that all he can say?" she grumbled to Marian. "As if nothing has happened?"

"How are we going to handle this, Tammy?"

Tammy sighed. "I don't know. I think we ought to keep him out of the way of Cynthia and Paul after their fruitless trip to Yorkshire. He's caused so much hassle it's unbelievable."

"Why don't you go down first," Marian suggested. "Meet him in the car park. I'll stay up here and then you can either text me to come down or bring him up to the room."

"Okay," Tammy agreed. "That sounds like a plan."

Marian laughed. "You look so relieved."

"I can't believe he's acting as if nothing's happened, though," Tammy said.

Soon, she was sitting outside in the pub's beer garden in bright sunshine waiting for Alan to arrive. She felt fuzzy and slightly disconnected from herself through lack of sleep. She couldn't shake the memory of the horrible dream about Jessie out of her head; she felt annoyed that it was creeping into her dulled consciousness when she needed to keep all her wits about her. She was desperate to speak to Paul, too, but Cynthia had caught her arm as she had raised it to knock on his door earlier. *'No,'* Cynthia had said, shaking her head. *'I'd leave them alone, Tammy. Paul needs some sleep.'*

There was very little traffic coming through the village, and she spotted her father's familiar car winding its way down the road in the distance. She followed it with her eyes and felt excited, like a child waiting for Santa. He was in for a surprise, though; she suspected it would take time for him to adjust to the brand new Tammy. She felt like a brilliant butterfly with still wet wings, newly emerged from her cocoon-like life in Yorkshire. He had set her free when he had reluctantly written out the list of names for her, and only now did she realise how difficult it must have been for him to wave her off last Monday morning, with only the plastic-coated voice of her new sat-nav for company, knowing she was driving headlong into thirty years of rejection and every single one of his worst nightmares, played out in a repetitive loop of lost years.

The sun reflected off the windscreen as he turned into the car park and she couldn't see his face. He reversed carefully into the parking spot beside Paul's car.

***

Pippa had loved music, poetry and the arts. She was always singing, or quoting little sayings or pearls of wisdom that took her fancy. She would coin phrases, turn them around and make them her own. Alan couldn't explain why, but snippets of prose that Pippa had sometimes quoted had been punching holes in his mind for the past week. He had kept hearing random parts of it over and over in his head.

Then, when he and Tammy had argued and she had slammed the phone down on him, it had been unrelenting in its assault and had kept him awake all night as he tossed and turned. Pippa's voice inside his troubled mind had finally bothered him so much that he'd had to go downstairs, switch on the computer and search for the words on the internet so that he could piece together the jigsaw puzzle that was tumbling around in his head.

> *'For everything there is a season,*
> *And a time for every matter under heaven:*
> *A time to be born, and a time to die;*
> *A time to plant, and a time to pluck up what is planted;*
> *A time to kill, and a time to heal;*
> *A time to break down, and a time to build up;*

246

A time to weep, and a time to laugh;
A time to mourn, and a time to dance;
A time to throw away stones, and a time to gather stones together;
A time to embrace, And a time to refrain from embracing;
A time to seek, and a time to lose;
A time to keep, and a time to throw away;
A time to tear, and a time to sew;
A time to keep silence, and a time to speak;
A time to love, and a time to hate,
A time for war, and a time for peace.'

On his computer screen, in the dead of night, the fragmented parts had flooded his entire world with its holistic significance. The words before him had made him realise he had flapped and floundered with his head in the sand for thirty years, hoping that, one day everything would miraculously resolve itself.

At that moment he had known that, for things to change, he would actually have to change them for himself instead of waiting for it to just happen. He knew the time had come to face up to the woodpecker inside his head and go back to Lyverton.

The last four words echoed in his mind.

A time for peace.

It was time. Smooth. Silky. Clean. The rough, gritty parts of the past must be erased from his mind and the beautiful memories savoured and preserved. He had to make things right. He had to face Lyverton, or there would be no point in living. It was now time for the final confrontation and then, and only then — a time for peace.

Alan had been tired, though, when he'd arrived in the village, and more nervous than he had ever been in his life. Then he'd had the shock of seeing Marian Troutman for the first time in over thirty years in a place he had not expected to encounter her and Tammy, relaxed and happy with her new sister and new friends. It had been too much, too soon.

247

He climbed out of his car in the brilliant sunlight, and took off his sunglasses, confident and assured in new denim jeans and plain navy polo shirt, bought hastily from a supermarket in Fawsden. As Tammy walked towards him, he could see in an instant that Lyverton had changed her. He had given her freedom, but she was coming back to him. He hadn't lost her. Sometimes you just had to set someone free in order to keep them close.

Alan suddenly felt like a naughty schoolboy. Tammy wasn't best pleased. She was bearing down on him like a Victorian schoolmistress. He wondered if staying at the Travelodge and keeping his distance until he could get his head around things had been the right thing to do, after all.

"Hello love," he said apologetically. "I'm so sorry about last night. Did you manage to get a good night's sleep?"

"No, I damned well didn't," Tammy complained. "I was worried sick about you, going off like that. Paul and Cynthia have been to Yorkshire and back in the middle the night, thinking you had gone home. I haven't slept a single wink."

Alan frowned. "I sent you a text to tell you I was staying in Fawsden. Didn't you get it?"

"No, I bloody well didn't. Where's your phone?"

Alan extracted his mobile phone from his jeans pocket. Tammy grabbed it from his hand and scrolled down the list of messages. "You sent it to Trevor, you idiot!"

"What?" Alan looked confused. "Why would I send it to Trevor?"

"Well, you did — and look, he's sent you one back asking what the hell you were on about."

"Has he? I didn't hear it go off."

Alan was bewildered. What the heck was Tammy talking about? The last time he had texted his mate, Trevor, who was a plumber, it was to arrange a time for him to come round to fix their broken toilet. He hadn't texted him for weeks.

"No, you wouldn't hear it because you had your phone switched off," Tammy said. "You are a complete prat, Dad."

"It ran out of battery. I had to charge it up overnight."

Tammy read the text again.

248

'I've got my head round things now. I am staying the night at the Travelodge in Fawsden. I am so happy that you have found Marian. Please apologise to everyone for me. It was stupid of me to just take off like that but it was such a shock to see you with her. I'll see you tomorrow morning and tell Marian that I am looking forward to meeting her again. Love from Dad. xxx'

Alan frowned. "Trevor? No I didn't. I couldn't have...." He snatched the phone back from Tammy's hand, and stared at the message on the screen.

Tammy pointed to the name on the display. "Look. Trevor is the next name down from me on your contact list. You scrolled down too far when you sent it and hit the wrong recipient!"

Alan shrugged and smiled through his teeth like a recalcitrant child. "Sorry," he said inadequately. He put his arms around Tammy. "You know I'm useless with the mobile phone. It took me ages to tap in that message."

Tammy punched him on the arm affectionately. "That's because you spell everything properly and put in full stops and commas. You gave me such a fright, Dad. We were all so worried about you."

"It's so good to see you, love, but why on earth didn't you tell me you'd been meeting up with Marian Troutman for the past week? What was the point in keeping it from me?"

"Because I hadn't yet told her I was her sister when you barged in on us."

"She didn't know?"

Tammy shook her head. "No, she didn't. But it took her less than two seconds to put two and two together when you just turned up like that. It was a terrible shock to her."

Alan turned around to get back into his car. "Come on, jump in, let's go and find her ..."

"No need. She's upstairs in my room. She's not left my side since yesterday evening when you stormed off."

They walked together into the Red Lion, through the ancient, heavy ledged-and-braced oak door and up the narrow staircase.

"I thought you'd betrayed me", Alan said. "I thought you'd spent a whole week with your sister without telling me, and I just didn't know what you'd been up to. I imagined you had found everyone in the family, had been welcomed into the fold with open arms and I'd be shut out of your life because they would never be able to forgive me for taking Pippa away from them. There seemed to be no place for me any more."

"Why didn't you tell me you were coming?" Tammy said.

"After we argued the other night, I knew I had to come back to Lyverton," Alan replied. "When you asked me if I was a man or a mouse — well, that just did it! What sort of a father was I, sending my daughter out on a mission your mother and I should have undertaken years ago. Sending her off to sort out things that were nothing to do with her. I was ashamed of myself, Tammy, really ashamed. At the very least I should have come here with you."

"I tried to tell Marian all week," Tammy explained. "But I kept getting interrupted just as I was about to tell her. Then she went off to stay with her auntie in Leicestershire and only came back yesterday morning. She's lovely, Dad."

"I know she is. She was a smashing girl when I knew her. As soon as I'd sent that first text, I regretted it and that's why I sent the next one straightaway, or so I thought I had. I remembered you'd said there was a Travelodge just outside Fawsden, so I went there and booked myself into a room, intending to make my peace with everyone today. I was tired. I'd had hell of a day. The journey was horrendous. I'll apologise to Paul and the landlady and I'll give Paul some money for his petrol and time."

They arrived at Tammy's door, Alan breathless with his hurried explanation. He ran his fingers through his hair three times and cleared his throat with a polite nervousness as Tammy opened the door.

**

As the door creaked open, Tammy didn't know what to say to introduce them to each other. There was something different about Alan. The woodenness had all but disappeared from his gait and he'd looked almost happy in the car park as he had leaned back on his car bonnet, annoyingly relaxed considering all the trouble he'd caused.

"Marian," she said, feeling suddenly like a gatecrasher at her own party. "The wanderer returns."

"Hi Alan," Marian said with a warm, friendly smile.

"Hi. Long time, no see."

Tammy shut the door behind her and leaned on it. Marian was fifty again. She looked exactly like her age, even though she had borrowed some of Tammy's clothes. She had showered, her hair was still damp and she wore no make-up, her fresh face intensifying the vulnerability in the atmosphere. The three of them stared at each other and the poignancy of the moment was mutually embarrassing. Alan extended his hand and Marian took it in a cordial shake.

"It is, isn't it? Too long," she replied with another smile.

"How are you?"

"Fine. You?"

"Fine."

Silence.

Tammy screwed up her face, looked up at the ceiling and sighed. Her father could be such a nerd at times and never more so than now, dressed in cheap, plain supermarket clothes, making polite small talk with his old girlfriend. She looked from her father to Marian and then back again before disappearing into the bathroom, glad to escape from the artificial, stilted atmosphere.

She turned on the shower and the hiss of water was somehow satisfying. The heavy silence coming from her room was unbearable and she just wanted to make as much noise as she could to drown it out.

Tammy peeped through the crack in the door.

Marian and Alan were standing, still and quiet. They had their arms entwined around each other and Tammy could see Marian's face, buried in the crook of Alan's neck. She had her eyes closed. Was it really going to be possible to mend her shattered family?

***

Tammy wandered barefoot along the landing with a towel wrapped around her wet hair. She could hear Cynthia's music playing behind her front door, so she knocked tentatively. Cynthia opened it with a

251

smile.

"Tammy my dear. Come on in."

"Have you had some sleep?" Tammy asked.

Cynthia wrinkled her nose. "I'm not really tired. I slept for a couple of hours in the car at the service station, and then slept most of the way back. Paul's much more tired than I am. What's happening with your dad? I saw he was back."

"Dad's really sorry about last night. After he sent me the first text, he immediately sent me another, apologising to everyone and telling me he was staying at the Travelodge, but he sent it to Trevor, his mate, instead of me. He hit the wrong recipient. Idiot! And then his phone ran out of charge."

"So Paul and I have been to Yorkshire and back, and you've been up all night worrying, for nothing?"

"Yep." Tammy rolled her eyes. "Sorry, Cynthia."

"Where is he now?"

"With Marian. The Head Teacher at the school has given her the day off on account of the unusual circumstances of finding herself with a long-lost sister. I've left them in my room. I had a quick shower, made them a cup of tea and then got out as fast as I could. I felt like an intruder — and I really didn't want to listen to what they had to say to each other."

"Probably for the best," Cynthia speculated. "As long as they're not at each other's throats."

"No, quite the opposite, actually. They're really pleased to see each other, I think, now they've both got over the shock."

"Actually, sit down, hen. It wasn't a complete waste of time going off gallivanting to Yorkshire with Paul."

"Why?"

"Because, my dear Tammy, fate dealt Paul a compassionate hand in giving him breathing space last night."

"How?"

"He needed to talk, Tammy. He desperately needed some time out to talk to someone who wasn't his parents, wasn't Claire and wasn't you. We talked things through while we were driving to Yorkshire and back."

"What did he say?"

"I can't betray his confidence, but I think the journey might have helped him put things into perspective. He is such a nice boy, you know. So caring. I just hope he's going to be all right. I'm really fond of him."

"Do you think he'll change his mind about going ahead with his marriage?"

Cynthia shook her head. "No, Tammy, he won't. He's made up his mind. He's going to go ahead and marry Claire and bring Lewis up as his own child. I think he's finally realised that she made just one mistake that was totally out of character. If she hadn't got pregnant, he would probably have never even known about it. He accepts Claire's decision not to abort her baby and actually admires her for the huge sacrifices she has made for Lewis and her honesty in not letting him think the baby was his."

For two or three glorious seconds Tammy had clung to a filament of hope that Paul was about to change his mind. Now she knew there was none.

No chance at all.

CHAPTER TWENTY-EIGHT

12.00 noon

Tammy found herself with nowhere to go.

After drying her hair in Cynthia's flat and spending a pleasant hour chatting, she stood on the landing, her towel draped over her arm, undecided as to what to do with herself.

"I'm really sorry, but I have to go out," said Cynthia. "I've got an appointment at the dentist, but I'd much rather stay here with you."

Tammy needed to get some shoes out of her room but was reluctant to intrude on her father and Marian. She looked down at her bare feet, wriggled her toes and took a deep breath before knocking on the door. She didn't wait for an answer. It *was* her room, after all.

Marian was sitting cross-legged on the bed, surrounded by dozens of torn-open envelopes, birthday cards of various sizes and letters written on blue paper, white paper, a notelet with a red rose on the front and even, Tammy noticed, a page torn out of one of her childhood notepads with a Winnie the Pooh motif in the corner. She looked incredibly sad and gloriously happy all at the same time. She twinkled like a diamond, only age was reflected off the multiple facets, not light. She was twenty, fifty, sixty, thirty, seventy, all at the same time. Her eyes were wet with happy tears, sad tears, tears of despair and tears of frustration and she was laughing and crying simultaneously. Alan was sitting in the chair, animated and alive for the first time in almost two years, listening intently to Marian pouring her life out of her heart. He was nodding and agreeing with her. Compassion radiated a long-forgotten warmth from within him and Tammy knew that, finally, they both had found someone who understood exactly what it was like to be in an age gap relationship and who, too, had suffered the pain of losing their soul-mate. How strange it was that they were ex-boyfriend and girlfriend. Did Marian still think of her father as a lover? Could it be that fate would stick back together that which had become unstuck, and would Alan and Marian connect at exactly the point their lives deviated over thirty years ago, when they had writhed around in the back of a steamed-up red Mini Clubman on Marian's eighteenth birthday? Would they fall in love? If they did, where would that leave Tammy?

"Tammy," they said in unison. "Are you okay?"

"I'm fine," Tammy replied, unable to hide the glorious landscape of pleasure on her face that her dad and sister were getting on so well; it masked the seed of dread that was germinating inside her that they would end up getting on a little too well.

"I'm going downstairs for some lunch" Tammy announced. "I've just come back for my shoes."

Was it her imagination or did she see a look of relief on their faces that she was not about to interrupt their cosy trip down memory lane.

Once she had thrust her feet into her flip flops and scooped up her handbag, she wandered down the stairs to the bar. She was a displaced person; a misplaced person. Paul was with Claire, their room was in silence and Tammy didn't want to think about them. Her dad was with Marian in some sort of weird Mobius strip of reconciliation, the two ends reconnected after flapping in the breeze for thirty years, and Cynthia was still at the dental surgery.

Tammy tried to project her mind into the future, but it was just a blank space. Was it legal for a man to marry his dead wife's daughter? Even if it wasn't legal, they would live together. They were not related, after all. Her father would whirl and twirl around the room with her sister, old songs from the 1970s would be playing in the background and they'd fall in a heap on the sofa. He would kiss her and love her, and Pippa's memory would fade to a distant star in a blackened sky.

Tammy sat at the same table in the alcove where, just a week ago, she had begun the helter-skelter journey of finding her roots. She gazed out of the window at the place where the teenagers had stood, smiling and waving at her. She remembered how she had burst into tears at the sight of the woman who was the same age as her mother, laughing and joking with her family over a red glace cherry. She looked at the cold, unfeeling jukebox in the corner and recalled how it had belted out *Don't go Breaking my Heart* as if it was an annoying television jingle, but the memories it had evoked within her had snaked their way into her soul and made her somehow stronger.

255

"Hi Tammy," Daniel called out from the corridor. "Cynthia tells me that all's well that ends well." He poked his head around the door and grinned at her.

"Thank you for last night, Daniel. You were a little star, driving round the countryside looking for my dad when he took off."

"That's cool," he said. "No worries. Oh, by the way, I meant to tell you yesterday, you're invited to Sophie's house this afternoon at two o'clock if you want to go. Soph's Auntie Wendy will be there — you know — old Philip Staverley's niece?"

"Oh, yes. That would be fascinating. I think I'll go if I can stay awake long enough. I need to give my dad and my sister some time to get to know each other again."

"Shall I text her and tell her you'll be there?"

"Yes, do that. Tell her thanks."

Tammy looked at her watch: it was just coming up to twelve thirty. She had one and a half hours to kill. From the cosy picture of her father and Marian drinking tea and reminiscing in her room, she thought they would be talking for a while yet. Now the Mobius strip had reconnected, she felt apprehensive and yet excited about her rapidly changing life.

**

They didn't see Tammy, sitting in the bar, but she could see them out of the window. They were sitting in the beer garden, deep in conversation. They were giving her no clues as they relaxed in the early afternoon sun, enjoying a cool drink in the colourful, fragrant garden. Paul smiled a lot, but didn't laugh. Claire laughed occasionally, loud enough for Tammy to hear. Then Tammy watched as Claire pulled a mobile phone out of her handbag and made a phone call.

Tammy leaned forwards so she could get a better view of them, her chin cupped in her hand and her elbow resting on the table. She wondered who Claire was ringing? Whoever it was, she was happy to be speaking to them. Her free hand was busy with gestures and her body language portrayed someone who was excited and elated. She had got her man back and she was full of exhilarated delight. Her face was flushed and, even at distance, Tammy could see the expression in her eyes as she chatted into her mobile phone.

Tammy imagined she was talking to Paul's mother, Rosemary, who, sitting in her living room in Norfolk, was beside herself with relief and pleasure that her precious son had come back to her. Not in person, because they were intending to settle in Lyverton, but he had come back to her emotionally. He was not lost any more. He was her son again: the umbilical cord mended and connected so that you couldn't even see the join. She imagined Keith Pepper standing beside her, taking the phone from her hand, impatient to tell Claire how he had taken Lewis for a walk along the seafront, and how he had dipped his little toes in the North Sea for the very first time. She imagined the two black Labradors, Zak and Barney, running around in the garden, playing with their ball and squeaky toys. It was a scene she would never be a part of now, and the strong sense of belonging she had felt in the company of Paul's parents on Friday only served to intensify her acute, painful feelings of loss.

Tammy sighed and leaned back in her chair. She didn't want to look any more. She just couldn't bear to watch.

She remembered a half-finished, tatty, pocket book of Sudoku in her handbag and pulled it out, along with a stubby pencil. "Daniel," she called out. "I'll have a ham salad and chips before I go to Sophie's."

"Coming up," he said, and wrote out the order for the kitchen staff to prepare.

Tammy wandered over to the jukebox to put on some music: not songs that would remind her of her childhood, but songs that reminded her of her teenage years and fun times and, as an afterthought, she added some that were bang up to date. Soon, she was engrossed in her puzzle, enjoying the music and feeling hungrier by the minute.

She didn't see someone walk over to her until they were right beside her table.

"That square's a nine," said Paul's deep voice in her ear, and his finger pointed to an empty square in her Sudoku puzzle.

Tammy looked up, startled and surprised and blushed like a schoolgirl. He bent down to study the grid and his smiling face was so close to hers she could see individual hairs of stubble around the dimple in his chin. Her heart did a somersault and then pounded behind her breastbone.

"Hi. Thanks. How are you? Did you manage to get some sleep?" she said as she inserted a number nine into the appropriate square.

"Oh yes. We've only just got up."

"Thanks, Paul, for last night. I'm really sorry about everything and especially about your wasted journey."

"I saw that he's back."

"Yes. He's okay. It was apparently the shock of seeing me with Marian that made him leave. He texted me before you left for Yorkshire to say he was staying at the Travelodge in Fawsden, but sent it to his friend Trevor instead of me by mistake."

Paul rolled his eyes and laughed out loud. "I've done that before. It's easily done."

"So have I — but don't tell Dad that!"

"Actually," Paul added, "Cynthia told me he was back safely. He's with Marian now, isn't he?"

Tammy nodded and grimaced. "They're getting on like a house on fire."

"Oh, that's good then." Paul pulled a face, reading Tammy's mind. "Or is it?"

Tammy shrugged. Paul could obviously see through her happy mask into the triangular-shaped jumble of mixed feelings in her head. He was the only other person, apart from Davey, the school caretaker, who knew what Marian had done with her father in the back of a red Mini Clubman over thirty years ago.

"Oh well, never mind. As long we keep them well away from red Minis," Paul joked in an effort to make Tammy laugh.

Tammy began to chuckle. "Don't ... please ..."

They both roared with laughter at the thought.

"Can you imagine it?" spluttered Paul.

"No! And I don't want to have to think about it."

They were giggling and laughing like sixteen-year-olds and Tammy saw the dark curtains lift in Paul's eyes as they twinkled, reflecting the light from the window. He looked straight at her. There really was no hiding place for her strong feelings for him, so she tried to change the subject, but he got in first.

"Can I get you a drink to say thank you?" he eventually said softly.

"I should be thanking *you* for chasing my dad half way across the country ..."

"Oh, no, believe me Tammy. I should be thanking *you*. For helping me sort my life out. If it wasn't for your moral support, I'd never have got my family back."

Tammy looked up at him again, and in his place saw the bald-headed old man with age spots splattered over his head. She imagined him scratching it and saying: *'I don't know what happened to her and I can't remember her name, but if it wasn't for her we'd probably never have got back together.'* The tunes on the car radio on Friday and the one that was playing on the jukebox at that very moment would be playing at his and Claire's golden wedding anniversary celebrations, and they would lever up some more fond memories, added to those of Paul and Tammy walking carefree along the beach on Friday. He would remember her, and the way she looked right at that very moment, and in some other place, in fifty years' time, she would be seventy-seven and she would be thinking of him too.

"I really do wish you both the very best of luck," Tammy said genuinely. "I hope you'll have a long and happy life together."

Paul looked at her. The smile died incrementally in his eyes, and the top of his cheek twitched, just a couple of times. He swallowed and his voice splintered.

"Thank you Tammy. And I wish you the very best of luck, too."

***

Feeling better now she had eaten a proper meal, Tammy made her way to Sophie's house. It was a gloriously sunny day and the familiar smell of hawthorn that pervaded the village mingled with wafts of honeysuckle and rhododendrons as she passed by neatly tended gardens. The sun was warm on her back as the buzz and whirr of various lawnmowers and hedge cutters competed with each other, a dog barked somewhere and it felt like summer.

She was speaking into her mobile phone as she walked along.

"… no, I don't mind at all. You and Marian have a nice meal in the bar, and I'll join you there about four o'clock."

"I feel really bad about neglecting you — and so does Maz," Alan said.

There. She just knew it! He had called her Maz years ago. He was acting like he was nineteen again, picking up where he left off.

"Tell her I'm going to Sophie's to find out about the twins and I'll speak to her later."

"To Sophie's? The twins?"

"The Staverley twins — Alice Thompson's companions — I told you about them on Saturday night on the phone," Tammy explained. "But then you yelled at me that I should be researching our own family tree and not that of complete strangers …"

"Oh, yes. I remember," Alan interrupted. "Oh well, at least you're not on your own and have got something to do. See you at four, then."

"Bye Dad. Love you. See you soon."

CHAPTER TWENTY-NINE

2.00 pm

Philip Staverley's niece, Wendy, was indeed the elegant, mature lady Tammy had watched getting out of the silver Range Rover at Alice Thompson's funeral last Tuesday. She held out her refined hand on a limp wrist and smiled at Tammy.

"I'm *sooo* pleased to meet you, Miss Hargreaves. I hear you have exciting news."

Tammy couldn't think what she meant for a moment. She hadn't done any more research on either Alice or the Staverley twins since Saturday, when she was at the care home in Fawsden with Sophie and her mother.

"Daniel told us this morning about you and Marian Troutman being long-lost sisters. Is that right?" Wendy gushed.

Daniel had struck again. It would now be all round the village that she was Marian Troutman's secret sister. Still, Tammy thought, at least it was the truth this time.

"Yes, we are. My mother was Tony Troutman's first wife ..."

Wendy threw her hands in the air before clasping her face in exaggerated surprise. "Phyllis! Don't tell me you're Phyllis's daughter! Oh my word, I can see it now! You are *so* like her. How is she? I haven't seen Phyll for years and years. Ever since she ... well ... I mean, you've only got to take one look at Tony Troutman to understand why she did it. And the lad she went off with *was* rather handsome in a foppish kind of way ..."

Tammy cut her off. "My mother died."

Wendy blinked furiously and her hand flew to her mouth.

"When was that? I didn't know. I'm *so* sorry, dear."

"It was two years ago. She had cancer. I came to Lyverton to find my sister."

"So you're not really a writer then?"

"Well, yes, I am, or rather I will be. I'm going to write Alice's life story. I want to do it because she had no family and accidentally attending someone's funeral was such an odd thing to happen. Then I found out she used to work at the hospital in Fawsden with my mother."

"Yes, she did, Tammy. She and your mother were great friends back in the 1960s. I think that's lovely — *so* exciting. Alice was such a marvellous woman. Anyway, I have lots of interesting things to tell you. I've had to be very *boring* and keep some old secrets while Alice was alive, and now she's gone I can reveal all. You see my mother, Polly, knew *everything*." Wendy flung her head back and her arms out in a theatrical pose, almost knocking a tea tray out of Sophie's mother's hands.

"Knew everything? What do you mean?"

"I've been itching to tell my mother's secret for years, but she swore me to secrecy while Alice was still alive."

"Your mother's secret? Your mother was Polly-Anne Staverley, wasn't she? The eldest daughter of Reverend Staverley?"

"Yes. She was a writer, too, you know. She wrote fifteen historical novels."

"Really? Did she by any chance write as Margaret Regent?"

"Yes, she wrote under several names. Margaret Regent was only one of them. I think it was her pen name for a women's magazine, if I remember rightly."

"It was! I have some of them in Alice's box. That must be why she kept them," said Tammy in admiration.

"Have you heard of Petra Pointelle?" Wendy said.

"Petra Pointelle. Yes, I have. My mother used to read all her books. She said she once knew the author ... oh, of course, she would have done when she lived here as a child. She would have known she was really Polly-Anne Staverley. And you have twin sisters, don't you? Susie and Sally?"

Wendy shook her head. "No, they weren't real; they were made up for the Hesitant Housewife column."

"What did your father — Polly's husband — do for a living, Wendy?" Tammy asked.

"My father was a vicar — not at the village church, though. I grew up in Somerset. My mother fell *madly* in love with a very serious young curate at my grandfather's church when she was only fifteen and eventually, when she was a little older, she managed to make him fall in love with her, married him, dragged him off to Somerset and became a vicar's wife herself. She was such a girl, was my mother. *Terribly* eccentric. My father, in contrast, was very serious and clever man. She based the fictitious twins on me and wrote about the dreadfully naughty things I used to get up to. She used to say I was double trouble. I can't *imagine* why!"

Tammy almost wanted to laugh out loud at the thought of Polly-Anne Staverley's long-suffering, straight-laced husband as he struggled to cope with his bubbly, eccentric wife and their equally extrovert daughter. It was almost another story in itself.

"Now, let me tell you my mother's story."

Tammy took a notepad and pen out of her bag.

"One day, when my mother was just a little girl, Jessie Smith and Harry Thompson turned up at the vicarage in Lyverton. My grandfather was the rector of the church — as you know. Jessie was only thirteen. It was dawn on the morning of midsummer's day in 1910 and my mother was laying the table for breakfast. Jessie fainted on the doorstep into my grandfather's arms and it was soon apparent that she was on the point of giving birth."

"Giving birth!" Sophie's mother, Sophie and Tammy all said in shocked unison.

"Yes — by the way — no one on earth knows any of this," Wendy said, looking round at Sophie and her mother who, by then, were hanging onto her every word. She waggled her finger at Tammy and her voice fell to a whisper. 'It was a *terribly* dark secret we shared, just my mother and I, but now poor Alice is gone, there's no reason why *you* can't tell the story, Tammy. The story deserves to be told. It's a wonderful heart-warming story. My mother was always rather galled that she couldn't be the one to tell it. It was too close to home, you see?

"My grandmother — the Reverend's wife — had coincidentally given birth just a few hours earlier, and my Great Aunt Gwen — my mother's auntie — was there because she was a midwife. People didn't go to hospital to have a baby in those days. They usually gave birth at home. Anyhow, Great Aunt Gwen delivered Jessie's baby just minutes after they turned up on the doorstep. It was a little girl."

"Jessie had a *baby*. At thirteen?" Sophie said with an incredulous, unbelieving look on her face. "In 1910?"

Tammy couldn't quite believe what she was hearing. Her high opinion of Harry Thompson took a serious nose-dive, like a World War One Tiger Moth in trouble.

"Yes. It was *very* premature. It was really more of a miscarriage, and the baby only weighed about two pounds."

Wendy closed her eyes momentarily and paused for effect. She leaned forwards and her eyes panned slowly from Tammy, to Sophie's mother and rested finally on Sophie's spellbound face. Her voice fell to a conspiratorial whisper.

"Great Aunt Gwen cast the baby aside; she thought it was dead. But it moved, and my mother picked it up. Great Aunt Gwen was going to smother it with a cushion to save it from suffering … apparently they did that with hopelessly premature babies in the olden days … but my mother screamed out: *Nooooooo* …." Everyone jumped as Wendy's voice shrilled out, at least thirty decibels louder.

"My mother was horrified beyond belief at what she was about to witness. She had nightmares about it for years and years," Wendy continued.

"So, are you saying that it was Jessie's baby that Harry tried to save in the incubator and not one of the Staverley twins, after all?" Sophie said.

Tammy scribbled on her notepad and then looked up at Wendy for an answer.

"There *were* no Staverley twins," Wendy said. "My grandmother had only one baby that day: the other one was *Jessie's* baby."

The three of them stared at Wendy in silence. She nodded at them knowingly. "And no one ever knew. Until now."

"It's a wonder Harry didn't get prosecuted for getting Jessie pregnant at thirteen," Sophie said with a disgusted look on her face. "He was nothing but a paedophile."

Wendy shook her head and waggled her finger. "No, no, no, Sophie, my dear! You shouldn't jump to conclusions. It wasn't *Harry's* baby. Jessie was raped by one of the Earl of Fawsden's sons: no-one believed her though — least of all her parents. Everyone thought it was really Harry's baby and so they ran away together. My mother found out later that it was Lord Frederick De Montpelier who'd raped Jessie. He had attacked her in his stables. *Terribly* frightening it was for poor Jessie. A horse reared up and its hooves crashed down just inches from her face while she was being attacked. She was almost killed in that stable. She suffered from dreadful nightmares for the rest of her life, according to my mother. Oh, they were great friends were Jessie and my mother. Do you know, at Jessie's funeral my mother collapsed at the graveside, she was so overcome with grief? My mother always said that Jessie Thompson was the best friend she ever had in all her life."

The room blurred in Tammy's vision, and she was conscious of over-breathing again. The tiredness that had been prowling around her head all day became heavy and dark, and she jerked her head upwards. It felt as if she was caught in cross currents in a swirling sea, unable to get back to shore.

"Oh my giddy aunt," she heard Wendy say. "She's gone as white as the driven snow."

When Tammy recovered her composure, she explained her funny turn away by explaining that she had been up all night, talking to Marian. What she didn't mention, though, was about her dream. She didn't tell them that she knew exactly how much Jessie had suffered; she didn't tell them about the terror and pain of her rape, or how she had smelled the horse's breath, Frederick's cigar and whisky breath and wriggled frantically around in straw and horse manure as she tried to get away. She kept quiet about the torn knickers, the horse rearing up and its hooves crashing down beside her face and being hit on the back of her head. Tammy could have revealed the rapist was a man called 'Frederick', had Wendy not mentioned it first. She could also tell Wendy something she didn't know. She could have told her that on the day Jessie had been raped, Frederick had brought back a rare albino Jacobin cuckoo from Kenya. She could have revealed that Jessie had fallen against the cage when she'd tried to escape and the white cuckoo had flown off into the countryside.

"Shall I go on?" Wendy asked.

Tammy nodded. "I'm all right now."

"No one expected the baby to survive, even my grandfather thought the poor little lamb would die because she was so premature."

Tammy shakily asked one more question. Everything was just too spooky to explain away with logical explanations. Her promise to her dying mother and her quest to find her sister had turned into something else entirely, something urgent and vital. All her life Tammy had felt as if she had been waiting for something — a point in her life where she could begin to live properly. On the first night in Lyverton, as she had sat sipping her drink by the window, and had watched the strange children, she had felt a warming feeling, deep inside. Over and over again during the last week, the feeling washed over her, making her feel alive and loved. Now the feeling was so strong, she almost wanted to jump up and down with joy.

"Which Staverley twin was Jessie's baby?" she said, suddenly desperate to know. Was it Lucy-Joy or was it Emily-Rose?"

Wendy shook her head. "I don't know, my dear. That's just it — my mother would never, ever tell — she said she had sworn on the Bible to keep it a secret. She told me it didn't matter anyway. I always thought it was Lucy, though, because she lived with Alice. They were so close to each other. I suppose that would have been a bit of a fairy-tale ending, but the truth was Alice was just as close to Emily-Rose. None of them married because they were content just to have each other and their wonderful careers."

"Auntie Wendy, are you sure you're not making all this up?"

Wendy spread her hand over her heart, closed her eyes momentarily and then fluttered her eyelashes indignantly. "Sophie my dear, I know I take after my mother in that I have the most *fabulous* imagination, but I cross my heart and hope to die that I have *never* told this story to a living soul. Now poor Alice has gone, the story can be told and who better to tell it than the daughter of one of my closest friends, who just *happens* to be a writer?"

Tammy stared at Wendy. She wouldn't have been a close friend of Pippa's. Her mother would have found her far too flamboyant and extrovert for her liking. Pippa had been down to earth, casting aside

266

glamour and elegance with a dismissive toss of her hand. She hadn't worn make up, or lots of jewellery, and preferred her garden and a good book to socialising with other women and indulging in a hectic social life. Unlike most women married to a much younger man, Pippa had steadfastly remained true to herself, had acted her age and had always been supremely confident in Alan's love for her. She'd had no need to turn into someone twenty years younger. She wouldn't have been close friends with Wendy. Tammy just knew.

"Why all the secrecy, though?" Sophie asked, interrupting Tammy's thoughts. "What was the point of keeping it all such a big secret?"

Wendy leaned forwards. "Because my grandfather — the vicar — did something very, very wrong. He could have lost his job, his home, everything."

"What?" chorused Tammy, Sophie and her mother, intrigued.

"My grandfather was a dedicated family man, but he was also a man of the cloth and a law-abiding pillar of the community. He would never deliberately have broken the law. No one expected Jessie's baby girl to live, least of all my grandfather. Jessie, Harry and my grandparents made a snap decision on the spur of the moment because they were convinced the baby was about to die."

"What did they decide?" Tammy said. "And how was it wrong?"

"They decided to baptise and register both babies as twins. My mother always said it was a decision my grandfather made as a father and a man. It was a human decision my parents and Harry and Jessie made together to give this tragic, tiny baby girl a proper family for the brief time she was alive and also access to the best possible medical care to alleviate her suffering. Think about it. The poor little soul was the product of an evil act — a rape. They all thought it would be the best thing they could do for her in the circumstances because she most certainly wouldn't live more than a few days at most. They thought no one would ever know the truth. Jessie wanted it, too. It meant she could help take care of and love her baby in peaceful, secure surroundings. She wanted to make the most of her brief time as a mother to her tiny daughter. But, you see, it was illegal. Because the baby lived against all the odds, my grandfather was put in a dreadfully untenable situation. He could have been prosecuted for registering the

267

birth falsely, and it would have *ruined* his career."

Tammy bit her lip at the weight of responsibility on her shoulders. She just *had* to learn how to write properly now because the story of the baby's survival against all the odds was so beautiful, it deserved to be told.

"So *that's* why they kept it all a secret," Tammy said. "I think I understand, now. But did Alice ever know which of them was really her sister?"

Wendy shook her head. "I don't think so. Alice was Jessie and Harry's only child. As it became obvious that the baby would live, my grandfather knew he had to take responsibility for Jessie and Harry too. He felt it was a true miracle the baby had survived and God had delivered Jessie, Harry and the tiny baby right into his hands to care for. That's why the Thompsons became so much a part of the Staverley family."

"Wendy," Tammy interrupted, "if Polly-Anne was a writer, why didn't *she* tell the story herself? She could have used different names, a different setting, or even a different period in history."

"She *so* wanted to tell it, Tammy. But while Alice was alive, no one could tell it, could they? Alice didn't know one of the twins was her half-sister, let alone of royal blood. My mother told me the secret because she didn't want it to die with her, but she wouldn't tell me which of the twins was Jessie's child. She said it wouldn't be right, because she had sworn on the bible."

Before Tammy left Sophie's house and said goodbye to Wendy, she learned more of how Emily-Rose Staverley had travelled the world, living amongst the under-privileged, the poor and the destitute. As well as working in the slums of India, she had taught English to African children and helped set up hospitals and medical centres where mass vaccination programmes were to be undertaken. Every two or three years she would return to Lyverton for a while. She'd come home to Alice and Lucy, and the three ladies would throw a party in their garden for their family and friends. Everyone would drink home-made elderflower, parsnip and rhubarb wine, eat fresh cream scones with delicious perfectly-made gooseberry jam and they would sing and dance the night away under an amethyst and butterscotch sky as a perfect summer evening turned to dusk.

Emily-Rose or Lucy-Joy. Which one of them was Jessie's baby? There must be a clue somewhere. Tammy just had to find it — it was absolutely crucial to the story. But she was certain of two things that Wendy didn't know. The first thing she knew was that Alice Thompson *had* known which of her two companions was really her half-sister. She must have done because second thing Tammy instinctively knew was that the few strands of blonde hair nestled in Jessie's golden locket had belonged to her premature baby. Tammy closed her eyes and imagined Jessie taking a pair of scissors and carefully snipping the lock of hair from her secret daughter's head, tying it securely with a piece of cotton and then placing it in her locket, to hold close to her heart every single day of her life.

***

As Tammy walked wearily around the side of the Red Lion, squinting against the afternoon sun, she heard laughter and jollity and wondered what was going on in the beer garden. As she peeped through the rose arbour she realised that everyone she knew in Lyverton was in the garden. They had pulled two tables together and sat drinking wine and cider under brightly coloured red and green parasols. Her father sat in the midst of them, laughing and joking and, for the first time in two years, relaxed and enjoying the company of other people.

"Here she comes," they all chorused.

"Tammy … whoo hoo." Cynthia called and waved to her. "Over here — in the garden."

Tammy's face broke out into a smile at the fantastic welcome, even though she was suffering from almost total exhaustion and just wanted to go to bed for a nap, having been up all night. She looked at her watch. It was almost four thirty.

Cynthia was sitting alongside Alan, Claire was lying on a cushion on a wooden sun-lounger, her bare feet in Paul's lap as he sat on the end, and Marian was deep in conversation with Daniel. Marjorie from the tea shop was there too, as was Davey, the school caretaker, and his wife, who were both thrilled to be reunited with their old friend, Alan.

Tammy opened the rustic gate to the garden with a squeak.

269

"Come on. We've all been waiting for you," Alan said proudly, as he pulled up an empty chair for her, and, before she could even be asked, Paul had leapt up to fetch her a drink.

Before Tammy wilted completely, she told everyone about the story of the Staverley twins, and how one of them was really Jessie's baby, saved from a certain death by the love of the Staverley family and Harry's home-made incubator. She told them that Jessie was raped in a stable by Frederick De Montpelier, and wanted to say about the rare, white cuckoo, but she didn't because that was part of her dream (which she wouldn't repeat to a living soul, because they would think she was crazy). It wasn't long before Tammy stopped talking and just listened to other people's conversations, her head resting on her crossed arms on the table. She shut her eyes.

"Tammy, come and lie down on here," she heard Claire say, and somehow found herself sinking gratefully into the warm, squidgy cushion of the sun lounger and then thankfully into a deep, welcome sleep.

CHAPTER THIRTY

9.30 pm

Alan and Cynthia sat in the beer garden, alone, side by side on a wooden bench seat, their heads close together, sharing a bottle of wine. Everyone else had gone, but they hadn't wanted to leave Tammy alone, asleep in the garden, and so they had covered her with a tartan blanket, opened another bottle, and waited for her to wake up.

Tammy opened her eyes to the deep blue sky of approaching darkness, the sound of a lone blackbird and the smell of food wafting into the garden from the pub kitchen, which made her suddenly hungry. Alan and Cynthia stopped talking as Tammy stirred on the sun lounger. She had been asleep for nearly five hours. She closed her eyes again and Cynthia and Alan resumed their conversation, in low voices, thinking Tammy was still asleep.

"I eventually did get over losing my Rabbie," Cynthia murmured. "But it was a long, long time, Alan. He was the love of my life. I felt I couldn't carry on without him, too. Who found you?"

"My friend, Colin. He followed me there," Alan said quietly.

"Oh, you poor, poor man. You must have been in the depths of despair to even think of it. What would have become of Tammy?"

"I thought she'd be okay, because Brenda and Colin would look out for her. They are like family anyway ..."

On the sun lounger, with her eyes still closed, Tammy was shocked. Had her father tried to take his own life? This was dreadful: she hadn't known. She wondered if it had been on that Saturday when he'd disappeared to Ilkley Moor on his own. And Brenda and Colin weren't family. Brenda had been Pippa's best friend. They had their own family; a grown-up son and daughter and grandchildren. There wouldn't have been room in their hearts for Tammy too. Not properly.

"Don't get me wrong, Alan. I do understand how dreadful you must have felt when Pippa died. It's a lonely old life, isn't it, when you've shared so many years together and then it's gone in the blinking of an eye. You can't quite believe you'll never see them again — well, not in this life, anyway."

There were a few minutes of silence and Tammy churned the revelation over in her head, thinking about the day when Alan had stormed off when *Close to You* by the Carpenters was playing on the television. She was just about to open her eyes when Cynthia spoke again.

"Alan. I know you'll think this completely presumptuous of me, but I have a spare bedroom in my flat. If you'd like to stay at the pub with Tammy until you go back to Yorkshire, you'd be most welcome. And to be perfectly honest, it would be lovely to have some company for a change."

"You must let me pay."

Cynthia sighed. "I wasn't thinking of any payment, but if you insist you can give me something towards food and stuff. To be honest with you, I've grown really fond of your Tammy over the last week, and I do have an ulterior motive. I know we hardly know each other, but I want us all to stay friends — both of you, if you'll have me. I'd love Tammy to come and stay with me now and again. I don't have any family of my own. She is such a lovely girl. You're very, very lucky to have her, Alan."

Her father's voice was still low. Tammy had to concentrate hard to hear him properly.

"I know that. I feel so bad about letting her come to Lyverton on her own. I should have come with her ..."

Cynthia cut in. "No, you did *exactly* the right thing. Tammy is a grown woman now, and you can't spend the rest of your life protecting her. You have to let her live her own life. You know what they say — you have to let someone go to keep them."

"I know. I've been so silly about Tammy since Pippa died. She's the light of my life, Cynthia. But I still think I should have paved the way — prepared the ground a little? I could have come here first and done all the hard bits. The thing is — and I've never even thought of this before — I didn't really have to make any difficult decisions about our life, other than to make sure I passed my exams and succeeded in my job so that I could provide for us all. When Pippa died I was somehow catapulted back to being nineteen again, and unsure of what to do next

272

or how to cope with life without her, especially where Tammy was concerned."

"Well, perhaps. But it's done now and everything is turning out just fine. You are a good man, Alan. Stop worrying and enjoy the rest of your time in Lyverton. When do you have to go back to Yorkshire?"

"I thought perhaps on Thursday. I've booked the dog into boarding kennels until Friday lunchtime, so I must be back by then."

There was another silence and Tammy opened her eyes, which were full of tears as, finally, she came to terms with her past. Alan and Cynthia were relaxed, completely at ease with each other. She closed her eyes again and savoured the warm glow that spread through her. She was loved. She was wanted. And above all, she belonged.

***

"Everyone else seems to be taking time off work around here," Cynthia announced as she bustled around her flat playing the perfect hostess. "So I have taken the night off too, in lieu of my birthday, which was six weeks ago."

Alan sat on Cynthia's sofa, sandwiched between Tammy and Marian, watching Cynthia pour the drinks. He had never met anyone quite like her. The hours they had spent together in the beer garden earlier had been like smothering himself in a soothing, healing balm as she had listened to his sorry tale of his attempted suicide a year ago, when he'd been unable to cope with the thought of spending the rest of his life without Pippa. She had poured her heart out about Rabbie, too, and her intense disappointment about never being able to have children.

It had been a strange sort of day, he thought to himself. Firstly, he and Marian had been surprised to discover that, despite the intervening years, they could just pick up their friendship as if nothing had happened. He instantly felt comfortable in her presence. Years ago, he had secretly sought to find similarities between Marian and Tammy and had found none. Tammy had been the image of Pippa, whereas Marian was dark, like Tony Troutman. But that morning, as he had sat in Tammy's room with Marian, watching her pore over Pippa's cards and letters, he could see so much of a likeness between them it had

273

caused a physical pain of regret that he and Pippa had kept them apart. They had been so, so wrong.

Then, in an afternoon of cathartic release, he had discovered the beautiful woman that was Cynthia McLaughlin. Everything about her was big, bright, fragrant and welcoming, like a lush, verdant oasis in the middle of a dry desert. He'd watched, mesmerised at her beaming smile, her florid, delicately flushed cheeks and her twinkling, kind eyes as they had talked. He'd felt a welcome sense of cleansing as Cynthia had gently brushed away the cobwebs of guilt at wanting to live again without Pippa, and had agreed to her suggestion that they should have a fun day out together that didn't involve old ruins or cathedrals. They should both enjoy themselves, she had said, with absolutely no inhibitions or backward glances at the past allowed.

"So how old are you then, Cynthia?" Marian asked boldly.

Cynthia brought the drinks over on a tray and rattled them onto the coffee table.

"I'm fifty …er …" she said, biting her lip. She sighed and chuckled. "Och Marian, I always was such a bad liar — I'm fifty-three," she said.

Alan grinned at her and Cynthia read his mind.

"I already know you're fifty, Alan Hargreaves. Tammy told me. When we go to the seaside tomorrow you can be my toy boy!"

"The seaside?" Tammy said, surprised.

Alan nodded and grinned again. It made him look like a naughty schoolboy. "I hope you don't mind, Tammy."

Tammy shook her head, hardly believing her ears. Her dad appeared to have a date.

"Alan. Can I ask you a question?" Marian said, changing the uncomfortable subject. "I know you changed your name, but where does the Hargreaves come from?"

Tammy smiled. She knew the answer to Marian's question, but she let Alan answer anyway.

"When we'd found a place to rent in Yorkshire in 1978, your mother decided that she wanted a new identity. She'd always hated being called Phyllis, or even Phyll, so I chose Pippa for her. From that day onwards I always called her Pippa and so did everyone else. It's so easy to call yourself by another name in a place where no one knows

274

you."

"Paul did that, too," Cynthia added. "He decided to call himself Paul when he first checked in here nearly a year ago, and now the name's stuck. No one in Lyverton knows him as Nick except Claire."

Alan nodded in agreement. "It's really easy to disappear too. One day, a couple of weeks later we decided that because it was so simple to change your first name, we'd go the whole hog and choose another surname. We picked up a telephone directory and made a pact that whatever name appeared at the top of the left hand page when we opened it up at random, we would adopt that name."

"Oh, I see — so it was Hargreaves," Marian said.

Alan laughed. Tammy laughed with him and the memory that had been stuck in the depths of her childhood rose to the surface, and she finished off the story. "No, it wasn't! The first name they picked was *Pepper.*"

There it was again. The peculiar synchronicity that was stalking Tammy rose to the surface like cream floating on the surface of milk. Tammy had known the name was significant as soon as she had heard Paul's surname but, until then, couldn't remember why.

Alan continued. "Pippa said that no way was she going to be known as *Pippa Pepper*, and so we opened the directory at another page and it was *Hargreaves.* So there you are. Two deed polls later and we were Alan and Pippa Hargreaves. And that is our name to this day."

Marian furrowed her brow. "No wonder I could never find you!"

"Sorry," Alan said apologetically. "I've had far more years as Hargreaves than I've had as Fielding."

Marian blew her fringe in amazement. "Wow," she said.

"Dad." Tammy said with a worried frown, remembering how he'd always been very careful to keep official documentation out of her sight since the day she had accidentally found his birth certificate when she had been ten years-old and curious about the different name. "You *were* actually married to Mum, weren't you? You're not about to drop another dark secret on me?"

Alan threw back his head and laughed out loud. "Tammy, you are as legitimate as they come. I can absolutely guarantee that you are the offspring of a perfectly respectable married couple, despite the history behind how they actually managed to extract a signature on divorce papers out of Tony Troutman and arrive at the registry office."

Tammy beamed, relieved. That would have just been the last straw if she had discovered her parents hadn't been married after all.

Alan was finally loosening up and enjoying himself, but there was something else about him. He looked the same, but he was subtly different. Somehow, he was more whole, real and substantial. It was as if the hollowness that resonated inside him was being slowly filled with life.

Alan put his arm around Tammy and drew her close to him. She rested her head on her father's chest. On impulse he put his other arm around Marian. "Friends again?" he said to her.

"Oh yes," Marian said with a wry smile. "But if you think you're dragging me around archaeological digs and old ruins, you've got another think coming."

Tammy leaned forward.

"What is all this I've been hearing about a fire in some old barns?" she said to Marian as Alan chuckled at her last comment.

Marian sighed. "It's a long time ago now. It was September 1978."

She looked at Alan. "Your brother, Simon, came to the door one evening and told my father that you and Mum were back in the village."

"Simon said that?" Alan gasped. "The little creep. Well, he was lying. I did come back, alone, that August to speak to my parents, but he was furious when I turned up. Then he threatened to beat me to a pulp if I ever set foot in the village again. I definitely didn't return in September."

Tammy turned from Marian to Alan. "Simon! You've got a brother, too, Dad? You didn't tell me I had an uncle!"

"There was a good reason for that." Alan said quickly. "You wouldn't want to know Simon, he was a right bad 'un. He was renowned for his violence — he almost killed a school friend once. He put him in hospital for a week. He was always getting into trouble with the police."

Tammy shot Alan a disapproving look. She would deal with him later. More secrets. How many more members of her family had her

276

parents kept from her? She not only had a sister, but an uncle, too. She turned back to face Marian. "What happened when my uncle turned up at your door, saying that Mum and Dad were back in the village?"

"My father went crazy. He took his shotgun out of his safe, jumped into his car with Simon and they went off together in the direction of Quarry Cottages, where Simon said he'd seen Alan and Mum go. I found out a few years later that my father had offered to give Simon five hundred pounds if he let him know when they were back in the village. I suppose he was just after some money. It was a complete lie."

Alan was shocked. He would never forgive his brother for this, even if he did eventually find his parents.

"If it wasn't my parents, then who was it that Simon had seen?" Tammy asked.

"That's just it," Marian replied. "No one knows who they were, or even if they had existed. By the time I raised the alarm, and told the police that my father had gone off with a loaded shotgun, the fire was, apparently, blazing out of control. The old barns were near Fawsden — where the development site now is — and the fire brigade was already there."

"There's a grave in the churchyard," Tammy said. "It contains the victims."

"Is there?" Alan raised his eyebrows.

"Yes. I saw it on Saturday when I was looking for Jessie's grave with the vicar." She turned to Marian. "It's tucked right into the corner of the churchyard. Have you seen it?"

Marian nodded, deep in thought. "For a couple of days, my father was in the frame for your murder, Alan — and my mother's. Everyone thought the bodies were yours."

Alan and Tammy spoke simultaneously.

"Murder!"

"Yes. Murder. Unbelievable, isn't it. Folks thought for years that it was really you and Mum who had died in the fire, despite the police saying that it most definitely wasn't, because the charred remains were much older."

"Tony was completely vindicated, though, wasn't he?" Cynthia said to Marian. "Or so I heard. The police let him go."

277

"Yes, that's right. Although there was no DNA testing in those days, and dental records and other forensic tests proved inconclusive, the police were absolutely certain almost immediately that the bodies found in the fire weren't those of my mother and Alan. There was then some speculation in the press that the bodies were probably those of Frederick de Montpelier and his daughter-in-law, who had disappeared off the face of the earth in the 1960s. The only thing the forensic scientists proved was that the bodies were those of a man and a woman who had died at least ten years previously. There was no jewellery at the crime scene that might have positively identified them and the bones were so charred with the heat of the fire it made further identification impossible."

"I can shed some light on that," Alan said in a serious voice. "I never knew about the fire, but just after we changed our names to Hargreaves, the police came knocking on our door. The police officer just asked us to confirm that we were Phyllis Troutman and Alan Fielding, formerly of Lyverton. Once we showed them our birth certificates and deed polls, they said that was all they needed and thanked us for our help. They never told us the reasons for their investigations and we were mystified as to why they'd followed up on our name change. After all, we hadn't broken the law."

Marian nodded slowly. "That fits perfectly," she said. "Out of the blue, my father was released from custody a couple of days after the fire, but the police would never tell us why. They just confirmed that the bodies found were definitely not those of Phyllis Troutman and Alan Fielding. It was way before the forensic results came back."

"But why wouldn't villagers accept it?" questioned Alan.

"I don't know," Marian replied with a sad sigh. "As I said, there was speculation that it was the missing Frederick de Montpelier and his daughter-in-law, but the then Earl of Fawsden and his family refused to comment or claim the bodies because they hadn't been positively identified. Rumours were flying around that despite what the police said, the bodies were those of Alan and my mother, and my father had got away with murder."

"So," Tammy speculated. "I wonder who they are? Do you think it *is* Frederick de Montpelier and his daughter-in-law?"

CHAPTER THIRTY-ONE

Day Nine
Tuesday, 2nd June: 8.00 am

Tammy awoke to the sound of birdsong, and a churning, grinding refuse lorry in the road outside her room, but the first thing she saw was Alice's box. She made herself a cup of tea and decided to sit for a while on her tiny roof terrace again. Perhaps now things had calmed down, she could just enjoy the rest of her holiday, get to spend some time with her sister and work out what she was going to do with the rest of her life.

Tammy knew she didn't want to go back to Yorkshire. Of course, she knew she would have to go back initially, but she was so certain destiny had led her to Lyverton, she was willing to leave everything behind: her father; her friends, her job and her home. She would never leave behind her happy memories of Pippa, though. They would be with her wherever she was. She sat, sipping tea in the early morning sunshine and tried not to think about Paul. Would there be another Paul? Another man in her life who would make her feel the way he had? Or would she have to settle for second best and try and build a life with a man with whom she got along quite amicably, but who could never make her feel cherished, precious and loved so unconditionally. It had been mutual love at first sight, and Tammy knew that it was special and rare and that she would never experience it again.

Tammy's thoughts meandered through the past week, and with a resolute determination to get to the bottom of the mystery of which twin had been Jessie's baby, she decided to spend a couple of hours going through Alice's box for more clues and then make a start on writing her story.

She wandered back into her room, tightened her dressing gown belt and picked up the tatty brown envelope containing Harry's letters, but something caught her eye on the cover of the top magazine in the box, beneath the envelope. There, running along the bottom of the page was a single, narrow strapline.

Fiction Special: A Ghost Story by Margaret Regent

Tammy picked up the magazine. How could she have missed it?

She flicked through the pages to find the story and settled down on the roof terrace to finish her tea and enjoy the read in the glorious morning sunshine.

Alicia's Letter
by Margaret Regent

Thirteen year-old Alicia was clawing her way out of a pit of grief when she came across the old letters from her father to her mother. The edges of the pit crumbled and Alicia's pale-grey eyes watered as an avalanche of memories swept her back in time to the days before the Great War when her family had all been so happy. She hadn't realised quite how much her parents had loved each other until she read the letters.

It was no fun being an orphan. She knew she was luckier than most girls in her situation because her friend's family had taken her in when her mother had died last year.

Tammy sat up in her patio chair, suddenly excited. This story was about Alice! She devoured the rest of the page with her eyes.

It was a broken heart, they'd said when they had revealed the awful news to her. 'Your mother's heart has given out, because she never stopped grieving for your poor father.'

'Home is Where the Heart Is '

The words of comfort were surrounded by intricately worked leaves and tiny white flowers. Alicia's mother had embroidered the cross-stitch canvass and it had been framed and hung on her bedroom wall beside her bed. Every time her gaze fell on the words they triggered a poignant, bittersweet memory of her parents and reminded her of the happy days they had spent together as a family. Alicia always imagined her mother in Heaven, sitting on a gate in the depths of a beautiful countryside, staring at slabs of purple and orange clouds gathering over a distant

280

red-bricked mansion house. Quite why Alicia had this vision, she didn't know, but it was always sharp and focused as she swam just below the surface of wakefulness and it was always the same. Her mother would look sad and lonely as the wind blew fluffy ringlets around her face and then the vision would fade as her mother's coppery-blonde hair obscured her features.

Alicia awoke from her dream sleep one bitterly cold Monday morning in February. The weather had been exceptionally harsh. People were saying that it hadn't been so cold for a hundred years. Freak weather fronts had caused the country to seize up, gripped by a hand of iron that was squeezing the life out of cities, towns and villages. The extortionate price of coal, coupled with the treacherous conditions underfoot, had driven many people indoors, huddled together around fires made of gathered firewood, rubbing their hands and shivering as they tried to keep themselves warm. It was so cold, people who didn't have to get up to go to work stayed in bed for an extra hour, just to preserve the warmth in their chilled bones.

Alicia was startled by a sharp knock on the front door. She pulled on a thick woollen cardigan over her nightclothes and made her way downstairs. No one else in the house was up because it was so cold. She pulled back the bolts on the heavy, oak front door and tugged it open.

Outside was a bright red painted motor vehicle such as Alicia had never seen before. The engine hummed erratically in the white, sub-zero conditions and Alicia couldn't take her eyes off it.

The golden letters that spelt out 'Royal Mail' told her that she was about to receive a parcel, or a letter, that needed to be signed for.

"Alicia Smithson?"

"Yes," replied Alicia. "That's me."

"Sign here," said the postman, thrusting a contraption into her hand before blowing on his chapped red hands to warm them.

"What's this?" Alicia asked, frowning in puzzlement at the long thin piece of plastic that looked like a pen, but with no nib.

"You write your name just there," said the postman. "On the little grey square."

Alicia was amazed to see her signature magically take its shape. Just how it worked she didn't know.

"Now put the date underneath," said the postman. "It's the twenty-second."

Alicia hesitated and the postman repeated himself. "The date?" He pointed to the screen again. " It's the twenty-second of February."

Well, I never! Tammy thought to herself as she sipped her tea, engrossed in the story. Polly-Anne was a very clever woman to project her writing into the future so accurately. How could she have possibly known in 1962 about the hand-held computers of today, where people simply give an electronic signature instead of signing a delivery note or receipt? She continued reading.

Alicia did as she was told, but scowled at the postman who said she had written the wrong date on the magic screen.

"Can you confirm for me, miss, that is your name and address?" The man pointed to a label on the envelope. He shivered and glanced skywards at the snow-laden clouds.

"Yes ... that's me."

The postman thrust the letter into her hand and shuffled back to his van. Alicia glanced at the church clock on the other side of the lane, but the hands were frozen solid and obscured by a thick layer of frozen snow.

In the dim light of dawn behind the closed door Alicia tore open the letter, frightened by the postman, the pen that wrote on the little grey square and the strange post van. Then she saw the date on the letter and wondered if someone was actually playing a trick on her: either that or had she somehow been transported forwards in time to 2009? The letter was handwritten in the shaky script of an elderly lady.

'Dear Alicia,

This is a letter from me to me, or me to you, whichever way you want to see it. Please don't be frightened. I can tell you that we will lead a long and fulfilling life and, one day a long, long time in the future, a woman you will never meet in life will be at your funeral. She will be the long-lost daughter of a special lady we know in the future. Her presence at your funeral is foretold, and I want you to, somehow, make sure you give this lady a message. You need to somehow let her know that the unnamed graves in the village churchyard are that of the rapist and his mistress, they were murdered in the spring of 1962, and she must use this knowledge to set a tortured soul free from the clutches of these evil ghosts of the past.'

The words began to swim on the page in front of Tammy's eyes. This was by far the strangest thing that had happened to her since she had been in the village. This letter was referring to her. It must be! She flicked back to the front cover of the magazine. The date indicated that it had been printed in August 1962. The words leapt off the page and hit her, hard, somewhere in the proximity of her breastbone making her breathe heavily. Could this just be a weird coincidence? Surely a fictional ghost story in a 1962 magazine couldn't possibly have been written just for *her*! She wasn't even born then and her father had only been two years-old himself. Tammy almost couldn't bear to read on, her heart was thumping so violently in her chest.

Alicia couldn't believe her eyes as she ran up the stairs and burst into her friend's bedroom. "Emmeline!" she cried. "Look at this."

Her friend sat up in bed, rubbed her eyes and then took the letter from her hand. "How very strange," she said after reading it, "is someone playing a trick on you, Alicia?"

Alicia climbed back in bed, clutching the letter in her hand. It was still very early and so cold in the house that bed was the best place to keep warm. As she dozed off to sleep again her eyes fell on her mother's cross-stitch canvass and she began to skim the surface of sleepiness again. In her dream, her mother was still sitting on the gate as if waiting for someone. Another lady approached and her mother had to climb down to let her through. The woman stopped and her mother passed Alicia's letter to her, as her fluffy hair blew across her face in the breeze. The other lady accepted the letter, put up her hand and stroked Alicia's mother's face. "Justice will, one day, be done," she said. "She will discover the truth and then it will be finished."

When Alicia stirred half-an-hour later she looked everywhere in her bed for the letter, but it had disappeared. She asked Emmeline about it, but Emmeline shook her head, bewildered. "I don't remember a letter," she said. "You must have been dreaming, Alicia."

Alicia reluctantly accepted that, indeed, she must have been dreaming, but she never, ever forgot the dream and carried it in her heart for the rest of her life.

Eighty-four years later, in 2009, the young author sat in the morning sunshine sipping tea. She recalled the misunderstanding the week before when she'd accidentally attended a stranger's funeral. "Come along," the rector had said to her, taking her by the arm and ushering her into the church. "The service is about to

283

start."

Had she not attended her funeral she would never have been given *Alicia Smithson's* box of old photographs, letters and magazines for research for her book about local history, and become caught up in the mystery surrounding the unmarked graves in the village churchyard. She picked up an old magazine from August 1962 and noticed the words along the bottom of the cover: "Fiction Special, a Ghost Story by Margaret Regent" She turned to the fiction page, where there was a ghost story entitled 'Alicia's Letter' by Margaret Regent.

The magazine fell to the floor as the ghostly message from the past was finally delivered.

The End

Tammy needed to know, too, right then, if she was dreaming. Everything seemed normal. Everything seemed real. The magazine slid off her lap and fell to the floor. Was she going to wake up any moment and realise that it was all just a dream, just like when she had been Jessie and dreamed about the white cuckoo and the dreadful rape in the stables?

Tammy picked up the magazine and ran her hand over the surface of the cover. She held it to her face and breathed in the mustiness. The distinctive smell of old paper hit the back of her nose and it prickled as she inhaled the pungent, sharp smell. On the spur of the moment she rushed into her room, grabbed her mobile phone and photographed the magazine story. It was there on her mobile phone screen. *Alicia's letter by Margaret Regent.* She wondered if Cynthia was awake and toyed with the idea of running along the landing, the magazine tucked under her arm, knocking on her door and asking to speak to her father. She paced up and down the room. The coincidences were getting much too intense, and had most definitely tipped over into something not only paranormal but urgent, too. Was she *really* the woman whose presence at Alice's funeral was foretold in a magazine in 1962?

No. Not 1962, thought Tammy.

The fictional Alicia was thirteen when the letter from the future was delivered to her. That was in 1926. Her presence at Alice's funeral was foretold on the 22nd February 1926.

284

No, not 1926 — if it was foretold, then that meant *before* 1926. A sudden vision of the church clock in the story, its hands frozen in time and covered in a thick blanket of snow flashed into her mind. Time. What *was* time? Did anyone really know? Could it be that time was not flat, smooth and constant. Could time be frozen, like the hands on the church clock? Could it be rippled like the surface of a pond in summer breeze, or form itself into mountainous waves in a stormy sea. Could it even get itself stuck, like a crease in a sheet of paper, and then leave its mark when the fold was smoothed out. Or perhaps time did not exist at all, and had been created just for the benefit of human beings, who needed order in their lives. Tammy's mind was spinning. The magazine story, if true, meant there was no past, no future, and the present was already past in less than the time it took to blink.

Could Alice Thompson *really* have known from the age of just thirteen that she was going to live to the ripe old age of ninety-six and, one day in May 2009 a stranger would attend her funeral by accident? Could she really have passed this information onto Polly-Anne Staverley in some way, so that Polly could write the story for publication in a magazine in 1962? Or was this just some weird self-fulfilling prophecy? A mere coincidence: just a very clever ghost story: a story within a story, like an image in a mirror reflected into eternity. Or did mankind look at the world through the wrong end of a telescope? Was there more to this beautiful earth than man had ever discovered by science alone? Was this unknown energy something wonderful and unique that silently guided everyone through their pre-determined lives in perfect synchronicity, the future just reflecting the past, rewritten, time after time again.

Was this ... *God*?

Suddenly, Tammy had a strong suspicion that Alice had known exactly when she would die. She remembered how Sophie's mother had said she had given away all her possessions before she had passed away. She had left the most personal, valuable thing until last.

Her box.

It had been carefully put together especially for Tammy — the locket, the photographs, the letters and the magazines. Alice must have had known of her existence, even though she had obviously lost touch with Pippa. And she had known she would be there on Tuesday, 26th May 2009 — sitting at the back of the church on the day of her own funeral. She had known since, at thirteen years-old, she had experienced a vivid dream about a letter. She had known, for most of her life, when she would die, but she wouldn't have been frightened when the time came, because she also knew for certain there *was* an afterlife.

Tammy shivered, suddenly cold. She felt small, but not quite insignificant. When people died, were the bodies they left behind just withered leaves on the tree of life? Just like the words of the *Immortal, Invisible* hymn they had sung in the church on Sunday morning. Was the soul, the human goodness and essence of humanity, drawn back into the sap of the tree and the past, present and future all rolled into one before the tree burst into leaf and blossomed again. Timeless. Ageless. Perpetual. Incredible. It really was true. Something *could* come from nothing. Everything on Earth had a purpose. Tammy took a sharp intake of breath as the knowledge flooded her consciousness. Her eyes filled with tears as she felt small and humbled and knew that her mother's soul lived on.

***

Tammy decided against running along the landing like a woman possessed. Instead, she resolved to keep her head. After all, if she lost it, and went around shoving a women's magazine from 1962 under people's noses and blabbering on about being in the fiction special, she would end up on Prozac or worse before she could even say the word.

She calmed down a little, but still had to keep checking to make sure the magazine hadn't disappeared. Before long, she was showered, dressed and ready to face the world, the logical, rational side of her having decided that Margaret Regent's story was nothing but a very clever twist in a ghostly tale. Pure fiction. But uncannily true … just like life, really. However, the image of the frozen church clock just wouldn't go away, and she couldn't stop thinking about the nature of time and the existence of God.

CHAPTER THIRTY-TWO

8.55 am

There was a knock on Tammy's door. It was Alan.

"Hi Dad," Tammy said brightly. "Did you have a good night's sleep?"

"I did ... but I don't think your friend, Paul, slept at all."

"Paul? Why?"

"He's in the flat with Cynthia. Claire's turned him down. Says she can't marry him after all."

Tammy's heart soared so high into the air, she almost let go and jumped up with it, punching her fist in the air in a triumphant victory. "Really?"

Alan smirked at her. "I can't imagine why you look so pleased ..."

"What's happened to make her change her mind?" interrupted Tammy.

"I really don't know. She's packing to go back to Norfolk."

"When?"

"Err ... now. Soon."

Tammy looked at her watch. "It's not nine o'clock yet, Dad. When did all this happen?"

"Last night, after you'd gone to bed and Marian had gone home, Cynthia and I stayed up listening to old CDs and playing cards. We didn't realise the time. It was way past midnight when Paul tapped on Cynthia's door to see if you were still there."

"Did they have a row?"

"No. I don't think so. They are parting amicably, so I hear."

Tammy wished her heart would stop beating so fast.

"Look, Tammy, I've offered to take Claire back to Norfolk. I want to repay Paul for his wild goose chase to Yorkshire on Sunday. It's not a long drive. Once we've dropped Claire off, we'll carry on with our plans for a day in Great Yarmouth. We'll be back this evening and then we can all have dinner together. Cynthia's booked a table. I've texted Marian and invited her. Cynthia suggested Daniel and Sophie could

287

come, too, so she's giving him the evening off."

"What's Marian doing today?" Tammy asked.

"She has to go to work because the children are back at school today after half-term. Yesterday was a training day, but the head teacher gave her the day off, as you know."

"So I'll be on my own then — great!"

Alan didn't say anything. The twinkle in his eyes said it all, but Tammy couldn't quite work out whether it was because he was spending the day with Cynthia, or because he was amused at her contrived indifference to the hugely significant fact that she and Paul would both be alone.

"Tammy. Can I come in for a bit?" Claire's voice followed a soft tap on Tammy's open door.

"Hi. Of course you can," Tammy replied. She could afford to be generous now Claire was bowing out gracefully from Paul's life.

Alan looked at his watch and then at Claire. "We'll see you in about thirty minutes, Claire. Is that all right?"

"Thanks, Alan. That'll be fine."

They stood in silence for a few seconds after Alan shut the door behind him.

"What happened?" Tammy said eventually.

Claire shrugged her shoulders. "I've spent ten months yearning for him. I've dreamed about him every single day. I've beaten myself up for being so stupid as to throw my life away on a single moment of madness, and on Saturday, when he agreed to come back to me, I was the happiest woman on the planet."

"I know. It was obvious."

"We've had three days together now, and I've waited patiently for the sparkle to return to our relationship. But it's dead, Tammy. The sparkle's gone. I realise now that the light in our relationship went out the moment I had several drinks too many and jumped into bed with a stranger. I've just been clinging onto a fantasy for the last ten months."

"You were so unlucky ..." Tammy began to say, but Claire stopped her before she could say any more.

"No. I'll never, ever say that. I wasn't unlucky. I was incredibly lucky, because I had Lewis, and I love him so much, Tammy. I really

288

miss him. *He's* my life, now. Do you know, I can't even remember his father's name or what he looks like? But it doesn't really matter, does it? He's *my* son and I love him to bits ... and that's all that matters."

"He's gorgeous," Tammy said. "A lovely little boy. I really enjoyed taking him out in his pushchair on Friday."

The futuristic scene Tammy had conjured up in her mind's eye, and played out several times over the last three days in various ways, shifted its focus a full circle. Lewis, grey and distinguished at fifty would say to his mother: *'she took me out in my pushchair, didn't she?'* An elderly Claire would smile at him and tell him how she turned down a proposal of marriage to a man who didn't love her, but who was quite prepared to sacrifice his own life and bring him up as his own. *'He must have been an incredible man,'* Lewis would say. And he would be so right.

Claire shook her head. "Friday. Doesn't it seem like a long time ago?"

Tammy nodded. "It does. Such a lot has happened."

"Hell yes, it has! Just look at what has happened to you this week, Tammy — finding a sister you'd never known about; being dragged into someone's funeral; researching a complete stranger's family tree and then charging off to Norfolk and back on Friday, not your regular type of week, was it?"

Tammy shut her eyes and then puffed the air out of her cheeks; there was more, much more, but she wasn't about to reveal any of the weird, paranormal stuff to Claire.

"No, not when you put it like that," she replied.

"Do you know what finally made up my mind, Tammy? What made me realise that Nick had gone forever and Paul had taken his place?"

Tammy shook her head. "What?"

"It was yesterday lunchtime. We were in the beer garden. I rang my parents in Spain from my mobile phone. It was so good to talk to them. They've been trying to get me to go out there with Lewis ever since they emigrated."

Tammy flinched inwardly. Her vivid imagination had let her down with that one. She had got it completely wrong. When she had watched them in the pub garden, yesterday lunchtime, she had been convinced Claire had been on the phone to Rosemary and Keith, having a cosy little chat about Lewis dipping his toes in the North Sea.

Claire took her hand and they both sank down onto the bed.

"Nick went in from the beer garden to get more drinks and I watched him through the window. You were sitting inside, weren't you, in the alcove."

"Yes, I was doing some Sudoku puzzles, killing time, waiting to visit someone about Alice's box."

"I saw him go over to you and bend down to whisper in your ear. Then I saw the look in his eyes as he smiled at you. Even through a glass window-pane, I could see that he was really Paul now and not the Nick that I'd known. Then he laughed and it was so loud I could actually hear him through the glass. He looked so happy and relaxed, but something niggled me. I just couldn't work out what it was, and then yesterday afternoon I saw the look on his face when you came back from Sophie Staverley's house and joined us in the garden. I realised that, in the three days we'd been back together, I hadn't seen his eyes shine like that. He hadn't laughed out loud with me either — not even once. Not like he'd laughed with you at lunch time."

Claire's eyes were bright with unshed tears. Once again, Tammy got the feeling that, in different circumstances, it wouldn't take much for them to become good friends. She toyed with the idea of telling her that Paul wasn't whispering endearments in her ear, but had merely pointed out where the number nine went in the Sudoku puzzle. She decided to keep her mouth firmly shut. People were too quick to jump to conclusions.

"I'm so sorry it didn't work out for you, Claire. Ten years is a long time to be with someone."

"I know. It was all my fault. I hurt him so much, Tammy."

"There's much more to life than meets the eye,' Tammy said, glancing at the old magazine on her bedside table. "I'm a great believer in destiny. You'll go to Spain to live with your parents, run a fantastically successful veterinary practice and meet a darkly handsome, totally passionate Spanish guy, who'll sweep you off your feet and shower you with red rose petals every single day. Lewis will grow up healthy and tanned, and will soon be joined by at least four brothers

290

and sisters. The children will play on the beach in the sun and will chatter away to local children in Spanish, and then speak impeccable English when they come home to visit."

Claire grinned, and thumped Tammy on the shoulder. "You are a one, Tammy. You make me laugh. *Four* more children. I don't think so!"

"Keep in touch?" Tammy asked.

"Oh most definitely. You can come and visit me and my dark, handsome, passionate Spanish lover in our million-pound villa. We'll have barbeques on the beach and our children will play together on the edge of the sea right into the evening. We'll dance to Spanish music, toast the setting sun and drink far too much red wine, which will give us all dreadful headaches the next day. And we'll exchange Christmas cards and birthday cards and ..."

Her voice broke like a snapped twig and she began to cry, covering her eyes with her hands. "It's just such a different life to that I'd imagined for myself."

"I know," Tammy sympathised, and put her arms around her. "Believe me, it will be okay. One day you'll see that it was all for the best. I promise."

"Will you and Nick get back together? Sorry ... not Nick ... Paul."

Tammy shrugged. "We were never together in the first place. We only met last Monday. We'd had just one date and he poured his heart out to me about you all night. Hardly a recipe for a successful relationship, is it?"

"No," Claire agreed. "Maybe you need to start again, from today. Put everything that's happened since last Monday right behind you and pretend you're meeting for the first time when you wave me off."

Tammy thought about what Claire had said. She didn't answer, but it seemed like a very good idea.

"We'll definitely keep in touch?" Claire asked.

"Yes. Definitely."

Claire gave Tammy another hug, stood up abruptly and then she was gone. The door shut with a click behind her and Tammy was alone in her room again.

***

"I really like your dad," Cynthia said to Tammy. "He's so witty and funny."

Tammy threw her a cynical look. "You *are* joking, aren't you?"

"No, hen. I'm not. I haven't enjoyed myself so much in ages. We had a lovely time together yesterday. We stayed up until nearly one o'clock this morning, just listening to music, playing card games and talking and laughing about this and that."

Cynthia was bustling around in her kitchen, packing an old wicker hamper with a colourful picnic. There was a bottle of expensive wine, cartons of fruit juice, sandwiches, pork pies, Scotch eggs, red grapes, juicy oranges and kiwi fruit. She bent down and extracted ice packs from the bottom drawer of her freezer.

"Do you think these will keep everything cold enough?"

Tammy shrugged. "I don't know."

Cynthia tutted and murmured something about young women today, and then her excitement at the prospect of a picnic on the beach transformed the look on her face into that of an excited teenager. She was a colourful sparkly firework, just like the design on the front of her expensive-looking black t-shirt. Loose, fine linen trousers complemented her full figure and her pink fingernails (the colour of which matched exactly the pink splashed in the design on her t-shirt) were perfect without any chips. Her hair was pulled back and clipped up on top of her head and her make-up matched her casual appearance: subtle and appropriate. Tammy admired her: she was so classy, was Cynthia. Always immaculate. Always matching. She was so different to gentle, soap-scrubbed, hippy-like Pippa, and yet to Tammy, the motherliness they both exuded was identical.

"There!" said Cynthia, as she packed the last of the food in the picnic hamper. "We're about done. I wonder where Alan has got to?"

"He's just having a word with Paul," Tammy said. "In my room."

***

"You *are* doing the right thing, you know," said Alan.

Paul turned around. He had been standing with his back to Alan, hands in his pockets, subconsciously jingling his loose change, staring at the church clock out of Tammy's patio doors.

292

"Am I?"

Alan walked over and stood beside him.

"I mean, you and Claire are doing the right thing. It might have worked for a while, and it would have been good for the kiddie to have a proper dad, but ..." Alan shook his head as the words died away. He stuck his hands in his pockets, assuming an identical pose to Paul's.

"But every time you looked at the poor little lad, you would have been reminded of Claire's infidelity," he continued.

Paul sighed. "I would have lived with it, but you're probably right, mate."

Alan looked down at his feet.

"You and Tammy should spend some time with each other today. Start again, lad. Press the rewind button and try to put this difficult week behind you."

Alan pulled out his wallet and extracted five twenty pound notes. "Here ... call it petrol money for your wasted trip to Yorkshire."

Paul smiled, but shook his head. "I can't take that, mate: It wouldn't be right."

"Why?"

"Because when you cleared off to sort your head out, you gave me a perfect excuse to do exactly the same thing."

***

"Where's Claire?" Cynthia asked.

"She's coming now. Just saying goodbye to Paul," Alan replied.

A few minutes later, Claire appeared at the open door. Her eyes were bright, but she wasn't crying. Paul joined her, but didn't look at Tammy as he lugged the suitcase down the stairs.

Everyone traipsed into the car park without speaking.

When they arrived at the car, Alan held the door open for her. Claire slid into the back seat and shut the door, looking straight ahead.

Paul lifted her suitcase and the picnic hamper into the boot, slammed down the lid and stood looking into the distance. What did you say at such times? *Goodbye. I'm sorry you slept with a stranger and spoilt everything, but hey let's keep in touch and stay friends?*

He hadn't yet spoken to his parents: Claire had called Rosemary and Keith that morning with the news she was coming back earlier than planned. They hadn't asked why, but Paul knew that his mother would guess; he knew how relieved she would be that it was finally all over. He'd have to talk to his father, but at least he had a foot back in the door again.

Alan opened the front passenger door for Cynthia who beamed with pleasure at the gentlemanly gesture.

Eventually, Paul opened the back passenger door again and gave Claire a peck on the cheek.

"Shall we stay in touch — try and remain friends, if we can?" he asked raising his eyebrows speculatively.

Claire nodded, and then looked down at her hands.

"Tell Lewis his Uncle Paul will be back to see him soon, and we'll go to the beach and he can have a little paddle in the sea."

Tammy and Paul watched as the car disappeared into the distant countryside and out of sight.

"I'm so sorry …" Tammy began to say.

"It's finished," Paul interrupted without looking at her. "You don't know how relieved I am that it's finally over."

"You were going to marry her and take on another man's child, I think that is just about the most selfless, wonderful, thing any man could do, Paul."

"Is it?"

"But you didn't love her."

"Nope"

"Could you have actually have gone through with it, knowing you didn't love her?"

Paul nodded and looked down at his feet. "Yep."

"Why?"

Paul finally turned his head to look at Tammy.

"My family — my mum, my dad and my sister — they're so important to me. But the real reason was Lewis," he said as he walked away, his voice breaking with emotion. "Every child needs a father, Tammy. Every child needs a proper family. I know that now."

CHAPTER THIRTY-THREE

10.15 am

Tammy was eating a full English breakfast in the sunshine outside Marjorie's tea shop, sitting at the same bistro table as when she had first arrived in the village. Daniel was hovering around in his blue and white striped apron, and the lone blackbird was back in the hawthorn bush, its clear tones forming a simple tune as it called for its mate. She could hear pigeons cooing in the distance and the smell of mayflowers was beginning to fade, as May slid into June, but it was still there. The sun was warm on her hair and she breathed in deeply. Unlike last Monday morning, though, Tammy was not alone at the table today. Paul sat opposite her, eating his breakfast. He was subdued and not quite himself, but that was understandable. Tammy was a little subdued, too, because, niggling in the back of her mind and lurking on her bedside table back at the Red Lion was the small matter of an uncannily true ghost story in a 1962 women's magazine.

"You needn't worry about your dad and Marian picking up where they left off," Paul said, as he finished his breakfast and his knife and fork rattled onto the plate. He wiped his mouth with a white serviette.

"Oh ... I'm not really. I was just being silly."

Paul grinned at her and the light began to flood back into his face.

"Cynthia thinks Alan's absolutely wonderful. I think she's got the hots for him. Says he reminds her of Hugh Grant. *Four Weddings and a Funeral* and *Love Actually* are her most favourite films of all time."

Tammy grimaced. "Even though she was annoyed at him for Sunday night's wild goose chase?"

"That was my fault, not Alan's. It was a bit extreme, you must admit. It wouldn't have happened if I'd not been in such a state over Claire and the thought of years and years of a grey, loveless marriage looming over me. I just had to get away, Tammy. Just like Alan did when he'd stood in the doorway and stared at his wife's daughter for the first time in over thirty years."

"So — let me get this right — you used my father storming off as

295

an excuse to storm off yourself?"

Tammy couldn't quite believe her ears. It was bizarre to say the least. It was funny how things fitted together though. If Cynthia and Paul hadn't gone chasing after Alan, she would never have spent the entire night with Marian. It was as if they had been encased together in Pippa's womb in the darkness and had been given a few precious hours of sisterly togetherness to make up for twenty-seven lost years.

"I wouldn't put it quite like that but, yes, I suppose I did storm off," Paul said.

"Cynthia's a diamond, isn't she?"

"She's the best, Tammy, just the best. She knew exactly how mixed up I was. There was no way she was going to just let me drive off on my own."

"Simply the best," Tammy repeated dreamily, and stared into the distance, thinking of Cynthia and wondering just how many people she could fit into her huge, welcoming heart.

On Monday last week, only minutes after she had first arrived in the village, Tammy had watched the strange children sharing sweets on the wall outside the post office. In her vivid imagination, two other children might be sitting on that same wall in a few years' time. They would be sharing a bag of sweets. *'You can have one of my white mice if you give me one of your fried eggs,'* one of them would say to the other. A large Scottish lady with a tartan shopping bag would step out of the door of the post office. *'Come on you two, don't eat all those before your lunch or else your grandad will smack my bottom,'* she would say. The children — a boy and a girl — would giggle at the thought, jump off the wall and run on ahead. Cynthia would shout after them: *'wait for me and don't go too far ahead.'* The children would skip happily along the main road, Cynthia hurrying after them, red-faced and puffing loudly. *'Come on Granny,'* they would shout, *'stop dawdling.'* Cynthia would call them cheeky little monkeys for teasing her about dawdling and then, when they arrived home for lunch, Alan would step out of the front doors of the Red Lion, squat down onto his heels and hold out his arms for them as they ran helter-skelter across the forecourt.

"What's up with you?" said Paul. "You're not about to cry again, are you? What have I said?"

296

"No, I'm not! I never cry," said Tammy cynically as she wiped a happy tear from the corner of her eye at the imagined scene in her mind. 'I was just picturing Cynthia and my dad living at the Red Lion in Cynthia's flat in a few years time. I think they are quite well-matched. Opposites, but they could be really good together. Actually, I quite like the idea."

Paul laughed, but then fell into a reflective silence.

"Did you mean it when you said you hoped that Claire and I would be happy together and wished me the best of luck?" he asked.

"Of course I did. I accepted your decision," Tammy replied. "End of story. We were never together in the first place. You were never mine to lose."

Paul shrugged. "It's just that I thought we meant something to each other. Hell, I was so devastated at losing you, it actually made me cry. Me ... a bloke, crying like some besotted teenager!"

Tammy sighed, remembering the intimate telephone call when she had just got out of the shower, and how the sound of Paul fighting back tears down the phone because of the huge sacrifice he had made, had tingled deliciously in every nerve in her body.

"We did — do — mean something. I *was* upset."

Tammy looked away and stared at the hawthorn bush as the tingling feeling began again. She leaned on the table, locking her hands together in a pensive pose and her thumbs took on a mind of their own as they circled round and round each other like Torvill and Dean as swans in *Bolero*.

"Look," she said. "Let's just start again, Paul. Let's just make today the first day. Let's rewind back to last Tuesday morning when you knocked on my door and asked if I wanted you to fetch me a newspaper. Only today is different because you don't have to go to work."

"I'd like that," Paul said softly, as he brushed her hair away from her eyes. "I think that sounds like a really good idea."

***

Paul and Tammy sat at the table outside Marjorie's tea shop all morning in the glorious sunshine of early June. Daniel cleared away the

297

breakfast things and after a while they ordered more coffee, which he brought to them with the morning newspaper and a grin so wide it almost split his face in two. Paul teased Tammy, telling her it was not a proper newspaper and it was just stuffed full of old rubbish, and then they turned to the puzzle pages and he completed the cryptic crossword, whilst Tammy half-heartedly turned her attention to the Sudoku, now and again stealing his thunder with a crossword answer he had become stuck with.

They became bored with the puzzles and the crossword, ordered more coffee and the conversation meandered around to Alice's box. Tammy needed to recap on Jessie's story for Paul's benefit (after all, he had been rather preoccupied with sorting out his life while she had been so busy delving into a stranger's family history).

"What a great story," Paul said.

Tammy nodded as she sipped her coffee. "Poor Jessie. How awful it must have been to be raped at thirteen, be made pregnant and then have no one believe you. Thank goodness she had Harry to stand by her."

"He must have been some bloke, you know, to give up his life and career prospects to look after her," Paul said seriously.

The distant hum of an electric lawnmower drifted through the mid-day sunshine and the blackbird sat in a nearby pear tree, trilling its little heart out. Tammy looked up and smiled at the bird; it was watching them; listening to the story and soon it would fly off and tell all its friends what it had heard, and the story of Harry and Jessie, their precious daughter, Alice, and the Staverley twins would be the topic of gossip amongst the entire bird population of the village. She really must stop daydreaming, she told herself. Her imagination had gone into overdrive since she had been in Lyverton.

A dog barked and a human reciprocated a reprimand. Everything was normal. Everything was fine. Nothing was weird and strange.

"Paul," she said.

"What?"

"Do you believe in the paranormal?"

Paul rolled his eyes. "What rubbish have you been reading in Cynthia's dodgy women's magazines in the foyer?"

298

Tammy laughed with him. "I know ... I know. Actually it's a 1962 women's magazine and it's a ghost story written by Margaret Regent, which was a pseudonym for Polly-Anne Staverley."

"Go on," he said as he leaned forward, interested, despite himself.

"This morning, I was up early and made myself a cup of tea. I was going to look through Harry's letters to Jessie again, and some old parish newsletters to try and find out which of the twins was Jessie's baby, when a strapline along the bottom of one of the old magazines caught my attention. It was about the fiction special in that week's edition: the ghost story."

"Wasn't she the Hesitant Housewife?" Paul recalled.

"Yes, that's right. So I settled down to read the story and realised that although the young girl in the story was thirteen and called 'Alicia', it was really about Alice Thompson. As I read on I realised the story was aimed at me."

Paul laughed out loud. "That's such an old trick," he said. "It's what dubious mediums use to make people think they are receiving messages from beyond the grave. My mother's completely taken in by it."

"Good," said Tammy. "Thanks for that. That's exactly what I thought."

After a few minutes of conversation about how gullible people could be, they fell into a harmonious silence for a while, but Tammy just couldn't let the subject drop.

"Paul?"

"Yes?"

"What about dreams. Do you think they can foretell the future, or relive the past?"

Paul frowned, considering the possibility. "They might do," he said. "I definitely think there is such a thing as telepathy. I think we human beings are capable of so much more than we realise. We haven't reached our evolutional potential yet."

"You know when you are floating just beneath the surface of full consciousness — you're not awake and yet you're not asleep — you know you're dreaming, but can't stop it."

Paul nodded. "I know what you mean."

"I had a weird experience on Sunday night. I couldn't move. I was completely paralysed and then I dreamed I was Alice's mother, Jessie, being raped by a man called Frederick who had just returned from Africa. He was a collector of exotic birds and had brought with him a rare, albino cuckoo — a Jacobin Cuckoo, he called it — he kept it in the stables with lots of other birds. He raped Jessie in the stables and I could actually smell the horse's breath and the manure, and the whisky and cigars on his breath as he leered and slobbered around my ear, and it was just as if I *was* her. I was absolutely petrified."

"Go on," Paul said, furrowing his brow in interest.

"Then I … Jessie … tried to get away. The man caught hold of my foot and I fell against the cage. The bottom came off and the white cuckoo escaped. Then everything went black and I woke up, just as I was being raped."

"It was just a dream, Tammy," said Paul. "I wouldn't worry too much about it. I saw a documentary about that sort of thing. It's called sleep paralysis and it's usually brought on by severe stress. People say they have hallucinations, too. It's when the body gets caught between being awake and being asleep. It's reckoned to be quite frightening. You've got lots of things on your mind at the moment. It's not surprising you're having bad dreams and your mind is playing tricks on you. It probably accounts for pretty much everything weird you have experienced since you arrived in Lyverton, such as the kids you thought were the ghosts of Harry and Jessie."

"I've never heard of that, but I did think it might be stress, until yesterday afternoon when I met with Sophie's Auntie Wendy. She told us about the twins, and how one of them was really Jessie's baby. She repeated almost exactly the scene I'd dreamed about only hours before and even said that the rapist was Frederick De Montpelier. But she didn't mention the white cuckoo."

Paul's eyes widened in disbelief. "Now that *is* odd!"

Tammy sighed. "That's it, really — apart from the unknown graves in the churchyard."

Tammy told Paul about how she had stood with the vicar at the grave of two unknown victims of a fire in 1978, and how later, in Cynthia's flat, Marian had said there was speculation that they might belong to missing Frederick de Montpelier and his daughter-in-law.

"Well, how do the victims of the fire fit in with the magazine story?" Paul asked. "It's completely unconnected."

"They *are* referred to in the ghost story," Tammy explained. "As the rapist and his mistress."

Paul looked confused.

"And last night, Marian told us how her father, Tony Troutman, was accused of murder and then released without charge."

Paul looked even more confused. "Come on," he said. "Let's pay the bill and then go and look at this ghost story in the magazine. I really can't get my head around all this."

***

Paul shut the door to Tammy's room behind him and his heart started to pound. There were no barriers; no lost directions; no secrets. He and Tammy were pure and fresh, the burdens they both carried just one week ago having been shed and disposed of like the discarded cocoons of butterflies.

It felt familiar and comforting when he wrapped his arms around her. It was like finally arriving home after a long, long journey and sinking down into a familiar armchair. He buried his face in her hair and inhaled, holding his breath. Tammy's fragrance, of citrus fruits and something as sweet as sherbet, invaded every pore, every cell, every part of his body and infused him with a happiness he hadn't felt for a very long time.

"Paul, are we officially together now?" she said breathlessly.

"If it's what you want."

"It is," she whispered, "very much."

"Me too. I meant every single word on the phone on Saturday, when you were standing naked and dripping wet. I haven't been able to get the image out of my mind. It's been driving me absolutely wild with frustration."

He felt Tammy's face crumple into a cringe on his shoulder.

"I just knew you would notice that," she said. "Can this, today, be our first date, Paul?"

Paul knew exactly what she meant. She was a nice girl, was Tammy.

She would never just leap into bed with someone, drunk or not. *If* she was the love of his life (and he knew she was, even though he hadn't known her for very long), she would never betray him. And he could never, ever do anything to hurt her, of that he was certain. She was unique, rare and something to be cherished for the rest of her life. He was so lucky.

"Oh, yes," he said. "As long as the second date is really soon."

It was almost three hours before Paul remembered the reason they had returned to Tammy's room. They were lying on top of her bed and he had fallen asleep with his arm around her shoulders, their lost night's sleep finally catching up with them. He had almost, but not quite, been a perfect gentleman. Paul opened his eyes and glanced sideways, half expecting the 1962 magazine to have disappeared into thin air, but no, it was still there. Tammy was reaching out, trying not to wake him, and she slid it quietly off her bedside table. Still lying on her back, she opened it at the story and began to read it again.

Paul shifted his arm from underneath Tammy's shoulders and sat up, shaking it. "My arm's gone to sleep," he said. "Is that the ghost story?"

"Yep," Tammy said with a sigh. "I still think it's aimed at me. I'm sorry I woke you up."

"Tell you what," said Paul, "I'll nip down to the bar and get a bottle of wine and some glasses, and then we'll read it together."

"Okay."

Ten minutes later, Paul almost shivered at the description of the cold winter. He had to keep telling himself it was just fiction, not a true story about Alice Thompson. He tried hard to read between the lines. How many churchyards held graves of unknown people? How many thirteen year-old girls suffered the horror of rape in the early twentieth century? How many people accidentally attended to the funeral of someone who, in life, they hadn't known? How many women would read the story and feel the same shiver down their spine and believe it related to them?

He had to admit to himself, the answers were probably very few, or even none.

***

Tammy watched Paul's face as he read the story. At first it was serene and calm. Then he furrowed his brow and it gradually turned into a frown as he read on. She watched the rise and fall of his chest, and then his jaw dropped slightly. He flicked the pages back to look at the front cover (she knew he was looking at the date). Then he did exactly as she had done and brought the yellow-edged paper up to his nose and breathed in its mustiness and age. He turned back to the story and re-read the ending. He looked up at her.

"Bloody hell, Tammy."

They stared at each other. Tammy was swirling her wine round and round in her glass.

"And the magazine *did* fall to the floor ... just like in the last line of the story, Tammy said."

"I don't know what to say. How did she know? It's impossible. Uncanny ..." Paul's words failed him, and he shook his head. "I don't know what's happening here, Tammy, but one thing is perfectly clear to me."

"What?"

"We need to resolve all this once and for all, or else you are never going to be able to put everything that's happened to you this week behind you and move on. We need to find out for definite the identity of the unknown people in the grave."

"How?"

"Tony Troutman."

"Oh no," said Tammy. "He's awful. What makes you think he can help?"

"You said people in the village were convinced he was the murderer when the bodies were found in the fire, even though the police had eliminated him from their enquiries. There must be a reason for that, Tammy, despite the disappearance of your parents earlier that year. We can kill two birds with one stone. We'll go and see him in a while. Has Marian told him who you are yet?"

"No. I know that for a fact. She doesn't quite know how to break the news to him."

"Right. So we can go and see him and introduce you as Tamasyn Hargreaves, the writer, and then just tell him that you're his ex-wife's daughter."

"No, Paul — you're such a bloke! We can't spring it on him just like that. We'll have to wait for Marian and discuss it with her. We can go and see him to try to get to the bottom of the story of the fire, but I don't think I should tell him who I am until Marian's with me."

Paul sighed. He had thought his helter-skelter week was over and he could just get on with his life, but it now appeared he had to start delving around into the murkiness of English nobility and an unsolved crime from over thirty years ago.

CHAPTER THIRTY-FOUR

2.00 pm

The Corner House in St Andrew's Lane was shabby and neglected. Tammy could see that Marian did her best with the garden, but the front door needed painting, the garden fence was all but falling down and whilst the upstairs windows looked bright and fresh with white net curtains blowing gently in the breeze from open windows, the downstairs curtains were drawn tightly shut and the windows closed. Marian had described her father as a recluse and Tammy was apprehensive of the man she had briefly encountered in the church. Paul knocked on the front door and stepped back.

"Are you okay?" he said to Tammy.

"Yes. He might not answer."

But he did, almost straight away, and the door creaked open. Tony Troutman peered through the crack.

"Hi," Tammy said brightly. "I'm Tamasyn Hargreaves and I'm visiting the village doing some research on local history for a book I'm planning to write. I wonder if I might talk to you, Mr Troutman."

Tammy was not sure if it was just wishful thinking but she could have sworn the look of surprise was mixed with something akin to self-validation in his eyes. His voice was gruff and his mannerisms were those of a man who couldn't care less about local history, but he sniffed, wiped his huge nose on the back of his hand and opened the door wide.

"Come in if you want," he said with a cough as he ran his fingers through his thin, grey, greasy hair which needed cutting.

It felt strange to step back in time across the threshold of her mother's former home. She felt as if she was voyeuristically stepping into Pippa's shoes and into her other life. The décor was most definitely 1970s vintage wallpaper, complemented by an orange and brown patterned, worn carpet. The door to the kitchen was wide open, and she could see right through to the back door. She visualised her mother, standing in that doorway with a black plastic sack in her hand

and her father washing up at the kitchen sink. In her head, she could hear Bill Withers singing *Lovely Day*. Nothing had changed. The hallway and kitchen was just as it was the day Pippa had left. The house was suspended in time, waiting for her to return.

"That's very kind of you, Mr Troutman," Tammy said, shocked by the time-warp in which she now found herself.

Tony opened the door to the lounge and waved them inside. The curtains were closed, but a lamp was on in the corner of the dull room. There were piles and piles of old newspapers, magazines, bills and unopened junk mail heaped on every available surface. He hunted around for the remote control and switched off the television, which had been blaring away in the corner of the room. Tammy felt angry on behalf of her sister. She wanted to pound on his chest and shout and scream at him that he had denied Marian the chance to see her mother before she died, but there was something very sad and buckled about him. It was as if the veneer of the horrible, insensitive, bawdy man who made jokes about poor, frail old ladies on the day of their funeral had been stripped away to leave behind someone uncertain and frightened.

"Sit down," he said, and belched. He cleared a space on the sofa.

Marian was obviously every bit as trapped by her father as Tammy was by Alan. The Tony Troutman slumped beside her could be Alan in twenty years' time if she hadn't forced him to face up to his future, come back to Lyverton and break free from a bleak, lonely life without his precious Pippa.

"Mr Troutman. I was wondering if you could tell me anything about the Fawsden fire in 1978?" Tammy said.

Tony Troutman shifted uncomfortably in his armchair. Tammy could tell she had knocked the breath out of his chest. The subject was obviously something he was very sensitive about.

"Why would I want to do that, Miss Hargreaves?"

"Because," Tammy said slowly, "I need to find out whose bodies were found in the old barn after the fire and why they had been there since 1962. I think you know exactly who they are, don't you? And how they died?"

Paul looked at her, alarmed. It was a shot in the dark on Tammy's behalf, but if the breathless hypothesis about the origins of Tony Troutman's former wealth she had hurriedly explained to him just before they had arrived was correct, either one or both of the victims had been murdered in 1962 and Tony Troutman knew all about it.

"It was a cover-up, wasn't it," Tammy continued. "And you couldn't tell anyone the truth because you were blackmailed?"

"Blackmail? What on earth are you talking about? I don't know nothing 'bout that ..."

"I think you might know what happened." Tammy continued.

Tony shook his head and pushed back with both hands on the arm of his chair, as if trying to disappear into the cushions.

"You're talking rubbish, woman. Absolute rubbish. It was nowt to do with me."

Tammy watched as Tony Troutman's face flushed to a deep crimson colour. He began breathing heavily and eventually he spoke, his voice a mere whisper as the redness drained from his face.

"How the bloody hell do you know that?"

Tammy didn't quite know what she was expecting, but it wasn't a total breakdown. The man put his head in his hands and started rocking backwards and forwards as his guilty, sordid, skeleton tumbled out of the closet.

"They bloody well destroyed me," he bubbled almost incoherently through his fingers. "The bastards — stitched me up they did. Shut me up good and proper. I thought it would be the end of it once they'd offered to pay to keep me quiet, but it was only the start."

Tony Troutman turned into an old man in front of Tammy's eyes. He took his hands away from his red, broken-veined face and his face contorted into an anguished grimace. "If they find out I've spoken to you, I'm a dead man. And you will be, too, if you speak about it. Even now they are dead, they're watching me — and they'll watch you too, if you start digging around too much. You can't fart against thunder, you know. They're all in it — the police, royalty — all in it together they are. Corrupt as hell."

"Go on, Mr Troutman," Paul said gently. "It's got to come out now. They can't do anything to you after all this time, they're all dead!"

Tony gulped, struggling to separate the past from the present in his

307

head as he told the story.

"It was early June 1962. Marian was just a toddler and my ex-wife, Phyll, and I were heading out in the countryside, on foot, for an afternoon picnic. Everyone went for picnics in the summer in those days.

"A white-haired man and a middle-aged woman in a black Humber Sceptre drove past us on a track out Fawsden way. It was a scorching hot day and me and Phyll and the nipper were walking to a very nice little place I knew by a stream, where we could eat our picnic and get away from the stresses and strains of life for a couple of hours. Just as the Humber Sceptre passed us, a red MGB GT came tearing past and skidded to a halt in front of it. A furious, middle-aged man jumped out of the car and yanked open the driver's door of the Humber."

Tony paused, his eyes wide with ancient terror and Tammy noticed a slight tremble in his voice as he remembered what happened.

"The MGB man shouted at the woman in the Sceptre: *'You dirty whore … and with my own father … don't you realise what he is? You dirty stinking slut.'* Then he yelled at the older man in the Sceptre. *'Don't think I don't know about all the little girls you've fiddled with over the years. Well, father, this is for them.'* He brought a shotgun up to his eye to take aim and a second later there was a single blast. *'And this is for my mother.'* Then there was another blast and the man reloaded the shotgun. *'And my daughter.'* A third shot. The old man was slumped forwards over the steering wheel, brains, blood and gore splattered all over the inside of the car like it was the inside of an abattoir. The woman screamed and screamed and then another blast rang out and she was silent too. Shot dead, both of them. Instantly. It was only then that the man saw us. We had stepped into a gap in the hedgerow when we heard the car coming down the track behind us. The murderer realised we had witnessed everything. He turned the gun on us in a panic and threatened us, too. He even thrust the gun into Marian's temple. I honestly thought we were all going to die. Then he made a pact with me. He wouldn't kill Marian and Phyllis if I helped him dispose of the bodies."

Paul and Tammy were silent, shocked. Tammy hadn't known quite what she was expecting to hear when she had — rightly as it turned

308

out — assumed that 1962 was significant in the case of the unknown bodies and she had surmised that Tony Troutman's sudden wealth during Marian's childhood might be connected to the mystery. Now the depraved, evil truth was tumbling out of Tony's lips, Tammy just felt sick at the vivid description of a violent murder.

"I thought I was going to die," Tony said simply. "I didn't think he would let me live, once I had helped him dispose of the bodies. I did as he asked to save my wife and daughter — to give them a chance to get away."

Tammy shook her head. "It must have been terrifying," she said quietly. "I think you were very brave."

Tony Troutman continued. "I had no choice. Once I realised the murdered man was Frederick De Montpelier, the then Earl of Fawsden, and the murderer was his son, I knew there was no way Guy de Montpelier would let me live. He was holding the gun to Marian's head, his finger on the trigger. I was almost demented with fear. My precious baby girl meant nothing to him. He would have blown her brains out, too, in the blinking of an eye and the merest twitch of his trigger finger, had I made just one wrong move."

Tony screwed his eyes shut and shuddered as he remembered what had happened afterwards.

"I was forced into helping him hide the bodies in the old barns. The roof timbers had fallen in, so we piled all the old timber on top of the bodies first. Some of the stone had crumbled into the barns, too, and so we piled that on top of the timber. We then cleaned up the Humber Sceptre as best we could with water from the stream and some spare nappies of Marian's. There was so much blood, bits of brain and grey-white splinters of bone, it took us absolutely ages. I threw up more than once, I can tell you. Marian was screaming her head off ... Phyll was trying to keep her from seeing what was happening ... wailing in terror ..."

He paused for breath, his chest heaving in distress as he shook his head in anguish.

"Then Guy De Montpelier forced me to drive the Sceptre back to Fawsden Hall down narrow, bumpy tracks and across open fields, its windscreen shattered by the shotgun blasts. I had to leave poor Phyll and Marian stranded in the middle of nowhere. Phyll knew that if she called the police, I would be shot dead instantly."

"How did you get back to Mum … er … I mean Phyll …? How did she and Marian get home if she was left in the middle of nowhere?"

Tammy blushed furiously and mentally kicked herself for the slip-up, hoping Tony hadn't noticed.

He had.

"Mum?" he said. "You called my Phyll, *mum*?"

CHAPTER THIRTY-FIVE

3:30 pm

Marian came home from school to find her father, Paul and Tammy sitting on white plastic patio chairs in her garden. She stood in the doorway, shocked, and let her heavy shoulder bag fall to the floor in disbelief.

"Dad?"

Tony's shoulders hunched over as if he was cowering from her. He flinched like a whipped dog, frightened of what she might say to him because he had let strangers into the house. His hands began to shake as he clutched the edge of his chair.

"Dad?" Marian repeated menacingly.

He didn't answer. Suddenly, Marian knew exactly how Alan had felt on Saturday night, because running away seemed a welcome option. Uncovered and stripped bare of the camouflage that had served her well for many years, she could hide no more. Of all the guilty secrets that that been churned up out of the earth in the last few days, her passive aggression towards her father was the last to be dug up and exposed. But Marian's secret was different, revealed not by words but by the reaction of her father when she'd come home.

"Dad. Look at me!"

Tony looked up. It was as clear as the blue sky overhead that he was the child and Marian the adult, and had been for some considerable years.

"I take it you know the truth about Tammy. Why did you deliberately hide my letters?"

The scathing words hit a wall of disbelief. Tammy knew Tony had not deliberately hidden Pippa's letters. Neglected, stripped of all respect for himself and his surroundings and hated by his only daughter for the huge mortgage that tied her emotionally and physically to The Corner House, Tony was a man who had been kicked mercilessly down the slippery slope of social decline. He truly believed he was nothing but a parasite to society, and he was the shield

311

behind which Marian could hide. When she had sobbed and cried in despair in Tammy's room the night Alan had shown up, it had not been because Tony had taken what was rightfully hers, it was because she had let him. She had always known he hid things, but it suited her. She liked playing Cinderella, the sympathy-drawing role of downtrodden drudgery. Keeping her father down helped her to act out her part on life's stage. Whilst he was cowering from that which he no longer needed to fear, she could roll her eyes, sigh dramatically and everyone instantly sympathised with her. It had been so easy to perpetuate the terror in his eyes and the guilt that had flowed through his veins every single day of his life since that fateful day in 1978 when she had discovered that her father had witnessed a shocking murder sixteen years previously. She had found out how he had taken the huge sums of money on offer to cover up nobility's dirty secrets, but Marian had known, then, that some things couldn't be bought at any price, and one of them had been her mother's happiness.

In a single, blinding flash of knowledge, Marian realised that she, too, had paid a heavy price for using her poor, broken father as a defence against the harsh realities of her life. The price she had paid was almost thirty years of the love of her mother.

"I didn't hide no letters, love."

"You did. You let my mother die without seeing me again!"

"Die? Phyll is dead! No. No. You're making a mistake ..."

Tony Troutman began to cry. Huge racking sobs shook his body and mucus bubbled out of his nose as tears trickled down his cheeks. "Phyll, Phyll ... my baby ... oh, no."

***

The truth rang out in Paul's head. It was as clear, real and solid as the village church bells on a crisp winter's morning. Once Tony had vented his anger on Alan for running off with his wife, and threatened to kill him if he ever set foot in Lyverton again, he'd withered and deflated like a punctured balloon. He had waited for Pippa to come back for thirty years, changing nothing in the house, keeping it preserved for her return, and all the time being trodden into life's carpet by his daughter, who despised him for being an accessory to murder and resented him for his financial ruin when the hush money had stopped with the death of Guy de Montpelier. Marian was completely unable to see the tragedy of it all. Now Paul had just watched the last vestiges of hope die in Tony's heart, he just felt sorry for the man. He might not have been a charismatic and charming character in his younger years, but Paul could see the real Tony Troutman as a loveable rogue, rather than an evil man. He had been a rough diamond with a heart; after all, he had thought he would be killed, too, in 1962 and had co-operated with a murderer only to save his wife and daughter.

Tammy knelt before Tony on the lawn and took his hands. Paul felt incredibly sorry for him: he was a man who had been haunted by a terrible, potentially scandalous, crime for almost fifty years, innocently caught up in the hard web of an exclusive society where money could buy everything and meant nothing. Money might have been able to buy silence and protection from long arms of a law tied back in straight-jackets of corruption, secret societies, promises and ridiculous paragraphs of legislation that let real criminals walk free, but it couldn't buy happiness, love and a clear conscience.

It was perfectly clear to Paul that the weight of the covered-up royal scandal and murder had destroyed both Tony's marriage and his sense of self-worth, despite the material luxuries the hush money had bought.

Paul watched as Tammy took Tony's hands in hers and he felt a sudden rush of pride for the incredibly strong woman it had taken only one week for him to fall in love with.

"Tony?" Tammy said gently. "My mother died of cancer two years ago."

Tony lifted his head. Mucus and tears were still running out of his eyes and huge purple nose.

Tammy continued. "Can you forgive my father? Can you let us back into your life? I promise I'll help you, every way I can. This is a terrible story, but I can't see you had any other choice. Anyone would have done the same to protect their family."

"You're a nice little lassie," Tony mumbled, deliberately not looking at Marian. "Clever too — just like your mother was."

313

Marian let Paul lead her back into the house as Tammy talked to Tony in the garden.

"You must think I'm a dreadful person ..." she began to say, but Paul cut her off.

"It's all about survival, Marian. Don't blame yourself. It's a shocking story."

"I saw him as a criminal when I found out the real reason I had been brought up in opulence and luxury. In my eyes he had sold his soul to the devil. I resented him when I found out the truth, but then people were so sympathetic and supportive to me when he suffered his breakdown, I lapped up the attention. But then he trapped me here, in this house. I couldn't see any escape and I hated him for it. God, I'm such an evil cow ..."

"You knew he hid letters?"

"Yes. I did try to sort through his piles once in a while, but then, instead of confronting the issue, I just got everything of importance — bills and personal stuff — sent to me at the school. It saved such a lot of hassle."

"You need to live for now, Marian," said Paul. "You need to forget about the past, let go of all this hatred and anger, and grasp your future. It's strange, but this week has marked a turning point in all our lives — you; me; Tammy; Alan; Tony and even Cynthia."

"How can I ever make it up to him, Paul?"

"That's easy. Just give him a hug and say sorry. He's your father and he loves you, no matter what you might have done. Tammy is talking to him right now, telling him that there's nothing to be frightened of any more."

***

They had a table already booked for eight o'clock that night. Paul spoke to the chef and increased the booking by one person, leaving Marian to sort out some suitable clothes for her father.

As well as Daniel and Sophie, Cynthia had asked Marjorie and her husband, and Alan's old friend, Davey, and his wife to join them all for dinner.

Tammy thought she ought to contact the police straightaway about her conversation with Tony, but Paul shook his head at the suggestion.

"Why rake everything up today, Tammy? Everyone's dead now and if you ask me, Frederick De Montpelier got his just desserts in the end. What is worse than being a depraved paedophile and rapist, then murdered by your son for sexually abusing your own daughter and granddaughter? Harry Thompson is the hero. It's his name that's carved forever on the war memorial in the village. He gave his life for King and Country and was an honourable man. Frederick de Montpelier was nothing but a wood louse. People will lay wreaths in Harry's memory for years and years to come. Who will remember cowardly, evil Frederick De Montpelier in his unnamed grave? Who will lay flowers in his memory? No one single person will grieve for him. Let sleeping dogs lie for a while. Don't ruin the rest of the time we have together before you have to go back to Yorkshire. We can decide what to do about it next week when Tony's in a bit better frame of mind about things. Not only that, we need to consider the potential repercussions if we go public with all this."

The mystery of who paid for the grave and headstone had been resolved, too. Tony had told Tammy that the three kind ladies, Alice Thompson, Lucy Staverley and her sister, Emily, had paid, because they felt so sorry that villagers were gossiping and accusing him of murder, and rumours had been rife that the bodies were those of Phyllis Troutman and her young lover. People had not believed the official line that the murdered bodies could be those of the missing Earl of Fawsden, Frederick de Montpelier and his daughter-in-law, Lady Teresa, because forensic evidence could not conclusively identify the charred remains and Guy de Montpelier refused to take responsibility for the unidentified bodies.

It was clear to both Tammy and Paul that Alice Thompson and the Staverley twins had been perfectly aware of the identity of the unknown bodies. Tammy imagined the creeping grapevine of nobility's secrets somehow reaching their ears and, tight-lipped and resolute, they had felt that justice for poor Jessie's suffering had, at long last, been done.

When they returned to the Red Lion, leaving Marian and Tony to

315

get ready for the celebratory dinner, Tammy discovered she hadn't got a single thing to wear.

"I'll have to go shopping," she said to Paul. "Have I got time?"

He looked at his watch. "If the shops shut at six, you have exactly one hour."

Tammy jumped straight into her car and headed for the shops in Fawsden. She just needed to buy a smart top and perhaps a skirt. She could wear the accessories she had bought on Wednesday last week.

Less than an hour later, Tammy drove back into the village, her hurried purchases on the back seat of her car.

She glanced into her rear view mirror to check for traffic behind her as she slowed down and approached the village sign. It was déjà vu as she noticed her mother's eyes once more. It was just a fleeting moment — a mere shooting star in the vastness of time — but just for a few seconds Tammy could hear Pippa's voice whispering to her inside her head:

'A time to keep silence, and a time to speak … a time to love … and a time for peace.'

Tammy shivered with a sudden tingle down her back as she glanced, once again, at the village sign as she drove past.

Lyverton was where she wanted to spend the rest of her life. She had never been so certain of anything: it sounded twee and clichéd, but she felt she had always belonged there. Her home in Yorkshire could be on the other side of the world it seemed so far away. She would have to go back initially, of course, to tie up the loose ends of her life, but then she would return, and this time she *would* be returning to Lyverton, having been there before, not like last week when she had realised that she wasn't actually returning to the village as it was her first visit.

As she pulled into the pub car park, she could see Alan and Cynthia were back from their day out, unloading the boot of Alan's car. She pulled in alongside them.

"Well? How did it go?"

"We've had a smashing day, haven't we Alan? Fantastic. We've really enjoyed ourselves," Cynthia said, her red, sun-flushed, florid cheeks almost disappearing into her eyes because her smile was so broad.

"I mean with Claire. Was she all right?"

"A bit quiet."

"Paul's parents seem very nice," Alan said as he slammed the boot lid shut. "I gave little Lewis some money for his money box. He's a smashing little lad."

"Your father is a very kind and generous man," Cynthia said. "He wouldn't let me pay for anything today. He's spoiled me rotten. I feel like a fairy princess."

"Where did you go then?" Tammy asked, trying not to laugh.

Cynthia and Alan looked at each other and giggled. "We went to the pleasure beach in Great Yarmouth," Alan grinned. "We went on the dodgems, the pirate ship and — you'll never believe this, Tammy — we went on the log flume. We got absolutely soaked and Cynthia had to dry her hair under a hand dryer in some public toilets. I haven't laughed so much in years."

***

Tammy sat next to Tony Troutman at dinner. She could see that he had a long way to go, and he seemed to be more accepting of her than of Alan, which was understandable, she supposed. He was quiet, hardly saying a word and his frightened dark eyes darted back and forth, startled and confused by the unaccustomed chit-chat of a social occasion.

There was much laughter and Tammy found it hard to believe that just over a week ago she could have been so upset at witnessing a scene so like the one she was now very much a part of. When the happy woman, who was around the same age as her mother, had enjoyed an evening out with her family, Tammy had felt envious. The laughter and togetherness of a happy family occasion had accentuated her own isolation and pessimism about her future. Now, just one week later, Tammy realised that life goes where destiny takes you; it might encourage you to sit back and do nothing or you could reach out and touch other people's lives with your own and change things with a snap of the fingers. Life was all about the love of a family, whether related by blood or not. It was about compassion and humanity — not

317

money; not possessions and most certainly not secrets, which were like immortal rats scavenging around the barrel of life.

Tammy glanced sideways at Tony, caught Marian's eye and smiled. Together they would coax him out of his shell and help him to live again. He would probably never completely be comfortable with Alan but they could all try to mend things the best they could. It might not be perfect, but it would be an improvement and any improvement was a success. Families were rarely models of harmonious perfection, anyway.

Daniel got up from his chair at the other end of the table and made his way over to Tammy. He crouched down and nudged her arm and then whispered in her ear.

"Your dad's holding hands with Cynthia," he grinned.

Tammy felt a pang of sadness for her mother, but she knew nothing would bring Pippa back, and Alan still had many years of life in front of him, as did Cynthia. She was nothing like Pippa and, Tammy suspected, Alan was nothing like Rabbie. Even if their relationship went nowhere (despite her glorious premonition that morning when she'd imagined her future children calling Cynthia 'Granny' outside the post office), and it was just a fleeting romance, it would be the first step on the dusty track of a new life for both of them.

Paul smiled at her, took her hand under the table and squeezed it. Tammy smiled back and returned the squeeze as they gazed at each other. She knew without any doubt she loved him, despite the short time she had known him, and it was a lasting type of love. Transparent and honest, she felt she could see right into his soul and, if she could, she would reach into it and gently untangle the knots that remained following the aftermath of a vandalised, tarnished love and the worst kind of betrayal a man could face. Tammy was not stupid though. She knew that only time and complete trust in each other could untangle those knots in Paul's heart.

The main topic of conversation around the table was the story of Alice's box and the secrets it had revealed about Harry and Jessie Thompson and the Staverley twins. There was much speculation about which one of the twins had been Jessie's baby.

318

"I think it was Emily-Rose," Sophie Staverley said confidently. "It must have been. I think she found out as a teenager and that's why she became a missionary. It would be terrible to discover that your parents weren't your mum and dad, after all, and that your real father was a royal paedophile and rapist."

Cynthia shook her head. "No, I think you're wrong, Sophie. It was Lucy-Joy. They were sisters. It's so obvious. Alice and Lucy were inseparable all their lives. I think they always knew."

"Who do *you* think was Jessie's baby?" Tammy asked Paul.

"I don't know and don't think it matters," he said. "But I tend to agree with Sophie, I think it was Emily-Rose, but I don't think she ever knew."

"You really must write about it," Cynthia said to Tammy. "Remember what I said to you last Thursday afternoon?"

"Dressmakers make dresses; photographers take photographs and writers write?" Tammy laughed.

"Exactly." Cynthia looked around the table. "Don't you all agree?"

"Yes!" Everyone chorused, nodding and chuckling and Tammy blushed, embarrassed.

"I don't know if I'm cut out to be a writer," she whispered in Paul's ear.

"Polly-Anne Staverley was," he whispered back, and kissed her ear. It sent a delectable tingle right down her back into her leg and she looked at her watch, wondering if she was going to be able to wait much longer before she showed Paul that really she wasn't quite the nice girl he thought she was.

"Perhaps I should write it as a ghost story?" she speculated.

Paul shook his head and grimaced. "I think we should keep well away from ghost stories, or else people will think we are complete nutters."

Tammy thought about what Paul had said. There really was more to this world than human beings had discovered and Polly-Anne, writing as Margaret Regent, had somehow tapped into this unseen energy. Or could it have been Alice herself who had set the tumbleweed rolling into the future? Did she have a vivid dream of her own funeral, just like Tammy had dreamed of Jessie's rape? Was that

319

dream so lifelike and sharp she wanted to share it with someone and Polly-Anne Staverley was the person she shared it with? Had Polly thought it would make a cracking good story, and used the dream as the basis for her fiction special? Tammy had no doubt at all that Polly wrote the ghost story as fiction, and probably had no idea that, forty-seven years later it would so magically touch her life and set a tormented man and his daughter free from a sordid and dirty past. She imagined her scribbling a plot outline for the story in June 1962. Her little blue netbook computer had finally come in handy earlier that evening, when she had spent a few minutes researching the De Montpelier family history on the internet. Frederick's reputation had been legendary, although he had always managed to escape prosecution for various accusations of sexual molestation of children. His lifetime of depravity and controversy had left people unsurprised when he'd disappeared in 1962. The consensus at that time seemed to have been that he'd escaped abroad and taken on a new identity because of huge debts and an impending nasty court case involving an accusation of incest by his own daughter.

Tammy had stared at old photographs of him. He appeared wild and unkempt for a member of the British aristocracy, with a cigar clenched between his blackening teeth as he grinned at the camera, his dicky-bow awry, obviously drunk, She shivered, remembering her dream and had to look away from the screen. Although he was much older in the photograph, the way he smirked at the camera and the look in his eyes told her he was undeniably the same man.

It was too much of a coincidence, though, that Polly-Anne had been so accurate in her predictions of the future, and Tammy wondered what ghostly hand guided hers as the story was written and published in 1962 uniquely for her in the here and now.

The evening was drawing to a close. Tammy had drunk too much wine again, but who cared? Alan walked over to her. He stood at the back of Tammy's chair and bent down to speak to Tony, who spun around.

Alan extended his hand and Tony took it. Tammy heard Alan say, " ... *for the sake of our girls* ... *for Marian and Tammy* ..." and then the uncertain, stilted conversation between them was drowned out by

Daniel telling everyone how Tammy had got it all completely wrong, and he and Sophie were not having a relationship, they were just good friends.

Tammy knew she would never forget the moment. It would shine in her lifetime of memories like a precious diamond necklace.

"Tammy," Alan said simply, his eyes shining with pride. "Thank you for having the courage to come to Lyverton and give me —us — our lives back. I love you, Petal."

She was reborn.

CHAPTER THIRTY-SIX

Day Ten
Wednesday, 3rd June: 7.45 am

Finally, at long last, Tammy woke up next to Paul. The sun was shining through the curtains in the blue-grey light of early morning, the birds were singing and Tammy was gloriously happy.

She wriggled slightly in Paul's bed. She had forgotten to take her mother's charm bracelet off last night in her haste to slide between the sheets with Paul. She slipped out of bed and tried not to wake him when she plugged in the kettle, but he caught her as she walked past and she fell back into his arms, laughing.

"What shall we do today?"

"Stay in bed," Paul replied, "all day." He grabbed her wrist gently and inspected her bracelet. "Was this your mother's?"

Pippa's charm bracelet was a curious hybrid of memories that connected the two halves of her life. Tammy knew there was only one person who should wear it now.

"I'd like to go for a walk on my own before breakfast," she said. "I have something I need to give to Marian."

"I think that would be a lovely gesture," Paul replied, reading her mind.

Once she had showered and dressed in her own room, she went back into Paul's room and gave him a kiss before she set off. It was still very early. Not too early, she hoped. As she walked down St Andrew's Lane, she glanced at the vicarage and smiled. She wasn't Jessie. Jessie wasn't her. Their souls were most definitely connected by something. There was a life force that joined them through the ripples of time, like twin stars, but they couldn't be the same person, could they? Paul had repaired Jessie's locket for her and, that morning, she had replaced it around her neck. It cemented the connection. It was as if it was just a sheet of the thinnest, gossamer silk that separated Tammy in the present day from Jessie in 1910.

Tony Troutman answered the door. Tammy almost reeled

backwards at the transformation. He was wearing clean clothes. A white shirt open at the neck, tucked into smart beige canvass trousers. He smelled of soap and aftershave and his hair was smoothed back. Even his nose didn't seem so big and bulbous.

"Tammy!" he said with something that she felt might, one day, develop into genuine affection in his eyes. "What a lovely surprise."

"Thank you for coming out with us last night," she said. "I hope you enjoyed yourself."

"Oh, I did, lass. I did. When you came round yesterday afternoon and said you knew about the murders, it lifted everything right off my shoulders. I'd been carrying that burden, you know, for nearly fifty years. I still can't believe my Phyll is gone, though. If only I'd read the letter, we could have both been there for her at the end and she could have died in peace. I don't remember signing for it, and I wouldn't have opened it, but I suppose it's here somewhere ..."

"Hi Tammy!" Marian ran down the stairs. "I thought I heard your voice; you're up early."

"I'm a woman on a mission," said Tammy, laughing.

"Not before you've had a nice cup of tea," Tony said and disappeared into the kitchen with a spring in his step. "After all, we're going to be a proper little family now, with you being our Marian's sister."

Marian and Tammy stepped into the living room. It was still a mess, but the curtains were thrown back, the windows were wide open and the sun, fresh pure air and a faint smell of summer was streaming in. Tammy put her hand in her coat pocket.

"I want you to have this, Marian." She held out her mother's charm bracelet.

Marian took it from the palm of Tammy's hand and gasped.

"Oh, Tammy — are you sure? It's so personal to her life with Alan. I don't know, It's too much." Her eyes shone with gratitude and Tammy knew she had done the right thing, even though Pippa's charm bracelet had been her most treasured possession.

Tammy explained to Marian the meaning of all the charms and Alan's life with his precious Pippa rolled out like a yellow brick road, way, way into the distance. Marian took the first step on the road as

Tammy told her the story of the moon and the stars, the key and the bird in the cage that Pippa had always joked looked like a cuckoo and not a canary.

They didn't realise Tony was standing in the doorway, holding two mugs of tea.

"I don't know where she got this one from. She'd never say. It was the only one I didn't know about," Tammy said.

"Is it a miniature bible?" Tony interrupted.

"Yes," Tammy replied, looking up at him.

"I bought it as a present for her on the occasion of Marian's christening," he said, very formally, and then cleared his throat, embarrassed. "The bracelet itself was my present to her on the day Marian was born."

"No wonder she'd never tell me what it represented! I didn't know about Marian until just three years ago." The secret, wistful reticence Tammy had sensed in her mother's warm, brown eyes loosened and dissolved into the treasure chest of her life.

"Thank you, Tammy. You don't know how much it means to me to have this," Marian said, inspecting the charms one by one.

Tony put the two mugs down on the coffee table.

"Can I have a look?"

Marian handed the bracelet to him. He inspected each charm in turn. Then he cradled it to his chest and his face distorted in anguish.

"When I bought her this bracelet, we were so happy. We didn't have two ha'pennies to rub together — really hard up we were. I had to save up for it for weeks and weeks. Husbands weren't allowed to be with their wives when babies were born in the sixties, but nothing could stop me bursting into the delivery room when I heard Marian's first cry. I can tell you, Tammy, there was no prouder bloke than me that day. It was the happiest day of my life and when I fastened this bracelet around my lovely Phyll's wrist I imagined it filled with charms, each one representing an event in our bright future. I don't know how many times I've regretted our picnic on that day in 1962. We nearly didn't go, you know. Phyll wanted to go to Hunstanton for the day, but I couldn't face the drive, and so we went for a picnic instead. If *only* we'd just gone to the seaside."

Tony shook his head, his eyes swimming with tears. "It all went wrong from then on. I can't believe I'll never see her again. I've waited so long ... and now she's gone."

Tammy surveyed the scene before her. The wreckage of lost years and lost lifetimes caused by evil and corruption was as bad as any road traffic accident. She wondered how many opportunities there had been over the years for a burying of the hatchet, or a compromise. How many times could her father jumped in his car, made a two or three hour car journey and knocked on the front door of this house? How many times could her mother have just picked up the phone and dialled her old friend, Alice, or anyone she knew in this village, and asked to be put in touch with her daughter, instead of relying on letters and cards sent through the post that would never be opened?

Tammy could almost see the metamorphosis of Tony Troutman beginning before her eyes. He was shakily grasping at his future as he struggled back over the edge of the swirling vortex. It wouldn't be easy for him, Tammy thought to herself. He'd need professional help to enter the world properly again, and Paul had been right when he said they needed to think carefully before going to the Police about the royal cover-up. *'A time to keep silence ...'* her mother's voice whispered, drilling deep and true into her subconscious mind.

***

Tammy closed her eyes and felt the wind in her hair. It lightly brushed her face in gossamer strands. She was so alive she could feel the blood of a thousand ancestors pumping through her veins. Who would have thought that just one week ago she could have squared up to, and conquered, her own destiny. Was it the spirit of her mother that had guided her here and given her the strength to face the tasks and challenges the complicated world had put before her? Tammy didn't know what her future held, but she did know she held it in the palm of her hand at that moment, as fragile, delicate and short-lived as a snowflake.

Tammy opened her eyes again and they sparkled in the sunlight as she smiled at Paul beside her and then gazed upon a landscape unchanged for a hundred years. Just a few thousand rising suns

325

separated Tammy and Paul from Harry and Jessie. Just ninety-nine years, practically nothing in the history of the Earth.

As Paul turned to look at her, he took her hand. His natural scepticism had been replaced by a unique kind of knowing.

"We are walking in their footsteps, Tammy," he whispered. "We are picking up the thread of their lives."

"Are we really them, Paul? Are *we* Harry and Jessie?"

Paul shrugged his shoulders. "There is so much about this world we haven't yet discovered. I think mankind has only scratched the surface."

The glorious Northamptonshire countryside fell away in front of her and the warmth of Paul's hand holding hers made her feel loved and safe. At the foot of the hill the breeze blew over the surface of the water in the old quarries, now home to greater-crested grebes, swans, geese and ducks.

Tammy stared at a row of derelict terraced cottages a hundred yards away. Quarry Cottages. It was obvious work hadn't yet started and the houses were sad and tired, waiting to be brought back to life by a property developer. A hoarding at the top of the track advertised the forthcoming development:

Lakeside Cottages
A unique development of four luxury properties

Tammy knew, then, as the words on the hoarding underlined the truth. They really *had* been visited by the ghosts of Jessie and Harry, just as they were in 1910, poised on the brink of their perfect, but short-lived, life together, but she wasn't frightened. She knew she would never see again.

"Thank you for coming to meet me," Tammy said. "and it was lovely of you to bring these." She inspected the bouquet of flowers in her hand, buried her face in the blooms and breathed in the heady smell of her future. She owed it to poor Jessie, her own life tragically cut short at twenty-eight, to make the very best of it.

It was still early — not yet ten o'clock. Paul and Tammy strolled, hand in hand, back to the village, into the churchyard and over to

Alice's grave through dancing shadows cast by the swish of wind through fir, silver birch and copper beech trees. The ground was heaped into a neat mound and tired, floral tributes still remained from her funeral last week. Tammy plucked a single red rose from the flowers Paul had brought, and then placed the bouquet on the mound.

"She drew so many people together," Tammy said. "I'm so sad I never knew her myself. She could easily have been a grandmother to me, you know, because she and my mother were such good friends back in the 1960s. Marian told me."

Paul nodded in agreement. "If you had decided to come to Lyverton just a few weeks earlier, you probably would have met her in person."

"No," Tammy whispered. "I know I was never meant to meet her — I think it has all happened exactly as it should."

Paul breathed in sharply as he suddenly understood. "It's like I said a while back at the top of the track to the quarry, there's got to be so much more to this world than meets the eye. Something breathtaking has happened to us all this week."

"Yes," Tammy agreed, remembering the hymn in the church on Sunday. "Something immortal, invisible and wise."

A nearby cuckoo began its distinctive high-low call. Paul and Tammy both looked up into the nearby trees but couldn't see it.

"I can't believe it. A cuckoo. Fancy that! I think it's coming from over there," Paul said, pointing towards the edge of the churchyard.

"Jessie's grave is under that tree," Tammy added. "Let's go and put this rose on her grave and look for it."

As they approached Jessie's graveside, hand in hand, a solitary magpie jerked its head around to look at them, then fluttered and flapped from the branches of an immature tree. They watched it disappear, high into the sky.

"It was just a magpie," Paul said as he took the rose from Tammy's hand. "How strange, it sounded just like a cuckoo."

He bent down and placed the single red rose on Jessie's grave. "One for sorrow — quite apt, really ..."

"Two for joy — look, Paul, there's another one!"

***

The village sighed, satiated and content as it held its long-lost daughter to its breast, having regurgitated the bitter secrets of her past. Like a lover savouring the last, sweet kiss, there was one, beautiful secret Lyverton would never, ever reveal. It would remain, buried deep within its heart until the end of time, the only clue being a tiny curl of golden hair clasped within the gold locket nestled between the breasts of its precious daughter.

CHAPTER THIRTY-SEVEN

21st June 1910: 7:00 am

The baby was born in a caul, almost completely encased in its amniotic sac. Polly's eyes widened at the grotesque, grey-blue mass that emerged from between Jessie's legs. There was no time to prepare for the birth. No time to decide what was to be done.

"Oh my giddy aunt," Polly's Auntie Gwen exclaimed as she tore Jessie's underwear from her, the baby almost slithering to the floor.

The child fitted almost entirely in Gwen's cupped hands. It was lifeless. Unmoving. Jessie's wailing began to subside and Harry fell to his knees beside the wicker chair on which Jessie half sat and half lay. He cradled her head into his chest so she couldn't see.

"It's dead," Gwen said. "It was much too premature to survive."

"It's all right, Jess," Harry said loudly, trying to drown out the fearsome-looking woman's harsh words. "You're going to be all right now. You're safe."

"We need scissors, and string — quick!" Gwen barked.

Polly stared as her father grabbed a roll of garden twine and some scissors from the windowsill of the garden room where he'd left them the previous day. Her Auntie Gwen deftly tied off the cord so that Jessie wouldn't bleed, and cut it roughly, holding the baby in one hand. A last heartbeat of blood spurted from the baby's untied end of the cord.

"It's stillborn. A miscarriage," she said, discarding the pitiful outcome of human violence and depravity onto the cold, quarry tiled floor. "Will someone please tell me what on earth is going on?" she added turning to Reverend Staverley. "What is this child doing here, miscarrying babies all over the floor?"

"They just turned up at the front door," he said, stunned and shocked at the bloody scene before his eyes. "Not two minutes ago."

Polly stared at the lifeless baby, still in its membranes, thrown away on the quarry-tiled, cold floor like a lump of something the dog had thrown up. She looked away feeling sick, but a slight movement caught her eye. Her heart began to beat faster. The baby had moved. She picked it up gently, and then pulled the membranes away from its face. The tiny baby opened its eyes and Polly watched, enchanted, as it took its first, painful breath. Instinctively Polly pulled her smock around the baby to keep it warm and cradled it in the crook of her arm.

"Auntie Gwen …"

"Not now, Polly. You really shouldn't be here …"

"But Auntie Gwen, the baby's breathing …"

The child in Polly's arms cried. It was a weak, pitiful, thin squeak, more like an animal sound than the cry of a human baby.

"Look." Polly showed the baby to her Auntie.

"Oh, no …" Gwen grumbled. "… I hate it when this happens. Polly give it here, and then go straight into the kitchen and put the kettle on for some hot water."

Gwen took the tiny baby from the crook of Polly's arm, held it in her hand and spun around on her heels as if looking for something. She grabbed a loose, chintzy cushion from the second wicker chair in the room and held it over the baby, pressing down hard.

Polly would never quite remember who it was screamed first. It might have been her, or it might have been Jessie. But for the rest of her life she would never forget what happened next.

"No!" cried Harry, in a squeaky voice, jumping up from the floor. "What are you doing?"

He tore the cushion out of Gwen's hand, scooped the baby out of her other hand and cradled it in his palms. It was flaccid, naked and the wet surface of its skin was cold. He put his mouth over the baby's nose and mouth and exhaled very gently and slowly.

"Come on, little baby. Breathe. Breathe. Dear Lord … please let it breathe. Please, please …"

Gwen began to complain. "It can't live, boy. It's too tiny. It's so early, I don't think it's even a seven-month baby. It's kindest — believe me — better to smother it quickly and painlessly with a cushion than leave it to die by an open window like some midwives would …"

"No!" yelled Harry and blew gently into the baby's nose and mouth again.

The baby squirmed in his hands.

330

"Harry?" Jessie's voice was bewildered and child-like.

Harry leaned forwards and tore open Jessie's clothes, the buttons popping off the front of her smock and rattling to the floor. He nestled the baby inside her clothes, next to her naked breasts.

"We have to keep it warm, Jess. This is the best place for it."

The baby opened its eyes again and instinctively began to root weakly for Jessie's nipple, blood trickling from its untied umbilical cord. Jessie guided her breast into position and the baby began to suck furiously as if it was desperate to live, frantic to make its mark on a wicked world where educated young members of the British royal family raped thirteen year old girls and got away with it.

"What is it?"

"I don't know." Harry peeled back Jessie's smock and underclothes gently.

"It's a girl."

"Harry," Jessie said in a weak, frightened voice. "Please don't let my little girl die."

Polly watched the scene from the corner of the conservatory. She knew she had just clutched the baby's life from the jaws of a cold, certain death when she'd scooped it up from the floor. She stared at her father and Auntie Gwen; their eyes were wide, speechless at the scene of the mother who was just a child herself and the tiniest baby they had ever seen at her breast, being cared for with such tenderness by a youth who was little more than a boy.

"It won't live," Gwen said, shaking her head. "It'll suffer terribly, and then it will die of suffocation anyway."

Reverend Staverley turned and left the room, his jaw set, looking straight ahead.

"God will decide when to call her home, Gwen, not you!" he said, unable to hide the disgust in his voice.

***

Polly ran after her father as he took the stairs two at a time.

"Stay in your rooms, please!" he barked out to Polly's younger brothers who were making an unholy din behind a closed bedroom door.

"Is mummy's baby here?" said a child's muffled voice.

"Yes — you have a baby sister but stay in your room. I have some important things to do."

"Can we see her?"

"Soon."

"Can we see mummy?"

"Soon. Stay there, boys. Polly will see to you in a minute."

Polly followed her father into his bedroom, where her mother was in bed, nursing her new-born baby sister.

"What on earth is going on?" her mother said. "What's all the commotion downstairs?"

Reverend Staverley sank down onto the bed and put his head in his hands. "You're not going to believe this, dear," he said. "But two children just knocked on the door, and the girl gave birth on the garden room floor."

"Gave birth?"

"Yes," Polly replied. "And I've just saved the baby's life. Auntie Gwen said the little baby girl was dead, but she wasn't. She's tiny. Really tiny …"

"Premature," Polly's father added. "Much too premature to survive, I fear. Practically a miscarriage."

"What are we going to do?" Polly's mother asked.

"I don't know. It's a child … it's alive … for now. We can't just pretend it doesn't belong in the world."

"What about the mother?"

"Not yet fourteen."

"Oh no — the poor little lamb. Is she all right?"

Reverend Staverley nodded. "Gwen's seeing to her now. They're both just children. The boy's only fourteen. He's insistent that he's not the baby's father, though."

"Is he telling the truth, do you think?"

"Yes."

"How do you know?"

"There's something about him. Something direct and forthright and I just believe him."

332

***

"Harry," Jessie whispered. "Are we safe here?"

"Yes," Harry breathed.

"She's asleep."

Harry gently peeled Jessie's shawl away from her and smiled. "She's perfect Jess. She's just beautiful."

"It's not her fault ..."

"No ... o'course it's not. She didn't ask to be born."

"She's so tiny, though. I've never seen a baby so small. Will she be all right, do you think?"

"I don't know, Jess. I can't lie to you. One thing I do know, though, is that we are all safe for the moment, and I can't think of any place we would be safer than here."

Harry brushed Jessie's fluffy hair away from her eyes.

"Remember when Molly died having her puppies and we had to hand rear them?"

Jessie nodded. "You made an incubator box and we fed them through a dropper."

"I could make one for our baby girl. Just the same as the one I made for Molly's puppies."

"Will they let us stay here for a few days, do you think?"

"I don't know. I could work for our keep." He looked around. "We could sleep in here for a few nights. You were so brave, Jess."

"I didn't feel brave. I was really frightened. I thought the baby was going to fall out on the doorstep."

"We were only just in time — she very nearly did."

"I know. Thank you Harry. Thank you for saving us."

Gwen bustled into the room, carrying a ceramic basin of hot water and some white cotton cloths.

"Young man, you'll have to leave us for a while."

Harry scrambled up. "Can I ... could I just 'ave a word, missus, if you please?"

"Just a quick one. I have to see to your ... your ... the young girl. She can't lie in her own mess all day." Gwen's voice was curt and businesslike. She showed no emotion or concern for either Jessie or

333

her baby daughter. Harry opened the door and stood aside to let Gwen pass through into the kitchen. He closed the door behind them so that Jessie couldn't hear.

"What are the baby's chances?"

"Practically nothing, I would say. It's just a matter of time ... and a mother's milk will be far too rich for her. Twice boiled sugar water, that's what she needs to start with, and wrapping up warmly in very lightly greased cotton to keep her skin from drying out. And even then you'll have a job keeping her at the right temperature. She'll either be too hot or too cold, and either extreme will snuff the life out of her — just like that!" Gwen snapped her fingers. "And, now, if you please, I'll see to the girl."

"Boy?"

Harry spun around. He wrung his cap in his hands and pulled himself up straight and tall. He looked the Reverend straight in the eye.

"Yes, mister Parson, sir?"

"I heard what Gwen said just now."

Harry lowered his head and shifted his position, as if squaring up to ask his loaded question.

"Please, sir, may we stay here until ... until ..."

"The poor little soul returns to the arms of Jesus?" the Reverend Staverley said quietly, finishing Harry's sentence for him. He closed his eyes momentarily, in silent prayer.

"Yes," Harry whispered.

Reverend Staverley took a step forwards and placed a fatherly hand on Harry's shoulder.

"I'd very much like you to join me for a few minutes," he said.

***

Polly watched from an upstairs window as her father and Harry walked across the road to the church. It was still early morning, and she could hardly believe that less than half an hour had passed since she'd sat on the back doorstep, listening to the birdsong and breathing in the heady smells of midsummer's day.

Torn between facing the boisterous excitement of three younger

334

brothers who were bouncing around on their beds in the next room, and the peace and tranquillity of the church, she made her decision.

She ran downstairs, out of the back door and across the road to join her father and Harry.

"Polly! Shouldn't you be seeing to your brothers?"

"In a minute Daddy. I want to pray for the little baby girl." She smiled at Harry, who managed a weak smile back.

The church was cold and Harry shivered, partly through inadequate clothing and partly through the shock of witnessing Jessie give birth. Sun streamed through stained glass windows and speckles of dust floated in the air. The trio knelt down in the front pew and Reverend Staverley said a prayer for the safe passage of the soul of Jessie's baby girl.

Afterwards, Harry spoke.

"Mister Parson, sir. I appreciate your kindness in our hour of need, but if I could just ask for some more help for a few days, I'd like to try and save Jessie's baby — if she survives the day, that is."

"How?"

"I am … was … a gamekeeper. I saved a litter of puppies last year when their mother died whelping them. If I could just get hold of some bits of wood, a good, large ceramic basin, a paraffin stove and kettle to heat water, I'd like to try. Please?"

"I'll help you," Polly said excitedly. "Please, Daddy, may I help Harry and Jessie save the little baby girl?"

Reverend Staverley stared at the image of Christ on the Cross in the stained glass window before him and closed his eyes. His lips moved silently.

After a minute or so he opened his eyes and said, "I'll have to baptise her now. Today. It must be done today."

Harry knew the vicar was secretly hoping that, when they returned to the vicarage, the matter would have been taken out of his hands and the baby would be dead. Whether Jessie's little daughter lived or died today, his own prayers had been answered and he was grateful. Jessie was safe and the baby was alive. That was all he'd asked for.

"You can stay with us until … until … well, things are a little bit more certain," Reverend Staverley said. He gave a resigned shrug of his

335

shoulders and a sigh of inevitability played around the edges of his voice. "I do have a plan, though. The child must be baptised as soon as possible because she might die. If my wife and Jessie agree, I'll baptise her and register the birth as though she is twin to my own baby daughter, born just a few hours ago. No matter how brief her life will be, this child should be loved, be a part of a family and have access to proper medical care. I fear she is too premature to survive, but I'll call in the doctor urgently and we'll see what he can do for her. As my daughter, the diocese will pay the doctor's fees. It's the best thing I can think of, boy."

Harry stared at the stone flags of the church floor and watched a wood louse disappear down a crack. If by some miracle the baby lived, it would lead a good, honest Christian life, much better than the life he could provide at fourteen with no job, no home and no money. Jessie would agree, he knew she would. She would want the very best for her precious baby daughter. He heard the distant call of a cuckoo and knew the Reverend was right. It was no more than what happened in nature all the time.

"All right," he said. "I agree, and I know Jessie will agree too."

Reverend Staverley stood up and climbed the three steps to the pulpit.

"Come here, lad. You too, Polly."

He took his daughter's hand gently in one hand and Harry's in the other and placed them on the bible.

"You must both solemnly swear before God that if a miracle should occur and this child should live, you will never, ever reveal to any person which of my daughters is Jessie's baby."

***

Later that afternoon, the Staverley family gathered around as the two baby girls were baptised together. The scene was surreal as Hannah Staverley lay in her bed, cradling one baby of a healthy size and another so tiny she almost disappeared in the folds of the cotton wrap. Both baby girls slept peacefully throughout the proceedings.

Downstairs in the conservatory, on a hastily made, makeshift bed created by the two wicker chairs pushed together, Harry held Jessie in his arms for the few anxious minutes she was separated from her daughter.

A couple of hundred yards away, on the edge of the churchyard a strange-looking white bird pecked at a hairy caterpillar, unaware and unconcerned that, in another tree nearby, one of its kind was laying a single egg in another bird's nest. The bird raised its head and its call echoed through the countryside.

"Listen, Jess. Can you hear the cuckoo?"

Jessie nodded. "Do you think it's the white Jacobin Cuckoo that escaped from the stables?"

"It could be, but cuckoos migrate to England from Africa in spring each year and by July they have all gone back to Kenya or Ethiopia. It was early December last year when the bird escaped from the stables. I don't think it would have survived the winter in this country, Jess. It would have died in the cold, although some experts say that the cuckoos come back to the same place to breed, if there is enough food. It lays its eggs in other birds' nests, and do you know, Jess, if it lays an egg in a robin's nest, the egg is exactly the same as a robin's egg? If the nest it should pick is a dunnock then the egg looks like a dunnock's egg. Then, when the young cuckoo hatches, it imitates the sound of the host's chicks, sounding just like a robin if the unsuspecting parents are robins."

"How does it do that?"

Harry shook his head. "No one knows. It's just one of those things in the world that can't be explained."

"Doesn't it push the other chicks out of the nest?"

"Usually, yes, because it's bigger than the other chicks. But our little girl is so tiny she will nestle in here and snuggle in with the rest of them. She won't be big enough to push any of the others out."

"I don't think I like cuckoos very much."

Harry pulled her closer into his chest. "They survive, though, don't they? Their young hatch, grow strong and then the whole cycle starts again."

Jessie started to cry. "I don't want my little Emily-Rose to be a cuckoo. I want to love her myself."

337

"I know you do — and you will. But this way the Reverend and his wife will bring a doctor in today. She will get the best of care and if I can make her an incubator box for her crib to keep her temperature exactly right all the time, she might just stand a chance. If we take her now, where will we go? The workhouse? She'll not be cared for in the workhouse and she'll die for certain. Here, our precious Emily-Rose stands a chance of life. A much better life than we can give her, Jess."

"Like a cuckoo, Harry?"

"Yes, just like a cuckoo."

THE END

338